Y0-BZB-549

CHINA GATE

CHINA GATE

WILLIAM ARNOLD

BALLANTINE BOOKS ● NEW YORK

Library of Congress Catalog Card Number: 83-48073

ISBN 0-345-30850-6

This edition published by arrangement with Villard Books

Manufactured in the United States of America

First Ballantine Books Edition: August 1984

FOR JANIE—AND ONCE AGAIN FOR KATHIE

CHINA
GATE

PROLOGUE

ON THE COOL, CLEAR AND UNSEASONABLY CALM MORN-
ing of December 6, 1949, a man stood with his five-year-
old son on the main deck of the S.S. *South China Sea* and
watched the crowd of refugees swarming down a rope-net
ladder into a bobbing landing craft. The craft was to take
them all to Keelung harbor.

The evacuation of the Chinese mainland had been
going on day and night since midyear. By aircraft, by
freighter, by junk and dinghy and sampan, tens of thousands of refugees crossed the hundred miles of the Formosa Strait in a frightened exodus from the victorious
Communist armies. Within a week the Nationalist reign
of China would be only a memory and all these people
would be faced with the task of starting their lives over
again.

The man on the deck watching them—an American
—faintly realized that he, too, would have to start his life
over again. He did not know how to begin.

The man's name was Whyte and for the past thirty
years he had been a prominent *taipan* of Shanghai—a
leading member of the elite foreign business aristocracy
that had supported Chiang Kai-shek and the Nationalists
to the bitter end. The last few years of the civil war had
been a terrible ordeal for him and his haggard face and
rumpled clothes betrayed that fact. He was, in every way,
a broken man.

As father and son stared at the spectacle, a handsome
young Chinese with a quick step and air of command
joined the pair and stood silently with them a moment.
From the way the deck coolies cowered out of his path and

bowed and groveled as he passed, it was apparent that he was a man of great respect, perhaps even a man to be feared.

This man's name was King Lu and, truly, he was a man to be feared. From Canton to Darien, he was known as heir apparent of the Green Society—the powerful Chinese underworld network whose *tongs* or gangs had, at least up until this week, controlled the economy of urban China and almost every overseas Chinese community around the globe. He was what Westerners would call a gangster, though that title did not have quite the same dark connotation in Chinese that it had in English. Like all the others gathered on the deck, he too was starting his life again.

King Lu took Whyte by the arm and the boy by the hand and led them to the stern of the ship to board his special launch. They climbed down the rope ladder together, the boatswain started the inboard motor and they chugged toward the harbor.

Once clear of the ship, King Lu pointed to the mountainous land mass ahead and said in flawless English, "Taiwan . . . means terraced bay. Portuguese sailors called it 'Ilha Formosa,' which means beautiful island. All throughout Chinese history it's been a refuge for outcasts, pirates, revolutionaries and political exiles. It is a perfect sanctuary for us—it will take years for the Communist bandits to build a navy strong enough to attack it."

The American said nothing to this, merely stared into the distance. Beside him, the boy leaned against the gunwhale and let the spray hit his open palm.

The boat pulled up to a dilapidated pier crowded with coolies and Nationalist soldiers, and King Lu helped the passengers out. In Chinese, he ordered the boatswain to wait for him.

"You're not staying?" the American asked with sudden interest.

"I'm going to Hong Kong. My master, Tu, is dying. I must be at his side."

A look of panic flashed across the American's eyes. "What do we do now?"

"Now we work to restore what has been stolen from us." He said this with strength and conviction and without a trace of the defeat that hung over the setting like a black cloud.

"How can we even hope . . . ?"

"We will do it. And we will do it from this island— just as you once said we would. Not soon, perhaps, but within our lifetimes."

Whyte gazed numbly off into the distance again. "There is no way for us," he said.

"There *is* a way. And your son will find it for us."

"My son?"

The boy—an unusually attractive child with large, captivating gray eyes—stiffened somewhat when he realized the men were speaking of him. He strained to understand their conversation, strained to appear strong in the face of the obvious weakness of his father.

"Chuang-tzu has spoken it."

"Chuang-tzu? The fortuneteller?"

"Yes."

The great Chuang-tzu was the most respected *hua-jen* or shaman of modern China. Some weeks before, as Shanghai was about to fall, King had gone to his bedside for a final prophecy. The ancient Taoist sage was over one hundred years old and about to die of assorted ailments of advanced age. But while the King stood before him, he had gone into a deep meditative trance and come up with a vision so startling that he had to cast sticks and consult all the learned texts for another whole day to make sure he could trust it.

"And you believe this?"

"I must." King said this with some embarrassment. He was not an overly superstitious man. He was raised in mission schools and had adopted many of the Western ways of viewing the world. But he was not about to question the deathbed prediction of a proven mystic with thousands of years of Taoist metaphysical knowledge at his fingertips. When Chuang-tzu was sure about a conclusion, he was never wrong. Never.

The American blinked several times, as if struggling to comprehend this, then looked away at another boatload of refugees pulling up alongside the pier.

"Chuang-tzu said that China will indeed fall to the barbarians; but it will be restored in some thirty years time. The instrument of this restoration will be your son. He is a messiah—what my people call a *beizo*—who will one day lead the struggle to regain the Mainland from the evil, foreign philosophy that has enslaved it."

The American seemed to have become keenly interested in the unloading of the boat. He watched the scene intently, tuning out King's voice.

King continued, though caught up in his memory of that historic moment at the bedside of the great prophet. "The boy will grow up on the Island of Taiwan. When he has gained his full manhood—when he has proven his full manhood—he will embark on a great journey. This journey will take him through many hardships and even more trials and tests of his endurance—both here and in his own country. But he will persevere and someday, many years from now, he will become the overlord of the entire Island. From this position, he will wage a war that will restore China to its rightful course in the flow of history. This is the boy's destiny—and it is the destiny of the rest of us to help him fulfill it."

King stopped to let this sink in, but it was apparent to him now that Whyte had not been listening. Seeing that it was useless to go on, King stared stoically at his friend for a moment, then embraced him. Then he squatted next to the boy, drew him near and kissed him.

King reached into his pocket and brought out a hexagonal *fu* or talisman on a gold chain and placed it around the boy's neck. "Wear this always," he said softly. "It is the symbol of my house."

Though he nodded and smiled, the child did not actually understand anything of what was happening. He did not understand what this man was doing or what had happened to his father to make him so distant or where his mother had been since the day of the great explosion or why they had been forced to leave their home in the first place.

He held his father's hand tightly and watched the man get back in the launch and chug toward the ship and had no idea that for the rest of his exile on this island he would be under the protection of the tongs of the mighty Green Society.

BOOK ONE
1961–1964

1

THE HONORABLE WARREN XAVIER STEVENS, FIRST Undersecretary of State for Asian affairs, leaned back in the huge black Cadillac limousine and suddenly realized that he could be in very big trouble—more trouble than he could even begin to handle by himself.

A tall, almost Lincolnesque, career diplomat of fifty with an aristocratic bearing and considerable political ambitions, Stevens had been a China specialist for the past twenty years. But as he sped through the streets of Taipei on his way to the Presidential Palace, it occurred to him once again that he knew as little about this world as the day he left Harvard. The street vendors, pushcarts, pedicabs, ox wagons, bicycles and tiny red Datsun taxis flew by his window. It was all still a mystery to him, an endless succession of incongruities and surprises.

It was January of 1961, the beginning of the second year of the second decade of the Nationalist Chinese exile on the Island of Taiwan. He was in town this time as special envoy for Senator John Kennedy, who this very week was to be inaugurated thirty-fifth President of the United States. All morning Stevens had been in conference with various uncooperative Kuomintang—the Nationalist Chinese party officials—rather desperately assuring them that the new administration would not make a change in China policy. Now he was on his way to make even stronger assurances to Generalissimo Chiang Kai-shek's general staff. But as he had stepped into the limo, an aide handed him a hastily decoded diplomatic message:

INTELLIGENCE SOURCES REPORT RUMORS OF
LARGE ANTI-AMERICAN DEMONSTRATION ON IN-
AUGURAL WEEK. INTENTION MAY BE TO EMBAR-
RASS NEW DEMOCRATIC ADMINISTRATION. PLEASE
INVESTIGATE AND TAKE STEPS TO PREVENT.

Stevens was baffled by the cable. Such a demonstration seemed highly unlikely. Taiwan was the most important strategic focal point of the entire Cold War. The
hordes of Communist China were a mere stone's throw
away and, even as he sat there pondering his predicament,
the offshore islands of Quemoy and Matsu were being
bombarded by a barrage of Communist artillery fire. The
people of this island fortress were totally committed to the
struggle against World Communism, and a serious incident aimed at humiliating their closest ally—the very ally
whose military power had guaranteed their existence for
the past eleven years—would have to be a suicidal gesture.

Yet, Stevens knew enough to take the message very
seriously. He was the State Department's top Taiwan expert and had been on the Island maybe a hundred times
since the Nationalists set up shop and the U.S. Seventh
Fleet moved into the Formosa Strait to insure Nationalist
integrity. He was quite familiar with the volatility and
unpredictability of Chiang Kai-shek's exiled government
and considered it capable of anything—especially when a
matter of face was involved.

He also knew that this government was so closely
linked to the underworld of the city that it could turn out
a violent demonstration at a moment's notice. Four years
ago, in fact, the U.S. Embassy in Taipei was sacked by
tong goon squads in a full-scale anti-American riot carefully choreographed by the Nationalists. Stevens couldn't
shake the gnawing feeling that something like that could
happen this week, especially since Chiang felt so threatened by the prospect of Senator Kennedy's election that
he had actively campaigned for Mr. Nixon. . . .

When the limousine made its way into the city center,
Stevens could see an immense crowd gathered around the

imposing, red brick Presidential Palace. The driver pulled up at a security station and a stonefaced guard with a machine gun jerked open the door. As the undersecretary stepped out and rose to his full six feet four inches, he could see that the crowd was even larger than he had earlier suspected. It was orderly but many of the faces displayed anger and open hostility.

As Stevens started unsurely toward the main steps, he saw something that made his blood go cold. On the outskirts of the crowd was a group of ten or fifteen fierce-looking Chinese in blue cotton jackets. He knew at once that the men were Blue Shirts—the elite fighting tong of the infamous Green Gang—and that they were here for trouble. They carried billy clubs and crude signs with anti-Communist, anti-Kennedy, pro-Nixon slogans.

Before Stevens could react, he felt something sharp strike his forehead. He staggered backward, into a shower of rocks and garbage and human waste. Instantly, a detachment of Chinese police made a circle around him. Two Chinese secret service men grabbed him by the arms and, with some difficulty due to his size, dragged him up the steps and into the building.

Shaken, Stevens felt blood oozing down his cheek from a gash on his forehead. His hand trembled visibly as his Chinese liaison helped him into a chair. "What . . . happened . . . out . . . there?"

The young Chinese major, livid with lost face, looked meekly at the floor around Stevens's feet. "Don't know, sir."

Stevens grabbed the man's arm, suddenly very angry, trying to hurt him. "This is only the beginning, isn't it? You bastards are going to stage a major riot! It's going to be 1958 all over again!"

"Donno, sir," the major, almost in tears, said again. "Donno, donno."

Stevens let go of the man's arm. He knew now that his mission was about to be scuttled by one senseless act of Chinese arrogance. It was too late for diplomatic overtures or political pressure or high level blackmail. At this point he only had one option to pursue and that option involved a young American by the name of Whyte.

Commander Floyd Harris, USN, executive officer of the Taipei Provost Marshal's office, sat at the end of a long teak table in the wood-paneled conference room of the Taiwan Defense Command Headquarters and scowled.

A short, burly Annapolis man (his despised nickname at the Academy had been "Stump"), a son and grandson of admirals and a former carrier pilot who had been twice decorated for valor in Korea, Harris was struggling with a particularly alarming crisis situation. The day before, a gang of mostly American kids calling themselves the Warlords had gone on a rampage of window-breaking and beatings over several blocks of the downtown area—apparently in an effort to enforce some crude protection racket. The damage had been so great and the beatings so severe that the story made the English-language newspapers that morning. It would also probably be picked up by the foreign wire services, embarrassing the Community before the entire civilized world right in the middle of inauguration week.

Sharing the table with Harris were the leaders of the four factions that made up the American Community of Taipei—missionary, business, diplomatic and all three branches of MAAG, the U.S. Military Assistance Advisory Group that had come to Taiwan in 1954 after the U.S. and Nationalist China signed their Mutual Defense Treaty. Most of the morning Harris had been forced to sit and listen to their theories as to how such an appalling incident could have happened here; why this community —a perfect, ideal little pioneer American community that had been built in the face of great adversity over the past eleven years and now prided itself in being a microcosm of traditional American values—should have such a problem with teenage gangs. Every person in the room seemed to have a different and equally useless hypothesis.

Beside Harris, a ruddy-faced Episcopal missionary

named Warner was whining on in deep, liturgical tones.

"The city of Taipei has, as we all know, the same kind of dark and evil underbelly we had to deal with in the old days in Shanghai. . . . There is more crime, more prostitution, more bars, more opportunities for trouble right here than in any other city in Asia right now. As long as the children are allowed to leave the sanctuary of the foreign compounds to roam the city at will, they will continue to be influenced by this atmosphere of lawlessness and gangsterism. This is our real problem."

The problem! Jesus Christ, he had only been on the Island six months but no one had to tell Floyd Harris the problem. The problem was that there was a wealth of economic opportunity out there for those kids and they were pursuing it with the same capitalistic impulse that had always attracted Westerners to China. The problem was compounded by the fact that Chiang Kai-shek had chosen to extend to the entire American Community a form of blanket diplomatic immunity—Chinese police had no clear jurisdiction over them. So, over the past decade, the children of this ideal little community had formed elaborate juvenile gangs—gangs whose members included sons of American generals and admirals, sons of senior foreign service officers and executives of large corporations, even sons of missionaries. Some of them had attained frightening power in the city. They owned property, operated rackets, black marketed PX goods, bribed officials and occasionally even did business with the Chinese underworld. As commander of the newly created Task Force on Juvenile Delinquency, it was Harris's job to control these gangs. This incident with the Warlords was now both a personal embarrassment and a threat to his whole naval career.

Harris picked up his cigarette lighter with an enormous hamlike hand and began clicking the lid methodically. He gazed out the window at a grove of wideleafed palms swaying gently in the afternoon breeze and wished he were somewhere else. Anywhere else. When there was finally a break in the tedious proceedings, Harris cut in and said, "Well, I guess I have all your thoughts on the subject and I believe we all understand the situation a little better. I'm hoping we can pool our efforts to get tough with these hooligans and make sure an incident like this never happens again."

He said these words with a certain conviction but they were hollow and he knew it and he loathed himself for having to say them. He realized and surely everyone around the table must have realized that they were all powerless in the face of this outrageous situation. The only thing he could do to control the excesses of the Warlords was to appeal to the one American youth gang in Taipei with anything like a social conscience. He would have to go to the Omega Chi and have another talk with their leader, Bryan Whyte.

David Butler, the new roving Southeast Asian correspondent for the Associated Press, rolled out of bed and realized that he had both a hangover and a very serious problem.

Butler was a talented, deeply ambitious but totally inexperienced young journalist who was in Taipei to research a feature that would sum up a decade of Nationalist Chinese achievements on the Island. He had spent last night—his first night in Taiwan—sleeping with a sassy little Taiwanese bargirl named Suzy. He had picked her up in one of the thousands of nameless little bars that dotted the grubby part of the city that Americans called "Sin Alley" and took her back to his hotel for a night of exotic sexual adventure. She had been everything the guidebooks promised, perhaps the single most enthusiastic and satisfying piece of ass of his entire life. But now, as the reporter put on his glasses and frantically searched the room, he could see that both the girl and his briefcase filled with passport, traveler's checks, important accreditation papers and a month's worth of dispatches for his bureau chief in Tokyo were gone!

He poured himself a quick drink, cursed his luck,

dressed and ran the short distance down Taipei's palm-lined main boulevard to the MAAG Provost Marshal's office. At a counter under a large sign stenciled "Complaints," he tried to explain his dilemma to a thick-necked MP sergeant who looked up at him from a Batman comic book.

"You see," Butler was saying, "everything I need to do my work is in that briefcase. If I don't get it back, I'm completely aced. I mean there's no leeway for me. I've only got this job on a trial basis. You understand? You gotta help me."

The MP handed him a stack of forms to fill out in triplicate and looked vaguely amused, as if he might be enjoying Butler's torment. There was an abrasiveness about Butler that often seemed to bring out the worst in other people. "You're wasting your time, friend," the man said. "There must be a million whores in this city and half of them are named Suzy. The passport alone is worth maybe a thousand bucks on the black market. You can fill out forms till you're blue in the face and you still ain't gonna get that briefcase back."

Butler left the forms on the counter and asked to use the telephone. He dialed the number of his one contact in town, a stringer who spoke Chinese and was the principal local news source for several of the foreign wire services. It was a long shot but the only straw he could think of to grasp.

"Well, it doesn't look good," the voice on the other end of the line said. "First of all, you can forget about the Provost Marshal and the Chinese police. Sin Alley belongs to the Tiger Eels, a Taiwanese gang, and they're the only ones who have any power down there."

"Can you get me in touch with them?"

"You don't know what you're asking. The Tiger Eels are the most bloody and unpredictable gangsters in all Asia. They have been for a hundred years. Even the Shanghai gangsters who came over with the Gimo stay away from Sin Alley."

"I'm going to see them."

"You can't do business with those animals."

"I have to try. Now are you going to help me or not?"

The stringer, an older, balding man named John Hay, picked Butler up in front of the Taipei Press Club. They drove his little Volkswagen to the Sin Alley area, past dozens of dark and nameless alleys, warrens and dead-end side streets, finally pulling up in front of a bar with a small neon sign flashing on and off in its single tiny window. The two Americans went inside and sat at a wooden picnic table. The air reeked of urine and cooking oil and that distinct sharp stink that Butler was beginning to recognize as the omnipresent odor of the Orient. Every eye in the room was on them.

They ordered a glass of rice wine each. Then another. After what seemed an eternity to Butler, a Taiwanese man with a large scar on his right cheek and half his nose missing entered the bar with two bodyguards. He sauntered over to join the Americans. His name was Loma and he was supreme overlord of all the Tiger Eel gangs of Taipei.

As Hay explained the situation in stumbling Mandarin Chinese and pidgin English, the gangster nodded thoughtfully.

"How much?" Hay finally asked him.

Loma reached for a cigarette. "Four thousand U.S. and favors," he said. "No haggle."

"*Bu hao,*" Hay said. "Totally out of the question. One thousand and no favors."

Loma said nothing. He knew he held all the cards here.

"Fifteen hundred and no favors. Last offer."

"No haggle," Loma said and looked as if he meant it.

Hay got up to leave. "Let's counsel," he said to Butler.

Back in the car, Hay shrugged apologetically. "That's about as good as we're going to get, I'm afraid."

Butler was close to tears. There was no way he could

pay anything close to that amount. He was only a year out of college and still deeply in debt.

He suddenly saw it all crumbling before him. The dream he had nurtured growing up as the son of the editor-publisher of the Eugene (Wyoming) *Gazette*. The dream of being a crusading foreign correspondent . . . exposing injustice . . . toppling tyrants . . . influencing the fate of nations. . . .

Well, he was not going to let it die. There had to be a way out of this.

Hay started up the engine. Then something seemed to jog in Butler's memory. Yesterday at the Press Club, there had been a big happy hour discussion about the American gang rampage in Shihminting that he had strained to overhear. He vaguely remembered that in the conversation several stories were told about one of the more enterprising of the gangs—a fraternity at the Taipei American School, really—that often helped out Americans in trouble. Supposedly the leader of this gang had closer ties to the Oriental underworld than any other Westerner on the Island. Yes, Butler remembered it all quite clearly now. The boy was the son of an old Shanghai taipan who had lost his fortune in the Communist take-over.

The boy's name was William Bryan Whyte.

2

WILLIAM JENNINGS BRYAN WHYTE, THE OBJECT OF SO much attention that hectic week of the big Democratic changeover, was himself among the dozens of Taipei

Americans making hurried last-minute preparations to celebrate the inauguration of John F. Kennedy.

He stayed home from his classes at the Taipei American School that day and spent most of the morning calmly haggling with "Snake-eyes" Lee Min, a wily old Shanghai merchant and caterer. Whyte was trying to close a deal for catering the gala inaugural party his fraternity was hosting that evening for the teenage foreign community of the city.

Lee Min cocked his ancient head, raised a bony finger and tried for the tenth time to score a point. "Bwyn, I makee you special deal. You getee—listen up now—soup, chicken, duck, shrimps, powk and all trimmings for two thousand New Taiwan dolla. Fifty dolla U.S. This plenty good deal I think. I even throw in wine and desserts, whataheck. I makee special deal only cause I do allatime business with Mega Chi, hey."

Whyte sat back in the wicker mandarin chair and looked impassive. He was, by any measure, a most impressive figure of a young man: tall, muscular, permanently tanned from many summers under the Taiwan sun; a long attractive scar on his chin, wide, steady gray eyes, and a likeable, commanding nature that radiated the same complete and overwhelming confidence his father had once had and lost. At sixteen, he seemed in every way a good five or six years older.

"You are a bandit, aren't you, Snake-eyes? You want me to pay you twice what you would charge a Chinese."

Lee looked suddenly distraught. "You makee me muchee sorrowful, Bwyn Whyte. I do business with you father before you born—now you wantee breakee old Lee's ricebowl when he ole and helpless. So sorrowful . . ."

"All right. Eleven hundred . . . but not one NT more."

The ceremony of haggling for price was second nature to Bryan Whyte. His father had been a titan of the Chinese banking and motion picture industries in the old days on the Mainland. Bryan had been born in the latter days of the war in Chungking in Szechwan Province after his family had fled the Japanese invasion of Shanghai. His

mother had been killed during the civil war in 1948 and he
and his father had been with the wave of refugees from
Shanghai in 1949 when the Mainland fell to the Communists. He had grown up foot-loose and fancy-free on the
mean streets of Taipei, and the complicated procedures of
doing business in the Orient came to him as naturally as
breathing did for other people.

"But this be for U.S. President honor!" Lee protested. "This be very special! You gots no patriotism?!"

Whyte could not hide his delight at this last, desperate tactic and he broke the ceremony by laughing outloud.
Then he made his closing offer. "You have my price. Now
make a deal or you forfeit all Omega Chi business. When
word gets out that Omega Chi has dropped Lee, he lose
so much face that pretty soon he got no American business
at all. Where will Lee be then?"

Lee mulled this over in silence.

"But because Lee is old family friend," Whyte continued magnanimously, "I will settle for fifteen hundred
NT dollars."

Lee made the deal and went away happy. This was,
of course, preordained from the beginning. The haggling
had only been a necessary formality. Lee knew that ultimately he had to accept any deal Bryan Whyte offered
him. He could not afford to offend Bryan Whyte because
everyone knew that Bryan Whyte was taipan of the
Omega Chi and thus the most powerful American teenager on the Island of Taiwan.

The Omega Chi House was a medium-sized, walled-
in, Japanese-style townhouse in a quiet residential district
in the eastside of Taipei that before the Second World War
had been reserved exclusively for the Island's Japanese
colonial administrators. It contained one large reception
room, two smaller council chambers, a library, sleeping
area and servants' quarters—all tatami-floored—and a
Japanese tea garden in the backyard which was kept in
immaculate condition by a scrub amah and part-time

yardboy. The fraternity was able to afford such a house by
virtue of the fact that for the past three years it had
managed to effectively dominate the black market on
American PX and commissary goods in the city of Taipei.

Whyte arrived there by taxi shortly after sundown
that evening. As he removed his shoes and stepped onto
the cool tatami floor, he could see the other brothers of
Omega Chi mingling with the guests that had already
arrived: maybe two dozen teenagers from the Taipei
American School listening to rock 'n' roll records, dancing
or sitting cross-legged on the floor drinking Filipino beer.
He paused a moment in the vestibule and experienced, as
he always did on entering this house, an instant rush of
pride in the place and a glow of affection for his friends.

His eyes searched the party until they landed on a
brown-haired girl sitting with a loud group in the corner
of the main room. She was easily the most beautiful girl
present, the most beautiful American girl Whyte had ever
seen in his life: with eyes, mouth, lips, teeth, hair and
figure altogether so unaffectedly and effortlessly perfect
that the sight of her intoxicated him. Everything about
this girl exuded wholesome sensuality—that prototypi-
cally American, high-school cheerleader kind of sexiness
—and, as she smiled at something that was said, he had
a strange sensation that he was looking at a model who
had somehow magically stepped out of a Pepsi-Cola ad.

When the girl noticed Whyte staring at her, she acknowledged him with a barely perceptible flash of her
green eyes. Then she looked away.

A clean-cut, cherub-faced boy wearing rimless
glasses and a flower-print luau shirt came up to greet
Whyte. "Where've you been?" Alan Phillips asked with
some urgency. "People have already started arriving. Everyone in the world is looking for you."

Phillips was acting as the unofficial host here tonight.
He was the oldest son of the head of the Taiwan branch
of the Agency for International Development (AID) and,
though his family had not been among the Mainland refugees in 1949, he had lived on the Island almost as long

as Whyte himself. He was the only member of the Omega Chi who was fluent in both Mandarin *and* Taiwanese and —almost inconceivable in free and easy Taipei—the only one of them who was still a virgin. He was also president of his class at the American School, an eagle scout of Taipei troop four fifty-one and chairman of the southend Taiwanese orphanage that the Omega Chi financially supported.

Whyte did not mind being bawled out by his friend. Phillips was an incorrigibly good and dutiful fellow who took all his responsibilities very seriously and Whyte depended on him to make things run smoothly. Phillips was something of a genius with figures; he served as the fraternity's secretary-treasurer, keeping track of the Omega Chi's considerable monthly income and putting Whyte's endless new business schemes into practical effect.

"There's an American newspaper guy who wants to talk to you," said Phillips. He motioned toward David Butler, who was standing unsurely in the main room staring at the same striking girl Whyte had been watching earlier.

"About what?"

"He needs a favor. Something to do with the Tiger Eels. He's a friend of John Hay."

Whyte frowned. "Later, Alan. I want to enjoy the party."

He grabbed a handful of pressed duck from one of the tables of Lee Min's catered food and said hello to John Casy, who was standing close by with his girlfriend.

Casy was a smaller, good-looking boy with an aura of intelligence, the son of an Air Force colonel stationed at the Taipei Air Station. He had only lived on the Island for three years but, because he was part of the Omega Chi in-crowd, was considered a part of the more clannish, permanent American Community. He was a very serious-minded and artistically inclined boy, equally talented at painting, writing (he had won several awards for his poetry and short stories) and music (he could play everything Chuck Berry and Duane Eddy ever recorded on the electric guitar). This multisided talent had always utterly fascinated Whyte, who had no artistic ability of his own. He had adopted Casy two years ago much as an aristocratic patron might adopt a struggling artist.

"Hey, Bryan," Casy said quickly, "some government honcho named Stevens was by here earlier. . . ."

"Stevens?"

"You know him?"

"Not personally. What did he want?"

"He wants to see you. He wants you to come to the American Embassy tonight." Casy was obviously very impressed by this. "Are you going?"

Whyte was not so impressed. "Maybe," he said and, stealing another quick glance at the girl across the room, stepped over to a cooler to help himself to a beer.

In the foyer that served as the Omega Chi library, a slight, horsefaced boy sat on the floor beside a row of empty beer bottles, loudly flirting with one of the serving amahs. Whyte joined Georgie Warner, who served as something of the court jester of the Omega Chi. Shy and reckless with an irresistible mischievous charm, Georgie was the son of Clifton Warner, the unofficial head of the missionary community. Like so many other missionaries' sons in Taipei, he seemed to be perpetually in trouble with the Provost Marshal's office. As at every social gathering, Warner was completely drunk, but he was such a good-natured and likeable drunk that he was always pleasant to be around; and always very funny.

Whyte exchanged some banter with Warner and then went out into the garden to check in with Mark Taylor, the fifth and final member of the fraternity.

Taylor was the most enigmatic of all the Omega Chi. He was a skinny, asthmatic boy whose parents had been killed in a Communist uprising on the Mainland in 1949, leaving him an orphan and ward of the Baptist Missionary Society. Despite an array of health problems, he had grown into an almost mythic figure in the city—an enormously cool, calm and dangerous character with considerable skill in the Chinese martial arts and a well-deserved reputation as a brawler and all-around non-conformist. When necessary, Taylor was a cunning and fearless enforcer for the Omega Chi. Usually just the mention of his nickname "Soldier"—the result of his longstanding ambition to go to West Point—was enough to discourage the Cavaliers, the Warlords, the Taipei Rangers or any of the other American gangs from encroaching on their black-market territory. He had known Whyte almost since they were toddlers and was frantically loyal to him—their longstanding friendship being the only stable personal relationship in Taylor's life.

Whyte found Taylor seated on a large rock under the cloudless, star-filled sky, smoking quietly by himself and listening to the sound of Ricky Nelson singing "Travelin' Man" from the hi-fi inside. When he noticed Whyte coming his way, he stood up.

"Guess you heard about the Warlords?"

"I heard."

"Bad stuff."

"Very bad."

"I think we should do something. Those bastards need to be taught a lesson."

"We'll have a meeting later."

"I don't think we should wait on this thing, Bryan."

"We can talk about it at the meeting. Let's relax and enjoy the party, Soldier."

Phillips soon called everyone together to drink a *gombei,* the traditional bottoms-up rice wine toast. By his calculation, the inauguration was taking place in Washington and it was now officially time to celebrate it. It was an event with a special significance to these people because it was the first real change of political power since the Taipei American Community was formed. Sensing that it was the beginning of a whole new era, they all made a circle and held their glasses to the air.

Later in the evening, the five brothers of Omega Chi —Whyte, Alan Phillips, John Casy, Georgie Warner and

Mark Taylor—left their guests and dutifully filed into a
tiny council room in the rear of the house. This inner
tatami room was decorated with framed candid photographs and other memorabilia celebrating moments of
Omega Chi glory over the years. It contained only one
piece of furniture, a large, knee-high round table with an
embossed fraternity symbol—a stylized X imposed on a
horseshoe figure—in its center.

When they were all positioned around the table, they
immediately fell into the usual teasing and horseplay. Despite numerous small jealousies and antagonisms, these
five had been a special kind of family for most of their lives
on the Island and they delighted in their private company.

Whyte took a sip from his beer and said, "Let's try
to make this quick. We've all got other things we want to
do tonight. Let's start with the newspaper guy."

Phillips opened the door and asked David Butler to
come in. The reporter stood before the table, looking awkward and uneasy, and feeling very foolish.

"You learned your lesson about bargirls the hard
way," Whyte said, not unpleasantly.

"Yes, very hard," Butler said.

"What bar?" asked John Casy.

"Some place on Chung Chun Road."

"Sin Alley? That was dumb."

"Yes, I know that now."

Whyte was interested. He studied Butler a moment,
admiring both the man's ingenuity at finding his way here
tonight and the guts it took for him to keep standing there
in front of them. "You spoke to someone from the Tiger
Eels and they actually wanted four thousand U.S. for your
stuff?"

"Yes."

"Crazy."

"I didn't have that kind of money."

"Good thing. The Tiger Eels would take your money
and you'd never hear from them again. The Taiwanese
gangs do not do business with tourists."

The use of the word "tourist" was obviously meant to sting Butler and it did. It was Whyte's way of telling him that, as an Asian correspondent, he should know better. But Butler swallowed the reprimand. There was something about the boy's lordly manner that offered some hope. "I was told you boys could help me."

"Maybe we can." Whyte turned to Warner. "Georgie, how sober are you tonight?"

"Sober as one of my old man's Sunday sermons."

Whyte smiled. "Then would you mind taking this gentleman back to Sin Alley to see Loma."

"I'd be delighted."

"Tell Loma we would consider it a New Year's act of friendship if he would help our friend here get his property back. Tell him we might just throw some regular business his way after such an act of friendship. That should do it."

Butler was fascinated now by this whole bizarre scene, fascinated particularly by this boy in charge. The journalist in him desperately wanted to stay and ask some questions. But before he could say a word, Warner led him out of the room and shut the door behind them.

When they were gone, Whyte immediately turned to Mark Taylor and arched his eyebrow. "Let's talk about the Warlords," he said.

"It's real ugly, man," Taylor said gravely. "Fatso Dave Magaha decided he would start a protection business on one of the blocks of Haggler's Alley. He took three other Warlords down there and demanded payments of about eight hundred NT dollars a month from each of the stallkeepers. These guys were already paying the Tiger Eels for protection so they told Magaha to stuff it. So Magaha and his stooges took clubs and started breaking up shops and busting heads to show that the Tiger Eels wouldn't protect them from an American gang. Apparently, the Chinese police stood by and watched the whole thing and didn't make a move to stop it."

"Bastards!" Whyte muttered.

"Commander Harris called today and he's frantic for some help. My personal recommendation is that we pulverize the shitbirds. Every last one of them."

Whyte considered this a moment. "What do you think, Alan?"

Phillips shook his head doubtfully. "I think that might be unwise. The Warlords have a lot of new blood this year. Mostly young Eurasians, Filipinos and Taiwanese, who can be very crazy. We're not a gang, for crying out loud. We can't just attack them like we're a bunch of hoodlums. That could engage us in a war we'd wish we'd never started. Let's give some financial aid to the shopkeepers and let Harris handle the Warlords himself this time."

A number of other suggestions for handling the problem were offered around the table and Whyte listened to each of them very attentively. Finally he said, "I don't see that we have any choice. Magaha must be punished and it's not likely that Harris will ever be able to build a case against him. Anyway, there's more to be considered here than just helping Harris keep the American image clean. If we let this go by, our face will invariably suffer. Not only will the Warlords go even further next time, but so will every other punk gang in the city. But Alan is right in that we must never act as a group—the Omega Chi against the Warlords. Magaha must be challenged by one of us on an individual basis. This is the way it has to be done and it should be done tonight."

Then, with a wave of his hand, he dismissed the meeting and his eyes sought out a private moment with Mark Taylor.

The object of the Omega Chi's concern was an obese, acne-ravaged boy named David Earl "Fatso" Magaha—a half-Chinese bully whose father had been an ace with General Chennault's famous Flying Tigers during the war and was now a top pilot for China Airlines. The Omega Chi all knew Magaha as a particularly hard case. His favorite story was of how he had once kicked a pedicab driver to death in a dispute over a fare, and he was known to frequent the notorious sadism brothels of the Lung Shan red-light district. He was also unusually ambitious in business, and he had recently been urging the Warlords into illegal moneychanging, protection and a renewed effort in the black market—which is one of the reasons Whyte felt a particular urgency about putting him in his place.

Whyte and Taylor pulled into the courtyard of the Tien Mou Teen Club that evening in a black Mercedes taxi. Magaha was in the back room shooting pool. A small Filipino boy having a cigarette outside saw the two Omega Chi and immediately ran back to the fat boy to announce their arrival. A frozen look came over Magaha's face but he continued to study the table. "So what?" he said. "What's that to me? I don't give a big shit what the Omega Chi do."

The American Special Services Teen Club was a single-story complex on a remote hilltop of the mostly American suburban village of Tien Mou, five miles north of Taipei. It had been built in 1954 as a social center for American teenagers, but the children of the entire non-Chinese population of Taipei were permitted as members and usually had the premises to themselves. There was a nicely furnished game room and a dance floor where a Wurlitzer jukebox blasted out all the latest rock 'n' roll hits from the States—a continuous stream of Sam Cooke and the Shirelles and Del Shannon's "Runaway" sounding all day long—and there were always several couples doing the fast dances they had learned from the American rock 'n' roll movies that played the downtown theaters with Chinese subtitles. The teen club was vaguely considered Warlord territory—they all hung out there on weekend evenings—and the instant the two Omega Chi walked through the door, everyone in the building knew there would be trouble.

Bryan Whyte and Mark Taylor nodded to each other and Whyte stepped over to the entrance of the game room.

As he watched Taylor happily enter the arena, he wondered suddenly if perhaps he should handle this matter himself. The Soldier seemed to enjoy these little disciplinary actions more than he was supposed to.

There was actually a hardness and cruelty about Taylor that often concerned Bryan. Taylor had started taking kung fu lessons when he was a tiny kid as a recommended therapy for his chronic asthma, and the martial arts quickly became his passion. Taylor's martial arts instructor had once told Whyte that he had never had a student of any nationality with more fighting confidence, a more natural killer instinct. At twelve, the Soldier was already going into downtown bars and picking fights with grown men.

Taylor slowly sauntered over to Magaha. "Hey, Dave, I hear you guys raised a little ruckus downtown the other day," he said cheerfully. "Boy, you just can't stay out of mischief, can you?"

Magaha didn't even look at him. He swaggered around the table, standing immediately next to Taylor, and tried a bank shot, missing.

"Geez, you know, Dave, I don't think those shopkeepers knew you were just having a little fun with them. I think they thought you were serious. Can you imagine that?"

Magaha picked up some chalk and dabbed at the tip of his cue expertly.

Taylor pressed on, an almost ludicrously skinny figure next to Magaha's two hundred pounds. "I think maybe you should make it up to those poor bastards. Maybe pay reparations for the damage you did. I think that'd be real sporting of you. Whataya say, Dave?"

Magaha continued to ignore him. The ceiling fan over the table hummed ominously, amplifying the silence.

"Hey." Taylor smiled at him. "I'm talking to you, Fatso."

Magaha hated that nickname more than he feared Taylor. He swung around in a blind flash of irritation. "Fuck you, Taylor."

Taylor sent his right fist smashing into Magaha's fat stomach like an iron spike. When the boy doubled over, Taylor's knee rose and rammed into Magaha's face, breaking his nose with a crack that echoed like a gunshot throughout the building. As Magaha fell to his knees, Taylor picked up the pool cue and, with a single savage stroke, broke it over Magaha's back.

"If you haven't paid by tomorrow noon I'll be back to see you," Taylor said, and calmly stepped over the body. He walked through the crowd, which parted before him like the waves before Moses.

When Whyte left Taylor in Tien Mou and took a taxi back into the city, he was still thinking about the Warlords. A year ago, they wouldn't have dared to make such a bold move right under the noses of the Omega Chi. Something was definitely inspiring them, spurring them on to such reckless acts, and he wasn't sure exactly what it could be. Sometimes he thought that all of Kennedy's campaign rhetoric and the success of the civil rights movement in the States was having its effect on the Filipino, Eurasian and Americanized Chinese who loosely belonged to the American Community—the very people who had always been on the lowest rung of the social order and who mostly made up the Warlords. Suddenly they were displaying a confidence and audacity they never had before. Whyte could sympathize with this in principle, but he was enough of a realist to see that in the case of the Warlords it could only mean trouble. He made a mental note to speak to Phillips about this if he saw him later that evening.

The taxi took him through the dark Taiwan countryside, over the Chung Shan bridge and down the city streets toward the U.S. Embassy on Chung Hsiao Road. Along the way, he watched the passing scenery with considerable interest. As he approached the downtown area, there was a view of miles and miles of dilapidated wood and stone buildings left over from the fifty years of Japanese rule that ended with the war. The streets were crowded with refugees who were still flooding out of Red China. In the near dozen years since the fall of the Mainland, Taipei had grown from a small town to a cosmopolitan city of half a million people, a city of great poverty and vast slums and unparalleled visual ugliness, but charged with an enterprising energy and optimism that never failed to excite Whyte.

At the Embassy, he paid the driver with a handful of rumpled bills, then paused a moment in front of the great walled compound, watching the lights, listening to the occasional peels of laughter from the inaugural party inside.

A marine corporal in the guard booth at the main gate took his name, phoned it in to someone inside the Embassy, then waved him on.

He walked slowly through the landscaped grounds, past clusters of formally attired couples catching a breath of cool night air. Several of them eyed his casual dress and black corduroy Omega Chi jacket.

At the Embassy door a second marine ushered him into an anteroom, where he sat on a sofa opposite a framed color photograph of Dwight Eisenhower. In a few moments, the door opened and an extremely tall, very dignified man wearing a tuxedo and a bandage on his head stepped hurriedly in. Beside him were two Embassy officials, also in tuxedos. The tall man sat down beside Whyte and attempted a smile.

"My name is Warren Stevens," he said. "I'm with the State Department."

Whyte knew who he was. He made it a point to keep track of the comings and goings of dignitaries in the morning *China Post.* But he decided to play dumb until he knew what the man could possibly want of him.

"I don't have time to beat around the bush," Stevens said stiffly. "The situation is too critical. Our intelligence sources tell us that the Nationalist Government may be planning a massive demonstration this week to protest the

Kennedy election and embarrass the new administration. It's supposed to take place somewhere in the American section and it's going to involve a lot of underworld types as demonstrators. Unfortunately, that's about all we know, but Washington has asked me to do everything possible to keep it from getting out of hand."

Whyte leaned back in the sofa and nodded thoughtfully. "I see. . . ."

Stevens was feeling a strange sense of déjà vu. Fifteen years ago, he had known this young man's father, and the similarity of their quiet, self-assured styles of carrying themselves was remarkable. "I'm told you have some kind of connections with the Taipei underworld. If there is anything you can do to help me get information I'd like you to do so. Specifically, I need to know when and where the demonstration will take place and an estimate of how many people will be involved."

Whyte thought about this a moment. He looked at the worried faces of the Embassy officials. He was rather enjoying the drama of the situation. "I think I know a way to prevent it entirely."

Stevens wasn't sure he heard the boy correctly. "You say, *prevent it?*"

Whyte looked at him very seriously. "At least defuse it."

"But how?"

Whyte edged a bit closer to the diplomat. "The Generalissimo relies on an organization called the Green Society to do jobs like this for him. They are almost certain to be in charge of both recruiting bodies and leading the demonstration. As you probably know, the Green Society is an ancient Chinese gang that helped Chiang come to power and practically ruled Shanghai for over a hundred years. . . ."

"Our intelligence sources say it doesn't exist anymore," Stevens said.

"They're wrong," Whyte smiled.

"I'm sorry I interrupted you. Go ahead with your

thought." Stevens realized that the boy's confidence and assurance was giving him the only comfort he had had in two days on this island.

"Well, above all else, the Greens are practical-minded businessmen. Right now probably their most lu-crative source of business income on the Island is Peitou, a little suburban village which has about ten really terrific whorehouses that are particularly popular with Ameri-cans. Say you were to announce tomorrow morning that from now on Peitou is off-limits to all American personnel —military, civilian, tourists, everyone. And that it will be enforced by nightly patrols. Say also that I get word to them that if the demonstration involves no destruction— and is just big enough so that no one loses face—then you'll lift the ban next week. I think it'll work. The Greens can't afford to have all their Peitou business move to Sin Alley and the Tiger Eels."

Stevens looked at the Embassy officials. "Arrange it," he said. "I don't care how many toes you have to step on. Make the announcement in the morning. Peitou is off-limits."

Whyte got up to leave. "Good. I'll take care of the rest."

At the door, they shook hands. "Maybe I can return the favor someday," Stevens said.

"Maybe." Whyte smiled. "But it's not necessary. We're all Americans, after all. We're all in this thing together."

His evening's obligations satisfied, Whyte hailed a pedicab—one of the thousands of little bicycle-rickshas that infested the streets of the city like so many mosquitoes —and took it to a large walled townhouse in a compound just off Roosevelt Road in South Taipei. He stood in the darkness outside the locked gate and made a low, distinc-tive whistle. Then he waited for an answer.

In a moment, he heard a window open and the sounds of someone crawling out of the house, moving cautiously across the yard and opening the gate. It was Shelley Spencer—the beautiful brown-haired American girl from the party. Around her neck, she wore a chain with his gold fraternity ring. When she came up and kissed him, her tongue darted playfully in his mouth.

"I have to be careful," she whispered urgently. "Daddy's getting suspicious again. When I got home, he gave me the third degree to end all third degrees."

They stepped inside the pedicab and Whyte mumbled directions to the driver. "The party at the House'll be winding down by now," he said, ignoring the remark about her father. "Let's go up to the Grand Hotel grounds. We can watch the fireworks over the river."

Shelley Spencer had been on the Island less than a year. Her father was an Army colonel who was transferred to Taipei for a two-year tour as a MAAG advisor on the Nationalist Chinese Nike missile project. She became involved with Bryan Whyte on her first day at the strange new international school. He came up out of nowhere and (rather nervously, she thought in retrospect) introduced himself, announcing that he would show her around. He was so clearly a popular—even awesome—figure among the American young people that she subtly encouraged him with every charm in her arsenal. As she gradually got to know him better, she discovered an extraordinary innocence and purity about him that was very appealing. Raised in an ultrapatriotic American Community without ever actually having been in America, he had never experienced any of the small setbacks and disillusionments that would have tempered his simplistic eighth-grade textbook view of his country and his place in it. He seemed to live in a world of utter confidence and limitless possibilities. This, plus the fact that his attentions gave her a queenlike status in high school society, made him quite irresistible.

"I'm dying for a cigarette, Bryan," she said hopefully. "Daddy's lecture has unnerved me."

"I thought we had a rule that you don't smoke around me anymore," he said.

"I'll just suffer in silence then."

"I'd appreciate that."

"Jerk."

"What?"

"You . . . are . . . a . . . jerk!"

"Oh, yeah?" He reached over and grabbed her waist and began tickling her. "*You* are a spoiled brat."

"Stop it," she giggled hysterically. "Bryan, I mean it."

"Why should I? I'm a jerk."

His hands moved from her waist to her breasts and he kissed her very long and very hard.

The pedicab swung a hard right on Chung Shan North Road, passed the neon fleshpots of Sin Alley and traveled on to the north end of the city, where the U.S. Officers' Club, U.S. Naval Exchange compound, U.S. Naval Support Activity Taiwan compound and Linkou U.S. Enlisted Men's Club made a little commercial American ghetto. The boulevard was crowded with people moving from party to party, drinks in hand. Wherever there was an American, there seemed to be an inauguration celebration going on.

As they sat back in the darkness of the rumbling pedicab, Whyte reached under her dress and slipped his hand under her silk panties. She resisted slightly, but gave in and moaned softly as he inserted his finger into her moist vagina, stroking it rhythmically. Remaining in this position, they rode through the wet, oily streets behind the oblivious, hard-peddling driver. Whyte had never gotten over his amazement at being able to touch Shelley there. Though he had gone all the way with maybe two dozen Oriental women in his young life, he had never before come close to such an experience with an American girl.

Shelley Spencer, in fact, had been a revelation to him in a number of ways. In their months together he had become attracted to her to the point of obsession. He was, of course, initially drawn by her beauty—which seemed to sum up that flawless American ideal that he only knew from magazine ads and Hollywood movies. But later, he

also became enchanted by her intelligence and sense of
humor; by her style and dignity and quiet faith in the
Catholic Church; by the thrilled and utterly believing look
in her green eyes every time he told her of his great plans
for the future. She was, in short, everything that Bryan
Whyte could want in a woman. The fact that her father
disapproved of him so vehemently that they had to meet
in secret was very upsetting to him.

As they began to cross the brightly lit Chung Shan
bridge, he removed his hand from her panties. "Why does
your father hate me so much?" he suddenly asked.

"He says you're a hood." The word "hood" seemed
such an inappropriate way of describing Bryan Whyte that
she giggled when she said it.

The injustice of this bothered Whyte so much that he
lost his erotic feeling. "He doesn't know a thing about
me," he said vacantly.

"Of course he doesn't."

Whyte was thinking that his connections with the
Oriental underworld were vastly overestimated by people
like Col. Spencer. Actually he only knew a few low-level
functionaries of the Greens that he dealt with in the course
of his black-market business. Still, since he was a child, he
had had an eerie sense of being watched over by them: the
Green Society *fu* he often wore around his neck had an
almost magical power to get him out of rough scrapes in
the city. Why this should be was a mystery he had never
really explored. He knew that his father was supposed to
have had some vague friendship with the *tai-lo* or overlord
of the Greens in the old Shanghai days. Undoubtedly it
was some holdover from that. But he never knew for sure
and he often wondered about it.

The pedicab crossed the Chung Shan bridge and
climbed the steep hill to the luxurious, government-owned
Grand Hotel, which overlooked the river and city like a
great medieval castle. Whyte came here often. He enjoyed
its lofty view of the city. He also had a favorite make-out
spot on the lower hotel grounds.

The fireworks display put on by the U.S. business

community had already started when they arrived. The couple lay in the grass under a gingko tree and watched the shooting stars and screaming meemies and the *pièce de résistance* that had reputedly cost the Taipei Harvard Club over five hundred U.S. dollars: a gigantic skyrocket that exploded into a crude outline of Kennedy's face in the clear winter sky.

"Do you really think it will be a new era?" Shelley asked.

"I definitely feel it," he said. "It's like a whole new beginning." He pointed to the sky and smiled. "You can even see the excitement in the air."

"It's going to be an adventure, huh?"

"Yes. One hell of an adventure."

Arm in arm, they walked down to the bluff overlooking the city and fell into reflective silence. As Whyte gazed into the distance he thought about this adventure, this future, and his thoughts filled him with a warm, familiar glow of confidence. He knew that he had a place in the future.

In the years since he and his father had come to Taiwan as penniless refugees, there had hardly been a single moment when he had not felt this sense of purpose. He had never exactly put it into words, but he somehow instinctively knew that he had a calling—a deep, sacred, all-consuming obligation to restore the fortune and face and way of life that had been stolen from his family. Indeed, everything about his world here was in some way structured toward that one end; and this was why he felt such loyalty to it, why he had made himself such an important, functioning part of it.

Looking out over the city, he experienced an overwhelming sensation of serenity and order and inevitability about his life. And if some crystal ball had told him that his whole world was about to erupt in disorder and violence and chaos, he would never have believed it.

3

THE FIRST SATURDAY OF EACH MONTH, ALAN PHILLIPS spent the morning in his makeshift office corner in the Omega Chi House. As secretary-treasurer of the fraternity, it was his duty to pay the bills of their orphanage, study the many requests for Omega Chi money and special favors and make dozens of phone calls to check on the progress of their various projects around town. This particular Saturday, he had just finished his last bit of business—acknowledging a belated thank-you note from David Butler, the newspaper correspondent whose stolen papers they had recovered from the Tiger Eels months before—when he picked up the telephone and discovered an extraordinary thing.

It was his custom to finish off the morning's work with a routine call to Johnny Hong, their contact with the Haggler's Alley Merchants' Association, to check the current rate at which the Chinese businessmen would buy unauthorized items from the Omega Chi to sell on the black market. This rate was a fairly standard figure determined each day by the law of supply and demand, usually falling somewhere between two hundred and fifty percent and three hundred percent of original purchase price. It had never, in anyone's memory, been lower than two hundred and thirty percent of original purchase price. But this time when Phillips called, Johnny calmly informed him that the rate was two hundred percent—a figure so ridiculously low as to indicate an enormous drop in demand. Or, more likely, Phillips instantly knew, an increase in supply.

The black market on Taiwan existed because U.S.

products were much prized on the local economy and totally unavailable except through the PX system. All an American had to do was buy a PX item—toothpaste, any article of clothing, a refrigerator, air conditioner, anything —and illegally resell it to a black-market broker for approximately two-and-a-half times the purchase price in New Taiwan dollars. In the mid-fifties, it became such a lucrative temptation for so many Americans and so many excesses took place that the U.S. Provost Marshal stepped in and deported most of the more flagrant offenders. The Marshal's office also began watching for anyone making a large number of purchases or trying to change a large amount of NT to greenbacks—thereby making it virtually impossible for anyone to do a volume business.

In early 1958 when he was no more than a child really, Bryan Whyte stepped in and, in one brilliant movement, took over the American black market for the Omega Chi by making himself middleman in the process. He let it be known around the appropriate people of the American Community that he would buy (in greenbacks) all U.S. items at twice the purchase price, eliminating for them the risk of being caught by the Provost Marshal or—as was frequently the case—swindled by the low-level Chinese and Taiwanese gangsters who served as black-market brokers. To the merchants of Haggler's Alley, who bought and resold the merchandise, he offered a steady volume business if they agreed to offer in turn a special preferred rate. Reportedly, Whyte also made a deal with the Green Society for protection, good will and initial financing, but Phillips knew nothing about this (nor did he want to know). The total system allowed them to take in several thousand U.S. dollars a week, a small fortune in a city like Taipei, where everything was so cheap.

Phillips had never felt comfortable dealing with the black market. With all his numerous community responsibilities, and as the son of an important U.S. official, he always felt he had a certain image to uphold. Somehow, dealing with Chinese gangsters did not go with that image. But Whyte had long ago convinced him that there was no other way to finance the Omega Chi and its special responsibilities on the Island. And Phillips was sure the money was being used for good purposes because he personally channeled most of it himself. So mostly he tried to ignore the black market and leave the day-to-day running of it to the others—except, of course, at times like this when it was impossible to ignore.

Phillips picked up the telephone and then paused. It had to be a mistake, he thought, or perhaps some devious Chinese ploy by Hong to test them. But what if—unlikely as it seemed—some new force was deliberately trying to muscle in on their longstanding business advantage? He went ahead and placed the call to Whyte's house in the Sung Shan District.

"Bryan," he said, "I think we may have a problem."

When the three Americans—Whyte, Phillips and Mark Taylor—entered his stall in the middle building of the crowded noontime Chung Wa Market, universally known as Haggler's Alley, old Johnny Hong was sitting at a small table stabbing chopsticks at a bowl of rice. Almost any time of the day, Hong could be found at this table listening contentedly to country-western music from his portable Sony radio, his great-grandchildren playing at his arthritic feet. The old man had a scraggly beard, a withered, prunelike face and an easygoing manner that disguised a shrewd business sense. All around him, his tiny place of business was stacked to the ceiling with boxes of black-market Pepsodent toothpaste, Brylcreem hair tonic, Dial soap, Halo shampoo, Right Guard spray deodorant.

Whyte had done business with Hong for years and was thoroughly attuned to his various nuances. The minute he looked into the old man's shifty eyes, he knew that something about their relationship had changed.

"Okay, so what is this about you no longer giving us a decent market rate, you old scoundrel?" he demanded in Mandarin, skipping the usual formalities.

Hong chewed his rice thoughtfully a moment and swallowed. Though all present spoke Chinese, he answered in pidgin, which was frequently preferred for haggling since it was so easy to hide behind its vagueness. "Rate two time now, Bwyn."

"Two times, bullshit. Three times all time same same."

"Me gotee too muchee sell. Rate down, Bwyn. Lookee you see." He motioned around the stall.

"I am to understand you have a new source of supply?"

The old man nodded. "You gotee competition, Bwyn."

"Who?"

"You buddies."

"What buddies?"

Hong's eyes danced merrily. "Davie Gaha gotee big supply to sell. Drive rate down two time."

Taylor grabbed Hong by the shirt and half-lifted him out of the chair. "The Warlords? Are you crazy? Those greasers will never keep you supplied with any volume. . . . One week, out of business. . . ."

Whyte calmly reached over and removed Taylor's hand from Hong's shirt. This was a break in custom that he could not allow. His eyes warned Taylor to back off.

Unruffled, the old man went back to his rice. "When that happen, we givee you two and haf, three time again. Same as befoh." He smiled devilishly, exposing numerous gold teeth. "Now two time."

Taylor turned to walk out. "Let's go, you guys," he said bitterly. "We don't need this old bandit. There are plenty of people standing in line to do business with the Omega Chi at a fair rate."

Whyte was also angry. "You should have warned us, Johnny," he said. "This is no way to treat old friends."

"Still friend. Busyness is busyness."

Out on the street again, they were all very grim. No organization had ever sought—had ever dared—to financially challenge the Omega Chi so boldly before. Whyte strained to remain impassive. The one thing he totally believed in was the principle of free enterprise and free competition. Taiwan stood for this principle. Now that he was being faced with real business competition for the first time he had to let it be a healthy thing. They could handle it.

But he still could not fathom how the Warlords could possibly scrape up the required capital for such an operation without him hearing about it. This worried him a great deal. "I think there is something we don't know and we better find out what it is," he told the other two. "Alan, call Randy Ortega and formally request a meeting."

Across town in a sweltering office in the U.S. Navy compound, Commander Floyd Harris was also having thoughts about the recent, curious activities of the Warlords gang. It was his responsibility to keep track of any unusual movements in the gangs of Taipei, and for the last twenty-four hours his informers had spoken of nothing *but* the Warlords' invasion of the Omega Chi's black-marketing operation and its possible consequences.

Harris paced under the spinning ceiling fan and tried to make some sense out of this troubling information. The Warlords seemed to be arrogantly challenging the supremacy of the Omega Chi and begging for a fight which they were in no physical or financial shape to win. It didn't make any sense at all and that made him very nervous. The one thing he had learned in his three months on this frustrating job was that the movement of the gangs almost always conformed to some logical sequence of cause and effect. There was obviously something he did not know and he was consumed with a fear that it would lead to some major catastrophe for which he, Floyd Harris, would inevitably shoulder the blame.

He sat down again and propped his feet on the desk. On the wall by the water cooler, there was a chart he had painstakingly constructed to show the structure of the underworld of Taipei and clarify the confusing maze of centuries-old Taoist secret societies, family associations, tongs, Taiwan racketeers, American street gangs and altruistic high school fraternities with which he had to deal. He lit a cigarette and studied the chart for some clue that would explain the Warlords' baffling action.

At the very top level of the chart was the *Ch'ing Pang*, or Green Gang. This extraordinary organization originated in Shanghai over a hundred years earlier and, though not much was really known about it, its name seemed to pop up regularly with all the major events of modern Chinese history. It was the Greens, in fact, who were largely responsible for Chiang Kai-shek's rise to power. In the twenties as a young man just making a name for himself in the Chinese Revolution, Chiang had actually been initiated as a member of the order. When the left and right wings of the Kuomintang split in 1927, it was the Greens who came to Chiang's rescue by brutally massacring the Shanghai Communists in one long night of terror. When the Second World War broke out, it was the Greens who made the most dreaded and effective force of resistance in occupied China. When Chiang was preparing his retreat to Taiwan in 1947, it was the Greens who went first and suppressed a Taiwanese insurrection with another massacre. Since that time, the Green Society (or Green Dragon Society or Green Association or *Ch'ing Pang*—as it was variously known in the history books) had remained a close ally of the Nationalist Government and served it in many strong-arm capacities, including bodyguard and political goon squad. It was also involved in smuggling, prostitution and gambling, and was thought to have intimate, Mafia-like connections with Chinese gangs throughout Asia and in every overseas Chinese community in the world.

On the level below the Green Society—far below, in fact, though they outnumbered the Greens many times— were the Tiger Eels. These were the direct descendants of the gangs of Formosan cutthroats, pirates and mercenaries who once were feared all up and down the China coast. When Chiang first came to Taiwan, he made a deal for support from the Tiger Eels and he had tolerated them ever since—though, of course, they were clearly subordinate to the Green Gang, which was made up entirely of Mainlanders. The Tiger Eels Gang was actually a loose network of separate (mostly teenage or *taibow*) gangs that were led by the elusive Taiwanese gangster named Loma —Taiwanese for "Big Eel." Each Tiger Eel gang had its own individual sphere of influence and political affiliation in West and Central Taipei. Each dealt in extortion and kidnapping and murder—their tools were acid bombs, butterfly knives (an Oriental stiletto that a skilled *taibow* could open faster than a switchblade), zip guns and straight razors—and the very mention of the name, "Tiger Eels" struck a chord of terror in the city.

Fanning out on a third level were the gangs of the American Community. These were mostly social organizations of the Taipei American School which had, over the years, become corrupted by the tong culture and their privileged positions and were now all marginally involved in hooliganism and petty rackets. The most troublesome of these were the Warlords, but close behind were the Taipei Rangers, Silver Knights and Cavaliers. Over all of the American gangs was the Omega Chi, which had some mysterious connection to the Greens. Bryan Whyte's gang was tolerated because its intentions were generally benign, because it kept the other gangs in some semblance of order and because Harris and his predecessors occasionally used it for their own purposes.

So, Harris thought, staring at his chart, the Nationalist Government cooperates with and uses the Green Society. The Green Society holds hegemony over the Taiwanese Tiger Eel gangs. The U.S. Government grudgingly tolerates the Omega Chi and the Omega Chi controls the American punk gangs and sometimes acts as a communication link to the Green Society. It was all very neat, a nice balance of power, he thought, and it seemed to work. But it was a fragile balance and he realized that the slightest upset could send it all toppling down around his feet. At best he could maintain a very precarious status quo, and at the worst . . . the worst was a black spot on his record that could deadend his career.

Harris crushed out his cigarette and thought about once again requesting a transfer to the fleet. Yet all his other requests for transfer had been denied without comment. Probably, he thought bitterly, because no one else wanted this job and because it was considered a suitable exile for an awkward bachelor who did not have a diplomatic personality or that proper Annapolis "look" suitable for the glamor jobs. Appearance was very important when there was not a hot war going on and—unlike his father and grandfather, both handsome admirals—he was cursed to look like a tree stump. It was so damned unfair!

The door to Harris's office opened; his assistant Hargrove, a young OCS ensign, filed in looking concerned. "We have a new report from a reliable informer, sir," he said as he placed a sheet of paper on the desk.

"What is it this time?"

"Seems Randy Ortega of the Warlords has had several meetings with Loma and the Tiger Eels in Sin Alley. We have no idea what they're talking about but we can be sure they're not just passing the time of day."

An ominous thought suddenly seized Harris. "Suppose, Mr. Hargrove," he said, looking intently at his chart once again, "just suppose that the Warlords and the Tiger Eels were to get together and form some sort of alliance? What would that do to our precious balance of power in the city?"

The ensign started to laugh and then quickly realized that the commander was not making a joke. "My God," he said. "I wouldn't even want to think about it."

Randy Ortega was a dark-skinned Filipino-American with an easy Latin charm that made him very attractive to women and a total ruthlessness that made him the most feared juvenile gang leader in the city. His father was a clarinet player in the U.S. Officers' Club orchestra who had served in the U.S. Army during the war and was given U.S. citizenship as a reward. Like Bryan Whyte, Ortega had grown up in the American Community and the two had known each other since they shared a tent at Y.M.C.A. summer camp in second grade. In eighth grade, they had an epic fistfight that had gone on for nearly two hours before it was stopped. Whyte still had the scar on his chin to remember it by, and there had been bad blood between them ever since.

When Ortega walked into the air-conditioned patio room of the U.S. Officers' Club for his prearranged meeting with Whyte, three of the other Warlords were with him. To his right was Lefty O'Hara, a short, tough American whose father fought Communists as a mercenary in Laos. To his left was Ya Ki Loi, a frail boy from Malaya whose father owned a shipping firm out of Keelung and who furnished the Warlords with their greatest source of show, or what the coolies called "looksee pidgin": a chauffeured limousine. Following them all by several steps was Ortega's little brother, Juan, who had not even reached puberty yet but who always trailed along with the Warlords like a shadow and was desperately eager to make a name for himself.

The rest of the Warlords—"Fatso" Dave Magaha, a Chinese-American named Clinton Chen, a bushy-haired Taiwanese named Amos Wong, and another American, a Presbyterian missionary's son named Tim Cutler—waited for their leader outside the swimming pool, where a small crowd of kids had gathered to speculate on what could be going on between Ortega and Whyte.

Whyte was at a table by himself. He stood up and ceremonially shook hands with each of the four Warlords individually. Then they all sat down together.

He came right to the point. "Yesterday," he said, "when I went down to Haggler's Alley to see Johnny Hong, I heard this incredible story. The story was that the Warlords were entering the black market down there in a very big way. Since I knew my friends the Warlords would never do such a provocative and unfriendly thing without even telling me, I immediately knew it was a lie. But I

thought we should get together and think of a way to stop
this story from spreading and giving people the impression
we are not friends."

As Whyte spoke, he felt his insides burning. He
couldn't help thinking of his famous fight with Ortega
and how it had started: He had seen Ortega break a rice
wine bottle over the head of a sleeping pedicab driver in
some perverted notion of sport. Whyte loathed these
people, and it was only with enormous concentration
and self-will that he was able to keep an outward balance
and calm.

Ortega listened to Whyte's words thoughtfully. Then
he lit a cigarette and blew a tiny smoke ring in the air.
O'Hara and Ya Ki Loi smirked disrespectfully. "But I'm
afraid it's not a lie," Ortega said, just as charmingly. "The
black market is the biggest profit business in the city and
it's getting bigger all the time. Surely the Omega Chi is not
so greedy that it can't share some of this business with us."

Whyte had expected this but had not expected the
uncharacteristic boldness with which it was spoken.
Something was giving Ortega this boldness—something
beyond the general audacity he had been noticing in people like the Warlords these past months. Ortega was holding a trump card. He had to find out what it was.

"It is true that the market is very profitable," Whyte
said, arching his eyebrow and breaking into a slight lecture tone, "and that is why we watch over it so closely.
The money we earn from it is used for all sorts of good
purposes and not just our own personal greed. As you
know, we support an orphanage, provide a fund for typhoon victims, help resettle Mainland refugees. . . . The
money is a by-product of the American presence and we
feel it is only proper that it be used for the benefit of the
people of the Island."

"Is it proper that you buy yourself a house and staff
it with amahs and houseboys?" Ortega laughed, as if to
answer his own question. "But it is no concern of mine.
What you do with your money is your business and what
we do with our money is our business."

The three other Warlords all nodded in unison.

Whyte went on, taking a different tack. "But how are you possibly going to finance such an operation? You need a lot of money—money to buy in volume, money to pay off the right people. And even if you were to get your hands on that kind of money, it would still be difficult because we have all the connections in the American Community. All the small buyers work for us. The only way you will ever get them to work for you on a regular basis is to force them and, of course, we will never sit back and allow that—it is all I can do to contain the Soldier as it is."

Ortega looked at him coldly. There was no fear in his small black eyes, only an extraordinary contempt that challenged Whyte like a slap in the face. He knew Whyte was probing for information and he did not want to tip his hand, but he could not resist: He wanted the satisfaction of delivering the news to his old enemy personally. "We have complete financing and protection from the Tiger Eels. Loma and I have signed a blood oath. From now on his enemies are our enemies and vice versa. The days when Mark Taylor can freely abuse us are over. The days when the Omega Chi owns the black market are history."

Whyte sat back in his chair. So this was it. The Tiger Eels and Warlords were banding together. He fought back a rising tide of panic. If he could not find a way to stop it, it would mean anarchy in his orderly world. The Warlords would be invincible. He continued to sit there a moment in silence and did not show the slightest expression. Finally he said, "Then I suppose we have nothing else to talk about."

Ortega stood up and smiled shrewdly. He nodded to the others and, without another word, the four Warlords shuffled out of the little dining room and joined their companions out by the pool.

When they were gone, Whyte immediately went to a phone and called Mark Taylor. He told him to leave whatever he was doing and get over to the Omega Chi House as soon as possible. They were in the midst of a crisis.

* * *

It was noon the following day at the Taipei American School—a muggy, blistering Tuesday in early May.

John Casy sat beside Georgie Warner at the rear of his Asian studies class, ignoring the instructor and gazing blankly out the window at a girls' physical education class playing volleyball. On his desk, his open notebook was filled with the senseless doodles and sketches he had drawn for the past hour instead of taking notes on the lecture.

The instructor—a burnt-out Ivy League Orientalist and borderline alcoholic like so many others that found their ways to teaching positions at TAS—finally noticed Casy's inattention and said to him: "Perhaps Mr. Casy will share with us his views on the origins of the Taiping Rebellion."

Casy smiled apologetically and shook his head negatively.

"You weren't listening, were you, Mr. Casy?"

"No, sir."

The instructor looked particularly vexed and, seeing this, Georgie Warner raised his hand and said enthusiastically, "I was listening, sir. I know the answer."

The instructor looked at Warner warily. "Okay, Warner. But make it short."

"The Taiping Rebellion was a revolution of all the secretaries of China in 1956."

"Don't start with me, Warner."

"They said, 'Hey, we're fed up with typing for these kind of coolie wages.'"

"That's enough . . ."

"Have you ever seen a Chinese typewriter? Those mothers have three thousand characters on their keyboards."

"I said . . ."

"Even the portable ones weigh over five tons. . . ."

The class was roaring so Warner settled down. He

glanced at Casy and smiled. The Jerry Lewis routine had been Warner's way of getting his friend out of a spot. A gift to a brother. Casy smiled back appreciatively.

Actually, under more normal circumstances, Casy enjoyed Asian studies best of all his subjects. Unlike his friends in the Omega Chi, he had not been raised taking traditional Chinese culture for granted—he was also the only one of them who did not speak Chinese—and he was fascinated by the beauty and order and harmony of it all. He had read around translations of the Confucian classics enough to have a superficial knowledge of them; he often visited the National Museum to view the extraordinary art treasures Chiang had brought with him from the Mainland; and he had made a serious study of Chinese music, which, to most Westerners, sounded like so much noise. He constantly tried to soak up every detail of Chinese philosophy and culture in the knowledge that someday it would come out as a strong influence on whatever art he chose to throw himself into.

But today, the only thing occupying his mind was the crisis with the Warlords. He really did not know what it would mean to them if that gang had truly formed a blood alliance with the Tiger Eels—he was not business-minded like Whyte and Phillips or military-minded like Taylor. He just assumed it would be very bad. He had gotten to know many of the Tiger Eels over the past two years. On one level he even sympathized with them because, as Taiwanese, they were treated like dirt by the Chinese Mainlanders in their own country. But he also knew that they were brutal, unpredictable and thoroughly unreasonable, and the thought of having them as adversaries paralyzed him.

Casy's fear was mitigated by the knowledge that at that very moment, Whyte and Taylor were out in Sin Alley somewhere trying to track down Loma. He knew that Whyte would use every skill he possessed to change the gangster's mind about such an alliance. He knew that if anyone could have success in that kind of mission it was

Bryan Whyte—who could convince anyone of anything
and had never gotten the short end of a negotiation in his
life.

Whyte had an uncanny ability to evoke blind loyalty
in those around him and no one felt a stronger loyalty than
Casy. Casy was attracted to him with that almost religious
devotion an artist or intellectual will often experience for
a man of action. He was utterly confident that Whyte
would pull something out of his hat at the last moment
and make things right. He always had before.

The bell rang and the class cleared the room. In the
passageway outside the classroom, one of the school cus-
todians stopped him and told him there was someone at
the back gate with a message for Mark Taylor. "Man he
say vely, vely portant."

"The Soldier is gone today," Casy said. "I'll take care
of it."

He usually considered it a privilege to fill in for
Whyte or Taylor but this was really inconvenient. It
meant he would have to walk all the way to the rear of the
school compound and be late for his next class. He
thought a moment of having Warner do it, but Warner
was already heading off in the other direction.

The American School was a small, walled-in compound constructed around a square courtyard—its buildings mostly bungalows built in prefab materials as an act
of faith that Chiang Kai-shek would retake the Mainland
someday and the school could be easily reconstructed
there. To get to its back gate, Casy had to walk all the way
along two sides of the square and pass through a large
playground where the grammar school was having recess.
Through the playing children he could see a heavyset
Taiwanese man standing at the gate waiting for him. The
man looked intimidated by the presence of so many
Americans.

As he approached him, Casy said, "Mark no here.
You givee me same same."

"Markee Tawyer?"

"Yes. Give it to me."

The man reached in his pocket and took out an object. He made a lightning motion with his wrist and a blade appeared in his hand, glaring in the afternoon sun. The hand lunged at him and the butterfly knife went into John Casy's chest and pierced a corner of his lung. The man withdrew the knife and stabbed at Casy's back, the blade lodging in a rib. When the man could not withdraw the knife again, he cursed, then broke and ran. Only then did Casy feel the sharp pains in his side and back. Only then did he fall to his knees, vaguely sensing his own blood all around him and the sound of little children wailing in horror.

Some miles away, Shelley Spencer was waiting for a prescription to be filled in the pharmacy of the big U.S. Navy Hospital near Tien Mou.

She sat in a waiting room filled with pregnant women and crying babies, flipping through the pages of a *Seventeen* magazine, trying to pretend she did not notice two sailors across the room ogling her. It was only in the past year that she had really become conscious of her beauty and the power it seemed to give her; it was still novel enough that she found herself delighting in the attention, casually moving her body every so often to give them a better view, casually crossing and recrossing her long legs under the tight skirt to subtly tantalize them.

She had missed school today to avoid an algebra exam and because she mildly felt the flu coming on. By afternoon, the symptoms disappeared but her mother—who was British and very conscientious about these things—sent her to the doctor anyway. She had obeyed because her father was home this week and a fight would be inevitable if she stayed around. These days, they couldn't stay in the same room for five minutes without getting into a screaming match, usually over Bryan Whyte. Last week, she had calmly announced that she was in love with Bryan and the colonel hit the ceiling. She had been under suspension ever since.

Shelley lit another cigarette and her name was called. She felt the eyes of the sailors watching her as she stepped to the counter, picked up the prescription and walked out of the hospital. Outside, she couldn't see a taxi so she stood in front of the Chinese bus stop, hoping some passing American would give her a ride into town.

As she stood there waiting, a black Volvo that had been parked across the street started its engine and pulled over beside her. Inside were three older Oriental men in business suits. One nodded to the other and rolled down the window. "Shelley Spencer?" he asked.

This surprised her. "Yes, why?"

"We are Foreign Affairs Police," he said. "There been lotta tlobah. You betta comee quick." He reached back and opened the rear door for her.

"What kind of trouble?"

"We takee you see Bwyn Whyte. He vely bad hurt. Big fight. Muchee tlobah."

"Oh God!" she cried and hurried into the car.

Whyte had called her last night and said there was probably going to be trouble with the Warlords but she had not paid any particular attention. He was always having trouble with the Warlords. She was instantly filled with guilt, fear, regret, anxiety and a not altogether unpleasant sensation of self-importance—the emotions of a martyred war widow.

The car sped through several miles of paddy fields while the two men chatted in the front seat and the one beside Shelley examined her from the corners of his eyes. The man reeked of garlic and he seemed to be sitting unnecessarily close to her. "What happened?" she finally thought to ask.

The man said nothing and kept casually examining her. She stared blankly at the passing scenery a few moments and then felt herself getting angry. "Where is he, anyway?" she demanded.

When the man still did not answer, it hit her all at once: *Chinese Foreign Affairs Police always wear distinctive blue uniforms.* "Stop this car," she yelled at the driver. "I want out right now."

The man beside her calmly flashed a six-inch butterfly knife and put it to her throat. She did not even think to struggle as the driver speeded up and her companion slowly put his hand up her skirt and between her thighs.

Several hours later, the afternoon crowds began to thin out around Haggler's Alley and the sweet and sour smells of thousands of small cooking fires began once more to fill the air of Shihminting, the city center area.

Old Johnny Hong impatiently switched off his radio and went to the front of his stall to look for his youngest daughter, who was late returning with the fish and squid that would be cooked out back for his large family's evening meal. Probably talking to some worthless boy, he thought irritably. What *was* becoming of this younger generation? The old man yawned into his hand and stood for a moment at the nearly deserted Chung Wa Road, watching the street vendors setting up their stands for the early evening crowds that would soon flock to the many Shihminting movie houses.

Haggler's Alley—so-called because the price of everything sold there was reached by the ancient Chinese custom of haggling—was situated in the heart of old Taipei. For years after the exodus of '49, it was a jungle of squatter shacks until the government stepped in and constructed large concrete buildings with hundreds of compartments from which the displaced Chinese merchants could sell their wares. As the oldest and most venerated of these exiled small businessmen, Johnny Hong served as president of their business association and made all the decisions regarding their participation in the lucrative black market on American goods.

The entry of the Warlords into the black market was regarded as a wonderful coup for him—even though Hong actually had little to do with it. Now that he had the

Omega Chi and the Warlords competing with one another as suppliers, he was in a position of power. His buying price was being driven way down and his selling price remained the same. His—and all the other merchants'—margin of profit was way up and there was no reason why this trend would not continue indefinitely and make him a wealthy man.

As Hong stood there in front of his stall waiting for his daughter, he noticed a fleet of cars rapidly coming his way—possibly the motorcade of some visiting dignitary. The cars screeched to a halt in front of his building and dozens of men rushed out. They were all Tiger Eels and Warlords and they carried billy clubs and axes. Hong then noticed that the policemen who were always on duty across the street had mysteriously vanished.

The seven Warlords—Magaha, O'Hara, Clinton Chen, Amos Wong, Ya Ki Loi, Tim Cutler and little Juan Ortega—reconnoitered in front of Hong's stall. Randy Ortega joined them, gave a nod, then each of them took a detachment of three Tiger Eels and fanned out over the other stalls. They proceeded to bust up everything in sight that looked as if it might have been black-marketed—liquor, cigarettes, cosmetics, food, detergent, anything with a label in English. What they couldn't break, they threw out into the street to be burned in a tremendous bonfire.

Ortega paced the pavement and watched the activity like a general contentedly inspecting the progress of a battle. Hong rushed up to him. "What for you do this?" he screamed. "We in busyness togethah!"

"Sure we're in business," the Filipino said, shouting over the sounds of breaking glass and splintering wood. "We just want to start fresh. We don't want anything to remind us of the Omega Chi, do we?"

"You no tell Johnny thisee happen. Stopee now!"

Ortega ignored him and looked up at his younger brother gleefully tearing up boxes of detergent from a second-story stall and letting it snow on the pavement below.

Hong was famous for not showing emotion, but at the sight of all this beautiful inventory being systematically destroyed, his businessman's heart was breaking. "Oh, please stopee," he cried. He grabbed Ortega by the arm.

It was a mistake. Ortega took Hong by the back of the neck and threw him tumbling back into his stall. Then he pointed a trembling finger at the old man. "From now on," he said, "you will do business only with the War-lords. The Omega Chi is finished down here for good."

Bryan Whyte arrived at the hospital just minutes after John Casy was rushed into surgery. He was completely numb, his heart pounding in his chest with the force of a sledgehammer. In the lobby he ran straight into Casy's father and near-hysterical mother. They told him that John's condition was serious—his lung had collapsed —but the doctors considered his prognosis reasonably good.

Colonel Casy, a tough and quick-tempered officer of the old school, glared an accusation at Whyte. "How did this happen?"

"I don't know, sir. They told me at school that it was a mistake. The guy who did it was apparently after Mark Taylor."

Veins bulged in the colonel's temples. "I want you to know that I hold you personally responsible for this. You and your hoodlum friends."

Mrs. Casy sobbed. "If he comes out of this, I don't want you ever to go near my son again. Is that understood?"

Whyte shared their grief. He wanted to say something reassuring but realized it was useless.

He waited with them for several hours and then called Georgie Warner at the Omega Chi House to check in. Warner told him in hushed tones that Shelley Spencer had been abducted, manhandled and terrorized, then set free downtown. When Whyte heard this story it was as if his whole world had become some nightmare version of itself. The old order had vanished, the old rules no longer applied.

He called Shelley immediately. "I want you to know that I'll get even for this," he said right off.

"I know, baby."

"Are you all right?"

"I was scared to death. They told me they were going to rape me."

"They didn't though, did they?"

"No."

There was a long pause, then Whyte said, "They wanted to demonstrate that they could have done it."

"But why?"

"I don't know. A warning. Or maybe a diversion to keep my mind occupied while they try something else. It was definitely timed to happen at the same time as the attack on Casy."

"What attack on Casy?"

He told her.

She started to cry. It was unbearable. Poor, sweet, gentle John Casy. "I'm coming to the hospital."

"No you're not. You're going to stay home with the door locked. Both of these things are only steps toward a larger goal that's not apparent yet. Until Ortega makes his big move, I want everyone to lie low."

"What are you going to do?"

"Nothing until I have more information."

He took a taxi back to his home in the Sung Shan District. It was a small and, by Taipei American standards, unimpressive townhouse several blocks south of the Taipei airport. He went inside to find that his father— known affectionately throughout the American Community as "Old Whyte"—was, as usual, not there and the amah was chattering away with some of her friends in the kitchen.

He went into his bedroom and shut the door. It was a tiny room with a depressing view of a back alley. It had a single bed, a teak desk, a chair, a barbell and a bookshelf that contained his favorite books: *The Power of Positive*

Thinking, The Wealth of Nations, American Capitalism, its Promise and Accomplishment, Capital Formation in Japan, 1868–1940; and biographies of John D. Rockefeller, Andrew Carnegie and Benjamin Franklin—worn volumes he had read and reread so many times that he had virtually committed them to memory.

On one wall was a large National Geographic map of the United States with little stars pasted on all the places he intended to visit when he finally went there to go to college. On the other walls were posters of Mount Rushmore and the Manhattan skyline. There was also a framed replica of the Declaration of Independence he had ordered through the *Reader's Digest* and framed photographs of his mother, whose memory he cherished, and Shelley Spencer, who faintly resembled her.

He sat on the bed and tried to force the rage from his mind. He had to be very calm and very rational. He had never been faced with a situation like this before and it would be very easy to do something stupid. His instinct was to regroup and go after the Warlords with a fury, but this was obviously what Ortega expected him to do and, with Tiger Eels lurking around every corner, it would be disastrous.

When he felt his emotions firmly under control he went into the hallway and made three phone calls.

The first was to Mark Taylor, who naturally insisted on immediate and total war. "Casy's blood is all over the playground," the Soldier said. "It's a symbol of our weakness. We lose more face every second that goes by while it remains unavenged. We gotta hit Ortega and Magaha tonight and forget about the Tiger Eels. Let's you and me beat them to goddamn . . . bloody . . . pulps." He was so enraged he was half bawling and could barely pronounce the words.

"Don't do anything until you hear from me," Whyte insisted, then abruptly hung up.

The second person he called was Alan Phillips, who told him about the takeover of the black market in Haggler's Alley.

"So that was it," Whyte said.

"They destroyed thousands of dollars' worth of stuff. Nobody lifted a finger to stop them."

"I never thought Ortega would go this far. I'd have bet a hundred bucks Loma would never have gone along with anything this outrageous. Christ, Alan, there's got to be some principle at work here that we don't understand."

"There's nothing we can do now, Bryan," Phillips cautioned, his voice unusually agitated. "We can't take on every Taiwanese gangster in town. They'll cut our throats without a second thought. We have to leave this to Harris and the Provost Marshal's office. . . ."

The third person he called was Commander Floyd Harris. Harris sounded frantic. "Where have you been? I've been trying to get you all day! Listen Bryan, I know you want to get even with those animals for what they did to Casy, but let *us* take care of it. I want your word that you'll do nothing. You can't single-handedly take on the Tiger Eels. And even if you could, there is no way I'd allow a major gang war to go on in the American Community. You're going to have to let me handle this."

Whyte paused for a full minute. The stakes involved here were tremendous. With the Omega Chi neutralized and the Warlords in charge of the American black market, this new coalition was going to become a powerful new force in the city. It was bound to touch every aspect of their lives.

Finally he said, "Commander, you seriously overestimate the Omega Chi. We are not crazy. The Tiger Eels have maybe two thousand warriors in the downtown area alone. Good lord, they outnumber the municipal police four to one. We're just five guys. What do you think we can do? What card do you think I have to play against those odds?"

On that note, Harris seemed satisfied and he hung up. What Harris did not know, however, was that Bryan Whyte did indeed have one very big card to play and, when the time was right, he had every intention of playing it.

4

WHEN MARK TAYLOR ARRIVED AT THE OMEGA CHI House, he saw that it was empty and unguarded. Considering the longstanding state of affairs in the city, this seemed criminally negligent to him and it made his foul mood even fouler. Cursing Georgie Warner under his breath, he fumbled in the dark with the lock on the door.

It was the big weekend of Chinese New Year's; the streets and lanes around the House were already alive with fireworks and noisemakers and gaudy papier-mâché dragons. He had just come from a late practice with the Taipei Outsiders rugby team and his taxi had great difficulty making its way through the mob of costumed dancers and excited children welcoming in the Year of the Hare. Usually he was able to get into the carnival spirit of Chinese New Year's, but this year was an exception. His lack of involvement in the merriment of the occasion was yet another painful reminder that his entire world had come apart in the past six months.

Randy Ortega and his Warlords had firmly established their control over the American black market in Taipei. They had effectively destroyed all the remaining back inventory of Omega Chi-supplied goods. They had consolidated virtually all of the smaller American gangs —the Taipei Rangers, the Silver Knights and the Cavaliers—and forced them to come up with monthly quotas of stolen American goods for the Warlords to resell. They were making Johnny Hong buy these goods at a three hundred fifty percent rate (which meant the man could make no money at all on the deal) and demanded he meet impossible monthly sales quotas. With Tiger Eel troops to back them up, they were beating, bullying and harassing anyone who dared defy them.

The Omega Chi had done nothing in these months to even try to stop them. There was no revenge for the knife attack on John Casy. There was no response to the humiliating abduction of Shelley Spencer. There was no reaction to the destruction of the goods on Haggler's Alley or complete takeover of their black market business. Bryan Whyte ordered them to stay in the American areas, out of the Warlords' way at TAS, and to avoid an incident or any kind of confrontation at all costs. Taylor, in particular, was being kept on the tightest of tight leashes and it was driving him out of his mind.

His business here tonight was to meet with an informer. Since the trouble began, Whyte had asked him to monitor the movements of the Warlords very closely and he dutifully had these little rendezvous once or twice a week or more. Whyte was always extremely interested in hearing the results of these meetings, though none of them had as yet been terribly informative. It was apparent that Whyte was waiting to hear something specific, something that would allow him to put some great master plan into effect—and this knowledge alone prevented Taylor from lashing out at their enemies in a personal suicide mission. Though Whyte never mentioned what it was he wanted to hear, Taylor assumed it had to be something that would bring the Warlords into conflict with the Green Society.

It was a very strange thing. Mark Taylor had been Bryan Whyte's best friend almost all his life. They had grown up closer than brothers, sharing all their deepest secrets—except one. He had always known that the Whyte family had some mysterious connection with the Green Society. As kids, it had often seemed that the Greens were looking after Whyte to make sure he came to no harm. Yet he had no idea of what that connection was or why it existed or even if Bryan himself knew what it was all about. All Taylor knew for certain was that the connection did exist and that it was now the Omega Chi's only hope of neutralizing the Tiger Eels and bringing down the reign of the Warlords.

He went in the House and looked around for Georgie Warner, who was supposed to be on duty tonight. Since they could no longer afford to pay servants, they were taking turns looking after the House. There was no sign of Warner (Taylor was not surprised, as he knew Warner had been sneaking off to the whorehouses almost every night since the crisis began) so he went to the refrigerator and pulled out a bottle of rice wine. Then he went to the foyer library, chose a copy of Eisenhower's *Crusade in Europe* and sat on the tatami floor to flip through it. In a few months he would take his first West Point preparatory exam and he was spending every spare moment cramming. It was the only thing that kept him sane.

There was a knock on the door. He stood up and opened it and a tiny boy with horn-rimmed glasses smiled at him. "Hiya, Soldier."

"Come on in, Dennis."

The boy was Dennis Chou. He was a Taiwanese who went to TAS and had lived in the States off and on over the years—the son of an executive for Firestone Rubber. He was a founding member of the Taipei Rangers and a sometime flunky of Fatso Magaha of the Warlords. Like many of the small-time gang members, Dennis Chou had grown up idolizing the legend of Mark Taylor and Taylor was now using that admiration to acquire information about the Warlords.

As he entered the House, Dennis Chou's eyes bulged at the stacks of black-market goods which they had managed to rescue before the Warlords got to them and which were now being hoarded until happier times—radios, toasters, toiletries and cartons of cigarettes piled from floor to ceiling in every corner.

Taylor opened the bottle of rice wine and took a mighty slug and handed it to the boy. The sound of fireworks crackled in the distance. "So what's new with our friends this week?" he asked.

Dennis Chou took a smaller sip and passed the bottle

back. He shook his little head slowly and methodically. "Un . . . bee . . . lieve . . . a . . . ble," he said.

"How so?"

"They had a big meeting this week and they decided they're going to expand all over the place. Ortega and Loma are gonna add a bunch of bars and whorehouses in Sin Alley and branch out into a lot of other business."

"Such as?"

"Gambling and moneylending."

"Really?"

"Yeah, and that's only the beginning. They got plans of eventually expanding all over the city. Shit, this time next year, those dudes are gonna own this town. You watch and see. That Ortega is a bigger fucking genius than Bryan Whyte himself."

Taylor experienced an intense, animal urge to kill Dennis Chou. He suddenly wanted to pound this thoughtless little puke into hamburger for even daring to mention that greaser Ortega in the same breath as Bryan Whyte. He dug his fingernails into the tatami and tried to smile. "And how is he gonna do that? Seems to me that he's gone about as far as he can go right now."

Dennis Chou grinned. "There's always Peitou."

"Peitou?"

"There's plenty of money there."

"Peitou belongs to the Green Gang. Does Ortega have a death wish or something?"

The boy shrugged. "I donno, man. Maybe Ortega thinks there's room for them both there. Maybe the Tiger Eels aren't as scared of the Greens as they used to be. Maybe we Taiwanese are tired of having our asses kicked around by the fucking Mainland Chinese." He paused and took another drink from the bottle. "And then again maybe it's all bullshit." He giggled. "You can't really believe a thing Magaha says."

Taylor tried to disguise his excitement. Adrenaline was surging through him. This was very interesting information indeed. This was something he should take to

Bryan Whyte right away. This could be exactly what Bryan Whyte was waiting for.

Dennis Chou's eyes wandered greedily to the stacks of merchandise around the room. "Say, Mark, can I have a radio or something?"

"Take all you can carry."

Two days later, Whyte called Taylor, Phillips, Casy and Georgie Warner together for an important meeting. They all sat cross-legged around the table in the Omega Chi council room; the houseboy had just served them tea and closed the door. It was their first official gathering since the night of the Kennedy inauguration party and the contrast in mood could not have been more drastic: The old Omega Chi morale and confidence had been devastated by the past six months. Not even Warner tried to make a joke or lighten the atmosphere.

Whyte began by reviewing the situation. He reminded them of the unpleasant fact that the Warlords had taken over the American black market, had ruthlessly squeezed them out of business and were using their profits and new position to create a reign of terror in the city that was growing more intolerable by the hour. The Omega Chi was helpless in this situation because the Warlords had the protection of the Tiger Eels, who were an overwhelming force. The only logical alternative for the Omega Chi, therefore, was to seek out the protection of an even greater force, and the only greater force was the Green Society. With the Greens checking the power of the Tiger Eels, the Omega Chi could handle the Warlords and everything would be as it had been before.

As Whyte spoke these words, several of the faces around the table visibly tightened. The Green Gang was probably the most powerful criminal organization that had ever existed in the world. Its name conjured up uneasy images of Shanghai back alleys and gangland murders and vicious tong wars.

But Whyte remained presidential in his assurance. "With the help of the Warlords and American black-market money, the Tiger Eels have been gradually expanding their influence and territory for the past six months. We now have pretty good evidence that they're finally making motions toward the lucrative Green territory in Peitou. If we could somehow get to the right people in the Greens, we could present them with the evidence and try to convince them that it's in their best interests to join with us and stop this coalition before it's too late."

Sensing the opposition of his friends, especially Phillips, Whyte let down a moment and his voice took on a very uncharacteristic desperate quality. "I realize this is a big step for us. When we formed this fraternity we didn't bargain on anything like this. Anyone who wants to step out should do it now. Honest to God, I won't think any the worse of you. The only reason I'm pursuing this is because it's the only goddamn way I can think of that has even a chance of returning things to normal."

There was a moment of silence. Phillips merely shook his head helplessly. He thought the whole endeavor was a terrible mistake, but his loyalty would not allow him to openly challenge Whyte. No one got up to leave.

Georgie Warner looked at Whyte incredulously. "I still don't get it," he said. "We've always dealt with low-level peons in the Greens—and even they're hard as hell to get to. How are you going to get to the right people? The honchos of the Greens are probably better protected than the Generalissimo."

Whyte's eyes followed the houseboy as he reentered the room with a fresh pot of tea and set it on the table.

"It won't be easy," he said. "But I know a way."

Bryan Whyte made his way through the regular crowd of pimps that congregated on the American strip of Chung Shan North Road. He passed the helmeted Chinese guard in the courtyard and stepped into the bright lights of the U.S. Officers' Club. His body tingled with excitement. For over six months he had patiently waited for the right opportunity to make his move, and now that the moment was finally at hand, he was not going to delay or procrastinate even another minute.

The O Club was filled with the usual Wednesday night crowd of diplomats and their families. Whyte walked through its ornate Ming-deco lobby, past rows of slot machines and loud clusters of Arabs, Africans and South Americans, and entered the immense, crowded ballroom. He was looking for his father.

The sizeable diplomatic community in Taipei was, for all purposes, a subdivision of the American Community. The staffs of over fifty embassies were extended full U.S. commissary privileges, sent their children to the American School, and had all the other special privileges of the American presence here. But the diplomats strove to maintain a separate—slightly more exclusive—identity. One of their traditions was Wednesday night bingo at the U.S. Officers' Club on Chung Shan North Road, for which the unofficial host was William Jennings Bryan Whyte, Senior, or, as he was better known, Old Whyte.

Old Whyte was himself a kind of institution in the American Community. As one of the last of the old-time taipans of Shanghai, he served as a colorful reminder of that older and more graceful time. With his white suits and snow white hair and full, colonial mustache, he played this role to the hilt, rarely missing an opportunity to tell an inconsequential anecdote about the old days or attend a social function of any kind. Underneath all the old world charm and quaint stories and refusal to talk about anything remotely serious, he was, everyone knew, a ruined and possibly crazed man. The Communist takeover of his businesses and the death of his wife had left him with nothing. He had survived since the evacuation on a charity "advisory" job on the Taipei stock exchange, arranged by his old friends in the Kuomintang.

Young Bryan Whyte adored his father even though he fully realized that the old man was considered something of a joke. He understood very early that his father drank too much and was not completely right in the head and, consequently, was extremely protective of him. Once, years ago, Bryan had seen a man making sport of his father at a community Fourth of July picnic. The man, a very large and very overbearing Army master sergeant, had egged Old Whyte on to tell stories of the days when he was taipan of the entire motion picture industry on the Mainland. The sergeant had listened patronizingly to all the stories, continually feeding him drinks, and when Old Whyte was finished, the man burst out laughing. In front of a crowd, he humiliated Old Whyte, calling him a fool and a liar. When Bryan Whyte witnessed this scene, he quickly gathered Mark Taylor and Georgie Warner and they followed the sergeant home. When the man got out of his taxi, they stopped him and, using Taylor's *nunchaku* or kung fu fighting sticks, and with a ferocity his friends had never seen in him before or since, Whyte beat the sergeant within an inch of his life. The man—and no one else, for that matter—was ever disrespectful of Old Whyte again. This was when Bryan Whyte was only thirteen years old.

When old Mr. Whyte saw his son, he joyously grabbed his arm and proceeded to introduce him around the ballroom. Knowing he was his father's greatest source of pride, Bryan endured this with a patient smile. He made small talk with the Argentine ambassador's visiting cousin (ironically, within earshot of Randy and Juan Ortega's father, who was playing clarinet with the orchestra providing background music) and then, when he saw his chance, he urgently whispered to his father, "I need to see you alone for a minute."

Father and son walked to the rear of the giant ballroom and stood beside a row of Las Vegas-style slot machines. The two lived in different worlds and the old man had only the vaguest notion of Bryan's troubles these past months.

"What's the rush, Sonny? You never get to any social events anymore. Enjoy yourself. There are people here I want you to meet."

"There *is* someone I want to meet. Can you help me?"

"Why, I think I can do that. Who did you have in mind?"

"King Lu."

The pleasant expression on the old man's face instantly changed. "What on earth for?"

"I want to do some business with him. Beyond that, I'd rather not say."

"I don't think that's a good idea, Sonny. No . . . I don't think you want to do business with the Greens on that level. . . ."

"You did."

"Yes, but that was in the old days. . . . Things were different then."

"Only the time and place are different. The Greens still call the shots."

"He can't see you. The Generalissimo put a ban on his doing business with Americans on the Island. Put it on years ago."

Bryan had not known this. He thought about it a moment and then took a deep breath. "Father, you've never spoken to me about it but I've always known that you were once very intimate with the Greens. It's even said that this King Lu has some sort of filial obligation to you. I've never pried into this but now I must because I desperately need to use that connection for the good of the Community." Whyte moved closer and squeezed his father's arm affectionately. "Believe me when I say I'm going to see the man one way or the other. Please help me."

Old Whyte examined his son's face carefully. He saw there the same determination and strength that he himself had once had as a young man just starting out in China. The sight of it suddenly filled the old man with sadness and an overwhelming sense of loss. In that other world, he thought, this would have been the face of a taipan.

* * *

Bryan Whyte peered absently out the tiny window and tried to focus his mind on the serious business ahead. The half-filled China Airlines DC-6 headed out over the busy harbor of Keelung and flew south along the Formosa Strait. Its flight path gave him a spectacular view of the western coast of the Island, its great jungle-covered, snow-capped central mountain range only partially obscured by the midday monsoonal rain clouds moving in from the south. As the path veered away from the Island and toward the Mainland, he moved to a seat on the opposite aisle so he could watch as they followed the brown, famine-ravaged Fukien and Kwangtung coastlines down to the little bastion of British capitalism on the great underbelly of Communist China.

The plane landed at Kai Tak airport shortly before noon. Whyte waded through the airport crowd and found a taxi. When he showed the driver the address his father had written down for him, a noticeable change came over the driver's face. "Sure, boss," he said. "I takee you, okay, you bet. . . ."

The taxi took him east for about half an hour through foothills with occasional glimpses of the ocean. It then climbed a steep, winding dirt road and turned onto a narrower gravel road that ended in front of the gate of a fifteen-foot tiled wall. Beyond the wall he could see the balconies and overhanging roofs of a Victorian palace that faced the ocean with a commanding view of Hong Kong Island.

The driver let him out at the gate and refused to accept payment. The man was not about to ask anything of a guest of King Lu, *tai-lo* of the Green Society.

A stonefaced guard led Whyte to the main house and down a long hallway to an elegant, high-ceilinged sitting room filled with exquisite antique furniture and delicate objects of art representing all the later dynasties. He sat in a wicker Mandarin chair while a moonfaced serving girl brought him tea in a covered bowl along with the customary hot rag. By the time he had finished the tea, he realized that a man in a conservative gray business suit had somehow, unnoticed, entered the room and was staring curiously at him. It was King Lu.

He was not very old, not much more than forty, but he had been a legend in the Orient for over two decades. His career started in Shanghai, where he served his apprenticeship as a young Green *boo hoy doy* or warrior in the endless gang wars, and where he attended mission school, learning economics, English and the ways of getting along with the international community. When the Mainland was about to fall to Communism, Tu Yueh-sen, his adopted father, the *tai-lo* of the Greens, had King supervise the evacuation of the Society's holdings and reestablishment in Taipei and Hong Kong. When old Tu died in 1950, King, still in his twenties, succeeded him as overlord. He was now a man of enormous influence and power and culture. On his trips to Taipei he dined with the Generalissimo like a head of state and from his Hong Kong retreat he controlled a criminal empire that extended throughout Free Asia.

King sat on a divan directly across a small teak tea table from Whyte. Up close, he was very striking in appearance with the clear, procelain skin and almost too perfect features of a Chinese film star. His look was hard, unemotional, displaying no hint that there was a bond between them. "So you are Bryan Whyte," he said in flawless English.

"I am honored that you would see me," Whyte said, also in English.

"I did much business with your father in the old days. I see you out of respect for him and our old relationship."

"I am with the Omega Chi. Do you know of it?"

King looked squarely at him. "Something."

"Sometimes we do business."

"I do business with many people," he said and reached in his coat pocket for a cigarette.

Whyte picked up the hot rag and ceremoniously wiped his hands. He noticed King staring at the *fu* around his neck.

"As you may know," Whyte continued, breaking into

Mandarin Chinese, "we have traditionally controlled the black market of American goods in Taipei, always giving a certain percentage to the Greens as tribute and always donating a large percentage to various charities. However, we now have a problem that has disrupted our business completely. It seems the Taiwanese Tiger Eels have joined forces with a gang in the American Community called the Warlords. Using the protection of the Tiger Eels, these Warlords have taken over control of the black market and have terrorized the city, paying no tribute to the Greens and supporting no charities. In past years, we would have stopped the Warlords but now we are helpless because of the infinitely superior presence of the Tiger Eels."

King Lu's hard black eyes watched Whyte closely. "I know of this alliance."

"What you may not know is that these organizations are planning on expanding into Peitou and the other forbidden areas in open defiance of the Green Society. The Tiger Eels have always hated the Greens because the Greens are Mainland Chinese. The winds of Taiwan nationalism are blowing strong and are fueling these ambitions of the Eels. As scattered gangs, they have no power, but united they could be very dangerous. Joined with the Warlords—who have the privileges and connections of the American Community as well as a tremendous source of revenue from the American black market—they could be a very serious threat to you someday."

King Lu looked at Whyte thoughtfully and blew smoke into the air. "And what do you propose we should do about this situation?"

Whyte took a deep breath. "I propose we form an alliance—a blood alliance between the Omega Chi and the Green Society." He sat back in the chair and waited for King's reaction.

There was no reaction. Whyte went on. "If the Greens will provide protection for the Omega Chi, the Tiger Eels will not dare strike against us without risking an all-out, Island-wide war which they could not possibly win. With your guaranteed protection, we can discipline the Warlords and restore order to the city. If we act swiftly together, we can check this threat before it gets any more threatening."

Whyte paused a moment to let this sink in. Then he continued. "There are other advantages to this design as well. Right now, the greatest single source of income on the Island for you is from Peitou—a direct result of the American presence. Yet, even though you are becoming more and more financially dependent on the Americans, you have no direct connections with the American authority. We can be that connection for you. We can be the agent who looks after your interests from the American point of view and points out financial opportunities that might arise. Think about it. Just as you and my father did business in the old days, you and I can do business now. It is time our houses were joined together again."

King Lu heard him out and then asked a few questions. He wanted to know specifics about the Tiger Eel ambitions in Peitou. When he was satisfied he knew the answers, he led Whyte around the gardens in the rear of the mansion and showed him his extensive collection of Sung Dynasty scroll paintings. Whyte, who cared nothing about flowers or art, tried to seem interested but did not feign enthusiasm.

Finally King ended the audience by saying, "Let me consider your most generous proposal for our mutual benefit. You will hear from me sometime this same week."

After Bryan Whyte left him, King Lu went up to one of the second floor balconies of the old British-built mansion and watched the taxi carry the boy back down the long gravel driveway. When it was finally out of sight, he realized for the first time how strangely emotional this meeting had been for him.

It had been over twelve years since he deposited this boy and his father on the Island of Taiwan. In the early years he had kept a watchful eye on the boy's development and had received many reports of his courage, his sound business judgment and his extraordinary ability to inspire loyalty in both Chinese and Americans. But seeing him in person was something else again. King saw that he was no longer a boy at all but a man, with his full growth and exactly the kind of manly beauty that the Chinese had been conditioned to admire in Westerners from Hollywood movies—the wide forehead, the firm jawline, the sensuous mouth and those confident, penetrating eyes.

There was no denying the emotion. King was filled with pride over the way his secret ward had turned out—an immense fatherly pride that was far in excess of anything he had felt for any of his own many legitimate or illegitimate sons.

He was especially pleased that the boy had done all the right things since the beginning of the Tiger Eels' takeover of the American black market in Taipei. He had not acted rashly. He had not let himself be provoked to a suicidal act by the humiliation of his woman or the attack on his friend. He had waited until he was able to come to the Greens with a plan that was well thought out, mutually beneficial and backed by indisputable logic. He had come up with a scheme that was so good, in fact, that King knew he was going to have to carry it out even though it went against the expressed dictates of the Generalissimo.

Since the evacuation, King Lu had strictly avoided all contact with the Americans of the Island. Because U.S. support was vital to the survival of Nationalist China, the Kuomintang insisted that the Americans be left completely alone and treated as privileged guests. The Greens' only contact with Americans was in the occasional riot they stirred up against them when the Generalissimo needed to make a point and in the operation of the luxurious whorehouses of Peitou—the Greens' chief source of revenue on the Island after gambling and moneylending.

But the rising threat of the Tiger Eels was going to force him—and the Generalissimo—to rethink this policy. With their added income from the American black market, these Taiwanese turtle eggs were already investing heavily in new bars and brothels in Sin Alley and this alone would eventually cut into the Peitou trade. If King didn't make some arrangement that would cut the Tiger Eels out of the black market and reestablish the old status quo, his only alternative was to assassinate Loma and perhaps start a messy war that could get much publicity. That would displease the Generalissimo much more than a Green involvement with a small segment of the American Community.

The scheme the Whyte boy offered was the obvious, best solution to the problem. Without a steady income of black-market money, the Tiger Eels were no real threat. If the Greens helped the Omega Chi reestablish control of the black market it could return the city to the old order overnight. Besides, as Young Whyte had pointed out, the Omega Chi could also give the Greens a link to the American Community that might prove increasingly valuable as the Americans continued to increase their presence in the Far East to fight Communist aggression.

Yes, it was a very good scheme. Almost a perfect scheme.

And even if the scheme had not been so perfect, he knew he would go along with it. The minute he saw the boy sitting there in the parlor, he knew it was preordained that they join hands at last, that it was the Tao telling him that the boy was ready. He thought back on the deathbed prediction of the great *hua-jen,* Chuang-tzu, that the boy would be a leader—no, a *beizo,* a deliverer—of the Chinese people, and he was sure this alliance had to be some small part of it, a first step toward a higher purpose that would transcend all these petty territorial squabbles. King Lu believed this because he was a man who believed in destiny. And he was absolutely convinced that his own destiny was to serve the greater destiny of Bryan Whyte.

It was dark by the time Whyte's plane landed in Taipei. Sung Shan Airport was close enough to his house that he was able to make the hike through a series of paddy fields and vacant lots and narrow residential streets in under ten minutes.

The street of small townhouses where he lived looked as it always did on a cool evening in late February. The usual circle of coolies stood gossiping around the noodle stand on the corner. A pedicab driver had parked his vehicle and was leisurely urinating against a wall. The singsong sounds from a phonograph filtered from a partially opened window and the putrid sewer smells of the open *benjo* ditch strangled the air.

He went in the house and saw that his father was asleep in his favorite living room chair. It was very dark and he had obviously been there for hours. The Armed Forces Radio Station was blaring an old "Great Gildersleeve" program on the console radio and an open bottle of Jack Daniels was overturned on the floor beside him.

Bryan quietly tiptoed over and switched off the radio, irritated at the amah for not even attempting to put the old man to bed. Old Whyte stirred, opened his bloodshot eyes and resettled himself in the chair. "Did you see him?" He sounded perfectly sober.

"Yes."

"How was the King?"

"Impressive." Bryan sat a moment on the wicker couch, resting his feet on the coffee table.

"Did you have any success with whatever it was you wanted to see him about?"

"I don't know yet. He said he would get back to me."

"Chiang has personally banned him from having anything to do with Americans on the Island, you know. He would have to petition for any change and that could take forever." His hand reached down to hunt for the bottle and found it on the third sweep.

Bryan handed him an empty glass from the table. "Father, I've met that man before, haven't I?"

Old Whyte clutched the glass and hesitated a full minute before answering. "Yes, years ago."

"Don't you think it's about time you told me about it?"

"That's what I've been sitting here all day thinking."

Bryan noticed that the old man's eyes had teared over and immediately regretted pressuring him. He could not bear the thought of his father suffering any more pain than he had already experienced in his life. He stood up to leave the room.

"No, wait. Stay. There are some things you need to know."

He sat down again and Old Whyte proceeded to speak to him. He spoke as he had never spoken to his son before and in the dim light he seemed a completely different man—a man not at all like the kindly, scatterbrained old gentleman who had been a joke in the American Community of Taipei for the past twelve years.

He carried on this monologue way into the night and the next morning he continued it and went on all that day and night and for most of the next week. These were not the usual anecdotes, but a detailed confession about his life that he had never come close to giving before. Aware that he would never have this opportunity again, Bryan dropped everything, stayed home from school and eagerly hoarded every sentence, every word, every nuance as his father filled in the many mysterious gaps in his knowledge of the Whyte family background in China in a single burst of long-suppressed energy.

One night later that week, while he was lying awake pondering his father's astonishing chronicle, Bryan heard the front door buzzer. The amah had gone to bed so he opened the door himself to find two Chinese thugs staring at him. Behind them, out in the darkness, Bryan could barely make out the outline of a limousine filling up the narrow street. There were a few awkward moments of silence and then Old Whyte came and stood beside him. "What is it, Sonny?"

King Lu suddenly appeared out of the darkness. He hurried up the three steps to the doorway and, tears in his eyes, he embraced Old Whyte. Then he turned and looked

at Bryan. Seeing in the boy's eyes the full recognition of
their bond, King put his arm around him as well and
hugged them both. The three were together at last. The
ban had been lifted.

——————————————————————————— 5

WHEN OLD WHYTE ARRIVED IN SHANGHAI IN THE
spring of 1915, China was a chaotic hodgepodge of fief-
doms ruled by feuding warlords and ruthless mercenary
armies. The Manchu Dynasty had just fallen; a frail, enigmatic medical doctor named Sun Yat-sen was trying to
restore some semblance of national political order; and the
country was split into economic "spheres of influence"
seized by the individual foreign colonial powers—France,
Germany, Great Britain and Japan—in a series of forced,
"unequal" treaties.

He was, of course, not known as "Old Whyte" in
those days. He was a lanky, affable young man with a wide
salesman grin and infectious laugh and everyone called
him "Billy." He had quit the University of Washington
within a year of a degree in economics and, like generations of his ancestors before him, experienced an irresistible compulsion to go west. He had simply said good-by
to his parents one gray Seattle morning and impulsively
booked steamer passage for the romance, adventure and
economic opportunity of the Orient.

The International Settlement of Shanghai in those
days was already an old and established society. The great
Shanghai Bund was lined with wealthy and prestigious
European and American trading houses like Jardine,
Matheson & Company, Dent and Company, and A. Heart

and Sons. Old taipan families who had made their fortunes in the opium trade of the last century sipped cool drinks in the magnificent old Shanghai Club ("No Dogs or Chinese Allowed") and contemplated an even more promising future. The International Community—including some four thousand Americans—gambled at its own racetrack, listened to its own symphony orchestra and strolled through its lush private gardens along the Wangpoo River much as it had done for the previous half century.

Billy Whyte took one look at this world—so exotic and exciting and alien from anything he had ever experienced, yet so comfortable for a white man—and fell in love with it. He immediately acquired a position as apprentice clerk with the American firm of Russell and Company and easily adapted himself to the Shanghai way of life. He hired two manservants. He joined a social club made up of other *giffins* or apprentice taipans and at nights they would haunt both the polite society soirees and the cabarets and jazz halls of Blood Alley, with its White Russian refugee whores and shady underworld characters. Most of all, as a practical-minded young man, he came to genuinely appreciate the perfection of the unique concept of International Shanghai—the only city in the world run by and for businessmen.

After a year in the Orient, Billy Whyte was struck with an idea that he was sure would make him a taipan. As a boy, he had been enchanted by the magic of moving pictures; and when he saw D. W. Griffith's grandiose *Birth of a Nation* shortly before leaving Seattle, he realized that the nickelodeons of his youth were about to grow into a major international industry. His idea was to get in on the ground floor of that business as it developed in China. Shanghai already had one small cinema but it catered only to the foreign concessions and no one had yet thought of catering directly to the general Chinese population. He knew that the great four hundred million of China would rather starve to death than miss the monthly traveling Chinese opera or puppet show, and he reasoned that they constituted an enormous consuming market that was just waiting to be tapped by an enterprising young *giffin*.

He quit his clerk job at Russell and Company and set about making his dream a reality. He borrowed money from everyone he knew and then cabled a proposition to the Famous Players Motion Picture Company of Hollywood, California. If the company would ship him a projector, generator and supply of films, he would give them part interest in his independent company, Omega Vaudeville Enterprises, which was already having "great success" introducing American-style entertainment into the great heartland of China. Based on a personal recommendation by two taipan firms he had charmed, the California company cabled back its acceptance on a three-month trial basis.

On June 14, 1917, he loaded up a river sampan with two servants and hundreds of dollars worth of motion picture equipment and headed up the mighty Yangtze River. His ultimate goal was a circuit of small cinemas between Shanghai and Hankow, and he intended to build initial audience interest by stopping at all the villages along the way and demonstrating movies to the river coolies and paddy farmers. "You watchee like Chinese opera," he would say as he stood before the crowd of puzzled coolies that invariably gathered, "and you see big, big magic."

But whenever he darkened a room and switched on the projector, it was the same story. The audiences reacted with horror. Usually the coolies would sit trembling through the entire ten-minute presentation with their eyes shut. Grounded as they were in superstition and Taoist folk religion, there was no way he could convince them they were not seeing demons and ghosts and the blackest of black magic. Soon word spread all along the river that Whyte was an evil sorcerer and he could no longer even get a crowd. Then the villages refused to let him dock; they threw stones at his passing sampan. Utterly defeated, he returned to Shanghai with a boatload of motion picture equipment and a broken dream.

A week later, Billy Whyte was at the warehouse he

rented across the river at Pootung wondering what to do next when he noticed a slightly cross-eyed man staring at him. Over the past month of preparations, he had seen this man watching him dozens of times. The man and his heavily pockmarked companion had carefully observed every step of the ill-fated business scheme. Each time his eyes met Whyte's, the man smiled and made a polite bow. It happened so often that the two of them had built a kind of friendly but as yet silent relationship.

This time, however, the man came up to Billy Whyte and frowned. "No joss?"

Billy Whyte shook his head. "No joss. Hopeless. Muchee hopeless."

"Try again. This time I helpee you. We split plenty moneys by and by, heya."

By that afternoon, this strange Chinese man had gathered a huge crowd of laborers and forced them to sit through Mary Pickford in *The New York Hat* over and over again until they had lost their fear and were screaming for more. He told Billy Whyte he would have his pockmarked lieutenant go into the Chinese district of Chapei and upriver to Hankow and set up as many cinemas as they could get equipment for. The man never asked for a signed paper or a verbal agreement, but from that moment on they were equal partners in the Chinese motion picture business.

The man's name was Tu Yueh-sen.

In 1917, Billy Whyte knew nothing about the Green Society or the ancient traditions of the Chinese underworld or the extraordinary genius of Tu Yueh-sen, but over the next ten years he would learn a great deal about these things and because of his knowledge he would prosper beyond his wildest dreams.

The organized underworld of China in the twentieth century had evolved directly out of the secret societies that had been an integral part of traditional Chinese culture from time immemorial. These societies or tongs (from the

Chinese word for "meeting hall") were originally Taoist religious organizations and totally mystical in nature. Over a period of a thousand years, the tongs developed not only a complicated philosophical system that governed the proper way to live but also a unique body of knowledge about a group of "forbidden" subjects that, if properly handled, greatly enhanced that life: the occult sciences, particularly fortunetelling; the martial arts, which were nurtured in the famous Shaolin temple of Honan Province; and sexual technique, which the early Taoists regarded as especially sacred and codified in a series of canons, culminating in the communal "union of breaths," a ritualized sex orgy that was reputed to be the most intense sexual experience possible for a human being.

In the second millennium of the existence of the secret societies, China suddenly fell under the domination of the Mongols and the Manchus for a period totaling nearly five hundred years. This cataclysmic development changed the nature of the societies in two very profound ways. The first was that they became strongly nationalistic in a manner they had never been before. With their clandestine organization already well formed, they became the natural repositories of all the accumulated Chinese traditions and culture and the source of most of the revolutionary activity against the hated foreign dynasties that sought to destroy them.

The second was that these societies became extremely capitalistic and business-oriented. Most China scholars agree that, had they not been under foreign control during the centuries of the rise of capitalism, the Chinese (whose Confucian tradition is very similar to the Protestant Work Ethic and who are naturally a very shrewd and business-minded people) would have developed a strong mercantile economy much like that of Europe and America—in fact, it was well under way when the native Ming Dynasty collapsed. But from 1864 to 1911, the Manchu rulers strictly forbade them from engaging in any but the most primitive business enterprise. Therefore, the frustrated business impulses of the Chinese had to be channeled through the

illegal secret societies—and what capitalism did develop
in China developed largely through them and behind a veil
of secrecy.

By the late nineteenth and early twentieth centuries,
the twin forces of nationalism and capitalism had caused
these numerous societies to merge into three huge illegal
organizations: the Reds, who reigned over the Yellow
River in North China; the Greens, who controlled the
Yangtze River in Central China; and the Triads, who
concentrated in the Canton-Hong Kong area of South
China. These groups engaged in a wide range of activity.
They ran businesses, looked out after their members' family welfare, settled community disputes, sponsored revolts
against the hated Manchus and warred with one another
for control of the overseas Chinese communities of San
Francisco, New York, Los Angeles and dozens of other
cities around the globe.

When China was forcibly opened to Western trade as
a result of the Opium Wars, the wealth of the country
inevitably began to flow to the immense treaty port of
Shanghai, and soon all three of these organizations gravi-
tated to the city to get their share. Since the Greens were
already established in the Yangtze valley and Shanghai
areas, they had the natural advantage. By the turn of the
century, they were in almost complete control not only of
Shanghai but all of China, having suppressed the Reds and
Triads in a series of bloody gang wars. From their headquarters in the French concession, the Greens openly
engaged in opium smuggling, casino gambling, moneylending, kidnapping, armed robbery, protection, political
strong-arming and every manner of economic manipula-
tion. Their profits were so staggering that, by the time of
the Nationalist Revolution of 1911, the Society had become
—even by the most conservative estimates—the largest,
wealthiest and most powerful criminal organization in the
history of the planet.

Tu Yueh-sen dominated the Green Society in the
period from the early twenties to the late forties.

He was born in Pootung, across the Wangpoo River

from Shanghai, and he had worked his way up the ranks of the Society by his cunning, his capitalistic genius and his ability to inspire loyalty in everyone around him. He was called the "Al Capone of Asia," but this was a considerable understatement of the facts because Tu had greater influence than any American gangster ever dared aspire to. At his zenith in the thirties, he had over a million men at his disposal and his finger on everything that moved in or out of the world's most populous country. He owned numerous estates, thousands of servants, more concubines than Genghis Khan, the nation's best legal brains and the entire detective squad of the Shanghai International Police Force (all of whom were loyal Greens and under the control of Tu's sadistic enforcer, the dreaded "Pockmarked" Hwang).

Considering the peculiar way capitalism had evolved in China and was practiced in Shanghai, it did not seem at all unusual for a man like Tu to openly run a criminal empire and yet still be so respectable that he could be named director of four of Shanghai's most prestigious banks.

This was the man who had befriended Billy Whyte that day in 1917 and who would grow and prosper together with him for the rest of their lives in China.

Tu had a natural fondness for Americans because they were the only members of the foreign community without a history of territorial aspiration in China. And he recognized in Billy Whyte a loyal partner who shared a vision of the end of China's colonial-like status and its capitalization along American lines. As a result, Whyte became the only Westerner that Tu ever completely trusted and the only one ever to fully understand the workings of the Green Gang. As Tu rose to leadership of the vast secret society, this association naturally put Whyte in a very advantageous position to do business. Soon every Westerner with a business problem was seeking him out and asking a favor, and Billy Whyte found himself becoming a wealthy and influential man.

By 1920, his business was booming. He owned cinemas all over Shanghai and the eastern Yangtze area. He constructed his own motion picture studio in Chapei and each month he was cranking out dozens of silent comedies, melodramas and histories that he would distribute all over China and the Chinese communities of East Asia. His Omega Enterprises had expanded into banking, export-import and tobacco farming in Honan Province. He bought himself a villa in Frenchtown and became a taipan, a respectable pillar of the foreign community.

One day early in their association, Tu brought an impressive young man to meet Whyte. He was a Chekiangese who had attended military school in Japan and had been very active in the Nationalist Revolution. He was then working as a minor clerk in the Shanghai stock exchange, but Tu was very taken by his keen mind and leadership ability and was giving him a number of important functions in the Society. He had dark, penetrating eyes and an air of authority, and Whyte immediately thought he was one of the most charismatic Chinese he had ever met. "This is Chiang Kai-shek," Tu said. "He will be a very important man someday."

It was a name that rocked China over the next decade. Using money he borrowed from Tu, this young man left Shanghai, became a protégé of Sun Yat-sen (who also had strong Green connections) and, within a few short years, leader of the fledgling Nationalist Army. After the death of Sun, he set out to finally unite China under the Nationalist flag once and for all. Because he was antiforeign and anti-Christian and had the support of the newly organized Chinese Communist Party, the other taipans were terrified of Chiang. Only Billy Whyte was not. He knew that the man was a Green at heart, which was to say he was anticommunist and procapitalist. Many times, he would argue the point with them into the morning hours in the smoke-filled stag bar of the Shanghai

Club. He was convinced that the Unequal Treaties had to go, that a strong nationalism was emerging that could not be held back, that Chiang Kai-shek was the personification of that nationalism and that the taipans *had* to do business with the man if they hoped to survive in China.

By April, 1927, Chiang and his armies had conquered most of North China and had encircled the foreign concessions of Shanghai. The International Community, under siege, did not know exactly what to expect. A large portion of Chiang's troops were Communist and they had been promised an end to the Western domination of the city that had existed now for over a hundred years. The taipans mobilized their tiny and ill-trained home guard and ordered in troops from their home countries to protect what property they could. But there was no doubt among them that if Chiang wanted to take the Settlement and fulfill his longstanding promises to the Communists, nothing could stop him.

Out of this chaos, Billy Whyte came forward with a plan. He met with a group of other prominent Shanghai bankers and got permission to represent them. Then he went with Tu Yueh-sen to have a frank meeting with Chiang and Chiang's Harvard-educated financial advisor and brother-in-law, T.V. Soong. Whyte put it to them succinctly. If Chiang wanted to unite China and bring it into the community of nations with any credibility, he would need the help of the Shanghai bankers. The bankers had always seen Chiang as a threat because of his Communist support and had fought him every step of the way. However, if Chiang would purge the Communist elements of the Kuomintang and leave the International Settlement alone, these same foreign bankers would stop fighting him and start financing him. If he would play ball with them, they would pay for his revolution and give it whatever it needed in terms of financial assistance and loan guarantees.

Chiang, who had successfully straddled the political fence all during the twenties, knew that he finally had to jump off. Was it to be on the left side or right side? The

Communists or the capitalists? He looked at his mentor, Tu Yueh-sen, for a moment and it did not seem a very difficult decision to make. He went with the capitalists.

In the early morning hours of the following day, several thousand members of the Green Gang assembled secretly at the Bund. Tu personally gave them their instructions and armed them with knives, axes, German lugers and Thompson submachine guns that had been borrowed from the U.S. Marine Corps arsenal. Under the command of Tu's lieutenant, "Pockmarked" Hwang, the Green troops fanned out over the Chinese city and proceeded methodically to murder every Communist they could find. The Communist Party headquarters in Chapei was set afire and the party members were machine-gunned as they fled the burning building. Two companies of Chiang's Communist troops were hacked to death with axes as they slept in their barracks. For one entire day, the streets and alleys of Shanghai ran red with blood in what was modern China's most ruthless and efficient massacre. Only Chou En-lai and a handful of other Communist leaders were able to make their way out of the city in time to avoid Tu's gangsters.

In one lightning action, Chiang seemed to have brilliantly dispelled the Communist menace in China and the Western powers flocked to him with money and offers of support. Nationalist China had at last been born and Chiang Kai-shek owed it to the Green Society.

William Whyte was now a man of great respect and singular influence in the new China. He was the only Westerner known to have the ear of the nation's two most powerful men, Chiang Kai-shek and Tu Yueh-sen. He was consulted for his opinion on every bit of important civic business that came before the Shanghai Municipal Council. His banking and vast motion picture interests soared, and to make life even sweeter, he had at long last fallen in love.

The young lady was named Jessica Wainright. She

had been born and raised in Shanghai, the daughter of a British executive for the venerable old firm of Jardine, Matheson & Company. Whyte first noticed her one evening in 1932 at a tea dance in the British Consulate, where she was being almost trampled to death by ardent suitors. She was a small, delicate and exquisitely beautiful woman who had been bred to be the wife of a taipan; and every eligible taipan, taipan son and *giffin* was after her.

As the most eligible of all the taipan bachelors, Billy Whyte had the inside track and he used it to launch an exhaustive campaign to win her. He courted her in several whirlwind weeks of parties and late-night, chaperoned strolls along the Bund under a big, star-filled sky. He escorted her to the Shanghai Symphony and the Shanghai Dramatic Society and the talking pictures that were just then appearing in the Settlement. He took her on a tour of his movie studio in Chapei and escorted her whole family on a luxury expedition to the Island of Taiwan to hunt wild boar in his favorite hunting grounds in the foothills south of Keelung.

She was, to him, a goddess. Everything about her was perfection—from the way she held a tea cup to the way she could control the amahs with an arch of her eyebrow. She somehow embodied all the grace and dignity—and physical beauty—of colonial Shanghai. He needed to possess her just as he had needed to be a part of this exotic world. Yet she held back from his advances. Friendly but distant. Noticeably indifferent whenever his salesman's charm became too effusive.

The tide did not turn in his favor until two weeks into the courtship. They were having lunch at the Astor House Hotel and Billy, discouraged and somewhat depressed by his lack of success with her, suddenly launched into a soapbox recitation of his "progressive" ideas about China. He said that maybe it was because he was an American, but he had come to believe that their lives here had to be devoted to something more than just making money. He told her how he believed they had a duty to help create a strong, Western-backed and business-oriented China that would lead Asia out of poverty and humiliation and into the twentieth century. He went on with these revolutionary ideas for hours, oblivious to whether or not she approved.

But she did approve. She was very impressed by his ideas and his seriousness. Her manner changed completely and she warmed to him. The following week, she allowed him to kiss her. The day after the kiss, he spoke to her father and they became engaged.

The marriage was the event of the social season in 1933. The ceremony was conducted at the Shanghai Episcopal Church by a young Episcopal missionary named Clifton E. Warner. Taipan families from some eight different nations attended. Tu Yueh-sen gave the couple a sumptuous new villa across the street from his own and they settled in for a life of parties, business prosperity and uninterrupted personal happiness that lasted right up to the time the bombs started falling all around them.

The war had officially started back in 1931.

The increasingly militaristic Japanese Government had watched the growing power of the Nationalist Chinese with a good deal of alarm, and abruptly they moved to prevent a strong, unified China by seizing a large section of Manchuria. At the same time, Chou En-lai, Mao Tse-tung and other Communists who survived the Shanghai purge of 1927 had regrouped and were gaining strength again in the remote countryside of Shensi Province. Throughout the early thirties, Chiang had been fighting both armies, concentrating especially on the Communists, whom he considered the greater threat. In 1936, just when the Communists were nearly stamped out, Chiang was kidnapped by his own officers in the north and forced to form a united front with the Communists against the common Japanese enemy.

With every month that went by, this newly escalated war intruded a bit more on the traditional life of Shanghai. One by one the great taipan families fled the country for the safety of Hong Kong or India or wherever home happened to be. The symphony concerts and cultural events ended. Business came to a dead halt. The Chinese sections were bombed almost daily. But Whyte refused to leave. He believed in Chiang's ability to defend China and he could not believe that Japan, a taipan power that had always been an integral part of the Shanghai scheme, would willfully destroy one of the most perfect business, social and governmental orders that had ever been devised by man.

One day in 1937, however, he came home with defeat in his eyes. Jessica met him at the door and knew at once that the unspeakable was about to happen. She hugged him and asked no questions. "Pack as much as you can in two suitcases," he said. "The plane leaves in an hour."

The plane took them to Chungking, deep in the rolling hills of Szechwan Province, where Chiang had moved the Nationalist capital. Whyte accepted a quick commission in the U.S. Army and was assigned to work as liaison officer attached to Generalissimo Chiang Kai-shek. His real job, however, was working with his old comrade Tu Yueh-sen in coordinating resistance to the Japanese occupation of eastern China. The thousands of members of the highly organized Chinese underworld were a ready-made urban guerrilla army; in Shanghai and Canton and the other big cities they could do real damage to the Japanese command. Tu and Whyte set up headquarters in an old Buddhist monastery and, answering to no one but themselves, established a third front of secret society gangsters that ultimately turned out to be more effective than all of Chiang's worn-out KMT troops put together.

The exile stretched on for years. America entered the war in 1941 and more years passed. During all this time Jessica Whyte never once complained about the damp, dreary city or the tedious, very harsh style of life it imposed on them. She never once complained about the constant Japanese bombing or the lack of a social life or the unsanitary conditions all around her. Even when she finally became pregnant after years of trying, she did not long to leave her husband for the safety of England or America. She was the daughter of a taipan and the wife of a taipan and she understood her husband's insistence on staying in China no matter what the personal cost.

Within a year of the birth of Bryan Whyte, the war was over. The first plane that left Chungking the day the Japanese surrendered contained three important figures— Chiang Kai-shek, Tu Yueh-sen and William "Billy" Whyte. Together they would have to survey the damage and pick up the pieces.

Shanghai was in ruins. Most of its fine buildings along the Bund and expansive parks and sumptuous villas in Frenchtown had been gutted, burned-out or bombed into oblivion. It was also not likely to get much better anytime soon. The majority of the old Shanghai people feared even more trouble and were refusing to return to China at all. Whyte, whose Omega Enterprises Ltd. was in hopeless disarray, estimated that even if everyone was back and pitching in enthusiastically, it would take years to restore the International Settlement to any semblance of business order or get Nationalist China back on its economic feet.

The main concern now that the Japanese were gone were the Communists. All during the United Front against Japan, Mao Tse-tung and his followers had been hoarding arms and supplies and increasing their troop strength. While Chiang was fighting the Japanese and losing credibility and support because of the corruption of his demoralized and weary army, the Communists had been steadily and very calculatingly gaining credibility and peasant support. The minute the war ended, both sides almost equally armed, raced to control territory. Civil war seemed so imminent that the Truman administration began sending a series of diplomatic missions to China to try and work out a Nationalist-Communist coalition government.

When these negotiations failed, the civil war broke out in a series of heated clashes all over the country. In a strange twist of policy, the U.S. decided to remain neutral and not support their wartime ally, the Kuomintang. Shocked by what seemed to him a complete betrayal, Whyte left his family in Shanghai and flew to Washington to try to change minds in the State Department. He spoke passionately to anyone who would see him. He argued that Chiang had only had ten years of rule before having to fight Japan and had accomplished great things in that time. He warned that the Communists were cultural anarchists who were already unleashing a reign of atrocity and terror in the Chinese countryside unequaled in this century. He insisted that with American support Chiang could put down the Communist threat just as he had done in the twenties and maintain a free China that would be very grateful to America and friendly to American business interests.

But—with the exception of a few powerless China experts, including a young and very sympathetic Warren Xavier Stevens—no one listened and Whyte returned to Shanghai in failure. It was soon obvious to the remaining business interests that, without U.S. support, the Nationalists would fall: Morale, after over ten straight years of war, was nonexistent and the economy was near collapse. Inflation raged out of control and the bureaucracy was so corrupt that virtually no tax revenue was making its way into the national treasury. The financial interests of Shanghai, who were largely responsible for Chiang's ascendancy, began to see the writing on the wall and one by one they deserted him, taking their capital with them. Before long, Whyte was the only taipan left and he was so pessimistic about Chiang's survival that he strongly urged the Gimo to move his government to the Island of Taiwan, where there were no Communists and where they could probably hold out until the U.S. came to its senses.

In 1947, the Island—which had just returned to China after fifty years of Japanese colonial rule—seemed an ideal place for such a regrouping. One hundred miles from the Mainland, midway between Shanghai and Canton, it had an advantageous location for establishing business connections with the rest of Asia and the United

States, was easily defensible and would be an excellent staging area for a return to the Mainland when the time was right. It was also, Whyte knew from his many hunting trips there, the most physically attractive place in China, with fertile soil, a spectacular array of plants and animals, and the highest mountains in East Asia. It was perfect.

But there was one small problem: The feisty native population of the Island—the descendants of the original Chinese settlers who had long ago lost any ties to the Mainland—did not particularly want to be part of Nationalist or any other kind of China. They openly advocated rebellion and independence.

Once again, the Green Society came to Chiang's rescue. Tu Yueh-sen sent his finest detachment of "Blue Shirts"—the elite of the Greens—to Taipei under joint command of "Pockmarked" Hwang and Tu's protégé and adopted son, King Lu.

The two men, who were rival heirs to the ailing Tu's throne, assessed the situation on the Island differently. King, a much younger man with a classical education and a statesman's sensibility, believed the Taiwanese were so disorganized and ill-equipped militarily that they offered no threat at all and would eventually accept Nationalist rule without a show of force. Hwang, who enjoyed killing the way a British aristocrat enjoyed cricket, was convinced that the Taiwanese dissidence was so advanced that a major campaign was needed to put them in their place. As senior commander, Hwang overruled King and put his own plan into action.

The first thing Hwang did was contact leaders of the Tiger Eels, a gang of unprincipled Taiwanese thugs, and paid them a large retainer for their services. With the Eels and Chinese troops loaned by the newly appointed Chinese governor, the Blue Shirts then reenacted the Shanghai Massacre of twenty years earlier. Machine-gun squads rode down Taipei streets in U.S. Army jeeps casually shooting innocent passersby. Taiwanese officials were taken from their homes and assassinated on the spot. The Tiger Eels gathered up government critics, lawyers, students and dissidents of all kinds and took them in U.S. Army buses to the Taipei racetrack where they were systematically shot by assembly-line firing squads or beaten to death with Japanese baseball bats. So many thousands of Taiwanese were senselessly slaughtered in the March, 1947, massacre that many of the Blue Shirt Greens themselves were sickened by it. Fearing a genocide of the Taiwanese people, King rushed back to Shanghai and convinced Tu to recall Hwang (and eventually banish him to French Indochina). But the campaign was successful in that any seed of rebellion or a Taiwan independence movement was put down for over a decade.

Now that the Island was secure, the last foreign residents of Shanghai began to plan an orderly evacuation. Billy Whyte sadly started the process of closing out his few remaining business interests and transferring assets to British banks in Hong Kong. One night as he was working late in the den of their partially bombed-out villa in Frenchtown, Whyte heard his wife crying. He went out to the parlor and he put his arm around her to comfort her. He knew there was probably no way they would ever completely bounce back from this disaster but he tried to reassure her. "We'll build it all over again, Jessica," he said. "It'll be the same. You'll see."

"It'll never be the same again," she said. It was the only completely negative thing he had ever heard her say —and the last thing.

While he was holding his wife, Whyte heard a noise coming from the rear of the big house—the sound of scurrying feet. He was instantly concerned because he knew he was at the very top of the Communist assassination list with an exorbitant price on his head. Tu had stationed bodyguards around the villa but, in these troubled times, anything could happen. He left his wife in the parlor and dashed back to check on the baby. As he stepped through the dining room, an explosion ripped through the building.

Whyte was in the hospital for three months and bedridden in King Lu's house for six more. He spent most of this time staring at the walls in silence. The bomb that destroyed his villa left him with a serious head injury which, together with the death of his wife, seemed to have drastically affected his mind. His charm and shrewdness and amazing foresight deserted him. Even when he finally got up from convalescence, he refused to attend to business or liquidate his holdings or take any interest in the outcome of the civil war. His hair turned snow white and people began to refer to him as "Old" Whyte. When the Communists finally cut off the city and it came time for him and his son Bryan to flee first to Hangchow and then to Taiwan, he was a ruined man.

Bryan Whyte knew only bits and pieces of this family history his father tried so hard to fill in that week in 1962. He did not remember anything about the explosion that had killed his mother. He did not remember being carried onto the S.S. *South China Sea* by King Lu that day in 1949 and crossing the Formosa Strait to a life of exile. He did not remember his father in any guise other than his present one—a harmless old rummy and community "character" who spoke only in vague trivialities about the days when he was a big-shot taipan.

He did not even remember that in the early '50s, there were grave doubts that Taiwan and Nationalist China would survive more than a year or two. But the Korean War broke out and it forced the U.S. to hastily take another look at its Asian policy. By this time, the threat of a new Yellow Peril of Chinese Communists had helped create the political climate in America known as McCarthyism and everyone suddenly wanted to know why the U.S. had "lost" China and deserted Chiang Kai-shek in his time of need. By 1954, when Bryan Whyte was barely ten years old, the U.S. and the Republic of China had signed a mutual defense treaty that would bind the two nations together as the closest of allies.

The Community in which Bryan Whyte grew to early manhood was a transplanted, miniature version of the

Settlement. As in Shanghai, servants did the work, sometimes three or four to a family. As in Shanghai, even the poorest Westerners lived well since the cost of living was so absurdly low for them. As in Shanghai, Chinese police and Chinese courts had no real jurisdiction over American citizens. As in Shanghai, the underworld remained a vital power and the city quickly became the sin capital of the Orient.

But there was one very important psychological distinction and it had been drilled into Bryan Whyte from his earliest years. While Shanghai had been a selfish colonial society dominated by the British, Taipei was a thoroughly unselfish society dominated by the Americans. The motives of the Americans were clear and simple and had been since the days of the clipper ships: America wanted to maintain a balance of power in Asia with strong, free, friendly nations with which it could trade. Unlike the foreign powers that had carved up and humiliated China for the last hundred years, America—itself born of an anticolonial revolution—generally supported the great anticolonial revolution that was taking place in Asia in the twentieth century.

The reason it maintained a military presence here was because it recognized that there was an international Communist conspiracy and that it was the Communists' policy to ride the back of these nationalist movements, creating a Moscow-run tyranny, as had happened in China. America, as leader of the Free World, would not allow this to happen again. It was determined to help these emerging nations resist Communism by giving freely of the fruits of its technology, by demonstrating the strength and viability of its free enterprise system and democratic institutions. The Taipei American Community completely believed it was carrying out altruistic principles and this belief made it as confident, complacent and cohesive a society as had ever existed.

In this unique environment, Bryan Whyte became a man at a very early age. Since his father was weak and ineffectual, he was determined to compensate by being strong and confident. Since he was poorer than most everyone he knew, he dreamed of one day being fabulously wealthy. Since the Communists had murdered his beautiful, self-sacrificing mother and stolen his home, he hated them with a passion that made his life seem very purposeful. Since he grew up in an exaggerated American community without ever once having experienced America, the country and the principles for which it stood in the world —freedom, justice, unlimited opportunity—were like a religion to him.

Since he possessed the natural charisma of his father, he became a popular figure at the American School and a circle of the outstanding boys naturally formed around him. This circle became the Omega Chi Fraternity and under Whyte's inspired leadership, enterprise and capitalistic instinct, it quickly became an institution with an important function in the Community. It took over control of the black market and used the money for a variety of charitable purposes. It used its influence to help the U.S. authorities whenever a problem arose with the Chinese underworld. It disciplined unruly American gangs who were ruining the American image by battling one another and operating rackets and committing acts of vandalism. It managed, remarkably, to keep the peace in the American Community of Taipei for years without a serious incident. It was effective and unchallenged—right up until the time the Warlords joined forces with the Tiger Eels and forced a Whyte to once again seek an alliance with the awesome and terrible Green Society.

6

GREEN TROOPS FLOODED INTO TAIPEI. THEY CAME BY the hundreds from Hong Kong and Manila and Singapore and from Chinatowns as far away as Honolulu. They brought with them axes, knives, revolvers, machine guns, hand grenades and a traditional Chinese contempt for the inferior Tiger Eel pirates of Taiwan. They joined the contingent of Taipei Greens in suburban Peitou to form an overwhelming military force and waited impatiently there for the command to storm the city.

King Lu remained in Taipei to take personal charge of the operation. Looking stern and committed, he met with Bryan Whyte and Mark Taylor for a quick strategy session in his makeshift headquarters suite in the Grand Hotel. He listened to their ideas very patiently—reliving for a moment his own days as a teenage gang strategist—and then dispatched a squad of Blue Shirts to Shihminting to retake the American black market for the Omega Chi.

Johnny Hong wept at the destruction of his Warlords-supplied inventory, but otherwise no resistance was offered. The squad did not even see a Tiger Eel or Warlord. It seemed that no one in the city—not Randy Ortega or Dave Magaha or Loma and all his gangsters—was brave enough or foolhardy enough to do battle with the force of invading Greens.

In a single morning, without a single drop of bloodshed, the old balance of power had been restored to the city—just as Bryan Whyte had said it would.

And yet, it was not exactly the same as before. To insure the status quo, the Greens remained in the city, a kind of army of occupation, and as the weeks and months wore on, their presence—evoking as it did the '47 massacre—came to be deeply resented by the great majority of the Taiwanese people of Taipei. Holed up in Sin Alley and South Taipei, the Tiger Eels began to acquire a credibility and political dimension they had never known before and did not really deserve—even among the very people they had been ruthlessly exploiting over the years. This was a curious and totally unexpected development. Soon even the Tiger Eels themselves began to see their struggle with the Green Mainlanders as a nationalistic one. It gave the gang an exhilarating new sense of strength and purpose and a whole new self-image. They were now the selfless defenders of the Taiwanese people.

It was another black, stormy day in early June—the longest rainy period anyone could remember this early in the summer—and Commander Floyd Harris sat in his newly air-conditioned office in the U.S. Navy compound lost in murky contemplation.

The spell was abruptly broken by the bleep of the squawk box, then his yeoman's voice. "He's here, Commander."

"Send him in, please."

The door opened and the yeoman led in an intense little man in his early thirties with thick glasses and an air of aggressive efficiency. Harris stood up to offer his hand and the man took it—with no warmth or pleasure—then removed his raincoat to get down to business.

The man was Harlan S. Bamcheck, assistant chief of the Asian Section of the Central Intelligence Agency in Honolulu. He was here concerning the recent migration of Chinese underworld forces into the city and Harris guessed it was more than a routine inquiry.

"What can we do for you, Mr. Bamcheck? The call I got from CINCPAC was vague as to the purpose of your visit to Taipei."

Bamcheck looked Harris over sternly, seeming to

study the Commander's rather odd, stumpy build, and then cleared his throat and sat himself in a chair. "I hardly know where to begin, Commander."

Harris swallowed nervously. "Oh?"

"In case you don't know it, Commander, we're in a very sensitive position in Asia this year. The famine on the Mainland has reached cataclysmic proportions. As a diversion, the Communists have invaded Tibet and are now massing troops across the Taiwan Straits and otherwise beating their war drums. At the same time the Kennedy administration feels it might be wise to take advantage of the famine and is seriously considering backing Chiang Kai-shek in a limited invasion probe into the particularly devastated parts of Kwangtung and Kwangsi."

"I'm aware of most of this, sir."

"Well, right in the middle of this crucial period, a time when the eyes of the world are upon us and our Asian Policy, my office is being flooded with reports of a situation in Taipei involving Chinese, American and native Taiwanese underworld factions that might erupt into violence and create a major scandal. And our intelligence people here don't seem to be able to do a thing about it! Can you understand how this might make us a bit cranky?!"

"I understand your concern, Mr. Bamcheck. We're very concerned too. Naturally. But you have to realize that this is primarily a domestic Chinese matter and there is very little this office can do about it. . . ."

"Our information has it that the principal reason the Chinese gangsters have invaded Taipei is to protect the interests of an American black-market gang called Omega Chi—a gang that has flourished under your nose for years. Can you give me even one good reason why these Omega Chi hoodlums are not in jail?"

Harris fully realized now that he was in for a rough time. His temperature was rising and so was an urge to strangle the sarcastic little bureaucrat. Still, he would be courteous. It was not good for one's military career to have the CIA as an enemy. "We could, of course, try to build a case against the Omega Chi but it would be very difficult. The Chinese police have no jurisdiction, and black-marketing is such an accepted part of the culture here it would be impossible to come up with a witness against them. . . . What you don't seem to understand, Mr. Bamcheck, is that the presence of these invading Green gangsters has *stabilized* the underworld situation in Taipei. What it has done is reestablish the old order that has kept the peace here for many, many years."

This seemed to make Bamcheck angry. "Mr. Harris, we don't think your judgment on this matter has been very solid from the start. We don't think it's in the best interests of the United States to let an 'independent' American power jeopardize our position here and we're not about to let it continue. I'm here to relieve your office of this case. I've got three new operatives on their way to Taipei at this moment and we're going to open a whole new field office to take charge of it."

Harris felt an enormous weight suddenly removed from his shoulders. He had been hoping for something like this ever since the crisis began. Now if the city exploded, he would have someone to blame. "I see. I see. Well," he said, surprising Bamcheck with a calm smile, "what can I do to help you?"

"I want to start by seeing every scrap of information you have on this Omega Chi gang."

"There's a good deal."

"I *have* the time."

Harris had the yeoman bring in the file on the Omega Chi. It consisted of five individual manila folders tabbed: TAYLOR, WARNER, PHILLIPS, CASY and WHYTE. Each folder was thick with notes, anecdotes, reports by paid informers, personal interviews and interrogations that Navy Intelligence had diligently gathered over the past several years.

Two hours later, Bamcheck had seen all of it. "You're right, Commander," he informed Harris. "You don't have enough to build a case. But when I get through, you will. I want you to begin by putting pressure on them individually—tails, formal interrogations, spot searches, harassment of parents and friends, the works."

"And how long do you want me to keep this up, Mr. Bamcheck?" He did not try to disguise his lack of enthusiasm.

"Until one of them breaks, Mr. Harris. Until one of them cracks wide open."

The week before the Whytes evacuated Mainland China in 1949, another ship carrying another five-year-old boy docked in Keelung harbor. The boy's name was Mark Earnest Taylor and his parents, both longtime China scholars and faculty members of the University of Tientsin, had been among those "enemies of the people" arrested, tortured and executed when Communist forces overran the city in January of that tumultuous year.

The boy had been smuggled out of Tientsin by Chinese Christians and sent on to Shanghai, Hangchow, Foochow and then Taipei. His presence at this final destination immediately caused a problem. The boy seemed to have no family in the States. His citizenship was questionable—his parents, like many idealistic Sinologists determined to stay in China after the fall, had officially renounced their American citizenship—and he spoke only Mandarin. The missionary groups that had reestablished themselves in Taipei wanted to keep him there as a symbol of Communist barbarism, but they couldn't very well put him, a white boy, in one of their crowded Chinese orphanages where he would not even learn English as a primary language. It was finally decided that he would be jointly cared for by both the Baptist and Episcopal missionary societies as a general ward of the Community.

With neither organization fully in charge, Mark Taylor grew up with very little authority over him. He became a kind of freewheeling Huckleberry Finn figure in the American Community: an odd, poker-faced, uncommunicative boy who was not exactly a troublemaker but always seemed to be up to no good. He became the first

American boy his age to venture into the whorehouses, the first to patronize the bars downtown, and the first to drink *kaoliang* wine and smoke *jin chu,* the powerful Taiwanese cannabis plant. Soon, inevitably, mothers began telling their children not to associate with "the Taylor boy." When the Episcopal Mission gave him an eleventh birthday party, the only child that showed up was Bryan Whyte, who did not have a mother to make him stay away.

Although they were best friends since those early childhood days, it was not until they were going into their teens that Taylor first became convinced that Bryan Whyte was a genius and thus became utterly committed to him. The occasion was Whyte's first major business coup—his entry into the pirated book business.

Since Nationalist China did not subscribe to any of the international copyright agreements, one of the biggest businesses that arose in the city in the mid-fifties was the pirating of American books, reprinted in cheap, rice-paper editions then legally sold in the dozens of Chung Shan North Road bookstores or illegally smuggled to other countries around the world. The business was very lucrative and efficient but it had one problem: There was usually a lag-time of several months between the book's initial publication in New York and the time a pirate could have a copy sent to him and begin putting out his own edition. So they were always behind in getting the current bestsellers to the stores. Whyte figured out that if he could print up a phony literary magazine, publishers would send him advance review copies through the APO mail. He could then get a new book to the pirates in plenty of time for a pirated edition to be out virtually simultaneously with the appearance of the original in Stateside bookstores. Using Taylor (and a skeptical group of English literature students from Taiwan University, who wrote the phony reviews that were printed and sent back to the publishers) as his staff, Bryan Whyte became the pirating industry's main supplier of source material—at the age of thirteen.

In those days, the American School was a blackboard

jungle of gangs made up of newly arrived military kids drunk on the freedom of the city and the big money they could make on the black market. When these gangs heard how much money Whyte and Taylor were making, several of them descended on the young pirates and demanded a cut. Whyte saw no choice but to comply but Taylor refused. Taylor had been studying the martial arts for years as an asthma treatment and he welcomed the opportunity for practical experience. Singly and in groups, he took on the older boys in a series of bloody fistfights and did not come out second in even one of them. This incident was the genesis of the Omega Chi: Soon the two had formed an organization around themselves that went by that name—Omega for Old Whyte's company in the Shanghai days and Chi (Ki) because Taylor thought the Greek letter X looked great on the back of a black jacket.

As the years passed, the Omega Chi became the American gang of gangs in teenage Taipei. For Taylor it was the family he had never known. Though he could be as remote and enigmatic—and rude—with the Omega Chi as he was with everyone else, there was no doubt that they mattered very much to him. He could be surprisingly mother-hennish—and so obviously devoted to Whyte that many outsiders suspected something unnatural at work. He loyally served the organization as its enforcer; he battled the other gangs into such total submission that, in time, an extraordinary legend of invincibility grew up around him. It spread all over the city—a legend that made possible all of Whyte's business schemes, including the takeover of the black market.

He was so naturally belligerent and ill-suited for anything else that it was taken for granted in the Community that Taylor would one day have a career in the military. Indeed, as long as he could remember, his single ambition was to go to West Point and become a professional soldier.

As his senior year in high school began, this goal seemed finally within his grasp. Because of his status as a war orphan, a political appointment was arranged by the Embassy. He sailed through the required academic tests and preliminary interviews and even passed his Academy physical, which, because of his asthma, had been a great concern. Furthermore, when the Greens invaded Taipei several months earlier and restored the Omega Chi to supremacy, Taylor did not go after revenge on the Warlords as everyone assumed he would. He simply did not want to risk getting in trouble, and thus jeopardize his chances of being admitted into the Military Academy.

On the second Monday in October, 1962, Mark Taylor was to have his last interview with the West Point selection committee. Very nervous, he put on his new three-button Hong Kong suit, went down to the U.S. Embassy and waited in a lacquered chair under a big color photograph of John F. Kennedy.

When his name was called, he went into the conference room to find three officers sitting around a table, looking at him sternly. Two of them were Army officers; the third was Commander Floyd Harris. Also at the table was a civilian, whom Taylor recognized from the numerous interrogations of the Omega Chi since the Green influx. It was Harlan Bamcheck of the CIA.

Taylor sat down uneasily as Bamcheck placed a piece of paper before him.

"What is this?" Taylor asked.

Bamcheck half-smiled. "It's a letter from me that's going to keep you out of West Point, should I choose to attach it to your application."

Taylor's face went pale but remained impassive. He assumed correctly that Bamcheck wanted to make a deal. "What do you want for it?"

"I want you to help me put Bryan Whyte in jail."

Taylor didn't answer; he took a deep breath and remained stoic, waiting for Bamcheck to finish.

"I need information that will help me build a case against him. No one need know where I got this information."

Mark Taylor stood up, calmly walked out of the room, out of the U.S. Embassy and out of any chance for a West Point appointment. Later, he would tell Whyte that he had been turned down by the committee but he would not say why and, as was his way, he would never mention anything about it again.

The Reverend Clifton Warner, the Old China Episcopal minister who served as unofficial leader of the missionary community and the man primarily responsible for the adoption of Mark Taylor, had a son of his own who was just one year younger than Taylor.

This boy, George Adam Warner, was a slight, rather unusual-looking child (his nose pointed to the left and his eyes were so close together they almost touched) with a quick wit who endlessly delighted his mother and three older sisters with his uncanny impressions of Disney characters. He also continually disappointed his father by showing no interest whatsoever in the daily Bible lessons that began in the Warner family at age three. Raised under such firm, old-fashioned discipline and the obligations of his father's position, young Georgie could not remember a time when he did not envy the freedom of his parentless friends, Bryan Whyte and Mark Taylor.

By the time he was twelve, Georgie had already started to rebel secretly against the strict hand of his pompous and impossible-to-please father. With Taylor and Whyte, he visited the whorehouses of Peitou, drank rice wine in the Japanese bars of the Yen Ping area and made money selling items on the black market of Haggler's Alley. He also began to skip school regularly and spend his days in the big Shihminting movie houses where he became hopelessly addicted to the exciting, perfect, larger-than-life world he found in the American Westerns of Randolph Scott and Audie Murphy, the B melodramas and the gangster epics of Samuel Fuller, the comedies of Bob Hope and Jerry Lewis.

He particularly liked the comedies. He would often see them three or four times in a single sitting. Afterward he would act out their routines in his room with the door locked. As he entered his teens, he found he had a genuine gift for making people laugh and he began to use that gift to get attention for himself. It made him a very popular kid, canceling out much of the stigma that went with being the funny-looking, head preacher's son.

When Bryan Whyte formed the Omega Chi, it was only natural that Warner would become a member. He too had family ties to the Mainland—his father had even performed the marriage ceremony for Whyte's parents in the thirties and he had always been a third musketeer of Whyte and Taylor. He was a kindhearted, good-natured and extremely likeable fellow and the two older boys were charmed by him—even if they didn't quite trust him with the more delicate fraternity business.

The Omega Chi quickly became the focus of Georgie Warner's whole life. The acceptance and recognition of Bryan Whyte and Soldier Taylor meant more to him than grades or women or achievement in sports. It was a feeling so glorious that it was absolutely inconceivable to him that anything in his later life could equal it.

Then, quite suddenly in 1962, all of it turned sour. First, Whyte began reminding him that the rest of the Omega Chi—all one year older than Warner—might be in college in the States next year. If so, it would be up to him to run the business and deal with both their Green allies and their increasingly restless Tiger Eel enemies—a prospect that terrified him. Then his father, who also terrified him, went on a campaign to convince him to quit the Omega Chi, subjecting him to marathon prayer sessions. If all that weren't enough, Bamcheck singled him out for special harassment, calling him in almost daily to threaten and interrogate him. It was making him feel so panicky and pressured that he all but dropped out of school, stayed drunk for days at a time and spent almost every afternoon hiding in the darkness of a movie theater.

When even this didn't alleviate the pressure he was feeling, he started going to Peitou. This was somewhat risky because it was technically illegal for an American dependent to be in a red-light district; Bamcheck would dearly love to catch him there. It also involved a certain loss of face to be seen whoring by oneself. But, in the past, he had discovered that the experience of secret whoring—the excited anticipation, the risk, the giving oneself over entirely to erotic pleasure with a stranger—was not unlike the experience of escaping into the fantasy world of a movie theater. On his first trip there, he picked a woman almost as old as his mother and copulated with her on a dirty tatami floor. Afterward he felt thoroughly disgusted with himself—so disgusted that it drove out any other emotion and left him with a strange sense of serenity and peace. It was such a relief that, as he kept feeling intolerably pressured, he found himself coming back to Peitou again and again.

When even Peitou lost its power of escape for him, Georgie began to sneak down to the Tiger Eel–run Lung Shan red-light district downtown. This was reputed to be the single most evil area in Asia and very few Americans —certainly no missionaries' sons—ever ventured there. Here he found the ultimate in sexual escape. Over the weeks of the Chinese New Year, he tried everything! He watched eight millimeter pornographic movies that had been smuggled in from Hong Kong and Yokohama. He participated in an orgy with three women and watched a woman have intercourse with a German shepherd dog. He visited a child brothel and smoked opium and even witnessed a demonstration in which a young Taiwanese prostitute was brutally tortured for the pleasure of a paying audience. The Lung Shan was a world of total depravity and he was totally fascinated by it. As his life became more and more pressured, he found himself escaping into it more and more until at last he realized he was no longer a tourist—he could not force himself to stay away more than a few days at a time.

The day after this scary realization hit him, he stepped into Bamcheck's office in the MAAG compound for his weekly interrogation. This time, however, Bamcheck did not greet him with his usual tirade of invective, insult and abuse. He merely smiled and placed three eight-by-ten snapshots on the table before him. They were grainy photographs of Georgie Warner in the sweaty midst of an orgy with three bored whores.

Bamcheck paced deliciously behind him as Warner's face froze into a mask of panic. "How would you like your father to see these pictures, Georgie?"

"How did . . . ?"

"We have our ways."

Warner started to sob. "What do you want?" he blurted.

"All we want is your cooperation, Georgie."

By that evening, Warner was back in a smoke-filled Lung Shan whorehouse, drunk and more pressured than ever and desperately trying to figure a way out of his dilemma. The more he thought, the more he was sure there was no way out. He could not betray the Omega Chi and he could not let his father see those pictures. The only way out was suicide. Yes, he thought grimly, that was it. He would throw himself in the Tamsui River; perhaps shoot himself with the pistol he always carried for protection. Relieved at this decision, he rose to his feet, shook off his drunkenness and stumbled down the tatami hallway with his whore for one more hour of pleasure before he ended it all.

In the narrow hallway, he bumped into a man who was just then leaving one of the back rooms with his arms around two giggling whores. As the dim light of a frosted overhanging light bulb flashed across the man's face, Georgie Warner knew in one astonished second that he would not have to commit suicide or give in to Bamcheck or worry about his father's reaction to those photographs after all.

The man was his *father*.

Alan Jeffrey Phillips came to Taiwan from a small farming community in upstate New York where the Phillips family had lived for more than five generations. His father, Seth, an agricultural engineer and professor at Cornell University, had grown dissatisfied with the quality of his life there. One day in 1950, Seth Phillips impulsively accepted a position with the Joint Commission on Rural Reconstruction (JCRR), a Sino-American agricultural aid group which had just relocated on the Island of Taiwan. At the time, he had never even heard of Taiwan.

The move turned out to be an unexpectedly rewarding one. Seth Phillips threw himself into the work (he was a farmer at heart, never happier than when knee-deep in paddy mud) and became the chief architect of the Island's land reform. His wife Mary enjoyed the experience of being a pioneer in a new frontier, living an existence of idealism, unselfishness and even occasional physical hardship. Both especially loved being part of the newly forming American Community, which in those days seemed a microcosm of all those cherished American values that had vanished from their former lives.

Raised within the framework of a healthy, confident community and a loving and fulfilled family, young Alan Phillips grew to be an unusually secure and unusually responsible individual. From early childhood, he was a very serious, clean-living, clean-cut and incorrigibly *good* boy. He loved his parents, was seemingly immune from all negative peer pressure and actively participated in sports, boy scouts, the Four-H, the Red Cross, the Methodist Church, the Sino-American Friendship League and practically every other service organization that existed on the Island. He became the ultimate community activist and was able to bring to all his responsibilities not just idealism but a hard organizational skill, a nit-picking thoroughness and attention to detail.

When Whyte got serious about the Omega Chi, the first thing he did was ask Alan Phillips to join them. At the time it was thought inconceivable that Phillips—the prototypical all-American boy—would join kids like Soldier Taylor and Georgie Warner in what amounted to a gang. But Phillips did accept. He had long been as intrigued by the glamor and mystique of Bryan Whyte as everyone else and had always felt particularly excluded from the inner circle of Old China hands. In time, he grew to be an integral part of this group—to give his supreme loyalty to Whyte, to laugh at the pranks of Georgie Warner, to enjoy being associated with the cool and dangerous Mark Taylor.

To a great extent, the Omega Chi that developed was as much a reflection of Phillips as it was of Whyte. Phillips organized their brilliant black-market system and put all of Whyte's other ideas into practical effect. He was their bookkeeper and day-to-day manager, the overseer of all their charitable activities. In a larger sense, he was also the morality of the Omega Chi. With typical idealism, he became convinced very early that the Omega Chi was a necessary underground element of the American presence and he intended to do everything possible to make sure it stayed an institution of nobility, honor and good works.

Phillips was disturbed by the conflict with the Warlords and Whyte's use of the Greens to protect Omega Chi interests. He had always known of Whyte's mysterious links to the Greens—he had even once been thrilled by the idea—but he was not prepared for such a public association. He was also not prepared for being regularly called in and shaken down by Harris and Bamcheck as if he were a common criminal. More than any of his brothers, he was susceptible to this kind of pressure—he *cared* very much how he looked in the eyes of his family and the Community—and his agony over it was making him question everything about his association with the fraternity.

As fears of imminent gang warfare spread through Taipei and Bamcheck redoubled his efforts to crack the Omega Chi, Phillips decided he'd had enough. There was only one course of action open to him: to resign. As much as he loved Whyte and the others, the Omega Chi simply did not make sense to him anymore.

The decision made, Phillips sadly went down for a final inspection of the Ta Tung Orphanage in South Taipei, which the Omega Chi entirely supported and which Phillips considered the major accomplishment of his life. With him, he took his longtime girlfriend, Doris Loo—a Chinese classmate at TAS, the daughter of a Chinese army general and, like Phillips, a strong Christian and civic activist.

After saying his good-bys to the staff and volunteers, he went back to the cafeteria to meet with a group of petitioners. It was Phillips's custom to meet there twice a month with anyone who had a request for money or service. This would be the last time.

After the pleas had been made and the petitioners sent on their way, Phillips noticed a small, nervous coolie with a pitifully scarred face standing in the rear of the cafeteria. "Who is that?" he asked Doris.

"This is my friend. I asked him to come today. I hoped there was something you could do to help him."

Phillips stepped over to the frightened man. "What is it, my cousin?" he asked in Mandarin.

The man was too frightened to speak so Doris spoke for him. "This man is Su Po-chuan," she said. "He owned a noodle stand near my house on Sung Chiang Road on the outskirts of Sin Alley. Every morning I see him as I wait for my car to take me to school and we talk. He is very proud to have four daughters and one of them is very beautiful. She is so beautiful that Loma of the Tiger Eels offered to buy her to work in his brothels. Mr. Su refused Loma's offer so the Tiger Eels burned down his stand and threw acid in his face. Now he is blind and without livelihood. He has no choice but to sell all his daughters to Loma. . . ."

Phillips listened to this story, nodding his head occasionally and choking back his outrage. When it was over, he said, "Tell Mr. Su that the Omega Chi will buy him a new stand. Tell him to move out of Sin Alley and set up in the Chung Wa Market. From now on he and his daughters will be under our protection."

As he spoke these words, Phillips suddenly experienced an overwhelming sensation of relief. In that moment, all the anxiety and confusion of the past year left him, replaced by a sense of strength and fulfillment and righteous indignation. He also knew that he could not quit the Omega Chi now. For a time anyway, it all made sense to him again.

In late 1954, the United States and Nationalist China signed a mutual defense treaty that pledged loyalty to one another for a period of twenty-five years. As a provision of this treaty, the U.S. formed a Taiwan branch of its Military Assistance Advisory Group (MAAG) and sent advisors to the Chinese military from all three branches of its armed services—Army, Navy and Air Force.

These advisers were normally stationed on Taiwan for short, two-year tours of duty but they were allowed to bring their families with them. Soon the military and their dependents made up the largest portion of the American Community. In most ways, they were an entirely different breed from the Old China hands who had come from the Mainland in '49 and the idealistic and stout-hearted civilians who had joined them in the early fifties. But they were no less committed to the *idea* of Taiwan and they added both a freshness and vitality to the Community, as well as a link to all the current Stateside trends in popular culture.

Among the second generation of these military dependents to hit the Island was a thirteen-year-old named John Patrick Casy. He was the son of a gung ho Air Force colonel whose new mission was to oversee the daily Chinese Air Force intelligence flights over the Mainland. By the time he came to Taiwan in the spring of 1958, Casy's family had already lived in Bordeaux, France; Frankfurt, Germany; Hickam Field, Hawaii; McConnell Air Force Base, Kansas; and various other air bases all over the American South.

Young John Casy was a sensitive boy by nature and all the moving involved in the life of a military dependent had its effect. Forever faced with having to adjust to new schools and new situations, he withdrew into himself. He lived in a world of books and his own imagination. This withdrawal—which particularly alarmed his father, who did everything possible to bring him out of it—would later seem a blessing to Casy and the genesis of his artistic sensibility. When he was ten, he was already a skilled cartoonist and watercolorist. When he was twelve, he wrote a short story that was published in *Boy's Life*. When he was thirteen, he had mastered the piano and guitar and was even composing his own music.

Still, Casy had been an outsider wherever he lived. When he became a teenager, the thing he wanted more than anything was to be accepted as an insider. When he came to Taiwan in 1958, he firmly determined to open himself up to people, to be a different person and start his life over again. For someone with a romantic nature, it was the perfect place for a new beginning. It was a world that made him feel special and alive—a world of alien new sights and sounds and smells; of whorehouses and pimps who grabbed frantically at his arm; of shocking slums and poverty; of streets crowded with humanity and jungle-covered mountains in the distance with their wild boar and monkeys and fifteen varieties of deadly snakes and aboriginal inhabitants that ten years ago were practicing headhunters; of constant military danger and dedicated, heroic people holding out against the forces of barbarism and anarchy just a stone's throw across the Taiwan Straits.

In his sophomore year, Casy had a class in which he was assigned a seat next to Bryan Whyte. Whyte had never met anyone quite like John Casy. He saw at once that Casy was an artist, with his own unique way of looking at the world and with drives and motives that he, Whyte, could not even begin to understand. Whyte became fascinated with Casy and his many talents. They became friends and Casy was eventually asked to be in the Omega Chi.

The Omega Chi Fraternity was the most incredible thing that ever happened to John Casy. It gave him, for the first time in his young life, stability, status and friends. He found that he thrived on being part of the ultimate in-crowd, on having money and power and girls at his disposal, on being brothers with the best-looking, most popular, most athletic kids in the school. Above all else, he cherished the closeness it gave him to Bryan Whyte. Sometimes Casy thought his whole purpose as an artist was to tell the world about the greatness of Bryan Whyte. Sometimes he suspected Bryan Whyte thought this too.

Casy loved everything about his life on Taiwan. So much so that he talked his father into extending their tour two times so that he could finish high school there. And his new life continued to be happy and fulfilled—right up to the savage attack on him by the Tiger Eels. After that, everything changed. He spent three months in the hospital and another two months at home. When the physical wounds had healed, he discovered psychological ones that had not. Every time he stepped out of the house, he felt himself surrounded by murderous Orientals with long knives. He could not be in a crowd without breaking into a sweat. No matter how hard he tried, he could not write or paint or make music. His confidence in *everything* had been shattered.

When the CIA interrogated Casy in the first part of 1963, Harlan Bamcheck immediately picked up on this wound and devised a whole strategy around it. One blustery March day, the little investigator called the boy into his office, sat him at the interrogation table and placed three eight by ten photos in front of him. They were grisly police shots of a recent Tiger Eel murder victim—the body dismembered and grotesquely mutilated.

"The reason I've called you in, John, is that our intelligence sources have reliable reports that the Tiger Eels are preparing another attack against you." Bamcheck lied. "We have reason to believe the murder in this picture may have been committed by the same fellow who's after you."

At the sight of the photos, Casy's last internal reserve of strength and resolve collapsed. As Bamcheck finally made his plea for cooperation against Whyte, Casy could not even speak. When dismissed, he took a taxi home and went directly to bed.

Over the next four days, Bamcheck called Casy in

once a day and forced him to view a new set of police
photos of Tiger Eel atrocities. On the fifth day, Casy got
sick with a soaring temperature and violent stomach
cramps and refused to get out of bed.

After he had been sick for nearly a month, Whyte and
Taylor appeared at Casy's house in Tien Mou one night
when his parents were gone. They had been by many times
trying to coax him out of bed, but these attempts only
made him withdraw deeper into himself. This time, without even a hello, they grabbed him, wrestled him into his
clothes and forced him into a waiting taxi.

As they drove along the Shih Lin Road, sweat began
to bead on Casy's face. As they crossed the Chung Shan
bridge and drove deeper into the city, Casy began to trem-
ble uncontrollably. He suddenly screamed at them to turn
around. But neither would say a word. They just stared
grimly into the night.

Whyte soon motioned the driver to stop.

They were at the entrance of Sin Alley. The heart of
Tiger Eel territory. Whyte opened the door. "Get out."

Casy panicked. "No!"

Whyte took him firmly by the arm and pulled him
out. Casy fought back. Whyte threw him against the taxi's
fender and held him until the fight was gone. "Now let's
go," he said.

They started to walk down the nearly deserted, neon-
lit street, Taylor a few steps behind them with his hand in
his pocket.

"Where . . . where are we going?"

"We're going to Loma's bar for a little drink."

"Oh, Christ . . . this is crazy. This is just asking for
trouble. They're going to murder us. This could start a
war!"

"Yeah, I guess it could."

"Then why are we doing it?"

"Because we're the Omega Chi," Taylor said.

A hundred Tiger Eel eyes peered at them from windows and side alleys and warrens. The three Americans
entered Loma's bar and ordered rice wine. Taylor stood

at the end of the bar watching the entrance and the handful of customers with the steely eyes of a gunfighter. He was enjoying himself to the fullest. "What shall we drink to?" he asked, laying his custom-made, pearl-handled forty-five caliber Smith & Wesson pistol on the bar.

"Let's drink to confidence," Whyte said.

"To confidence," Taylor said.

Whyte looked at Casy and held up his glass. "You can't do business without it."

They gulped down the wine and Casy found, to his amazement, that he was beginning to feel better. "Okay, let's go," he muttered.

"Not so fast," Whyte said, smiling calmly. He ordered another round. They drank it and Casy found himself feeling better still, feeling safe and secure in their company. They drank two more and Taylor described in semidrunken detail how they could hold off an attack almost indefinitely from this position. By this time, Casy was actually enjoying the sheer recklessness, the ridiculous grandeur of being there.

As they finally walked unmolested back up Sin Alley, Casy was brimming over with love for his two friends. Later that night, he forced himself to sit down and write a song about it.

Over the course of her senior year in high school, Shelley Spencer's infatuation with Bryan Whyte matured into an emotion she could, for the first time in her life, clearly identify as "love."

This extraordinary process took place in the face of enormous opposition: from her parents, who no longer forbade her to see him openly but still disapproved of him so vehemently his name was not allowed to be mentioned at the dinner table; from Bamcheck and Harris, who followed her, regularly harassed her and put relentless pressure on her to sell him out; from her own secret fears that something like the kidnapping of 1961 could happen again.

But, in the end, these obstacles only served to feed her

love. She discovered she actually thrived on the controversy, that she was able to find a total identity in being the woman of such a rebellious and glamorous figure. It made her feel special and vastly important in this strange world to which, otherwise, she had never fully adjusted.

Their intimate life during this trying year had been fumblingly carried on in the Omega Chi House, Shihminting hotels, taxis, pedicabs and wherever else they could steal a moment alone. Their love-making was always passionate and usually very inventive and sometimes it was marginally satisfying. But it had never been fully consummated. Shelley was a practicing Catholic. She would not use birth control or permit Bryan to have complete intercourse with her. Despite all his best efforts, she remained a "technical" virgin.

However, toward the end of the year, she began to have some hard second thoughts about this policy. Bryan had been accepted to the University of Washington, his father's alma mater, and he would be leaving Taipei at the end of summer. Shelley was going to the University of Missouri, near her father's new station, and would be leaving in June. After that, they would not see each other again until the next summer—an entire year!

One day, just two weeks before graduation and three weeks before she was scheduled to go back to the States, Shelley decided to finally, irrevocably commit herself to Bryan Whyte. She checked her calendar to make sure it was the safest time of her month. She said a prayer, asking God to understand what she was about to do, and called Bryan, telling him she wanted to be alone with him, and soon.

That afternoon, not knowing exactly what to expect and very much aware of her unusual nervousness, Whyte took her to the Omega Chi House. He locked the door, put a Johnny Mathis record on the hi-fi, then carefully laid a pillow and comforter on a corner of the tatami floor, as was their ritual. He slowly undressed her, then himself, and pulled the large down comforter over them. They kissed hungrily and proceeded to exchange the oral foreplay which he had learned from a Peitou girl when he was eleven and she had learned from the Japanese pornographic pictures Georgie Warner had once gleefully used to shock her.

But this time, when he was ready and full, she rolled on her back and spread her legs. She pulled him on top of her and guided his erection into her, gasping from the sting. Realizing now what was happening, he moved gently and evenly with her; the sensation of being inside her—this perfect American beauty—was so intense, so deeply satisfying, so different from what he had experienced with a succession of Oriental prostitutes, that he was shocked. The orgasm he experienced within seconds seemed not so much a sexual culmination as a revelation, a glorious affirmation of his lifelong dream of America.

Afterward, they lay on the tatami for nearly an hour, occasionally whispering vows of love, mostly just holding one another tightly. Bryan was overcome with such a sense of excitement and joy about his future he was near the bursting point. The sexual experience had triggered a flood of optimism; he felt himself on the threshold of the most fulfilling period of his life. He wanted to express this feeling to her, but couldn't quite find the words.

Laying against him, Shelley could feel his excitement. "Thinking about going to the States, aren't you?" she said, finally breaking the quiet.

"Yes."

"It won't be long now."

"I'm counting off the days."

"Are you scared?"

"A little. Mostly it's just hard for me to believe it's actually going to happen. I've spent my whole life thinking about the place. Now I'm going to see it, touch it, smell it, walk on top of it. It's almost more than I can bear."

As she listened to these words, Shelley experienced a wave of melancholy. She felt so sad she wanted to cry and she had no idea why. She did everything she could think of to escape this feeling of doom but it stayed with her for the rest of the day, marring what was otherwise the most important experience of her life.

Aside from his sexual adventures with Shelley Spencer, Bryan Whyte's senior year of high school proved to be an ordeal. Bamcheck and Harris kept the pressure on twenty-four hours a day, seven days a week, never letting him forget for a minute that he was an outlaw. They had him followed and publicly shaken down at the most embarrassing times. They threatened to have him deported or thrown in jail. What bothered him most about it was that they steadfastly refused to believe that his only goal in bringing about the occupation of the Greens was to serve the best interests of the American Community.

During this year, he found himself being drawn deeper into the mysterious world of the Green Society. From numerous strategy sessions, he got to know many of the more prominent *boo hoy doys,* and among his friends, he now counted such legendary figures as "The Elephant," a jovial yet much-feared three-hundred-pound master of kung fu and all-around enforcer for the Greens who had been in Taipei since 1947; "Terrible" Ding Tze, a silent, moonfaced, old-time hatchet man who had supposedly killed in excess of a thousand men in his lengthy career; Samuel Yin, King Lu's cool, American-educated, military-minded second in command; and Johnny Yen, a very handsome and charismatic young Green lieutenant who was an addict of American popular culture and who dreamed of being a Hollywood movie star.

As he became more familiar with the twilight world of this Chinese secret society, more and more questions came to his mind about it. He read many volumes on Taoism and Chinese history, trying to learn everything he could. In the course of time he developed a strong respect and deep affection to go along with his instinctual awe and fear of the Greens. Their beliefs seemed to be very much in line with his own. They believed in the supreme importance of the family. They believed in religion (almost any religion would do, they were not particular). They believed in swift justice, public charity and an orderly society. They also believed in capitalism as a moral force, in enterprise and thrift and competition and free trade as bringing out the best in a people—just as Whyte so fervently believed.

King Lu flew to the city every month or so to keep an eye on the situation. Whyte was quite fascinated with the man and eagerly looked forward to his visits. King seemed to possess all the magnificence and contradiction of China itself. He was nominally a Christian but he believed in Taoist magic and superstition, and in his bearing and his personal conduct he embodied the Confucian ideal of order and decorum. He was a devout Chinese nationalist but seemed to believe in America and what America wanted to do in Asia. He made a foreboding figure but was always very warm and affectionate with Whyte, hugging him in greeting as he would a favorite son, patiently instructing him in the ways of the Greens.

Yet there was much about King and their relationship that Whyte did not understand and which was not perfect. King always seemed to be scrutinizing him, testing him in little ways that made Whyte uncomfortable. The gang lord was aghast that Whyte was determined to go to the States for college and tried to argue him out of it. They also could not agree on what to do about the rising threat of a war with the Tiger Eels—Whyte wanted to preserve the balance of power but to avoid a violent confrontation with the Taiwanese gang and its Warlord allies at all costs; King did not think it would be possible—and this, particularly, drove a wedge between them.

On the busy week before the TAS graduation, King made one of his periodic trips to town and sent a message requesting to see Bryan Whyte.

Whyte left his graduation practice and went directly to the Grand Hotel. King received him in his suite with an embrace and a smile, but his manner was tense and businesslike.

"Welcome once again," Whyte said in Mandarin.

"Thank you." They stood facing each other as King said, "I have come to Taipei because I have received more alarming reports. These reports tell me that the Tiger Eels have continued to build up their strength over the past six months. They tell me that the hawks of the Tiger Eels are actually calling for a military confrontation with the Greens. My advisor, Samuel Yin, insists that all it will take is a minor incident for the rest of the Eels to go along with them and force an attack. I think I must move before that incident takes place, Little Brother."

"Sir. Please. I think this is unwise and unnecessary. Surely the Green presence alone . . ."

"I too thought our presence would be enough," King cut him short. "But I was wrong. There is something very powerful in the wind giving them strength—some force that I do not fully understand. They are very dangerous —and should be stamped out while we still have the overwhelming advantage."

"Yes, I feel this force too. But we don't know how strong it is or how long it will last. I want to avoid bloodshed. I simply cannot believe that, in the end, they will dare attack us."

"It goes against my instincts to wait. Strongly."

"Any large-scale violence would be disastrous for the Island, disastrous for the cause it serves. I beg you to wait."

King stared at the floor and blinked several times. His jaw muscle moved up and down. "I will wait a little while longer," he said.

With this uneasily settled, they stepped out on the balcony. The sun was beginning to go down over the city. "You are still leaving after the summer?" King asked.

"Yes."

"May I ask why?"

Whyte smiled. King had asked this question many times before and always got the same answer. "Because America is my home," he said. "Just as China is your real home. I need to have my schooling there, to gain strength and identity. I will be back."

"I think maybe this is your home," King grumbled angrily.

The graduation of the Taipei American School's class of '63 took place in the school's new auditorium on a sweltering night one week later. Alan Phillips was class valedictorian. He spoke earnestly for twenty minutes about "American Responsibility in the Pacific" while Whyte, Taylor, Casy and some seventy other graduates sat in heavy blue caps and gowns sweating in the front two rows. After the diplomas were handed out, the class and its friends and parents went in a caravan of taxis to the Grand Hotel for a gala champagne reception.

The ceremony put Whyte in an unusually bittersweet and sentimental mood. As much as he wanted to go to the States and have the adventure of his real life begin, he was shaken by the realization that nothing would ever be the same. In the following summer months, all of these friends —the entire Omega Chi except for Warner—would be leaving Taiwan. His whole world would be breaking up. The first to go—in less than a week, in fact—was Shelley Spencer. Bryan spent most of the evening tearfully dancing with Shelley to a small combo on the patio under the light of a full moon. He was blurry-eyed with appreciation for her. She was, as usual, a vision of beauty: with a sky-blue *chong-sam* split skirt, no make-up and an azalea twisted in her long brown hair.

But she had become more than just beauty to him these past two years. Much more. She had been as loyal to him as any of the Omega Chi, suffering the physical abuse of the Warlords, the wrath of her father and the harassment of the American authorities to stand by his side. She had been everything to him his mother had been to his father—and more. And someday—when he had made his mark in the States and restored his family's fortune—he would marry her. He would make her a queen.

The mood was abruptly broken by a hand on his

shoulder. He turned around to see the pale and drawn face of Alan Phillips.

Even through the haze of melancholy and drunkenness he knew at once that something was terribly wrong.

"Bryan, I need to talk to you. . . . It's very important."

He took Shelley by the hand and followed Phillips back to the Omega Chi table. Phillips reached for a champagne bottle and poured himself a drink. Alan Phillips had never had a drink in his life.

Whyte said nothing. He knew his friend would speak as soon as he was able.

Phillips's hand trembled as he set the empty glass back on the table. "It's Georgie," he said. "He was arrested this afternoon."

"Why?" Whyte's voice was even, calm.

"He was down in Lung Shan in some godforsaken brothel—drunk as a sailor."

"Yes?"

"He ran into Ortega and Magaha and there was a fight. Bryan, he had a pistol and he shot Ortega!"

In an instant, Whyte threw off his drunkenness. Without a word, without a trace of expression on his face, he motioned to Mark Taylor and started out the door. Every eye in the ballroom followed him.

The great gang war of 1963 had begun.

7

THE DRIVER PULLED THE BIG MERCEDES TAXI UP TO the curb on Roosevelt Road. Whyte rolled down the window and waved. Mark Taylor got in and closed the door. "Any word yet?" Whyte asked him eagerly.

"Nothing." Taylor tried to exhale his tension away. "Not a goddamn thing."

The shooting of Randy Ortega was taken by everyone involved as the incident that would finally bring about a violent confrontation between the Green Society and Tiger Eel gangster armies. From the sulphur spas of Pei-tou to the opium dens of Lung Shan and all throughout the American Community, people were holding their breaths, waiting to see if the Tiger Eels would join the Warlord retaliation. But the retaliation still had not come.

Forty-eight hours later, there had not been a sound from the Warlords or the Tiger Eels.

Bryan Whyte was caught completely off guard by the incident. He had simply not anticipated that the first un-provoked shot would come from one of his own people. As the facts became known, it made them look even worse: Warner had shot Ortega knowing he was unarmed and had apparently sought him out for that purpose. Even though Ortega had only been hit in the legs and would easily recover, Whyte had sent the Warlords restitution money in Warner's name. He had gone so far as to send Ortega a personal message, deploring the incident and begging him not to do anything foolish. Writing such a note had not been easy but it had to be done—there was simply no way he could justify Georgie Warner's incred-ible action.

"Maybe they won't retaliate," he suddenly consid-ered. "Or maybe they'll retaliate without the Tiger Eels. Maybe the Tiger Eels don't think it's provocation enough to stumble into a showdown fight with the Greens."

Taylor thought about this idea before rejecting it.

"I doubt it. Ortega's been badly humiliated. He's lost all kinds of face and for him that's worse than being killed. The Eels also have great face involved—they have a blood alliance with Ortega, don't forget. They probably figure it was a planned assassination attempt. No, they've both got to do something. I think we can assume they're just wait-ing for the right opportunity. And why shouldn't they? It's their move and they can make it without any pressure. That's why my advice is that we get King Lu on the stick and move against them *now* with everything we can muster. Strategically, the smartest thing we could do is follow up on Georgie's action."

"No, Soldier. Warner did a despicable thing. To follow up on something like that would be to condone it. We can't act without honor, even against our worst enemies."

"Then all we can do is wait for them to retaliate. And it'll come, Bryan, believe me. It will come."

Whyte was quiet for a moment. He watched the passing headlights making shadowy designs on the driver's back as the taxi turned off Canal Road and whined on toward the Omega Chi House. "How do you think it'll happen?"

"The most obvious thing is for them to move against the black market again. The Tiger Eels are very, very strong in numbers downtown. But . . ." Taylor paused, enjoying the analysis of the situation, thrilled at being so close to the smell of battle. "Since Ortega is their leader and he was the one humiliated, they may try to get you alone to even the score. They may just be content to humiliate you in public. In any case, if the Eels are going to be involved, they're not likely to do anything too major without one of those Taiwanese hatchets sticking in our door one night as a declaration of war. They're very big on symbols, I understand."

Taylor reached over into the front seat to push in the cigarette lighter when the first shot crashed through the windshield of the taxi, showering the compartment with glass. Taylor grabbed at his forehead and fell back almost in Whyte's lap. The driver screamed and instinctively stepped on the gas. Two more bullets from a small caliber rifle whizzed through the open window, hitting the driver in the arm and face. He lost control and the taxi crashed into a parked car.

The impact of the collision sent Whyte through the door, rolling into the *benjo* ditch. He opened his eyes in time to see a large black limousine disappear around a corner a block up the street. Stunned and bleeding from a dozen tiny cuts, he stood up, straining to recover his

senses as he surveyed the scene. The driver was impaled
by the steering wheel, glassy-eyed and dead. Taylor was
on the floor, unconscious, bleeding from a large gash on
his forehead. Whyte reached in and tenderly pulled his
friend from the hissing wreck. "Hold on, Soldier," he
muttered steadily to himself, "hold on, hold on."

While the crowd gathered and the police roped off the
area, Whyte tried to stop the bleeding from Taylor's head
wound. He rode to the Navy hospital in the police car with
him and waited outside his room until he was assured that
Taylor's condition was not critical. Only then did he let
the doctors treat the cuts on his own face and check him
out for injuries.

When he was released from the hospital, Whyte
spoke to the Chinese police, the Chinese Foreign Affairs
Police, and made a statement for the U.S. Provost Marshal's office. He told each of them he had no idea what had
instigated this unprovoked attack but, yes, he supposed it
could have something to do with the Warner incident.
When, totally exhausted, he finally returned to the Omega
Chi House, there was a bloody hatchet stuck in the door.

Whyte did not go to bed. His body ached for sleep but
there was too much that had to be done. His mind was
racing with fragmented images of his father and Tu Yueh-
sen and all the stories he had heard his entire life about
the great tong wars of Shanghai and Penang and San
Francisco that had raged out of control for years, even
decades. He was aware that if he did not make the right
decisions tonight, it would happen in Taipei as well.

He called King Lu in Hong Kong. He was not surprised to learn that King knew all about the ambush and,
by this time, even the names of the Warlords responsible
—Fatso Magaha and little Amos Wong. King said he had
been trying to reach him for an hour, that he was ready
to move all over the city. He said he could assassinate
Loma. His troops could attack Tiger Eel strongholds in
Sin Alley and Lung Shan and end this thing in a matter

of hours. "Even as we speak, my men are leaving Peitou and getting into position."

"I don't want that," Whyte said emphatically. "Call them off. If you miss Loma or misjudge the Tiger Eel strength, you could start a war that will go on forever and take hundreds of lives. There must be a way to retain face for this attack and still avoid a long war in the city. I want your permission to try and work this thing out on my own —to keep it between the Omega Chi and the Warlords."

"The Tiger Eels are already involved."

"Not really. Not yet. Not in any numbers. We've still got time to head it off."

King was dubious. He hesitated a long time before he answered. "You have twenty-four hours, then we move." He did not wait for Whyte's reply.

Whyte next called Alan Phillips, who had heard the news and was beside himself with worry. "I heard all kinds of stories," he said. "I heard you were dead. That Mark was in the hospital and nearly dead. Nobody there would tell me anything. Why didn't you call me sooner? Does this mean we're in a war with the Tiger Eels?"

"Not if I can prevent it. Now listen to me very carefully. I want you to call Casy. The two of you stay in your houses until you hear from me again. Call Commander Harris at home and tell him we're not going out of our heads. Tell him I intend to answer this challenge and still avoid a war between the Greens and Tiger Eels."

The third number he dialed was that of someone he had hoped he would never have to use. But Taylor was out of commission and he needed muscle. He had no choice.

He listened to the ring and then heard a deep, rough Chinese voice. It belonged to the gigantic three-hundred-pound Fukienese who King Lu had placed at Whyte's tactical disposal: the chief enforcer of the Taipei Greens, known and feared all over the Island as "The Elephant."

Whyte told The Elephant the situation, then gave him detailed instructions. He repeated the instructions so the giant would know exactly what he was supposed to do. He cautioned him to be very careful and not to go too far.

No one was to be killed. No harm was to come to any Tiger Eels. When he was satisfied that everything was understood, Whyte hung up, took the phone off the hook and waited.

From his home on Nanking East Road, The Elephant immediately made calls to his network of informers. Within fifteen minutes he knew everything he needed to know.

He started to leave the house quietly when he heard the shrill Mandarin voice of his wife. She only weighed ninety pounds—not even a third of his bulk—but he was thoroughly intimidated by her.

"Where are you going *now?*"

"Business, my pearl. Emergency business."

"Business. All the time business. Any excuse to get out of the house, eh?" It was true. The house was filled to the rafters with children and his wife's freeloading relatives.

"I will return within two hours, my lotus blossom." He was halfway through the door now.

"In two hours I lock the door. You can sleep in the *benjo* and disgrace all your ancestors back to Buddha!"

"Good-by, my sweet."

The door slammed and he breathed a sigh of relief in the steamy night air. In a minute, his two associates picked him up in a battered '59 Chevrolet. The younger of these men was the handsome Green warrior and martial arts expert, Johnny Yen. The older was "Terrible" Ding Tze, the grumpy Green assassin who was every bit as ugly as Johnny Yen was handsome.

The Elephant gave the two Green warriors the Young Taipan's instructions, and they drove directly to a snooker hall, a familiar Tiger Eel hangout near Taipei New Park. They waited in the shadows to watch the comings and goings.

"Why is it that my little wife gets more impossible with every passing day?" The Elephant lamented.

"Women are a curse," said Ding Tze absently. He had heard this before.

"In the old days a woman knew her place. Gave her man respect. Now . . ." He hawked and spit out the window.

"Nothing is the same as it was in the old days, my brother."

Young Johnny Yen ignored this conversation. That afternoon he had seen his favorite Western, *The Magnificent Seven,* for the fourteenth time. He was imagining he was the character in it played by Steve McQueen. "Shall we take care of these turtle eggs now?" he said.

The Elephant nodded unenthusiastically and they got out of the car. Ding Tze took a sawed-off shotgun from the trunk and they entered the snooker hall.

Inside, five Tiger Eels, Amos Wong and Fatso Dave Magaha were playing snooker and drinking plum wine from the bottle—celebrating the demise of Soldier Taylor. When they saw the unmistakable figure of The Elephant, they froze. Magaha knew at once what was happening and he ran for the door. The Elephant took two steps and caught him with an easy open-palm blow. The American boy crashed to the floor. Ding Tze pulled out the shotgun and stood the others against the wall while Johnny Yen relieved them of their pistols, butterfly knives, straight razors, brass knuckles and other assorted armaments.

The two Warlords—the fat, pimple-faced Eurasian and the wiry little Taiwanese—began to beg The Elephant not to kill them. The Elephant listened impassively to their pleas and then, with lightning quickness, grabbed each of them by the neck, one with each enormous, ham-like hand. He hurled them against the wall like two basketballs. As they bounced off the wall with a mighty thud, the giant stepped over to them. Letting out an animal shriek that was so bloodcurdling it startled even Ding Tze and Johnny Yen, he kicked one Warlord in the face, then whirled around to kick the other. Then he kicked them in the back, the stomach, the groin. With the grace of some great, grotesque ballet dancer, he continued screaming and kicking in a ritualized, rhythmic frenzy until his victims were bloody and unconscious.

When the job was completed, the three Greens went back to the Omega Chi House and reported in to Bryan Whyte. Whyte thanked them and asked Johnny Yen— since The Elephant said he had to rush back home—to please get a message to Randy Ortega. He asked him to tell Ortega that there had been a lot of unfortunate events over which they had no control. He would take no further action and he hoped Ortega would act accordingly. If he did, they could both get out of this dangerous situation with their face intact.

When the Greens were gone, Whyte did some *tai chi* breathing exercises to try and relax. There was nothing else to be done. It was now up to Ortega.

After the graduation day shooting of Randy Ortega, two MPs came and arrested Georgie Warner as he was waiting for a bus back to the Omega Chi House. He was taken to the Provost Marshal's office in the Navy compound where he was placed in an interrogation room and questioned by Commander Harris. When Harris saw that the boy was intoxicated, he suspended the interrogation, had him fingerprinted and photographed. Then he put him in a cell to sleep it off.

The next day was a nightmare for Warner. He awoke to a blinding headache and the sound of his father's booming liturgical voice. When the guard finally got rid of Reverend Warner, Harris came in and told him about Ortega's condition and exactly how he, Warner, had made an incalculable mess. After that, came a parade of psychologists, sociologists and one of Bamcheck's CIA investigators who asked him the usual questions about the Omega Chi, the Greens and the gang structure of Taipei —all of which Warner ignored.

The following night, Harris came back and told him about the retaliatory strike made against Whyte and Taylor. His rash and juvenile action had probably started a shooting war that would engulf the entire underworld of Taipei. Mark Taylor was in the hospital. An innocent taxi driver with a large family had been killed. The American mission in Asia would be damaged. It was all his fault.

When Whyte finally got in to see him the next morning, Georgie Warner was in a suicidal depression. He was holding his face in his hands and moaning. "I didn't mean to let you down like this, Bryan."

"What happened?"

"I was in this Lung Shan bar, drunk as a skunk and . . ."

"Why Lung Shan, for Christ's sake?"

"I donno. My life has been such shit lately. . . . It seemed like a good place to get away from things, to be anonymous."

"What happened?"

"Ortega and Magaha came in the bar. When I saw them I guess I just went crazy. I don't even remember exactly. It seemed like it was them or me, you know? I was *sooo* drunk. Oh, God, I'm sorry, Bryan."

Whyte decided not to make his friend feel any worse than he obviously already did. This was Harris's doing, he thought angrily. Harris and Bamcheck had pressured him into this. Goddamn them. He placed his hand on the boy's shoulder and squeezed. "The thing we have to do now is get you out of here."

"They tell me Ortega won't press charges. The bastard told them it was an accident, that he and I were fooling around and the gun went off—three times. Can you beat that? The asshole has a sense of humor after all."

"Ortega isn't the problem. Harris is holding you for being a public nuisance and possessing a firearm."

"How serious is that?"

"Serious enough to give them an excuse to keep you for a week or so and try to break you down. Can you take that?"

"Yeah, I can take it. I guess."

"They'll threaten you with deportation and then offer you a deal if you'll sell us out."

Angry resolve came over Warner's frightened face. "They'll never break me, Bryan. Never."

"Good."

On the way out, Commander Harris was waiting for Whyte. He was angry and desperate, knowing that if this war got any hotter he was somehow going to end up taking the blame for it. "Wonderful state of affairs," he said. "Congratulations."

"How long do you intend to keep him?"

"As long as I can."

Whyte moved closer and lowered his voice to a conspiratorial tone. "I've made a peace overture that will have to be accepted. I'm waiting for an answer now. Why not let Georgie go?"

"Forget it," Harris said sharply. "Until peace is made, every Taiwanese punk in the city is going to be after his ass. Anyway, you should be happy I'm keeping him for you. At least you know he'll be safe here."

But Harris was wrong about that. That very night a teenage Tiger Eel somehow managed to change places with one of the scrub coolies who regularly cleaned the brig every evening around midnight. The *taibow* worked the entire night shift without being spotted by the sergeant on duty. At a little past midnight, he took a vial of sulphuric acid—the traditional Oriental gangland instrument of nonlethal revenge—and threw it into the sleeping Warner's comical face. Miraculously, Georgie Warner was not blinded, but he was burned so badly that he would carry deep, hideous and very uncomical scars for the remainder of his life.

Whyte had been given his answer.

Within twenty-four hours the city was a war zone.

Just before dawn, the Tiger Eels made a raid against the Haggler's Alley black market in the downtown area, killing two Green Gang guards and Johnny Hong's youngest son. Loma, the half-nosed head Tiger Eel, personally led the raid, dispelling any notion that the Eels were not operating as a vigorously united front with their Warlord allies.

By midday, Whyte could clearly see that the situation was beyond him. The brutal assaults on the black market and on Georgie Warner had to be avenged and avenged quickly. He now had no choice but to let the Greens do it with force. He called King Lu in Hong Kong. "I have failed," he said. "I gave Randy Ortega a way out and he refused to accept it."

"What you did was the correct thing," said the somber voice over the phone. "It is not your fault that Ortega is stupid. But now we must work fast."

"Yes, I will put it in the hands of The Elephant."

"Guards are already placed around your home and all the homes and families of the Omega Chi. Go there and don't leave until you hear from me again."

That evening, eighteen hours after the assault on Warner, The Elephant gathered his troops and carried out a counterattack. Green Gang soldiers assembled at Taipei New Park, then fanned out over the streets of the theater district, Sin Alley and Lung Shan in one massive maneuver. While the city police looked the other way, every Tiger Eel, Tiger Eel sympathizer or suspected Tiger Eel sympathizer the Greens could find was executed on the spot. "Terrible" Ding Tze took a Blue Shirt squad from snooker hall to restaurant to movie theater, shooting anyone that was pointed out by their informers. The element of surprise was so overwhelming that the victims did not have time to understand what was happening. It was very much the same kind of coordinated, all-out effort that had worked so well for the Greens in both '27 and '47.

But when the smoke cleared, it was soon apparent that the tactic was not going to work quite so well in 1963. The Elephant knew at once that they had waited too long and miscalculated both the numbers of the Tiger Eels and their surprising support among the Taiwanese people, who were hiding them at great personal risk. His men killed a hundred Tiger Eels in two hours but twice that number had escaped—including Loma and his chief lieutenants—and were already retrenching in the various all-Taiwanese sections of the city. The surprise attack had by no means wiped out the Tiger Eels. The Greens could be in for a long, drawn-out and very costly war.

By the second day, fragmentary reports about the tong war in Taipei appeared on the front page of the San Francisco and Hong Kong papers—though no mention was made in the English-language *China Post* or *China News* or in any of the Chinese-language newspapers of Taipei. The China News Service said that certain acts of violence had occurred in various parts of the city on the evening of June 14, but it termed them merely unrelated "acts of hooliganism." The U.S. Embassy, when pressured by reporters, said it was purely an internal Chinese matter that did not involve Americans.

The one out-of-town reporter who did not believe the official pronouncements, who fully understood the roots and grasped the significance of the gang war, was David Butler.

Since his first exposure to the Taipei underworld back in 1961, he had used his trips to town to carefully cultivate his contacts with the gangs. He now knew most of the Omega Chi personally and was even a regular drinking partner of Georgie Warner. He had also allowed himself to be used by Whyte on occasion—had allowed Whyte to talk him into toning down several news stories that mentioned Omega Chi friends in a critical light. He did that because from that first meeting, his instinct told him that Bryan Whyte would someday turn out to be a major story for him, the kind of story that might make his whole career, the kind of story that was worth nursing and developing, even if it took years.

When the fighting broke out on June 14, Butler was ready to move. He flew in from another assignment in Manila, raced to the AP office near the Taipei Press Club and stayed on the phone for twenty-four straight hours, using all his skills and all his contacts to gather the story that he was sure would be his first big break.

Finally, after four more hours of catch-up sleep, he typed it all up. He wrote that the violence in Taipei of June 14, 1963 had originated in certain rivalries and social conflicts in the American Community. He wrote of two American teenage gangs which, because of their privileged status as Americans on Taiwan, had attained enormous power and had each become allied with a different Mafialike Oriental tong. He wrote in some depth about the tangled underworld structure of Asia and, as a parting shot, he mentioned that Chiang Kai-shek himself had once been a member of the Green Gang.

Before this story was dispatched, however, Whyte obtained the discarded carbons of it through one of his sources at AP. He instantly called David Butler. "That story will do great damage," he said curtly. "It'll hurt me, the American Community and everything America is trying to do on this Island. And for no purpose."

"I'm sorry but . . ."

"I want you to kill it."

"I've never killed a story for anyone in my life."

Whyte did not try to be charming or cajoling. He had neither the time nor the energy. He was very angry. "Kill the story. You owe us. This will make us even."

"Look, I'm a journalist. You don't know what you're asking here."

"Yes, I do."

"Then you know . . ."

"There's more involved here than your integrity. I'm asking you to pay your debt. Now kill that story."

"I can't."

"I'm going to say this one more time. Kill the story."

"No."

Whyte paused for several moments. "Listen, Butler. This is a small story. A minor, pissant story that nobody will care about after this week. But there'll be other stories. Big stories. And you're not going to get any of them. You'll never have another decent source or another decent story. Anywhere in Asia. You'll be a marked man wherever you go. I promise you that. So you better decide if this story is important enough for you to burn all your bridges to tell it."

Butler thought about it for a day and night and then

killed the story. But he would never quite forgive himself for it—or Bryan Whyte.

Shelley Spencer paced nervously before the U.S. military gate of the big, crowded lobby of Sung Shan Airport. Her mother had already boarded the aircraft. Her father —a large, unpleasant man with a red face—stood impatiently beside her. "Shelley, this is ridiculous. Get on the plane with me."

"We've got three minutes yet. Now, *please*, leave me alone."

As she anxiously watched the entrance of the terminal, there was a sudden commotion and the sounds of angry people being pushed out of the way of something. Through the stampeding crowd, she saw Bryan Whyte and a phalanx of Green Gang bodyguards storming their way toward her.

Rushing ahead of him, several of the guards made a protective circle around her and her father. Bryan took her in his arms. "I thought you weren't coming," she sobbed with relief.

"King Lu tried to keep me away. Said it was too dangerous. I came anyway."

Colonel Spencer angrily pulled on his daughter's arm. The guards tensed. Two of them reached in their pockets and pulled out pistols. The colonel backed off, stumbling toward the gate. He was plainly frightened. "I'm getting on the plane. You can stay with your hoodlum friend forever for all I care."

Shelley didn't even hear him. She clutched Bryan Whyte with all her strength. "I love you," she said. "Oh, God, I love you so much. I just wish you were coming with me."

"I'm coming. Don't you worry. Just let me finish up this business with the Warlords and I'll be on the next plane. One year of school and then we'll be together. It'll be a summer we'll never forget."

She clasped both hands around his left arm and

walked with him toward the gate. "Next summer, huh?"

"You can count on it." His soul ached at the thought of losing her but he was tremendously relieved to be getting her safely off the Island.

She kissed him. "I adore you," she said, beginning to cry.

"Me too," he said, momentarily inhibited by the presence of the Greens. "Don't miss your plane." Then realizing she would soon be half a world away, he grabbed her and kissed her long and passionately. "I . . . love you too."

She started into the gate. Tears streamed down her cheeks. "Next summer, then."

He nodded, afraid he would choke on another word. She ran for the plane.

The war of June became a stalemate that stretched into July.

The actual violence had subsided very quickly: The threat of adverse Stateside publicity frightened the Nationalist Government into sending troops into the streets to keep order. Similarly, Harris stepped up his patrols of MPs and clamped a tight 8 P.M. curfew on all American teenagers. King Lu immediately called off The Elephant from his mopping up operations and each of the principals —the Warlords, Tiger Eels, Omega Chi and Green Society —soon settled into their secure areas, waiting for the opposing side to make the next move.

This stalemate put the Omega Chi under even more pressure than in the unpleasant months leading up to the violence. It was now genuinely unsafe for them to venture out on the streets. Bamcheck and the CIA maintained twenty-four-hour tails on each of them. Warner, awaiting a deportation proceeding, was still being held in protective custody; no one had seen him since the acid attack. The black market had all but closed down and the Omega Chi had once again lost its primary source of income. Whyte's dream of college and a life in America would end if it continued much longer. Casy, Phillips and Taylor were all due to go back to the States at the end of the summer—and this gave the utmost urgency to ending the war they had inadvertently started.

As more days passed and nothing changed, this urgency began to cause a split in the Omega Chi.

Mark Taylor came from his hospital bed demanding they make King Lu follow up on The Elephant's action and force their enemies into capitulation while they still had the military advantage—to hell with the KMT and its Stateside image. Alan Phillips, taking the exact opposite view, wanted to break the alliance with the Greens and make a separate peace with the Warlords—no matter what the cost. The two argued about it every time they met and vied for the support of John Casy, who went back and forth.

No one was satisfied with Whyte's nonpolicy of laying low, leaving all initiative with the Greens and waiting for something to happen. Every time he spoke to one of them, he felt their confidence in him growing weaker and their confidence in their own points of view growing stronger. He had to do something soon or the Omega Chi was going to explode.

When the stalemate continued on into late July, Phillips asked for an emergency meeting in the protected Green stronghold of Peitou.

Whyte spent most of the day mentally preparing for the meeting. He knew that, for the first time in his life, his leadership was about to be questioned. Also for the first time in his life, he did not have any answers—he did not know *what* he was going to tell them.

He opened the door of the Literary Inn spa that evening and saw the rest of the Omega Chi positioned around the natural sulphur water pool waiting for him—Phillips, Casy, Taylor and Warner, who had just been released prior to his deportation hearing later that week. Three nude young women with waist-long black hair were serving them drinks. Phillips and Casy sat on wicker pool chairs. Taylor stood impatiently by the door. Warner was in a corner, sitting in such a way as to hide his mask of horrific scar tissue. Of the four of them, only Taylor was able to look Whyte straight in the eye.

One of the serving girls, a willowy and beautiful young Taiwanese named May Lin, rushed up to Bryan as he entered. She was Whyte's regular courtesan now that Shelley Spencer had returned to the States, and he was spending all his spare time in the safety of the little Green-run village of pine trees and sulphur spas. "What wantee Bwyn?"

"Bring me *peijo*," he said. "*Bing peijo*. Very cold beer."

"No wantee boom boom?"

"Not tonight, May Lin. Business."

"*Hao*," she said, disappointed.

Taylor closed the door behind her. Then he joined the group. "They want out," he said to Whyte, his voice icy with contempt. "These brave warriors here have had it with the struggle. They're ready to cut and run and turn their backs on everything the Omega Chi stands for. So what if the Warlords control the black market and terrorize the city? So what if we have a sacred alliance with the Greens and they're depending on us? None of that matters as long as their precious asses are safe and their daddies don't get angry with them!"

Whyte surveyed the room, his eyebrow arched suspiciously. "Is this the way you all feel?" It was a challenge.

Phillips accepted it. He stepped forward and said, "We must end this thing soon for the good of everyone. It's not a matter of bravery or cowardice. Most of us will be gone within two months. It would be easy to just get out of here and forget it. But how can we leave our home in a situation like this? A situation we started? No, we have a responsibility to end this thing, even if it's at our disadvantage."

"I admit it," John Casy joined in. "I'm scared shit-less, Bryan. I never bargained for anything like this. The Greens killed a hundred Tiger Eels on the fourteenth of

June. And it didn't settle anything! How many more people are going to die the next time this thing heats up? How are we going to live with even *more* lives on our consciences?"

"Look at us, Bryan," Phillips continued, picking up momentum. "Just look at us. Mark has been shot. John has been stabbed. Georgie has been . . . disfigured." He didn't look over at Warner. "It's a miracle that none of us has been killed yet. We can't go on like this. We're not gangsters. We should never have gotten involved with the Greens in the first place."

Whyte looked at Warner. It was obvious that he would have the deciding vote. "How do you feel about this, Georgie?"

Warner shrugged. There was none of the old audacity and mischief left behind those watery, sad eyes. "I guess we have to do something . . . to end it," he said.

Whyte sighed and sat down beside the pool. Well, he couldn't blame them. The situation was as intolerable to him as it was to them. But he was not about to just give up. He said, "I understand how you feel. This has not been an easy year for any of us. But if we make a peace with the bastards, if we give in to them now, it will all have been for nothing. Are you prepared to live with *that?*"

But Phillips was firm, as firm as anyone had ever seen him. "We've taken a vote already, Bryan. The war must end. Either you end it or we'll end it without you."

Whyte took a taxi back into the city by himself. As he sat watching the five miles of black countryside roll past his window, he thought of how wretchedly everything had turned out: Taipei engulfed in a bitter gang war, the Omega Chi breaking under the strain, all Omega Chi business activity at a halt and their income dried to a trickle. If something was not settled immediately he would have to forget his dream of college and the States and stay in Taipei.

He left the taxi near one of the old city gates that now

stood as a memorial to the ancient walled city of Taipei. He walked by the city bus station, deserted at this hour, around the imposing statue of Sun Yat-sen down to Chung Shan North Road. Then he walked the entire length of Chung Shan, oblivious to the danger of being exposed and unprotected so near to Sin Alley and Tiger Eel territory.

His mind ached. He was sure now that there had been some basic flaw in his thinking about the Omega Chi-Green alliance all along. He had made some terrible conceptual oversight—something beyond merely misjudging the strength of the Tiger Eels and the cunning and determination of Randy Ortega. But what? *What was the missing element?*

He continued on down Chung Shan, past the Four Roses Bar and the Chesterfield Bar and the other cheesy dives that catered almost exclusively to American fleet sailors on liberty. He passed a couple of pirated book stores, a flower shop, and crossed the wide boulevard. He walked the block in front of the walled, palatial residence of the U.S. ambassador. Then, suddenly, it came to him.

Like a flood of sunlight finally breaking through a bank of morning fog, the realization of what was missing from his scheme dawned on him. Suddenly, walking down Chung Shan North Road before the U.S. ambassador's mansion, he knew exactly what the role of the Omega Chi should, *had to* be on the Island of Taiwan. Suddenly, everything made perfect sense and his excitement was overpowering. An extraordinary vision of what they could be came to him—a vision that would later seem almost mystical—and to a large extent that single vision would determine the rest of his life.

He broke into a run and ran all the way to MAAG-ville, a bachelor officers' housing compound near the Officers' Club at the northern end of Chung Shan. He ran past a Chinese Army guard, down a sidewalk and up the steps to Commander Floyd Harris's quarters. A light bulb over the door illuminated a swarm of insects. He pushed the doorbell.

Harris opened the door in his bathrobe and looked very surprised. "Bryan Whyte? What . . ."

Whyte stepped in without being invited. He looked at the stocky little Naval officer excitedly and said, "I've come to end this war."

Floyd Harris was wary. He was also exhausted from worry and weeks of sixteen-hour workdays. The gang war had been just the career-breaking nightmare he had feared it would be and he was expecting any minute to be transferred in disgrace.

"The problem is . . ." Whyte began excitedly even before he was through the door, "the problem is that you and I have been fighting each other when we should be cooperating. Our interests are now and always have been exactly the same. We must become allies."

"What?"

"We have to join forces to end the war. The first step is to get rid of the Warlords. They're responsible for all this trouble."

"And how are we to do that?" Harris said sarcastically as he closed the door and looked at his watch. "Do you know it's after midnight?"

"Deport them on black-market charges."

Harris looked at him incredulously. "But *you* control the black market!"

"It doesn't matter. I can get you all the evidence you'll need to nail them."

He was looking at Harris with such uncomplicated sincerity that Harris had to laugh. "And why would I want to do that?"

"Because they're the enemy. Because, at heart, they're . . . Communists, or at least communistic."

"Be serious."

"They want to destroy the Community. I want to protect it. *That's* the difference. Listen, can we sit down and talk about this?"

Harris woke his amah and had her make them a pot of coffee. Then he and Whyte stood in the kitchen and spoke about this idea way into the early hours of morning. Whyte was selling hard and Harris—despite his initial hostility—was buying. Not only did the commander immediately see cooperation with the Omega Chi on its terms as the only possibility of ending the crisis, but he also saw the outline taking shape of a far-reaching and mutually beneficial arrangement that might prevent such a crisis from ever breaking out again. If it worked, he might just end this tour with captain's boards on his shoulders after all.

The next day they met again at Harris's office and hammered out details of a plan of action: In the face of massive evidence, the most troublesome Warlords were to be deported, thereby ending their influence over the Tiger Eels. Then Sin Alley would become off-limits to all U.S. personnel so that the Greens would get the business in Peitou—thus the economic base of the Tiger Eels would collapse. Finally, if that didn't put the Eels in their place, U.S. intelligence would come up with enough evidence of Communist infiltration to justify the Nationalist Army moving against their strongholds.

When the gang war was over, the Omega Chi would give up all the old trappings of a teenage gang—its black jackets and such—and strive to become recognized as a legitimate business and charitable organization. The Omega Chi would serve the U.S. authority in any way it could and would use its influence with the Green Society to aid the American mission anywhere in Asia it might need help. In return, the Omega Chi would be allowed an unofficial concession to the American black market in Taipei and other business advantages. There would be, for all purposes, an alliance between the Omega Chi and the U.S. authority aimed at keeping an orderly community geared toward their common objective: to free the Mainland and fight the spread of Communism in Asia.

"You take it to your people and I'll take it to mine,"

said Harris. "We'll meet again tomorrow and see how we do."

Whyte called a meeting of the Omega Chi and offered them the deal. It was, he told them, a way to rid Taipei of the Warlords, end the war with the Tiger Eels to the Omega Chi's advantage and establish an order over the city that would hold forever. "The thing that has always been missing from the scheme is the participation of the U.S. authority. We've been fighting them, honoring some senseless outlaw code of silence that has always worked to our disadvantage. The fact is we should be as much a part of the U.S. authority as Harris or Bamcheck. . . ."

They liked it. Even Phillips. Even Taylor. It seemed a way to solve their problems and give them the respectability and credibility they all craved.

"But what about King Lu?" Taylor asked. "Will he go for it?"

"Leave King Lu to me."

King Lu stood unhappily before the large map of the city on the wall of the Green war room that had been hastily set up in a suite of the Grand Hotel. His chief lieutenant, Samuel Yin, pointed at the various Tiger Eel strongholds and offered suggestions on what tactical methods would best wipe them out.

King rejected them all.

He knew that he had to do something soon to break the stalemate and end the Tiger Eel threat completely. The Generalissimo was demanding it; frantic directives were coming to him from the Presidential Palace every hour. Procrastinating was only giving his enemies more time to regroup and rebuild their strength.

But he was simply not sure that another military operation would do the job any more effectively than the last one had. The Tiger Eels had surprising support from the Taiwanese people. They could hold out in a guerrilla-type struggle for months, years. What to do? What to do?

The door opened and Bryan Whyte was escorted into the room. King was irritated to see him. He did not want to be bothered at a time when he felt so exposed and disoriented. "What is it?" he barked unpleasantly in Mandarin.

"I know a way to break the stalemate, to solve all our problems without firing another shot."

King looked at him icily. "How?"

"We will let the U.S. Government do it for us."

King thought a moment, then waved the rest of the Greens from the room. Samuel Yin shut the door behind himself.

Whyte continued excitedly. "We will make an alliance with the U.S. Government."

"Please explain."

"The Greens have always had an alliance with the KMT. There is no reason why you should not have an equally beneficial one with the U.S. Government. All of us —the Omega Chi, the Greens, the U.S. Government and the KMT—have the same goals and, really, the same values. It's time we formally recognized this."

"But how will that end this situation?"

"Follow this. With the U.S. authority here and the Omega Chi as partners, they will simply find a way to deport the Warlords and end all American influence over the Tiger Eels. Then we'll place the brothels and bars of Lung Shan off-limits to Americans. The economic base of the Tiger Eels will eventually collapse. It's that simple."

"The Americans will do this?"

"Of course they will. It is obviously to their advantage to do so."

King struggled to take it all in. He rubbed his forehead with his palm and began pacing before the big map.

"Do I have your permission to pursue this goal, Elder Brother?"

King stopped pacing. He suddenly, fully, glimpsed the beauty of what young Whyte was telling him. Not only would this plan solve their immediate problems, it would create a whole new order in which the Greens and the U.S.

Government would be connected through Bryan Whyte. Yes, truly this was destiny working itself out. . . .

He quickly nodded his approval.

Warren Xavier Stevens flew in from Saigon the next morning. Commander Harris had called and told him there might finally be a creative solution to the crisis. Harris said that Bamcheck, however, would probably veto this solution and so they needed someone of the highest authority to take on the responsibility.

Over the past two years, Stevens had become a roving troubleshooter for the Kennedy administration in Asia. As such, the major concern on his agenda was South Vietnam. The Diem regime was becoming impossibly corrupt and unmanageable, the threat of a Communist takeover much more alarming. The U.S., in his opinion, would have to do something soon—either go in with troops or quickly install a leader who could regain the support of the people. It was a perplexing problem that was requiring all his time and energy.

In the midst of this, the Taipei crisis had popped up out of nowhere. He knew all about the Green invasion, the bloodshed, the stalemate, the possibility of more violence and damaging publicity. He also knew that the young gang leader Bryan Whyte had played a part in it all. It was a mess—and one that he wanted to rid himself of quickly so that he could get back to Saigon. If Harris and Whyte had come up with some sort of Band-Aid solution to the problem, he intended to grab it—and put the stamp of the U.S. Government on it, Bamcheck and his CIA clowns be damned.

Stevens walked into Harris's office in the Navy compound. He shook hands with the commander, and together they went into an adjoining conference room. Bryan Whyte was waiting for them there.

Stevens studied Whyte's beaming face as Harris went over the plan. The diplomat decided to accept the proposal the moment he looked into young Whyte's confident eyes. He had long thought it would be advantageous for America to establish some sort of unofficial relations with the Chinese underworld. He had never forgotten how effectively this fascinating young man had used the Greens to snuff out that riot in 1961. This whole situation suddenly seemed heaven-sent.

He took a few puffs from his pipe and restrained his excitement. "You understand, Mr. Whyte, that this would be strictly unofficial and that all communications with the Greens would be conducted through you. I wouldn't want to see any Chinese gangsters sitting across the desk from me asking for favors. Do you understand that?"

Whyte nodded, surprised by Stevens's lack of resistance to the idea. "Of course. That's the way we all want it."

"Then I think we have ourselves a relationship," he said.

They all shook hands. Whyte handed Harris the address of Ortega's black-market depot in Sin Alley and a list of a dozen convicted Chinese black marketeers who would agree to testify that they had engaged in black-marketing activities with the Warlords.

In the afternoon of July 24, 1963, the Island suddenly went into typhoon condition two—which meant a three-day storm was imminent. All activity came to an abrupt halt as Typhoon Billie—the biggest storm to hit the Island since the forties—lumbered in from its Pacific spawning grounds, battering and drenching the northern half of the Island for most of the last week of July. Before it passed, some fifty people lay dead, hundreds injured, perhaps several thousands homeless.

Most of the Warlords waited out the typhoon in the comfort of their apartment headquarters above the Hollywood Bar in Sin Alley. Fatso Dave Magaha, Lefty O'-Hara, Ya Ki Loi and Randy Ortega partied with a group of Sin Alley bargirls for almost three solid days and nights. By the time the typhoon condition was lifted, the debris and bodies cleared from the streets and the electricity restored, Randy Ortega was sick of the drinking and fucking and eager to get to Loma. He wanted to finalize his plans for an urban guerrilla war against the Green army of occupation.

Ortega awoke that next morning to the sound of a bullhorn telling him and his men to come out with their hands over their heads. He stumbled to the window and looked out to see a combined force of MPs, CIA and Chinese Foreign Affairs Police standing out in Sin Alley. The downstairs door was broken in and the building was flooding with uniforms.

The premises were searched, evidence was confiscated. Ortega, Magaha and Ya Ki Loi were arrested and taken in handcuffs to the Naval Support Activity compound.

The following morning, a deportation hearing was held at the Taipei Municipal Police station. Commander Harris presented a parade of witnesses and a mountain of evidence against the trio, linking them to black-marketing and numerous other crimes, including sympathy with Communism. The three-man tribunal heard the evidence and deliberated for five minutes before it reached its verdict: The defendants would be jailed for six weeks then deported. They would never be allowed to return to Taiwan again.

Dazed by rage and incomprehension, Ortega stood up to protest the injustice of the sentence. But as he looked at the stone faces of Harris and the Chinese judges, he realized it was useless and he sat down again without a word. Ya Ki Loi, always more sensitive and babyish than the other Warlords, broke into tears and ran to embrace his parents. Dave Magaha merely looked at his father, the airline pilot, and shrugged insolently.

As the three were being led back to their cell, a Taiwanese attorney, long suspected of being active in the outlawed Taiwanese Independence Movement, whispered to Ortega that the Green Gang—this time aided by Nationalist Army troops—was in the process of another all-out attack on Tiger Eel strongholds throughout the city. Any hope of a massive Taiwanese demonstration in support of the defendants would have to be abandoned.

Little Juan Ortega maneuvered his way through the police guards and frantically grabbed his brother's arm. "What do we do now?"

"Tell Loma to make a peace."

"No."

"As quickly as possible."

"Never."

"Do as I say. We must preserve what we can for the next battle."

That afternoon, the remaining Warlords—Little Ortega, Lefty O'Hara, Clinton Chen, Tim Cutler, Amos Wong—and Loma and his lieutenants stood by in submission and humiliation while Bryan Whyte and Samuel Yin presented a lengthy list of demands. These included a severing of any ties between the Warlords and Tiger Eels, payment of reparations to the family of the taxi driver killed in the ambush of Taylor and banishment from the Island for all Tiger Eels who participated in the attacks on Casy and Shelley Spencer in 1961. The demands were accepted without argument and the gang war of 1963 officially ended.

Two weeks after the peace conference was concluded, Bryan Whyte finished his final marathon business meetings with Georgie Warner and Johnny Hong, packed his suitcases and, after a round of emotional farewells, boarded an airplane that would, at long last, take him to the United States of America.

8

A BRIGHT BLANKET OF SNOW ILLUMINATED THE NIGHT all around Bryan Whyte. He clutched the heavy load of textbooks tightly to his body and trudged slowly across the main quadrangle of the campus, occasionally slipping on the icy cobblestones in his haste to be back in the warmth of the men's dorm. After a lifetime in the subtropics of Asia, even the comparatively mild winter of western Washington State seemed unbearable. His bones ached from the incessant, the immobilizing, the inescapable cold.

It was February of 1964 and he was a freshman at the huge University of Washington in Seattle. He had been in the States for the better part of six months and it had been a miserable, heartbreaking, soul-wrenching experience for him.

After his plane landed in Los Angeles in mid-August, he spent nearly a month hitchhiking up the coast, almost frantically trying to take in and experience every aspect of this great country he had worshiped and dreamed about for the past eighteen years. The journey had been without a single truly unpleasant incident, yet when he got into Seattle a week before classes started, he was thoroughly disappointed.

He was not exactly sure why he felt this way. Perhaps he had built up an impossibly idealized image of a perfect country and the reality could not come close to matching it. Perhaps he had expected to be hit by a super-sensation of home and belonging—the way he felt about the Taipei American Community amplified a thousand times. Perhaps he was merely overwhelmed by the bigness of it all, the being lost in crowds of people just like him, the feeling of being insignificant and no longer special by the mere fact of his nationality. He knew now, he thought, what it was like to be Chinese in China.

When he started school, the disillusionment became worse. He found he was entering the university with the largest freshman class in its history—the vanguard of the post-Second World War baby boom and by far the biggest generation in U.S. history. He was a buck private in an army of kids, kids who were raised on Davy Crockett and hula hoops and Elvis, kids who had absolutely nothing in common with him and who seemed so laughably immature he did not even want to make friends with them.

He was also unable to escape into his work. The courses and curriculum of the business school bored him; they did not even begin to fit his goals of becoming a successful international businessman. He was shocked to find that virtually no one—including his professors—seemed to share his uncomplicated faith in the strength and built-in morality of capitalism. In fact, the general consensus among them was that the system was corrupt, dying and that the day of the great individual capitalists was long over in American business. At first he argued with them, then he became angry, resentful of the whole educational process. Was it not insanity for him to drown himself in triviality for four years to get a degree that would qualify him to be someone's clerk? What could these people possibly teach him about doing business that he didn't already know from intuition and experience?

The more lonely and disillusioned he became, the more his mind dwelled on the Omega Chi, which was now spread all over creation. John Casy was down at the University of California at Berkeley, majoring in English literature. Mark Taylor was at some small college in South Carolina, where the Baptist Mission Fund had set up a scholarship for him. Alan Phillips was in prelaw at Cornell University in New York State. Only Georgie Warner was still on the Island looking out after their business interests. The single thought that came to dominate his fantasies was of somehow preserving this unit of friends, of using their diverse talents and loyalty in the hazy future to build the Omega Chi to its full potential as a perfect business machine. He was convinced that, together, they could conquer the world—but only if they were together.

He went in one of the great hotel-like dormitories on Campus Parkway. As he started to pass through the lounge to the bank of elevators, he noticed a mob of students hanging around the communal television set waiting for something to happen.

The tableau immediately reminded him of the horror of the Kennedy assassination two months before. "Is something wrong?" he asked one of the crowd.

A pimply-faced boy in a UW sweatshirt and Bermuda shorts looked at him shrewdly and grinned. "Nah, it's those queers from England. They're gonna be on the 'Sullivan Show' tonight. Everybody's waiting for the show to begin."

After an avalanche of publicity, a band of British musicians called the Beatles were finally showing themselves to the American public this Sunday night. Though he had never been a particular fan of rock 'n' roll music, Whyte was fascinated by the way these students were being manipulated into lining up to consume a product they had never even seen. The possibilities of the communications business were especially intriguing to him, perhaps because his father had done so well in the movie business on the Mainland and it was in his blood. He watched for a few moments but couldn't hear anything over the sarcastic jeering of the students, so he went up to his room to write a letter to Shelley Spencer.

Shelley was at the University of Missouri and writing to her was his single emotional release. Over the months, he had poured out his feelings in letter after letter. He opened himself up to her in a way he never had to another human being. He confessed to her the central irony of his existence: His entire life had been a preparation for coming to the States and now that he was finally here he could not stand it. There was no place here for an individual with his own ideas. There was none of the endless possibility he had anticipated. The people here had none of the commitment and spirit of patriotism and self-sacrifice he had grown up with in the Taipei American Community. Even the assassination of the President had not shaken them out of their hedonism and selfishness.

Within the last month, he had become so thoroughly discouraged that he had pretty much given up. He had dropped out of most of his classes and was spending most of his time, as tonight, hiding in the Far East Department library, reading everything he could find about the history and culture of China. On weekends, he almost always took the bus to Seattle's Chinatown district, where he soon struck up friendships with some of the younger members of the Hop Sung Tong, a branch of the Green Society that was very powerful in all the West Coast U.S. Chinatowns. He particularly relished the time spent with the Hop Sungs—and, appropriately enough, it was only while associating with them that he found himself once again sparking with creative business ideas, including one very exciting importing idea he hoped to work out before the school year was over.

In his room, there was a message from his roommate that John Casy had called. He eagerly picked up the phone and made a station-to-station call to Berkeley. A girl answered. There was the sound of the telephone dropping on the floor, then Casy came on the line.

"Bryan!"

Casy's voice was pure music to his ears. "How's life treating you, champ?"

Casy sounded ecstatically happy. "Wonderful. I like school. I'm on the newspaper staff. On Fridays and Saturdays I play guitar at a beatnik coffee house. Everything is great. Hey, didja see the Beatles?"

"For a second."

"Aren't they something?!"

Whyte laughed. "Yeah. Something."

"How's Seattle?"

"Cold and boring."

There was a pause. Casy had never heard Bryan Whyte complain about anything before. It was simply not in his nature to verbalize things that bothered him or express pessimistic thoughts. "Why not come down here for spring break? There's all kinds of things I wanna show you, things I want to talk about."

The idea was appealing to Whyte. "Maybe I will. I could conduct a little business in San Francisco while I'm there."

"Screw business. Just come down and we'll let it all hang out. Things are happening down here, Bryan. This is the center of the world."

Whyte laughed again.

"I'm not kidding, Bryan. This is incredible. There is so much excitement and energy here you won't believe it."

Casy put the girl on the phone to talk him into coming down and Whyte soon said yes. When he hung up, he sat by the phone a few minutes, thinking about the conversation. He wondered how it could be that Casy's experience was so totally different from his own. For some reason, it depressed him. It made him feel he was losing John Casy.

When he got off the Greyhound bus in San Francisco, John Casy was waiting for him on the loading dock. Casy wore his Omega Chi jacket, an almost comic touch under the circumstances. He also held a bottle of Taiwan rice wine.

"Cost me two bucks in Chinatown," he said disgustedly. "That's a nine hundred percent markup."

"I understand these Chinese here are real gangsters," Whyte said and offered his hand.

Casy took it and held it. "God, it's weird to see you in this place."

"It's weird to be here, my friend."

They looked at each other a moment and then spontaneously embraced.

Casy drove him around San Francisco then down to

Berkeley and around the University of California campus. As they cruised the school, Casy handed him a stack of poems and short stories he had written over the past six months—unlike Whyte, he seemed to have been very creatively inspired by his new surroundings. Whyte looked through them very carefully, reading some, not fully understanding what all of them were about, but very impressed by the dedicated work behind them. He was particularly pleased and flattered that some of them seemed to glorify him personally. It gave him great satisfaction to believe that someday Casy's talent would give him a kind of immortality.

"Have you been able to keep in touch with the guys?" Whyte asked as they were having lunch at a Big Boy Drive-in.

"Somewhat. I get letters from Georgie all the time. Alan wrote me once. He was running for some student office at Cornell. I haven't heard anything from the Soldier. But then he isn't exactly the kind to write, is he?"

Whyte had heard from Taylor and it was not good news. "He's having a hard time. He hates the States. His grades and asthma are both terrible. He's been in six fistfights already and it'll be a miracle if he makes it to the end of the year without getting kicked out on a disciplinary."

Casy bit into his Big Boy Burger and shook his head helplessly. "I guess it's really tough for a guy with Mark's background and temperament to adjust to all this. The poor guy must really feel out of place."

"Yeah."

"It makes you wonder how he would have ever made it at West Point. I mean, as much as he loves the military, I just can't imagine him taking orders and bowing and scraping to a bunch of upperclassmen."

"That thought has occurred to me too."

"Hey, maybe we should give the old Soldier a call after we get drunk tonight."

They went to Casy's tiny apartment off-campus; some of his friends came over to drink beer and meet

Whyte. Most of them were politically minded freshmen and sophomores who worked with Casy on the school paper and who were all planning to go to Mississippi in a group over the summer to work in a civil rights voter registration drive. The leader of this circle was an arrogant teaching assistant from New York named Marco Bellini and Casy introduced him, with obvious pride, as "the nightmare of the university administration and a genuine radical." Bellini took one look at Whyte, recognized a rival for Casy's admiration and went for the throat, subtly baiting him about his background, his politics and his belief in capitalism throughout the afternoon.

That night, many of these same people were at the coffee house where Casy played guitar and sang for tips. The conversation—led and dominated by Bellini—was about Bob Dylan and Joan Baez and the civil rights situation in the South. It was very animated and filled with repeated use of the words "we" and "us" and "them" and "injustice." Whyte didn't know what they were talking about and didn't even try to enter in.

Casy sensed Bryan's discomfort and was feeling considerable anxiety over it. He had never dreamed a situation could exist that Bryan Whyte could not master.

"Something's wrong, isn't it Bryan?"

Whyte tried to look surprised. "Not at all. I'm just enjoying being a spectator."

Casy smiled dubiously. "After tonight, we'll lose these characters and spend some time by ourselves."

Whyte strained to focus his mind on more positive things. "John, you *are* still going back to Taipei for the summer?"

"Yeah, but it may be for the last time. My old man isn't going to extend his tour of duty again."

"I want you to get back as soon as you can after finals. This summer is going to be very important to us. I've had a lot of ideas about expanding our business and bringing in more income. It could make a big difference to all our futures."

Casy didn't seem to hear him. It was time for his set.

He picked up his acoustic guitar and told Whyte he would be back. He started off with a number called "Blowin' in the Wind," and as he fingered the chords and sang the lyrics, Whyte was astonished at how good he was. There was a power and beauty and earnestness in the singing that Whyte had never heard before and of which he had not really thought Casy capable.

He gazed around the room and noticed that everyone in it was hushed in awe and respect and philosophical oneness with the music. Casy had been right. There was something unique going on here.

And whatever it was seemed very threatening to Bryan Whyte.

Early the next morning, he took a bus—Casy offered his car but Whyte had never learned to drive—into San Francisco. He got out at the Mark Hopkins Hotel on Nob Hill and walked down Mason Street. Within minutes he was at the entrance of the largest Chinatown in America.

He checked his map, then climbed several steep, narrow streets until he found Waverly Place. On the corner of Waverly and Washington Streets, he stood a moment gazing at the signs and buildings and thought that it looked much smaller than he had imagined. This tiny cross street was the traditional headquarters of all the major Chinese-American tongs and as famous in the mythology of the Chinese underworld as Broadway was in the acting business. He had heard stories about it all his life.

He knew, for instance, that down the block the Kwong Dock Tong and the Suey Sing Tong had fought the city's bloodiest tong battle in 1875 for control of gambling in the area. In the center of the block was Ross Alley, where, for well over a hundred years, rival tongs had posted their *chin hungs,* or public notices, challenging one another to do battle. Behind him, in one of the older buildings, Little Pete Fong, the overlord of Chinatown, had been assassinated by a rival *boo hoy doy* while having a haircut in 1897. He stood taking in all this history for a few more minutes, then walked into a building marked with Chinese characters and a large English sign inscribed "Hop Sung Tong."

Through his association with the Greens, Whyte had come to learn a great deal about the tongs of America. They were essentially the foreign branch offices of the ancient Chinese secret societies, brought over by the hordes of Chinese who crossed the Pacific to serve as coolie labor in the nineteenth century. At first they were entirely fraternal and social in nature and their function was to make life easier for the poorly treated immigrant Chinese. They always retained this aspect, but they soon also became an outlet for capitalistic impulses, which led to their takeover of the flourishing trade in prostitution, opium and gambling in the Chinatowns. As business increased, so did competition, and in the late nineteenth and early twentieth centuries, the Chinatowns of the country exploded with dozens of bloody tong wars fought for economic supremacy and territoriality.

In New York's Chinatown, the fighting between the On Leong Tong and the Hip Sing Tong was so fierce in the year 1910 that the U.S. Government stepped in and asked the Chinese ambassador in Washington to negotiate a peace. At this time, the various tong leaders met in San Francisco and decided that the situation was out of hand —the newspapers were covering tong wars like sporting events, keeping box scores of the day's casualties: On Leongs five, Hip Sings four. It was bad for business and worse, bad for the Chinese national image. A council of tongs was formed and from that moment on, the U.S. tongs strove for an image of respectability and community service.

There had not been a major tong war in America since that day and the tongs prospered in peace and obscurity for the next half century. They continued to control the illegal and legal activities of the Chinatowns and in-

vested their money very wisely: The Hop Sungs even
bought controlling interest of a major Las Vegas casino in
1962. Still fiercely nationalistic, they helped finance the
Chinese Revolution of Sun Yat-sen. They retained strong
ties and paid tribute to the Green Pang Society of Shanghai and the Triads of Hong Kong. When the Mainland fell
to Communism, they became the strongest supporters of
Chiang Kai-shek, invested heavily in the Taiwan economy
and acted as political agents of the Kuomintang in the
United States.

Whyte walked up a flight of stairs and into an office
where an old man in a gold short-sleeve shirt sat behind
a desk reading a *Playboy* magazine. "I'm looking for Mr.
Chu," Whyte said.

The man studied the *fu* around Whyte's neck a moment and then stood and offered his hand. "You are Bryan
Whyte. And you are very young."

Mr. Chu Yung-liu was the reigning community
leader in San Francisco's Chinatown. He was a member
of the Green Society, the Hop Sung Tong and the Kuomintang, for which he served as district political chief. He
was said to control all the illegal activities in the Chinatowns of San Francisco, Los Angeles, Seattle and Vancouver, B.C.

In Mandarin, Whyte said, "I have come to pay my
respects to you. I bring the good wishes of King Lu, our
honored brother."

The old man nodded. "I accept them and welcome
his little brother to San Francisco." He motioned to the
chair opposite him.

Whyte took a seat. "I have also come to speak to you
about a matter of business."

"What business?"

"The business of pool cues."

Mr. Chu noticeably stiffened. "I don't understand.
You are speaking of billiard cues?"

"Yes. I want to import them from Taiwan and sell
them on the U.S. market. I want the Hop Sungs to join

me in this endeavor and distribute them through one of their wholesale companies."

Mr. Chu waved his hand negatively and smiled for the first time. "The Hop Sungs are not in the business of foreign trade."

"You're not, but you should be. Given the huge amount of cheap labor and materials in Taiwan, given your special connections with the government there, given your knowledge of the U.S. market, it is a crime that you are not in this business."

Mr. Chu leaned back in his chair. He seemed vaguely interested now. "We have thought of it, of course. Often. But there are many, many problems. The U.S. market for the kinds of things we could import has been completely captured by the Japanese. Our limited efforts have been unsuccessful."

"But I think I have found a way to get our foot in the door."

"The pool cues."

"Yes. During the year I've lived in this country, I've observed that the game of pocket billiards is having a massive resurgence—particularly on college and high school campuses. This is mainly because of the popularity of a movie called *The Hustler.* In this movie, Paul Newman is a pool shark who savages his opponents with a fancy, two-piece, screw-together pool cue. In America, these custom cues are actually very rare and prohibitively expensive. But in Taipei, where snooker has been a mania for a decade, these hand-carved, breakaway cues are sold on every streetcorner for less than a U.S. dollar. Why could we not import them and sell them here."

"How could you manufacture them in enough volume to be profitable? I know of no large-scale manufacturing of pool cues on the Island."

"My own company, the Omega Chi, will manufacture them."

"Have you calculated what kind of markup you could get by with?"

"Roughly one thousand percent."

Mr. Chu's eyes danced. "Would King Lu stand behind you in such an enterprise?"

"I am sure of it." Actually, he was not sure of it at all, but nothing about his manner gave this away.

"How would we split such an enormous profit?"

"The Hop Sungs would take one-fourth for its distribution fee."

"No, we would need half. That is only fair."

"One-third is my final offer."

"I am sorry."

Whyte stood up to leave. "I will relay this to King Lu."

"Wait. Since we are all brothers of King Lu, that will be agreeable." Whyte sat back down. "How long will you need to set up such an operation?"

"Six months."

"But are you not going to school in this country?"

"I am quitting and going back to Taiwan." He had not consciously made this decision until that very moment.

Mr. Chu smiled and offered his hand. "Then we will do business."

When Whyte left the building, he was elated. His mind was swimming with a thousand possibilities; his body pulsated with a sensation of being reunited with his true self. The feeling was so strong it lasted all the way through Chinatown and down Powell Street and did not disappear completely until he stepped on the bus back to Berkeley.

Shelley Spencer watched the two-engine Ozark Airliner taxi up the Ft. Leonard Wood Airport runway. She saw Bryan climb out of the cabin of the plane and walk toward the shabby one-room terminal where she was waiting. She met him at the gate. He observed that she had a cigarette in her hand. She kissed him and the kiss told him that some vital ingredient of their old chemistry was missing.

She had spent the past year at the University of Missouri at Rolla, the closest college to her father's new station. It had been a very exciting time for her. In one year she had had it all—homecoming queen, pursued by the biggest men on campus, the subject of an entire photo essay in the university magazine. Somehow this magazine had found its way to one of the top modeling agencies in New York. Now that agency wanted her to come to New York and work for them.

Whyte had phoned the day before and she had told him about this offer. They argued about it on the phone for an hour. She wanted to go, at least for the summer. He wanted her to go back to Taipei with him. He told her again how he hated being in the States—how the only thing that had made him stay on at school after spring break was an impassioned and unusually lucid plea from his father—and how he needed her by his side. When he couldn't convince her, he impulsively flew across the country to see her.

It was a typical Bryan Whyte stunt, she thought. He would do anything or go anywhere to get what he wanted. He was so determined, so sure of himself, so unashamedly ruthless. This was what she had loved and now what she was beginning to resent about him.

He stood before her looking very grim and resolute. "I have something very important to say and I only have a few minutes before this mousetrap takes off again."

She couldn't look him in the eyes. She was afraid that if she did he could convince her of anything. And she was sure this call to New York would be her only chance to do something special and exciting with her life before she got married and settled down to a family.

"I want you to come back to Taipei with me. I'll pay your way and we can get the hell out of here this very day."

"Please don't do this."

He put his arm around her. "I'm going back to Taipei to stay. I'm never coming back. I want you to marry me."

Tears welled in her eyes. She shook her head sadly. "How can I do that? I'm not ready to be married. Maybe in a year or so . . ."

"I need you now."

"How would we live? The black market? Good God, Bryan."

He removed his arm from around her. "The Omega Chi is going into legitimate business. It's going to make a great deal of money. I'll be able to support you in style."

"No. I have to stay. You should stay too if you really want to make something of yourself. Even your father can see that."

"I have to go back. I'm needed there. There is nothing for me here. Nothing at all."

"I know that," she said, very distantly.

Looking at her, he felt helpless and impotent. She had become a stranger. "Please change your mind. This is the last time I'll ask you."

She looked into his unsteady gray eyes a moment and suddenly realized that, standing there in the middle of the United States, he did not seem at all like the powerful taipan figure she remembered. He seemed more an object of pity, a little person who could not adjust to the big world—desperately trying to hold on to his former glory and former friends like some pathetic aging athlete who hangs around the high-school football games in his letterman's jacket.

"I just can't, Bryan."

"Then I'm leaving." He kissed her quickly on the cheek and walked back to the plane.

Whyte returned to Taipei just before noon on the last Saturday of April—a full month before the end of spring quarter. As he waited in line to clear customs at Sung Shan, his heart pounded wildly. In the taxiride to his house, he looked out at the old familiar scenes, smelled the old familiar smells and experienced a sense of security and self-importance he had not known for almost a year. It made anything in the world seem possible.

Old Whyte was reading the morning *China Post* in the living room when Bryan opened the door. The old man dropped the paper and rushed to embrace him, his eyes brimming with tears, hugging him for a full minute. Then he realized that his son was not supposed to be here. "You're . . . early. I didn't expect you for another month."

Bryan gently took his father's hands and looked him squarely in the eye. "I didn't come back early. I've come back for good. I quit school."

The old man stuttered. "Sonny! . . . Oh, no! No. This is awful. What . . . what will you do?"

"I'm going into business right here on the Island. I'm going to manufacture and export pool cues."

Old Whyte sat himself on the arm of the sofa looking very sad and confused. "I don't know, Sonny," he said. "I just don't know. . . ."

Bryan smiled. "Trust me, okay? I know what I'm doing."

"What was it like? . . . the States."

"Big. Crowded. Well regulated. Very stifling. Probably just the way it was when you decided you had to leave it. Only more so."

"But Sonny. Ever since you were a little, little boy, you wanted to go to America and make something special of yourself. It was your dream. It hurts me to see you lose your dream. . . ."

"I haven't lost anything, Father. I'm just wiser about it now. I know who I am and where I belong. The dream just works better here. For me, *this* is America."

The other Omega Chi began to trickle back to Taipei a month later.

Mark Taylor came first. His year in the States had been as disastrous as Whyte's. He had not even attempted to adjust. On first sight, he hated everything about the

State of South Carolina, the city of Charleston and the Smith Bible College. He was also not too shy to tell people about it. He shocked the conservative little college community by getting drunk every weekend and starting a fistfight with anyone who looked at him cross-eyed. He was a very miserable and totally frustrated young man, wound up to his breaking point and ready to explode into violence.

His frustration also did not find relief on his return to Taipei. The first thing he discovered was that, in his absence, Randy Ortega and Fatso Magaha had bribed their way back on the Island. He immediately, happily, set out to discipline them. But Whyte forbade it. Instead, Whyte located the Warlords through informers, tipped Harris and waited until a combined squad of MPs and Foreign Affairs Police arrested the culprits. Through an unprecedented arrangement with the U.S. Embassy (a deal personally negotiated by Warren Xavier Stevens), jurisdiction over the Ortega-Magaha case was then given to a Chinese court. A trial was held, a verdict of guilty was handed down on the charge of illegal entry and the defendants each received a one-year sentence in the dreaded Nationalist Chinese prison on Green Island, thirty-five miles off the shark-infested southeast coast. Taylor had been rendered totally unnecessary.

Alan Phillips returned to the Island just after the trial and was delighted to learn that a Warlords threat had been so easily put down by proper, respectable channels. His year in the States had been much more successful than Whyte's or Taylor's. He adjusted well to Cornell, made the honor society and immediately became the most indispensible person in five separate college service organizations. Yet he too had deeply missed Taiwan, missed the authority of Bryan Whyte, above all missed the sense of purpose and power to do good works that being in the Omega Chi gave him.

He also missed Doris Loo. His feelings had become much stronger for her in his year away. He had dated others at Cornell but these had been bad experiences: The girls were frivolous and empty-headed children who were disappointed when he kept his hands to himself. Doris was more serious-minded and mature than any American girl he had ever met; she shared his sense of responsibility and high moral values. In the past, he had been a bit afraid of his growing relationship with Doris, afraid that it would invariably lead to a marriage that would limit him, keep him tied to Asia. Now he was pretty much convinced that he wanted that tie.

John Casy came back a week after Phillips. He alone of the four had completely adjusted to the States. He managed to stay excited about most everything he found there. In fact, he had almost not come back at all. He was tempted to go to Mississippi with his friend Bellini or to Greenwich Village with a musician friend to play folk music in a coffee house. In the end, he decided to come back only because he knew Whyte—whom he still worshiped—would be disappointed if he didn't.

Georgie Warner was relieved to have his friends back. He had spent the year successfully avoiding the responsibility of the Omega Chi and feeling guilty about it. He had had only one business conversation with King Lu during the entire time and the Green overlord was so uncordial that Warner never went back to see him. Warner then proceeded to let the Omega Chi black-market system atrophy, quit his senior year at TAS, move out of his house (without even consulting his estranged father) and bury himself in the whorehouses of Peitou.

Whyte told each of them individually about his decision to stay in Taiwan and put the Omega Chi in the pool cue business. Each reacted in a somewhat different manner, in accordance with his individual experience of the past year. Taylor was delighted and Warner was relieved. Phillips was surprised and troubled by it, though he was not sure exactly why. Casy simply didn't believe it. He bet Taylor fifty U.S. dollars that Whyte would come to his senses and change his mind by the end of the summer.

* * *

Bryan Whyte decided that the first stage of his new plan for the Omega Chi would be to suppress his vaulting ambition and learn all the things he did not know about the legitimate American business community in Taipei. At least partially to fill the void in his life without Shelley, he threw himself into this task with a single-minded dedication.

He began in the offices of Kurt Perkins, the blustery and cantankerous head of China Petroleum, the biggest company on the Island. Perkins was Old China, a friend of his father's, and he hired the young Whyte as a general gofer, with a minimum of responsibility and a maximum of opportunity to study all the facets of the business.

Under Perkins's auspices, he made a concerted effort to meet (and do small favors for) everyone who counted in the Taipei business world, including speculators, corporation executives, economists, international lawyers and government officials. He soon found that he liked most of these people and, perhaps recognizing a kindred spirit, they tended to like him back. The more he mingled in this world, the more he became convinced that it would be possible for the Omega Chi to become an accepted part of it, that the transition could be made quickly and that the key to their entrée would be wooden, screw-together pool cues.

In July, Whyte left Perkins. Using all the money Phillips could squeeze out of their bank accounts along with a substantial sum borrowed interest-free from King Lu, the Omega Chi bought a small pool cue factory in the nearby port city of Keelung.

To run it, Whyte hired that craftiest of old Shanghai merchants and longtime Omega Chi cohort, "Snake-eyes" Lee Min. In this factory, Lee supervised fifteen workers who began to turn out five hundred handcrafted cues each week. These were crated and sent airmail to the Hop Sung Tong in San Francisco, then distributed nationally through one of the Hop Sungs' several small wholesale companies.

By the end of the month, a first batch had been shipped, immediately sold out, and the Hop Sung distributor was screaming for more. Whyte was able to pay back King Lu and have enough left over to make a down payment on another small pool cue factory.

The summer of 1964 was generally the most peaceful in years for most Americans in Taipei. It was so peaceful that they soon forgot there had ever been any trouble with their children and Oriental gangs. It was so peaceful that the curfews were dropped, the MP patrols discontinued and Commander Harris had nothing to do in his little office in the Navy compound but count the days until his tour of duty was up. It was so peaceful that all the old complacency returned to the missionaries and businessmen and military establishment who had been so on edge since the assassination of President Kennedy.

Then, in the first week of August, something happened that shattered that sense of peace forever.

When the word first reached Taipei, most of the Omega Chi were at the American beach area in Ching Shan lying in the sun and listening to the "Tops in Pops" program on Armed Forces Radio. The announcer interrupted a song by the Beach Boys to report that a U.S. destroyer had been unexpectedly attacked by North Vietnamese gunboats in the international waters of the Gulf of Tonkin.

All motion ceased in the American Community of Taipei as suddenly and completely as if an atomic bomb had been dropped on Los Angeles. The military went on immediate alert. The various American schools, social clubs and swimming pools were closed. The Naval Exchange and commissary and various American compounds tripled their security. Bomb shelters were prepared and air-raid sirens wailed their drills into the night. Evacuation plans for American dependents were frantically made and the Island braced itself for a possible follow-up from the Communist Mainland.

On the second day, there were reports of even more attacks on more U.S. destroyers in the Gulf of Tonkin but there was no discernible movement, no massing of invasion troops on the Mainland coast. The reaction in the American Community settled into relief and then flared up in righteous indignation. *This was the most unprecedented cowardly attack since Pearl Harbor and it had happened practically on their front doorstep!* When President Johnson ordered a military build-up in South Vietnam and air strikes against the supply bases of the offending gunboats, the cheering from the Taipei Press Club, where hundreds of Americans were gathered to follow the developments, could be heard three blocks away.

On the third day, news flashed over the wire that the U.S. Senate had passed a bold new resolution that would allow American forces to retaliate on a continuing basis. It authorized the President to "take all necessary measures to repel any armed attack against the forces of the United States and to prevent future aggression." It was just the kind of strong measure that the Americans of Taipei always knew was necessary if they were ever to have anything more than a perpetual stalemate in this part of the world.

Like everyone else, Bryan Whyte dropped everything to follow these great unfolding events very closely. His emotions during the week of crisis ran the gamut from shock to grim concern to outraged anger to pep-rally patriotic excitement. When it was over, he was left with an exhilarating certainty that they were all entering a whole new age: that, for the first time in his life, America was finally going to seize the offensive in Asia.

BOOK TWO
1965–1970

9

THE YEAR 1965 WITNESSED AN UNPRECEDENTED EX-
pansion of the American presence in Asia.

As the year began, it became apparent that the Vietcong rebels were following up the incomprehensible attacks in the Gulf of Tonkin with a wave of new guerrilla
activity in South Vietnam. To counter this aggression, and
to continue the policy of firmness set during the crisis,
the Johnson administration initiated regular air strikes
against both guerrilla positions in the South and their
supply bases in the Communist North. At the same time,
more American military advisors were dispatched to the
area and a large U.S. Naval Task Force moved into the
South China Sea to show the flag and demonstrate once
and for all that the U.S. would not tolerate South Vietnam
going the way China had: This time it would stand by its
ally with all its might.

By midyear, troops from Communist North Vietnam
directly entered the conflict for the first time. The U.S. did
not hesitate in its response. It rallied to this new escalation
with regular U.S. Army and Marine combat troops of its
own. The number of American military personnel in the
area suddenly doubled, then tripled, then quadrupled. The
message being sent to world Communism was clear: This
U.S. administration simply would not budge even an inch
in its determination to keep South Vietnam free—even if
it meant having to draft thirty-five thousand of its young
men per month, even if it meant spending millions of U.S.
dollars a day to arm and supply them, even if it meant
hundreds of their number would have to pay the ultimate
price.

By the year's end, it dawned on the Americans of Asia that this was not building up to be just a war, but *the* war—the long-awaited showdown with Communism on their continent. To fight it, billions were appropriated for men and supplies and ground was hastily broken on dozens of enormous permanent bases around the Orient— strategic bomber bases on Guam and Taiwan, naval bases in the Philippines, supply bases on Okinawa. By Christmas, so many men and so much hardware had been brought to Taiwan, the Philippines, Japan, Okinawa and South Korea that an immense American arsenal seemed to form a contiguous semicircle around Communist Asia —a vast empire of men, matériel and logistical support fueled by that traditional, philosophical confidence and spiritual commitment that had never allowed America to lose a war.

The rapid build-up of the American presence to fight the Vietnam War had its repercussions all over Asia that year. One of them was to dramatically change the economy of the city of Taipei almost overnight.

The economic structure of Taipei had always been greatly influenced by the presence of the two thousand or so Americans whose living standard was so out of balance with the rest of the population. Now, as the Island became a major staging area for the war, the American Community began to look like a boomtown. Hundreds, then thousands of new Americans flooded into the city with each month that passed. They came as families of Vietnam servicemen using the city as an official government "safe haven." They came as soldiers and sailors and airmen to serve on one of the new U.S. installations that were springing up all over the northern part of the Island. They came as opportunistic businessmen eager to pick up government contracts and set up shop under the assumption that the American military expansion in Asia was assurance that capitalism would be safe there for decades to come.

In the summer of 1965, they began to come in a way

that would have an even more profound impact on the city: as R&R soldiers on leave from the war zone. With its other world of bars and whorehouses, Taipei naturally became a popular rest-and-recreation center. It wasn't long before hordes of American servicemen could be seen on any night of the week prowling Peitou and Sin Alley, looking for the cheap sex that Taipei offered in such abundance. To accommodate them, a whole new district of R&R bars and black-market dealers soon sprang up on Min Chuan East Road within a few blocks of the American compounds.

On the heels of the R&R was another phenomenon that Taipei had never really experienced before in any number: tourists. As word of the city's charms spread with the coming and going of American GIs and American journalists, it gradually found itself with a new international notoriety. It wasn't long before the whorehouses of Peitou were being written up in *Esquire, Playboy* and *Time.* The word "Taipei" began to become synonymous with Oriental vice and exotic evil. The tourist industry got off the ground for the first time in 1965 and soon adventurous Americans, who had nothing to do with the war effort, were coming to the city by the thousands to sample its delights and to bring home stories of the magnificent scenery, the exquisite Chinese cuisine and the carnal pleasures of Peitou and Sin Alley.

The net effect of all this activity was a continual infusion of U.S. dollars into the economy of the city, the Island and, eventually, the rest of Free Asia—first as a small and steady stream and then as a raging and uncontrollable torrent.

At first, Bryan Whyte saw the American build-up and its inevitable economic consequences as a threat to his ambitions. Gradually, however, he perceived it as an extraordinary opportunity—the great opportunity of his lifetime.

After all the Omega Chi, except Warner, returned to

the States for another year of college, Whyte stayed on in Taipei. He moved into the Omega Chi House and threw himself into his fledgling pool cue business. He cut himself off from any social distractions, spent hours on the phone with the Hop Sings in San Francisco, made endless trips to Hong Kong to seek advice from King Lu, rode Georgie Warner, rode his manager, Lee Min, until the old merchant threw a cue at him, and worked impossibly long hours in a determined effort to expand on his initial success.

Before the end of 1964, he had three more back alley factories turning out several thousand pool cues a week along with a full year's contract to supply three major U.S. sporting goods companies. With this plus the money he was already making off the black market, he had enough to support himself, his father and Warner and to pay for the college tuitions of Casy, Phillips and Taylor—should they need the help. There was even enough left to start building a substantial savings account, which he hoped eventually to invest in other Taiwan-based businesses.

The success of these months went a long way toward repairing the damage done by his traumatic year in the States. He realized now that, as for all true taipans, his strength was China; he had no business ever leaving it again. He realized also that he had expected too much of the States—had expected a fantasy—and with this realization his strong American identity began to heal and reassert itself in a slightly more realistic shape. Furthermore, the American response to the Gulf of Tonkin—which he continued to follow breathlessly—had restored all his old confidence in America's commitment to its sacred mission in Asia.

As the American build-up got fully underway, however, it immediately created several problems for him. First, the sheer number of new Americans in town was making it next to impossible to control the black market; the volume of new supply that came with them was driving the rates to an all-time low. Secondly, the sudden influx of R&R had created a bonanza in the bar and whorehouse business and everyone was scrambling to get in on it. Directly competing were the Greens of Peitou, the Tiger Eels of Lung Shan and Sin Alley and the independents of Min Chuan (who were Green financed but had ideas of their own). It made for a desperately unhealthy situation that he felt he had to stabilize somehow before the city erupted in violence once again.

During the opening months of 1965, Whyte spent a good deal of time trying to figure out just how far this American build-up was going and what it was going to mean to him personally. When he fully grasped its scope, he realized that not only was his boyhood dream of an American military crusade against Communism in Asia actually coming to pass, but that it fit in almost uncannily with the mystical vision of the possibilities of the Omega Chi that had come to him that night nearly two years ago.

It was all coming together like some inexorable divine plan. With the U.S. expanding its presence and building bases all over the Orient in the coming years, it would find that in order to operate efficiently, it *had* to have some link with the Chinese underworld. Who else could this connection be but the Omega Chi, which had already established itself as an intermediary between the U.S. authority on Taiwan and the highest level of the Green Society? Who else would function in this scheme with unquestioned loyalty to both sides? Who else would be smart enough to profit from the business opportunities this unique position would invariably offer?

By the time the summer of 1965 came around, Bryan Whyte had formulated a concrete plan to remobilize the Omega Chi to seize all the opportunities created by the American build-up. And he was aching to move on it.

The first thing he had to do was convince Mark Taylor and Alan Phillips to stay out of college for one year to help him. These two opposing personalities gave the Omega Chi the balance that made it such an effective unit: Taylor was brash, fearless and instinctive; Phillips was methodical, cautious and highly organized. He could do it without Casy perhaps. His input to the fraternity was mainly spiritual. He could also do it without Warner. His contribution had been almost nonexistent since the acid attack on him two summers before. But he knew there was no way he would ever fulfill the visions of wealth and power that burned in his brain without the skill and support of his strong right and left arms.

Taylor agreed immediately. He had not told Whyte but he had been kicked out of school on a disciplinary— for fighting again—shortly before the end of the term. At that point, he immediately went to his nearest Army recruiter and tried to enlist but was turned down because of his asthma, which had gotten drastically worse over the past two traumatic years. Now that he was nearly twenty-one, the missionaries were washing their hands of him. The fact was, he was counting on holding a position in the Omega Chi business until he could somehow think of a way to get in the Army.

Phillips had mixed feelings about Whyte's request. The U.S. AID program had ended during the year—it had been so successful that Taiwan no longer needed U.S. economic aid—and his family was moving back to the States after fifteen years. He was looking for an excuse to stay actively involved with the Island—he had lived there most of his life and he considered it home—but he was still reluctant and somewhat troubled. "I'll consider it, Bryan," he said after Whyte approached him about it several times, "but I have a condition."

"Name it."

"I'm concerned about our change of emphasis. Making money is fine. But we started out as a fraternity of service to the community and I haven't heard you mention this once in all these plans. I would expect at least a fourth of our income each month to go to the orphanage and other charities. I mean, this is what we're supposed to be doing here in the first place, right?"

Whyte thought about this quickly. "Of course," he said. "That was always my intention. There is no change of purpose. We're going to serve the same function we always have."

"Then I'll stay a year to help you get the organizational structure set up. But only a year. Then I'm going back to finish school."

The following day, they met with an official of the financial committee of the Legislative Yuan to apply for a license to incorporate under Chinese law. The official told them it was out of the question at the present time. They came back the next day, spoke to the full committee and were informed that there would be a year of red tape before they could get an answer and no amount of *cumshaw* or squeeze could change that. That evening Whyte telephoned King Lu and asked him if he would expedite the matter as a personal favor. The proper papers were hand-delivered to Phillips the next morning. Omega Chi Enterprises was born.

Whyte's basic scenario went like this: The Omega Chi now had a steady income from the black market, the pool cue business and a tiny cut King had granted them from the Green bar and whorehouse business in Peitou. It would use this income first to branch out into more export businesses, more small manufacturing and numerous retail businesses such as book and record pirating. Then it would invest in more income-generating pieces of real estate in Peitou and Min Chuan and other areas where the R&R was creating an unprecedented boom.

On another level, the Omega Chi would begin to act as a consulting firm to the Chinese business community. It would use its special relationship with the U.S. authority to help certain Chinese firms who desired to do business with the U.S. Government on Taiwan. The competition among these companies for U.S. contracts was fierce and they were eager for this kind of service. In return, the Omega Chi would collect a percentage of the contract, which in the case of a large construction project, for example, could be considerable.

The Omega Chi would be able to keep this kind of continuing influence with the U.S. authority by helping it in any matter involving the Chinese underworld. It would merely maintain the terms of the deal Whyte had made with Harris to end the gang war of 1963, continuing to serve the function the Omega Chi had always served on the Island. If the U.S. Government had a Chinese labor problem, the Omega Chi would fix it. If the U.S. Army was being strangled by underworld squeeze at a certain installation, the Omega Chi would step in and control it. If the U.S. Embassy ever needed the help of the Green Society for any reason whatsoever, the Omega Chi would get it for them.

"Basically, we're the same fraternity," Whyte explained to them at the end of the summer. "But we've got a larger role to play now and more business to worry about. We've got to be more sophisticated."

"What's this going to mean to each of us personally?" Warner asked.

"We're a privately held American-owned Taiwan corporation now. The stock is split between the five of us and cannot be transferred, sold or bequeathed without our unanimous consent. Each of us is on the board of directors with an equal vote and an annual salary of, for now, twenty-five thousand U.S. We'll be paid by an accounting firm that will be working with Alan. They'll be taking care of your taxes and other complicated matters."

"What about Casy?" Phillips asked.

"We're not about to bust up the fraternity. Even though he's chosen to remain in the States for now, Casy gets exactly what we get and has the same vote. However, he will not be able to exercise that vote unless he is actually physically on the Island—nor will any of the rest of us for that matter."

"One other thing," said Mark Taylor. "We'll lose our college deferments. Has anyone considered that? I can always be a 4-F for asthma but you jokers are gonna get your asses thrown in the Army as buck privates."

Whyte arched his eyebrow. "I've already spoken to the Embassy. Since we will be aiding them on intelligence matters on a regular basis, the Omega Chi has been deemed vital to the war effort. We'll all be deferred, at least for the time being. Any more questions?"

The three looked at each other blankly. There was nothing to ask. As usual, Bryan Whyte had thought of everything.

The following weekend, Alan Phillips attended a dinner party celebrating the arrival of Warren Stevens, the new U.S. Ambassador to Nationalist China.

Stevens was one of the few Kennedy favorites to keep favor with the Johnson administration. His handling of the Taiwan gang crisis of 1963—a success he owed to Bryan Whyte—gave him a considerable reputation as an innovative peacemaker. That reputation was largely responsible for his appointment to what was considered one of the five most important and prestigious U.S. ambassadorships. In this post, he could have an enormously beneficial influence on the future of the Omega Chi—so Whyte dispatched Phillips to welcome him and make sure the man knew he was in their debt.

The party was given by Kurt Perkins, the Old China hand, president of the China Petroleum Company. As one of the few oldtimers to make it off the Mainland with his fortune intact, Perkins was able to live in a fine estate on Grass Mountain, an exclusive residential area north of the city, where he and his Chinese wife—a distant relative of Madame Chiang—ran the most exclusive salon in the American Community.

Phillips arrived that evening with Doris Loo—to whom he had become formally engaged that summer—to see virtually all the American businessmen, missionaries, military and government people who counted on the Island elbow to elbow in one room. They were mostly chattering away about the Vietnam situation with that strange glow of confidence and pride he had noticed at these kind of gatherings ever since America had seized the initiative in Southeast Asia.

Phillips mingled easily with these people. He found

he was no longer considered a child by them. The Omega Chi was beginning to be accepted as an increasingly important element of the business community. As its most visible figure in the community, he was now regularly invited to the best soirées, where he hobnobbed with some of the most distinguished people in America—who invariably stopped over in Taipei on their way through Asia.

Dinner was a sumptuous Chekiang feast of salted shrimp, sautéed crab meat, duck, sweet and sour pork, rice, lotus soup, chicken, prawns and fried bananas. The conversation was about the administration's recent decision to commit even more U.S. ground troops to bring the war to a speedy conclusion. Stevens was for it. He outlined in some detail the administration's strategy and the distinguished heads around the table strained to listen, hanging on the ambassador's every word.

After the last course, the guests moaned at the fullness of their stomachs and adjourned to the parlor for a special performance by the Taipei String Quartet. Ambassador Stevens strolled out onto the patio to listen to the music and enjoy a brandy. Seeing his opportunity, Phillips followed the tall, craggy diplomat out into the warm night air. "I wanted to tell you how pleased we all were to hear of your appointment," he said, approaching Stevens with a smile. "It's the smartest move Johnson has made so far."

"Mr. Whyte couldn't be here?"

"No. He sends his apologies. He's tied up with business tonight."

Stevens chuckled. "He's become a busy man, has he? Well, you boys—excuse me, you *gentlemen*—have come a long way."

Phillips smiled. "So have you, sir."

"Yes, and I suppose I owe at least part of it to Bryan Whyte."

"We're hoping we can continue to help you while you're ambassador," Phillips said, relieved that the man was getting the message so easily.

"That's very kind of you."

"In fact, there's a problem brewing here right now that we might be able to head off together."

Stevens sipped his brandy and eyed Phillips coolly. "And what kind of problem is that?"

Phillips pushed his rimless glasses up the bridge of his nose, a signal that he was ready to get down to business. Stevens thought that the boy looked like a nervous high-school debater; there was something almost comical about the two of them standing out on the patio conspiring to the strains of Haydn.

"As you know," Phillips said, "American money has been pouring into the economy of this island so fast that no one can keep up with it. Naturally the various under-world elements have gone after this money and the Tiger Eels have been getting enough of the spillover to give them ambition again. They're expanding their operations in certain areas of the city. There is going to be trouble over it someday."

Stevens seemed surprised. "I thought you had a mo-nopoly on the black market here. We agreed to let you have it. You said that would be the end of the trouble."

"The black market is no longer where the real money is," Phillips went on. "The black market rate is way down because of the increase of supply since the middle of this year. Too many Americans with too much to sell. No, the real money is in the R&R—the bars and brothels."

"Mr. Phillips, my first action as ambassador is going to be to sign the long-talked-about Status of Forces Agree-ment between our country and Nationalist China. The effect of this agreement will be to give Chinese police full jurisdiction over all American citizens. This should end any problems with the Warlords once and for all."

"Pardon me, sir, but all this will do is ensure that a great many Chinese policemen will get rich from bribes."

"What do you suggest be done to stop it?" Stevens demanded abruptly.

"Bryan Whyte believes that the smartest thing you could do is strictly enforce the off-limits ruling on Sin

Alley and Lung Shan. That's certainly in your power. It would have the effect of moving all the U.S. R&R business to Peitou and Min Chuan, where the Greens can control it."

Irritation flashed in Stevens's eyes. "Whyte would get a cut of all the R&R business if I were to do that, wouldn't he?"

Phillips strained to maintain a reasonable tone to his voice. "Whether or not the Omega Chi would profit by the move is really beside the point, isn't it? The point is that we have a problem and a potential disaster. You can avoid that disaster by keeping the R&R money out of the hands of the Tiger Eels. With your GIs patronizing only the Green establishments, you will also—through us—be able to exercise a certain amount of control over them and avoid any serious incidents that might get in the papers and cause embarrassment."

Stevens sipped his drink and stared out into the darkness. Crickets chirped in the distance. He knew he had no choice but to do what Phillips suggested and for the reasons he so logically outlined. He had not even been here a full day and he was already being manipulated by Bryan Whyte. It fascinated him more than it made him angry.

"You know," he said after several moments of hesitation, "your man Whyte is a damned interesting fellow. There's something so pure about him, yet at the same time he's ruthless to the point of corruption. Something very admirable and very seductive yet . . . frightening. Do you know what I mean?"

"I think so, sir." Phillips knew exactly what he meant.

"What is it that Whyte is after?"

"He wants to restore his family's fortune."

"There's more to it than that."

Phillips smiled knowingly. "He's a man with a vision. I don't pretend to know exactly what that vision is, but I trust it—and him—completely."

"It must be nice to have that kind of confidence in another human being."

"He's never let me down yet."

"Still, sometimes I think he may be too ambitious. I think he may want real wealth and power. Like certain Westerners had in the old days. If that's what he wants, we could all be in for a rough time. In this day and age that could prove to be a very dangerous ambition."

Phillips stared noncommittally at this. But inside he was also wondering about the direction Bryan Whyte was leading them—and Stevens's warning made him very uncomfortable.

Even though there had been no war or hint of war in the Taipei underworld for nearly two years, King Lu's new townhouse on Canal Road was full of armed bodyguards. They stood sentry in the front street and back alley. They congregated in little groups at the end of the block. They loitered in the hallway. They were all stern-faced Blue Shirt soldiers, the elite of the Greens—men trained in the various Oriental arts of killing since childhood, men who had all taken mystical vows of service to King and whose loyalty to him was as certain as the setting of the sun in the west.

Whyte made his way through this mob, noting with pleasure how they seemed to stiffen with respect as he passed, and went upstairs to King's office. The Green leader was sitting behind his desk going over the annual statement of the Bank of Taiwan, of which he had recently become a major stockholder and board member. When he saw Whyte, he smiled and stood up to greet him. *"Hao, hao,"* he said.

"Welcome back, Older Brother," Whyte said in Mandarin and respectfully embraced him.

Over the past two years, Whyte had come to experience a genuine filial affection for King Lu. On King's increasingly frequent trips to Taipei, they spent many hours together. During this time they had developed the bond of master and pupil, one of the most sacred of Chinese relationships. When Whyte reached his twenty-first birthday in August, King came to town with his entire entourage, bought himself a luxurious townhouse and began to have a series of long counseling sessions with his pupil, telling him for the first time as much as there was to know—and much more than his father had ever known —about the complicated organizational structure and philosophy of the Green Pang Society.

King gave him a detailed accounting of the Greens' financial portfolio—gambling operations, brothels, securities, real estate, and whole banks in every major city in Asia and dozens of others in Europe and the United States. He told him about the complicated oaths and initiations all Greens had to take, about their schooling in the ways of killing enemies and disposing of traitors, such as the traditional ritualized dismemberment by hand ax (reserved for the most hated enemies). He told him about the ancient Taoist rites still practiced by the Greens, among them the legendary Union of Breaths which was the ultimate sexual communion between two lovers. And he told him about the Greens' use of magic and soothsayers to forsee the way of the great Tao in a generalized manner.

"I have heard the news," King said immediately, continuing to speak in Mandarin. "My informers tell me that Randy Ortega and Dave Magaha have returned from their year on Green Island and are running with Loma and his Taiwanese pirates again. They have opened some new 'specialty' operations in Lung Shan and Sin Alley to lure the R&R business." He laughed humorlessly. "It seems prison has taught them nothing."

"It was to be expected," Whyte said. "There is so much money flowing these days that the temptation for them to grab for it must be overwhelming."

"What do you suggest we do?"

"I suggest we do nothing for the present time," Whyte said. "The establishments of the Tiger Eels will remain off-limits to Americans. Ortega may help them pick up a few daring GIs who will risk the brig to go there, but not enough to concern us."

King looked pleased. "A good decision. We can afford to be generous. Another war would only hurt business for us at a time when we have never had it so good."

"I have actually come on another matter of business, Elder Brother. I have learned today that the U.S. Government intends to build a large air base near Taichung sometime next year. It will be the largest military installation ever constructed on this island and it will play a major role in the Vietnam fighting."

"Truly?" King's eyes registered a keen interest.

"Yes. I want to be able to tell Ambassador Stevens that the Green Society will cooperate in this worthy venture. I want to tell him that there will be absolutely no problems in acquiring the proper local materials or sufficient coolie labor at a reasonable price. I want to tell him that there will be no interference from the Taichung underworld."

"And what compensation was the Ambassador thinking of?"

"The normal fifteen percent squeeze. In this case, that amounts to a substantial sum. You will also obtain the fringe benefit of the business the base will bring to the Island. The men stationed there will have to engage in the normal activities of soldiers on leave. They will be able to do so only in the places of business you will build in Taichung. As in Taipei, all other establishments will be off-limits and the restriction will be strongly enforced."

King remained very poker-faced. "This is satisfactory. And what do you get out of it for your services?"

"The normal percentage plus a favor from you."

King couldn't help but grin. Though it was totally unnecessary, they found themselves going through the formal ritual of haggling, of coming to a fair deal for each of them. It was old custom and both enjoyed it. "And what is that?"

"I want to become involved in the Taiwan movie industry."

This shocked King. "Whatever for? There is no

money in this worthless business. Not even the Tiger Eels would bother with it."

"Perhaps because it is in my blood. Because it was the business of my father on the Mainland."

"Yes, but on the Mainland it was indeed a business. A real business with thousands of theaters and profits in the millions. Here it is nothing."

"Maybe it will be big again. It is, after all, a business that grows hand in hand with mounting prosperity."

King frowned. "It will only occupy your time and take your attention away from the truly important matters."

"I will let Georgie Warner handle it. I need something for him to do. He loves the movies and he is not capable of handling anything of real consequence."

King frowned more deeply. He was clearly disappointed in his pupil. "I recommend against it strongly. Find something else for your acid-faced brother to do."

Whyte was determined. "Can you get me control of one of the studios? Is this possible?"

King sighed and gave in. "It is possible. Which one do you want?"

"The National Film Studio in Shih Lin. They do not want to sell but I have heard they are in deep financial difficulty."

"Let me see what can be done."

Whyte bowed his head as a sign of gratitude and started to leave but something about this victory left him vaguely dissatisfied. "Elder Brother," he suddenly jerked around and said, "why do you always concede to me so easily? Why do you do all the things you do for me? What is it about the Whytes that makes the Greens so protective of them? What *is* it that I do not know?"

King sat and stared at Whyte for a long, uncomfortable time without speaking. Then he said, "I suppose you should know this. When you were a child staying with me after the Communist murder of your mother, the famous soothsayer Chuang-tzu predicted that you would someday be instrumental in the restoration of the Mainland."

"How?"

"He was not specific."

Whyte sat down in the nearest chair. "That does explain a lot," he said.

"You may believe it or not, of course. But you must understand that Chuang-tzu's prestige is so great that the Green Society will always regard you as a man of special destiny, a man who will help determine the future of China."

Whyte did not know exactly how to react to this revelation. He was strangely not surprised, having always suspected something like it as part of his heritage. But as he came to terms with it over the following weeks and months, it pleased him and began to fill him with new determination and boundless new ambition—not only because it confirmed what he had always known about himself by intuition, but because it made him realize that he had a hold on this powerful secret society that was very near unshakable.

Georgie Warner stood before Whyte with the look of a man who had just witnessed a miracle. "Well, I've finally found her," he said.

"You've found who?"

"The most beautiful woman on the Island. Just exactly what you ordered."

"I've heard this before."

"Get your coat. This one you have to see to believe. Bryan, I'm in love."

Two months ago, the Omega Chi had acquired a controlling interest in the nearly bankrupt National Film Studio in Shih Lin. With Warner as president and Old Whyte as consultant, they had great fun playing at getting the business started again—at the expense of all the Omega Chi's other, vastly more lucrative operations. They chased the ducks and chickens out of the single sound stage, rented some modern equipment from Hong Kong and were now (on the insistence of Old Whyte, who knew

about these things) frantically searching for a beautiful
girl to promote into a star.

Whyte knew that the most beautiful women on the
Island were often sold into prostitution by their families
and—to meet the demand of the American R&R—the
profession was now, as never before, overcrowded with
beautiful women. Since Warner spent more time in the
whorehouses than all the rest of the Omega Chi combined,
Whyte had him constantly on the lookout. Every day he
appeared with a different candidate, but Whyte had never
seen him this excited before.

In the car, Warner explained a certain complication
to the situation which immediately discouraged Whyte.
"Her name is Su Ling and she was sold by her father to
an old Tiger Eel cannibal named Anwah, who is the personal pimp for Loma himself. Anwah uses the girl as the
star attraction for one of the illegal sex shows he stages for
American GIs. She's making the old bastard a mint."

"I don't like it. It all sounds like trouble to me."

"You've just got to see her!"

"Where are we going?"

"Sin Alley."

"Christ, Georgie."

"I guarantee you she's worth it."

"All right, but we better swing by and get The Elephant."

They picked up the Green Gang enforcer at his home
on Nanking East Road and took a series of side streets
north toward Sin Alley. Whyte had not been in this part
of Taipei for years and he commented on how different it
looked. Several blocks of slums had been leveled, replaced
with low-income housing. The pedicabs that once clogged
these narrow streets had now been officially banned as a
nuisance. Television had come to the Island in 1963, and
the roofs of the buildings were now jammed with antennae. Yes, the city was changing. . . .

But not Sin Alley. Sin Alley looked just as run-down
and gaudy as it had in the days when he and Taylor used

to sneak out of elementary school and come down there
to flirt with the bargirls.

They drove to the Theater of Ten Delights in one of
the back warrens off the Alley and got out. They paid an
old woman at the door five U.S. dollars each—an outrageous sum, indicating a very special show—and took seats
around a small, elevated stage area. The rest of the audience consisted of three American R&R soldiers who
waited in silent, lusty anticipation.

Warner was almost on top of Whyte; the closeness of
his acid-scarred face made Whyte vaguely uncomfortable.
"Actually," Warner was saying, almost whispering in his
ear, "we have a legitimate claim on this girl. The Eels
wanted her so badly that they blinded her father to force
him to sell her. Apparently, Phillips heard about this and
put her under our protection. Her old man sold her anyway. . . ."

A moment later, the lights dimmed, a record by the
Rolling Stones came on and two women entered the shadowy room to begin the performance. They stepped onto
the stage and slipped out of their panties and bras. It was
going to be the standard lesbian act but Whyte saw at once
why it rated such an exorbitant price. The younger per-
former was simply extraordinary. She had the body of a
barely pubescent teenager and her waist-long black hair
framed a delicate, innocent, mystically lovely face. She
had a pouty mouth and big green eyes—obviously the
legacy of some Western ancestor—that were so beautiful
and so striking as to be almost hypnotic. With one look
at her, Bryan Whyte forgot all about Shelley Spencer for
the first time in two years. Never in his life had he seen
any woman—Eastern or Western—with such obvious star
quality.

The two women lay lengthwise on the stage and proceeded to kiss and fondle one another's breasts for several
moments. When the record changed, they gradually
crawled around into a sixty-nine position and began enthusiastically tonguing each other in time with the music.

Overcome with lust, a quartermaster sergeant sitting near the stage area stood up, lowered his pants and held out a U.S. ten dollar bill. The younger woman, Su Ling, quickly got up and grabbed the money. Then she got on her knees in front of his erection and took it into her mouth.

Whyte immediately shot to his feet, his whole body trembling. "The show is over," he announced at the top of his lungs.

The woman backed off and the sergeant pulled up his pants, angry and embarrassed. "You just bought yourself some big trouble, sonny boy."

As the man fumbled to fasten his belt, Whyte stepped over and hit him in the chest with a single, powerful karate punch. The man went down gasping for breath. Whyte looked quickly at the man's two companions. "Get him out of here."

At the sight of The Elephant looming behind Whyte, the GIs meekly obeyed.

The music stopped. Anwah, the owner of the theater, came out of nowhere and let loose a tirade of pidgin. "You clazy boy! You luin my busyness. Thisee my gwyl!"

"Not anymore," Whyte said. "I'm taking her." He stepped over and grabbed the frightened girl by the arm. The touch of her sent thrills of delight throughout his body.

The Elephant looked uncertain. "This no good, boss. She thisee man plopety. Go against custom."

"We have a prior claim to her," Whyte said shortly. "Phillips put her under our protection two years ago."

This made The Elephant look happier. He and Anwah began bantering back and forth in Taiwanese, which Whyte could not understand. The Elephant looked worried again. "He say gwyl's father sellee her to Anwah. This the father's right, boss."

"All right, dammit," Whyte muttered. "I'll buy her back then. What is a fair price?"

The Elephant scratched his head. "Maybe two hundred dolla U.S. a fair price."

Anwah screamed his rejection. "I no sellee. *Ayee yo!* Su Ling my licee bowl." He hawked and spit on the floor around Whyte's feet.

Whyte nodded to The Elephant. The *boo hoy doy* pulled out his thirty-eight caliber revolver and put it to Anwah's temple. He was not bluffing.

As the gun cocked, the frightened, indignant man changed his mind just in time to prevent it from being spread all over the wall.

They took Su Ling to the Omega Chi House. Whyte put her in his private quarters and dismissed The Elephant and Warner. Warner didn't want to go. He was as taken with the girl as Whyte was and he felt she should be his by right of discovery.

"I'd like to stick around, Bryan."

Whyte could see the conflict brewing but he had no intention of being noble. After all, Georgie had hundreds of Lung Shan and Peitou girls. Another one more or less would make no difference to him. He decided quickly that it would be better to be firm from the start. "I want to be alone with her, Georgie. I feel very strongly about this."

Warner hesitated a moment. He did not quite realize what was happening. "But . . . Bryan . . ."

"Go."

Whyte whispered but it was a cold and powerful whisper and it made Warner stop and stand absolutely still. He stared at Whyte with a sense of shock and betrayal. And fear. He did not, finally, have the strength to challenge Whyte—any more than he could challenge his own father. Instead he turned and stormed out of the room without a word.

Whyte watched the door close. He felt bad for a moment about the ugly scene and thought about calling Warner back. He could explain—explain how he desperately needed this particular girl at this particular time. But he didn't. He just turned to the girl and smiled.

The girl was Taiwanese but she spoke Mandarin and

even some English. When she saw they were alone, she said very angrily, "What for you want Su Ling, anyhow?"

Whyte didn't answer. He merely locked the door and continued studying her, marveling at her physical presence, wondering if she could possibly photograph as stunningly as she came off in person.

She tried to act confident but inside the girl was near panic. She was thinking of the beating Anwah would give her when she returned. She was also very uneasy being completely alone with an American. She didn't like their boisterous manner or hairy bodies. She had also heard stories that some of them were cannibals who cooked and ate young Taiwanese girls.

"We do boom boom now, then I go back, okay, hey?" she said.

"You're not going back," he said.

"I gotee job. Good job with Anwah."

"I have a new job for you."

"I am slave to Anwah," she insisted.

"There are no slaves anymore."

She looked very worried. "Anwah angly with Su Ling. Beat Su Ling."

"Don't be afraid of Anwah," he said, switching to Mandarin. "You will never have to see Anwah again."

She thought about this a moment. She had heard of this taipan Whyte, knew him to be truly powerful and much feared. But could anyone escape the wrath of Anwah?

"Would you like to be an actress?" he asked suddenly.

She looked surprised. "I am an actress," she said. "What do you think I do on the stage of the Ten Delights?"

"I mean really act. In movies."

She went back to English. "I makee two movie for Anwah. One with big doggie, hey. Maybe you see, what?"

"Not that kind of movie."

"Likee in Chung Wa movie theater?"

"Yes."

She didn't quite understand. She shrugged. "Donno," she said.

"I own a studio in Shih Lin. I want you to be in the films I'm going to make there."

"I good actee," she said, matter-of-factly.

"I'm going to make something very special out of you. People are going to think you're a goddess from another world. Not only on Taiwan but all over Asia. What do you think of that?"

She listened to the intense, utterly confident way these words were spoken to her, and she believed them. "Why so?" she asked. "Why so you want to do thisee for Su Ling?"

"Because it pleases me. And because it's a wise business decision."

She stared at him a moment and then placed her hand on his knee.

Her touch made him unbearably excited. He reached over and kissed her on the mouth and felt her tongue dart expertly into his. Using both his hands, he unbuttoned her thin silk robe and let it fall to the tatami. He removed his own clothes as she stood watching him, curiously examining his muscular body, noting with a certain pride that he was already fully aroused by her.

He kissed her breasts and dropped to his knees before her, almost as a sign of worship, kissing her tiny navel and smooth, flat stomach, burying his face into the patch of silky black pubic hair between her legs.

He pulled her down to the tatami floor, where he entered her and made love to her with uncharacteristic lust and abandon. He had not made love to anyone in well over a year.

Afterward, they went to the hot tub room and bathed together. Then she spread him on the tatami and rubbed his back with oils while he told her about how he was going to buy a great house soon, a house like his father had once owned on the Mainland, and he would teach her how to be the *tai tai,* the lady of that great house.

As he told her these things, he experienced an overwhelming sense of contentment with himself. He had obviously found the thing he most needed to feel complete, the one thing he was sure would finally and completely liberate him from the States and the hold of Shelley Spencer.

—————————————————— 10

FOR HIS TWENTY-SECOND BIRTHDAY ON AUGUST 14, 1966, Bryan Whyte bought himself a great house on Grass Mountain. It had been originally built as the residence of the colonial officer of one of the immensely wealthy prewar Japanese *zaibatsu*, or family-owned corporations, that had formerly run the economy of the Island. The estate had eight bedrooms, a billiard parlor, separate servants' quarters, a natural sulphur hot spring and five acres of cherry and azalea trees. Whyte staffed it with three amahs, a crew of yardboys, a houseboy, a chauffeur, a private secretary and Su Ling, who moved in with him and valiantly tried to take over the duties of mistress of the house while being tutored daily by a team of drama coaches in preparation for her film debut in the fall.

Before he made the down payment, Whyte took his father through the main house to look it over.

"This will be your room," he said, leading the old man into a large bedroom just off the end of the long stone hallway that echoed with their footsteps. "I hope that eventually you'll sell the old house and move in with me."

Old Whyte was not able to find words. He just stood with his son in the empty room of the empty mansion looking out over the stunning view of Taipei and the northern suburbs.

Bryan put his arm around old Whyte. "I'm going to name the place China Gate," he said. It was the favorite Kuomintang nickname for the Island of Taiwan—a term that embodied for them the belief that the Island would be the base from which they would someday recover their lost homeland.

At this, the old man's eyes teared over and his jaw trembled with emotion. Bryan assumed the emotion was joy, but when his father turned and looked at him with fearful eyes, he saw that it was something else.

"Don't try to do too much, Sonny," the old man said. "This is enough for us. More than enough."

But Bryan Whyte refused to hear this. "No, Father," he said, seething with confidence and determination. "This is only the beginning."

In early September of that year, a combination house-warming and birthday party was held at China Gate. It was the social event of the Taipei season.

Old Whyte prepared a guest list of the most important business, diplomatic, military and missionary people deemed worthy to honor the young taipan of the house of Omega Chi. Among them were a number of old friends: David Butler, now assistant chief of the Hong Kong AP Bureau; Ambassador Warren Stevens, his wife and two teenage children on vacation from boarding school in the States; and the newly promoted Captain Floyd Harris, in town on his way to his new station with Navy Intelligence in Saigon.

The party also served as a reunion for the brothers of Omega Chi, whose frantic activity over the past six months had kept them away from the city for long stretches of time. Like Whyte, each of them had bought homes in the city, each had large staffs and large responsibilities and each had long-ago given up any thought of returning to the States.

Alan Phillips drove in from Taichung, where the

construction firm selected by the Omega Chi had already broken ground on the new U.S. air base. He came early to help organize the party, but he and Whyte spent most of the morning talking business. Their profit from the construction project alone was staggering and they could not completely agree on what to do with all the money they were making—Phillips wanted to give it to their various charities, Whyte wanted to invest it in new business schemes.

Still, Phillips was reasonably content with his life and had felt settled enough to finally marry Doris Loo late in the summer. Bryan Whyte served as best man at the ceremony, though, in fact, he was an immediate source of tension in the new marriage. Doris was jealous of his influence over her husband and was even trying to convince Alan to break with Whyte and go back to college. She particularly hated any kind of social affair with Whyte because she was expected to associate with Su Ling, whom Doris, a staunch Methodist and a Mainlander, considered beneath contempt. She had no trouble whatsoever developing a very real headache that morning as an excuse to avoid the party.

Georgie Warner showed up midmorning in his brand new Jaguar XKE. He too had been avoiding Whyte: He had not recovered from the shock of having Su Ling so casually stolen from him. As compensation, Whyte had put him in charge of the Omega Chi Studio in Shih Lin. Warner liked this job. Most of the real decision-making was handled by his Chinese staff yet he had an impressive title, a spacious office and a great deal of free time to spend in nearby Peitou.

Mark Taylor arrived just before noon, flying in from Okinawa, where he was negotiating to buy two more factories that would produce sporting goods accessories to augment the Omega Chi's line of pool cues. Whyte was trying to mold Taylor into a proper businessman but was having no luck. Taylor had little patience in negotiations and did not even try to hide the frustration and edginess that came from the lack of excitement in his life. For the most part, he spent his days working out in The Elephant's martial arts gym, playing war games with the Greens or reading military books in the library that filled one whole floor of his new townhouse on Fu Hsing North Road.

Of the original five Omega Chi, only John Casy held out, still struggling away as a writer and musician in San Francisco. However, he drew his full monthly salary from the company and that caused considerable bitterness. Taylor frequently complained that he did not think it fair that they were expected to work their asses off while Casy got away with doing nothing. But Whyte was always adamant about Casy. "He is an artist," Whyte would say and that would be the end of the conversation.

In the heat of the afternoon, the guests all assembled under the shade of a large cherry tree to watch Whyte open his gifts. It seemed that every business of any consequence in the city had sent an extravagant present in hopes of gaining favor with the Omega Chi. The front lawn of China Gate was soon filled with television sets, radios, appliances, furniture, carpets, oil paintings, lamps, porcelains, jade sculpture. The high point came when a Lincoln Continental limousine, handcrafted and monogrammed with an Omega Chi symbol, was driven through the front gate—a special gift from King Lu, who thought it inappropriate to attend the party personally.

There was a stack of congratulatory telegrams to be opened—from John Casy in California, from the commander of the Taiwan Defense Command, from dozens of important and influential American and Asian businessmen he had never met. As he went through the telegrams, he found himself looking for something from Shelley Spencer. It was maddening the way he had started thinking about her again lately, despite the fact that they had not communicated since the final good-by in Missouri, despite the fact that he was now completely happy with Su Ling. A few weeks ago, he had seen Shelley's picture in a Winston cigarette ad in *Look* magazine and, surprisingly, the sight of it had been like a stab wound.

When the amahs handed out a round of champagne glasses, Whyte offered a small toast: "To all of my friends. May we all prosper together. May we all work together for a free Asia."

There were a few echoes of "a free Asia" and "here, here" and the clinking of glasses.

A little while later, while the guests were still toasting his honor, Whyte left the group. He followed Phillips and Ambassador Stevens into the privacy of the billiard room for a special meeting Stevens had requested.

"Thank you for coming to my party, Mr. Ambassador," he said, closing the door. "I realize that it is an honor you don't bestow very often. Now what can I do to repay it?"

The two Omega Chi could tell from the uncomfortable look on Stevens's face that he needed something from them. "Maybe we can do you some service," Phillips said, to make it easier for him.

"Yes," said Stevens, clearly not enjoying the position. "We've got an ugly situation developing and we think maybe you could give us a hand."

"That's why we're here," said Whyte. "Just tell us what we can do."

Stevens sat his lanky frame on the edge of the pool table, picked up the cue ball and bounced it gently in his hand. "It's like this," he began uneasily. "The American build-up since last year has had a negative side effect that none of us could have foreseen. The U.S. money that's been pumped into Asia has been a bonanza for the underworlds of the various countries in which we maintain a presence or do major business. These gangs have been demanding more and more squeeze and have been getting more and more belligerent, powerful, uncontrollable. In Hong Kong, Manila, Singapore, Okinawa and Saigon. Everywhere except here. Here in Taiwan there has been a difference. That difference has been you and the control exerted over the underworld by your organization."

Whyte nodded thoughtfully as Stevens spoke. "And you'd like us to work the same miracle in the other cities of Asia?"

"If it can be done."

Whyte sat on the table edge next to Stevens. "Intriguing idea," he said. "What do you think, Alan?"

"It can't be done," Phillips said. "We have no influence, no leverage in those cities."

"But we would if we had the cooperation of the U.S. Government," Whyte said. "American money is the dominant force in Asia right now. Anyone in a position to channel the flow of that money is in a position to exert influence."

"We desperately need to get control of the situation," said Stevens. "If we can't, the underworld of Asia will become increasingly powerful. One day it could possibly compromise the entire American mission."

A flush of excitement came over Bryan Whyte. These were exactly the words he had wanted to hear from Stevens, exactly the invitation he had been waiting for to extend his vision of the Omega Chi over all of Asia.

Watching Whyte, carefully attuned to his every nuance, Phillips guessed this emotion and it frightened him. "Don't overestimate what we can do, Bryan," he cautioned. "These gangs will fight us every step of the way. It could be very costly."

"We must show them that it is in their best interests not to fight us," he said firmly. Then he looked at Stevens with a challenge in his eyes. "How far will you back us up?"

"All the way. Privately, that is. Officially we don't have a thing to do with you."

"Go over it one more time, please," King Lu said without looking up from the water buffalo he was leisurely sketching on a large scratch pad before him. He was sitting in the semidarkness of a conference room at a table opposite Bryan Whyte. Samuel Yin and Mark Taylor were also seated at the table but neither had spoken during the course of the half-hour meeting.

Whyte was very tired. He had been up all night talking to Taylor and Phillips, then he had flown to Hong Kong to present the idea to King Lu. King was intrigued but annoyingly cautious. He had asked Whyte to go over it again and again.

"The situation is like this," Whyte began once more in Mandarin. "The war and all the money that is pouring into Asia to fight it has caused a very unstable condition in the underworld of Asia, as you well know. Numerous gangs are fighting one another over this money, putting the big squeeze on the various American installations and generally creating a very unhealthy atmosphere."

"Yes?"

"The U.S. Government is very alarmed by this situation. They want stability and order in the countries of Free Asia. Therefore, they would be happy if we—the Omega Chi and the Green Society—brought all these underworld factions under our control."

"How?"

"By regulating the flow of squeeze from the U.S. presence. By saying where American servicemen can take R&R and where they cannot. By being able to say who gets construction contracts and who does not. By aiming all U.S. business into the coffers of the Greens and their allies and away from anyone who makes themselves our enemy."

"And why should we want to do this?"

Whyte was sick of going over and over the same scenario and the exasperation showed in his voice. "Because it will be to all our benefit. The Greens will become more powerful than they have been since the fall of the Mainland. The Omega Chi will get its cut and will be able to use its relationship with the Greens to expand its business interests in half a dozen market areas. The U.S. will get stability and order and, through us, a certain control over the Asian underworld. We will all have the satisfaction of knowing that we are creating a condition that will aid the war effort and help fight Communism and make another small step toward the return to the Mainland. . . ."

King kept drawing.

"Above all, it is an extraordinary opportunity and one must always take advantages of one's opportunities. That is the number one maxim of the Green Society."

King continued sketching. "I see many problems."

"What problems?" Whyte demanded in exasperation.

"There will be stiff resistance. In Manila, the Fortune of Man gang is more powerful than our ally, the Ah Ching Tong. In Saigon, the Greens are firmly in control but they are under the leadership of 'Pockmarked' Hwang, who is a renegade and my sworn enemy for nearly twenty years. In Hong Kong, the underworld is under the control of the Triads, who have graciously granted me asylum in their territory all these years and who I must be careful not to offend. None of these groups are likely to accept your plan without a major war."

"There need not be a war. There need not be any bloodshed. We have the power. It has been given us by the U.S. authority. All we have to do is exert it skillfully. These are businessmen. They will listen to reason."

King was expressionless. "It's very bold."

"Yes."

"So bold it approaches recklessness."

"You don't like it."

"On the contrary, I do like it—as much of it as I understand. Are you sure your government will support us?"

"I'm positive. They're the ones who came to me with the suggestion. Stevens says we can even have the assistance of the CIA if we need it."

"I will send invitations to all our competitors in Asia, suggesting it would be to their advantage to unite under our hegemony. When they refuse, as they most certainly will, you can go to them under a flag of truce and try to convince them otherwise. If they refuse again, we will have to take other measures."

"Good," Whyte said. "Let's get started right away." He got up to leave.

"Little Brother." King finally looked up from his drawing.

"Yes?"

"Understand that, once started on this course, we can't back away when we meet difficulties. If we begin, our face will be on the line and we will have to finish it—or die in the process."

"I understand, Elder Brother."

Whyte and Phillips were on the morning China Airlines flight to Manila a week later. As King Lu had predicted, the proposal that the gangs of Asia unite under the overlordship of the Green Society and Omega Chi had hardly been greeted with enthusiasm. Only in Singapore, Okinawa and Bangkok did they get some positive reaction and a definite agreement to begin friendly negotiations later in the fall. In Hong Kong, Manila and Saigon—the places where American money flowed in largest quantity and the need for control was the greatest—the suggestion was bitterly rejected.

Manila, some six hundred miles due south of Taipei, was chosen as the first target. It was under the control of a vicious Filipino gang called the Fortune of Man, which had parasitically fed off the American presence ever since the end of the Second World War. The gang's main host was Clark Air Base, just outside the city, which was the largest U.S. installation in Asia. Here, the Fortune of Man stole supplies, furnished all the base's civilian employees, demanded payments for protection and controlled gambling, prostitution, the black market and every politician within a radius of a hundred miles. Since the big Vietnam build-up, its squeeze had become so tight that it was said that a U.S. plane could not take off or land without the permission of the gang.

At a strategy session before leaving, Taylor, who had been briefed by Bamcheck of the CIA, briefed Whyte on the overall situation in Manila. "The city has traditionally been run by two big organizations," he said. "One is the Chinese Ah Ching Tong, which controls things among the city's large Chinese population, and the other, more powerful one is the Filipino Fortune of Man. Until 1962, the Filipino gang was run by an American named Hiram Rockwell. A former American who stayed on after the war and built himself an empire. He practically owned the Macapagal administration."

Whyte nodded. He remembered the story. "Who took his place when he was deported?"

"Rockwell's most treacherous lieutenant, the man you are going to meet. His name is Antonio Sanchez."

"What should I expect?"

"A monster. A man with no class at all and no loyalty to the United States, the Philippines or anything else except his own personal greed. Last week, in fact, the guy put the squeeze on the Clark base commander for a flat thirty percent."

"You're not serious? Thirty percent?"

"Yes."

"Unbelievable."

"The man is a menace. He has to be brought under control."

"What about the Ah Chings?"

"As allies of the Greens, obviously it would be to our advantage to have them in control of the city. But Bamcheck does not think that would be possible without a major war."

"Our problem then is to convince this Sanchez to ease up and accept our authority."

Taylor did not look optimistic. "It won't be easy, Bryan. You're going to have to play it very tough."

As Whyte, Phillips and their three Green Gang bodyguards drove through the streets of Manila, Phillips commented humorlessly that the passing scene resembled some Hollywood version of Dodge City in the 1880s. The city had the highest rate of murder, robbery and kidnapping in the world. With absolutely no restrictions on fire-arms, every other citizen seemed to wear a pistol strapped to his waist for protection. In the first two hours in town, they witnessed a holdup and two minor shoot-outs. Not once did they see a policeman.

That evening they went to the Palacio Hotel in down-town Manila for the prearranged meeting with Antonio Sanchez. The gangster was waiting for them in the hotel dining room with two Filipino bodyguards and two strik-ingly beautiful French women hanging on his arms like permanent appendages. He was a fat, dark-skinned man with two long, intersecting scars on his right cheek and a carefully trimmed pencil moustache. Phillips immediately thought the man could be Randy Ortega twenty years and one hundred pounds from now.

Sanchez took one look at the two Omega Chi, threw back his head and roared with laughter. "You are chil-dren! They send children to talk to me. You waste my time, little ones."

"I was told that Antonio Sanchez was a serious man," Whyte began stiffly as they joined the group at the table. "I have come in hopes that we might do serious business."

Sanchez's beady eyes danced merrily. "And why should I do business with you? What could you possibly have to interest Antonio Sanchez? I should spank you and send you back to your dung-heap of an island."

Whyte did not react to the insult. Instead he smiled and poured himself a drink from a bottle of mineral water on the table. "Let's be frank a moment, Mr. Sanchez," he said. "It is well known that your income comes almost entirely from squeezing Clark and the U.S. Naval installa-tions to the south."

"And what if it does?"

Whyte sipped the water. "Mr. Sanchez, we represent an American-owned business corporation that has been asked to regulate that squeeze, to withhold that money from you as we see fit and, if necessary, start it flowing into the hands of your enemies. Either you will accept this authority or we will simply put an end to your greed once and for all."

The face of Antonio Sanchez became a sudden mask of rage. His eyes bulged in their sockets and a rivulet of drool made its way from the corner of his mouth to the cleft of his chin. "You dare . . ."

Whyte did not blink. "Yes, I do," he said. "I make this demand on the highest authority of the United States Government. You will comply with it, my friend, or you have seen your last American dollar. You will cooperate with us or the U.S. Government will put all its power behind the Ah Chings to make war on you and wipe you from the face of the earth."

Sanchez's whole body was trembling. He had never been spoken to in this manner by anyone, let alone a mere youth, in a business situation. He slammed his fist on the table and spit on his plate. "I will have your testicles cut off and stuffed in your mother's mouth, you son of a donkey's whore. . . ."

Whyte let Sanchez rave on. He had seen enough. He concluded that it would be impossible to do business with this unprincipled and untrustworthy buffoon; nothing could be done here until the man was eliminated from the scene. He nodded to Phillips, and the two of them stood up. "There is nothing more to talk about," Whyte said civilly.

As they started to leave, Sanchez made a little gesture as if to stop them. But they continued walking. "I will not be threatened by children!" he shouted after them.

By the time they were back in Taipei, all American squeeze to the Sanchez people had ceased and was being paid instead to the Ah Ching Tong—which, at King Lu's request, had been steadily moving its forces into battle positions for the past week. Within twenty-four hours, a bloody war broke out between the Ah Chings and the Fortune of Man.

Sanchez was assassinated while on his way to a meeting with the commander of Clark Air Base. By the end of September, the Ah Chings were in total control of the area around Clark and the Fortune of Man—already a shadow of its former self—agreed to pay tribute to the Ah Ching Tong and the Tong's overlord, the Green Society.

Georgie Warner gently pulled back the curtain of his hotel room window and gazed down on the crowded Kowloon street. Ten stories below he could see a living stream of R&R American servicemen moving snakelike from bar to bar. He watched a moment, then sat back on the bed. The sight of them and his knowledge of the lucrative business they represented only heightened his sense of frustration and failure.

The underworld of Hong Kong was composed of a hierarchy of gangs known collectively in the West as the "Triad"—a name often mistakenly used to refer to the entire Chinese underworld. This organization, more properly called the "Heaven on Earth Society," used a triangle representing heaven, earth and man as its symbol. It originated in the seventeenth century as an anti-Manchu secret society based in a monastery near Foochow in Fukien Province. In the mid-nineteenth century, it took political refuge in the new British Crown Colony and more or less stayed ever since. Over the next hundred years, it developed into an efficient and very orderly criminal league which maintained a fairly constant peace operating with the grudging acceptance of the British colonial authorities. The American build-up since 1965, however, had dramatically upset the delicate balance that had always existed within the Triad. With the majority of the hundreds of thousands of Americans in Asia taking their leaves in the bars and whorehouses of Hong Kong, there was a sudden bonanza available that instigated a stampede for profit and dominance among several factions. The traditional peace within the Triad soon broke into open civil warfare, firebombings, executions and kidnappings—with American servicemen right in the middle.

The chances of convincing these factions to quit

squabbling and accept Omega Chi-Green overlordship seemed less than auspicious. The Triads were all from South China and thus had an instinctive mistrust of the Greens and all other wheat-eating Northern Chinese. They also pledged no allegiance to the Kuomintang and its zealous determination to return to the Mainland. And since there were no American bases in Hong Kong, they received no direct American squeeze which could be used to blackmail them. Besides all this, the Triads had graciously given asylum to King Lu and Tu Yueh-sen after the Nationalists fell in '49; King's taking part in an attempt to usurp their authority now would seem the basest form of ingratitude—a quality particularly loathsome to any Chinese.

Nonetheless, some measure of control of Hong Kong was essential to Whyte's master plan and he was determined to make it the next stage of his campaign. Because Taylor and Phillips were still busy straightening out the situation in Manila, Georgie Warner had been chosen as advance man.

"Your job is to talk to them and try to make them see reason," Whyte told him in a quick briefing at China Gate just before he left for the airport. "Remember that you have the power of the United States of America behind you. Use it forcefully but don't get needlessly tough. Don't make idle threats. This can be very counterproductive with these people. Make them see that it is in their interests to work with us, to cooperate with us in a spirit of friendship for our mutual benefit. The Chinese invented logic and they're very susceptible to it."

But the Triad leadership refused to be swayed by logic or anything else. Warner spent the better part of a week petitioning the individual rival leaders. No matter what argument or threat he brought forward, they all politely but firmly refused even to discuss it. To make his sense of failure even greater, he committed the tragic blunder of threatening a leader of the Triads in the name of the Greens and the man responded by dispatching a group of

Triad warriors to burn down the famous Hong Kong
mansion of King Lu, who, fortunately, happened to be in
Taipei at the time.

Warner spent the last twenty-four hours moving
from whorehouse to whorehouse trying to relieve the unbearable pressure he felt and pondering his next move.
Over and over again he asked himself: What would Bryan
Whyte do in such a situation? What manner of maneuver
would he come up with to manipulate the Triad leaders
into a peaceful settlement? Use the power of the U.S.
Government, he would probably say. Think big, he would
say. But what did that mean in a British Crown Colony
in which America had no power or authority? It was
simply an impossible situation.

Gradually his sense of incompetence gave way to
bitterness toward Whyte. More than anything he had
wanted to make good on this mission—to justify Whyte's
confidence in him and his ever-increasing salary. But
Whyte had given him the dirtiest, most hopeless job of the
entire campaign so that failure would be guaranteed.
Sometimes he thought Whyte liked to see him humiliated.
Why else did he so casually take Su Ling off his hands
without so much as a word of explanation? Why else did
he install him as head of a movie studio, for crissakes,
when he had no business competence whatsoever? Sometimes he thought he hated Bryan Whyte more than he
loved him, hated the constant pressure and expectations
of being in this new corporate Omega Chi just as he had
once hated the constant pressure and expectations of being
a missionary's son. All he really wanted was to be left
alone to his private vices.

Finally, he got drunk enough to call Whyte in Taipei.
He told him about the failure of his mission and the destruction of all of King Lu's Hong Kong property. There
was a long pause at the other end of the line. Then, very
cool and collected, Whyte said, "Assemble all the leaders
of the Triad. Tell them I would respectfully like to address
them one time and then I will never trouble them again."

"It won't do any good."

"Just arrange it."

Warner did it and now, as he got up again to look out the window, everything was in readiness. The leaders of the Triad were waiting in a banquet room of the hotel. Whyte had already arrived at the airport and his limousine would reach the hotel any minute. Warner looked at his watch again and decided it was time to go downstairs.

He got off the elevator at the Manchu Room and opened the door to peek inside. The leaders of the warring factions and their assorted entourages were there, each group in its own hostile corner. No one was speaking and it was obvious that if Whyte didn't arrive soon the whole room was going to erupt in violence. Whyte had to be out of his mind, Warner thought again. What possible argument was going to convince these greedy gangsters to accept his authority?

He went down to the lobby and waited until Whyte's limousine pulled up. Whyte strolled into the lobby with three Green bodyguards and spoke calmly to Warner. "Where are they?"

"Upstairs. Follow me."

"Are they all here?"

"They're all here and the atmosphere up there is cold as whale shit. Sure you wanta go through with this?"

Whyte didn't answer him. He seemed to be deep in thought. They walked upstairs and into the banquet room. The Triads watched in attentive silence. What was this young taipan possibly going to offer them?

Whyte stepped before the crowd of gangsters. He took a piece of paper from his suit pocket. Since the Triads spoke mostly Cantonese, he addressed them in English. "Gentlemen," he said, "beginning tomorrow morning at 9 A.M., Hong Kong will be off-limits to all American servicemen. Because of the unstable conditions here and your unwillingness to cooperate with us, all R&R leaves will henceforth be taken in Taipei, Bangkok and Singapore. This is the authorization signed by the U.S. commander in Saigon and approved by the commander of all U.S. Pacific Forces in Honolulu." He handed the paper to the Triad sitting nearest to him to pass around. "Thank you for your time."

As he turned to leave, the Triads gasped in confusion and disbelief.

Warner and the Greens followed him out of the hotel. They all got in the limousine together and went directly to the airport. In the car, Whyte winked and arched his eyebrows slyly. "You have to think big, Georgie. We *are* the United States."

"Is that paper for real?"

"No, it's a phony. But I could make it real given a week or so."

When they reached the airport, a delegation of Triads was waiting for them with the not-totally-unexpected news that there had been a sudden and dramatic change of heart regarding the petition of the Omega Chi and Green Society.

A limousine sped through the bustling Tran Hung Dao Boulevard three weeks later. Inside, Bryan Whyte and Mark Taylor were having a last-minute strategy session, giving themselves shots of confidence for the difficult meeting ahead. For months they had been scoring one success after another in Asia, and now they were ready to tackle the most crucial and most challenging stage of the campaign—Saigon.

They had flown into Tan Son Nhut late the day before and stayed the night in an old French colonial hotel near the airport. Floyd Harris met them for breakfast that morning and surprised them by being totally pessimistic about the outcome of their mission. Harris was now Saigon Provost Marshal, in charge of all U.S. intelligence operations within the metropolitan area. He was cranky and he looked weary and overweight as he gulped down two Bloody Marys before breakfast was served. "I've been briefed about your trip here," he said. "It's a waste of time. A good college try—but a complete waste of time."

Whyte felt Harris looking at him for a reaction but

he didn't give one. "How so?" he merely asked as he deliberately buttered a croissant.

"You're simply not going to get any cooperation out of these people."

"We've been successful everywhere else," Taylor said, arrogantly.

"It's different here. The Greens here are different. They have no loyalty to the order. There's nothing you can offer them and nothing you can use to threaten them. They're unprincipled and greedy and they have their fingers in every pie. Even if you established a relationship with Hwang, you'd never be able to trust him. You certainly would never be able to control him."

The underworld of Saigon in late 1966 was led by "Pockmarked" Hwang, a legendary Chinese gangster who had been the enforcer of the Green Gang and a partner of Tu Yueh-sen in the glory days of Shanghai. He had been in Saigon since his falling out with Tu over the Taipei massacre of 1947, but it wasn't until the big American build-up began that he suddenly found himself a major power again. Within one year, his monopoly on the bars, whorehouses and black market of Saigon and his squeeze on all commerce and the flow of all war materials had made him the wealthiest man in Southeast Asia.

Whyte knew it would be very difficult to convince this man to do business with them. The Omega Chi simply had no leverage here. Here, Hwang told the Americans what to do and when to do it and he had hundreds of them on his payroll. He had untold thousands of Chinese and Vietnamese gangsters in his organization—probably more manpower in the city than the Thieu government. The relationship with King Lu also meant nothing here: King and Hwang had disputed with one another for leadership of the Greens for nearly two decades and were the bitterest of enemies.

Harris was right, Whyte thought as their car maneuvered through the dense late morning traffic, it would be very difficult. . . .

The limo pulled up before an old walled mansion on

a tree-lined street just north of the National Assembly Hall. Whyte and Taylor got out and walked up to two armed Vietnamese guards at the gate. A gentle wind blew through a grove of palms that rose from behind the wall. "We're expected," Taylor said to them in English.

One guard leveled a machine gun at them while the other searched them. The man found Taylor's pearl-handled forty-five, smiled knowingly and handed it to his companion. The two Americans then followed the guards into the compound.

Hwang received them in his council room, which was painted a gaudy orange and was filled with cheap, tourist-stand wicker furniture. The gangster was in his late seventies and he looked even older. Old and ugly and crafty and beguiling.

"So you are the son of Billy Whyte," he said immediately in Mandarin. "I knew your father well in better days. I have heard that his son has become a powerful taipan on the Island of Taiwan. It is even said among some of the Greens that you are a *beizo*—a man of destiny to the Chinese people." He broke into giggles, exposing his few remaining teeth, all capped with gold.

This was Hwang's way of telling them that he did not accept the prophecy of the great Chuang-tzu and thus Whyte had no special hold over him. Whyte arched his eyebrow. He spoke back in Mandarin. "I bring greetings from your nephew, King Lu."

"I have not seen the little *tai-lo* for many years. I hope his health and fortune are intact and that he is enjoying his exile among the Triads."

"I also bring the respects of the Omega Chi and a hope that we might do business someday for our mutual profit."

Hwang poured three glasses of tea. "Now why should I, a successful but simple merchant, want to expand my business with an American partner? I am not a greedy man. I have more than enough in this city to satisfy my meager needs."

Whyte sipped from his tea, savored the unusually

sweet flavor of the Vietnamese blend, and swallowed. "Every businessman needs to think of growth. To cease to grow is to begin to die. We must all take advantage of our opportunities."

"This is so. But what opportunity could you possibly have to interest me?"

Whyte was experiencing a great discomfort in this old man's presence. There was an aura of evil about him that he had never sensed in another member of the Greens. It also threw him off guard for Hwang to come to the point so early in their first meeting: It was very un-Chinese. He sipped from the tea again and nodded to Taylor to play their hand.

Taylor lit a cigarette and blew the smoke in the air. He looked steadily at Hwang. "It is well known, Honored Uncle, that after the Chinese civil war, the remnants of the Third and Fifth Kuomintang Armies fled across the Yunnan border to the safety of northern Thailand. Ever since then, these troops—the Chinese Irregular Forces—have stayed in this remote area and continued to fight the Communists. To support their ongoing struggle, the leaders of these forces—General Li Wien-huan and General Tuan Shih-wen—have gone into the business of opium, which is widely cultivated in this particularly fertile part of the Golden Triangle and used as a currency.

"It is also known that many years ago Hwang went into business with these generals. They have since been the supplier for the raw opium which he converts into heroin and smuggles in small quantities around the world. Last year, Hwang and the generals went into a whole new business together: *jin chu,* marijuana, which the generals grow in great fields in Chiang Mei Province near the Burma border and which Hwang sells in staggering quantities to American GIs in Saigon. Since 1965, this *jin chu* business has given Hwang the greatest margin of profit of all his many businesses.

"It is further known that Hwang would like nothing more than to sell some of this huge crop in the increasingly profitable American market but is prevented from exporting it by the diligent American authorities, who watch any shipments out of Saigon very closely for contraband and would surely spot anything as bulky as *jin chu*. This is Hwang's dilemma. We offer him a solution."

Hwang's eyes narrowed into slits. He looked serious for the first time in the meeting. "It is said that the Omega Chi does not deal in the drug business."

"This is true," Taylor acknowledged. "We will not tolerate anyone dealing in drugs on the Island of Taiwan. We often cooperate with the Kuomintang in putting offenders in prison. However, we have a different attitude toward *jin chu*, which has been grown and used in China since the time of Confucius and is known to be harmless, even beneficial to the user. If Hwang is determined to pursue this business, we will help him because he is our uncle."

"What can you do?"

"We will let you use our protection, the U.S. military transportation system and whatever connections we can make in American colleges—which are becoming the greatest market for *jin chu*. It can be shipped without inspection to Keelung by sea and Taichung by air. From there we can guarantee its shipment via military transport to Travis Air Force Base outside San Francisco."

Hwang played thoughtfully with a hairy mole on his ancient pockmarked chin. His eyes gave a hint of the greed that was behind them.

"If you don't deal with us," Taylor continued, "your only other alternative to reach this market is the American underworld—the Mafia—and they take half of your profits right off the top because of the great risk involved. With us, there is no risk and you keep everything. Our sources tell us that with a continuous pipeline into the United States for *jin chu*, you could double your yearly net income. Do you comprehend that, my uncle? Double your income."

Hwang's eyes flashed and Whyte knew it was done. The old butcher would go for it. "And what exactly do you want in return for this service?"

"We want your friendship and brotherhood," Whyte

said. "We want your good faith and cooperation in the war against the Communists. We want you to deal, through us, with the American authority as various situations present themselves. We want you to unite with King Lu and the rest of the Greens in our effort to control Asia for our mutual benefit and noble purpose."

The old man blinked hard at the mention of King. He said nothing for several moments. Then he asked several questions and wanted an assurance that the arrangement would not call for him to take orders from King Lu. Satisfied, he broke into a larcenous grin and agreed to begin negotiations—provided everything they said about the *jin chu* was true.

When they were clear of the compound, Taylor put his hand on Whyte's shoulder. "Are you going to tell Harris or Stevens about the terms?"

"No," he answered. "They'll be surprised and delighted an agreement has been reached with Hwang. They won't ask about the terms. They won't even want to know about them."

Some weeks later, Whyte sat behind his large mahogany desk in his private office at China Gate. He was trying to dictate letters into a machine while being constantly interrupted by telephone calls. Outside, the air around the big house was damp and chilly and the immense wrought-iron front gate was already decorated with a Christmas wreath.

There was a light tap on the door then Ah Chin, Whyte's new private secretary, quietly entered. He was a recent business school graduate of Taiwan University and the son of one of Old Whyte's former *compradores* or Chinese business associates, on the Mainland. He was very efficient, but rather stuffy and humorless. The other Omega Chi referred to him as "the old maid."

"There is more update coming over the AP wire now, sir."

Whyte quickly got up and followed Ah Chin down the main hallway to the communications room. Here he had recently installed the most sophisticated business communications equipment available—including a telex, Xerox dry copiers, direct phone lines to branch offices in downisland and two wire news-service machines.

He picked up the AP print-out and read that the Chinese Red Guards had seized power in Tientsin and several other cities in the north. The Chinese Cultural Revolution had been raging for nearly a year now and at last seemed to be coming to some climax of national insanity.

He smiled. "They've finally gone off the deep end, Ah Chin."

"It certainly looks like it, sir."

"They're closing down their major cities."

"It's scary, sir."

"What do you think we should do?"

"Do, sir?"

"As businessmen. How should we react to this latest development?"

"Well, sir, it will no doubt cause a panic all over the Asian market. I suppose a smart businessman would wait until the smoke clears before making any other sizable investments."

"You're wrong, Ah Chin. This is the best possible investment climate for us. We have confidence that this Communist madness will never overrun Asia, therefore we buy cheap while everyone else is waiting for the smoke to clear." He smiled and put his hand on Ah Chin's shoulder. "We believe in something other than dollars and cents. This is our edge."

"Yes, sir," Ah Chin said and went back to the office feeling appropriately castigated.

Whyte walked farther down the hall past several offices filled with Chinese employees finishing up an early evening shift. After selling the old Omega Chi House last year, he had moved the Omega Chi corporate headquarters to these rooms. Any time of the day or night this part of the house always seemed to be humming with activity.

He entered a large room that had once been the gymnasium of the estate and was now refurbished into a luxurious council room. In the center of the room was a round table surrounded by five chairs—one for each of the five directors of the Omega Chi. In direct view of the table and taking up one whole wall of the room was a map of Asia dotted with dozens of tiny blue pins.

Over the past several months, Whyte had been frantically investing their new income and new influence to expand their holdings all over Asia. Each pin in the map represented a place where the Omega Chi now had a business interest: a construction company in Saigon, a hotel in Manila, bars in Okinawa, a shipping company in Singapore, an export house in Penang. Djakarta, Bangkok, Phnom Penh. A budding empire.

Ah Chin came in behind him and handed Whyte the pile of telephone messages that had accumulated in the few minutes since he had left his desk. "The Reverend Warner is holding for you on line three. I think it's about a donation to his mission."

Even though Whyte did not particularly believe in the presence of a divine being, he went way out of his way to be supportive of all the missionaries of Taipei. But he was investing every penny he could get his hands on these days and he simply had no cash to spare. "Tell him I'm busy but that I'll get back to him later in the week."

"Yes, sir."

"By the way, is Su Ling back yet?"

"Yes, sir. Hours ago."

"Christ, I've lost all track of the time."

He walked farther down the hallway to the master bedroom, a spacious wing that in daylight had a sweeping view of the city and the mountains to the south. Su Ling was in bed reading a magazine.

"I'm sorry," he apologized in Mandarin. "Work, work, work."

"You look tired."

"I'm not."

"You should rest."

"Maybe after Christmas. There's too much to do

now. Too many opportunities that cannot be ignored."

Su Ling looked unusually petulant. In English, she said, "Muchee tlobah. Bigee headache. Why so you care?"

Whyte smiled and sat on the bed beside her. "Because I was born to it. Just as you were born to be worshiped by men. And because it is necessary."

She was not convinced. "Why necessary?"

"I'm serving my country."

"Bah."

"No, Su Ling. It's true. We are the fine line between order and anarchy. Between the corruption of Asia and what America is trying to do for Asia. We are a vital part of a noble cause." He repeated this last sentence in Mandarin so she would better understand it.

She hugged his body and put her head on his lap.

He looked down at her, caressing the soft, silky black hair with his fingertips. "You don't understand, do you?"

She shook her head. "No. But you are a great, good man. That I understand."

Whyte kissed her on the forehead and chin and nose. Then they lay on the bed together and Su Ling told him about her day at the studio.

No matter how hard he pushed her, she was not going to make it as a *tai tai*. She was worthless as a hostess and so intimidated by the servants that she spent all of her time in the house hiding in the bedroom. But at the studio it was a different matter. There, she worked tirelessly and had already completed her first film. Whyte intended to spend so much money publicizing it that in six months' time hers would be the most famous female face on the Island. The idea of deifying the woman he loved deeply excited him.

The phone rang. Whyte answered it and spoke to Mark Taylor for fifteen minutes. Su Ling fell asleep. When he hung up, the phone rang again and he quickly unplugged it. Then he pulled the covers up around Su Ling and went in the adjoining bathroom to shower and shave. He undressed and looked at himself in the mirror, experiencing a rush of contentment at being utterly alone and unpressured for the first time that day. He paused, examining the face in the mirror, noting its full maturity —the face of a man at least ten years older than twenty-two. He studied the wide, commanding eyes, the attractive scar on his chin, the aristocratic jawline, the dark hair now fashionably cut to touch the top of his ears. It was a good face, he thought. A proper face for a man who was well on his way to being the most wealthy and powerful American in Asia.

11

IN MARCH, THE FIRST HEAVY RAINS OF 1967 ARRIVED. The gray skies poured for two steady weeks, flooding the paddy fields and riverbeds, eroding the mountain terraces and sloping suburban tea crops to a soupy muck, generally bringing commerce in the city to a standstill. It was the earliest summer monsoon in living memory and the numerous Chinese fortunetellers, soothsayers and astrologers all shook their heads and agreed that it was an omen of much trouble in the year—perhaps many years—ahead.

Alan Phillips was mindful of this omen as he ran through waves of heavy rain to the front steps of China Gate. He slid his umbrella in the slot by the entrance and vigorously shook the water from his raincoat. Ah Chin let him in and he followed the secretary through the foyer, down the long stone main hallway of the mansion.

Whyte was waiting in the office area. He noticed the drawn and worried look on Phillips's baby face at once but didn't comment on it. He embraced him, feeling the tension in his body. Ah Chin left them alone. "Welcome back," Whyte said, taking a seat behind the desk.

He smiled broadly when Phillips made no move to speak. "I was by to see Doris yesterday. She looks like she swallowed a medicine ball. You're going to have one hell of a son."

Phillips had been married only six months but his bride was already hugely pregnant. True to his principles, he had remained a virgin right up to his wedding night. The universal comment about the instant pregnancy was that Phillips was "making up for lost time."

"I haven't seen her yet. I came straight from the airport."

"How did everything go?"

"Well, as I cabled you. The Hop Sung Tong has used the money and influence we've loaned them very wisely to consolidate their financial control of the Chinese communities of Honolulu, San Francisco and Seattle. I was very impressed with your Mr. Chu Yung-liu and what he's been able to do in just one month. The old guy is tough as nails and has a mind like an abacus."

"There was trouble in Vancouver?"

"Yes. The Suey Sing Tong is still very strong there. They're stubborn and individualistic and they've resisted the intrusion of the Hop Sungs in their territory. If we continue to push it, we may have the first tong war in fifty years there."

"Then let's ease up. Three out of four isn't bad. You've done very well. You can afford to relax and forget business for a while. Go home and spend some time with your wife. You look worn out."

Phillips pulled up a chair and collapsed into it. "Bryan, when are we going to start channeling some of this squeeze money into our charity programs? Aside from the new wing to the Ta Tung Orphanage, we haven't done a thing."

Whyte leaned back and arched an eyebrow. Ever since he had convinced Phillips to quit college and stay with the Omega Chi, he often detected a certain testiness and challenge in his manner. He was getting tired of it.

"We've been investing that money in business opportunities that are just too good to pass up. That has to come first right now. Surely you know this better than anyone."

"What happened to our big plan to establish a major relocation facility for Vietnamese refugees?"

"It's still in the works. But that sort of thing takes time. We've been spending our time expanding our financial base so that someday we can build a dozen relocation centers if we want to. You know all this. Why do you look so worried?"

"Because I *am* worried!" He shot to his feet and began pacing in front of Whyte. "There's trouble brewing for us in the States, Bryan. Something is happening back there and you have to experience it to know what I'm talking about. This antiwar stuff is becoming a way of life for some people."

"I appreciate that, Alan. I read the papers too. But it's nothing I'm going to let affect us or the operation of our business."

Phillips paced over to a window and watched the rain beat against it. "I saw Casy while I was in San Francisco. Did you know he's playing full time with one of those rock 'n' roll bands now? He's really in this hippie thing and he's changed so much I hardly knew what to say to him. . . ."

"Is that what's bothering you? Christ, you have to expect that from Casy. He's an artist and very impressionable and he's bound to pick up on whatever happens to be the rage. This time next year he'll be on to something else."

"I don't think it's that simple."

"Alan, the name of Omega Chi is known and respected all over Asia. The U.S. Government depends on us. Our business is growing by leaps and bounds. We've never been in a stronger financial position. The doors to a thousand opportunities are open to us. What is there you can possibly find to worry about?"

Phillips turned around to face him. He looked positively hostile. "It's this war. It's going so badly that it's changing the way our own countrymen see us over here. I've never in my life experienced anything like it. Everywhere I looked I saw pictures of long-haired college war protesters and Vietnamese babies horribly burned by napalm. Everywhere I went I heard talk about the 'morality' of the American role here. They talk about us being colonialists here, of us supporting corrupt little dictators who can only rule by martial law and American guns, of us *exploiting* the people of Asia. . . ."

"That's just Communist bullshit propaganda," Whyte said, "and you know it."

"The talk really bothers me, Bryan. Confuses me. We're vulnerable to these arguments. No one is making more money off this war than we are."

Whyte dismissed the whole thing with a wave of his hand. "Let me worry about the criticism," he said. "We've never done anything dishonorable. We've always acted in the best interests of the people of Asia. As a matter of fact, we're going to break ground on the new refugee center next month. I was just waiting for you to get back to surprise you."

But Phillips was not to be comforted. "There's going to be big trouble for us," he said again and his persistence troubled Whyte. He knew Phillips had a sixth sense about these things.

The trouble that Phillips feared came within two months of the time he predicted it, and when it did, it came in a completely unexpected, almost inconceivable fashion.

On the first day of May, 1967, a U.S. Government courier arrived at China Gate and presented Bryan Whyte with a brown manila envelope. When he opened it, Whyte discovered that he was being invited to testify before a special U.S. Senate Foreign Relations subcommittee in Washington D.C. under the chairmanship of one Senator John Randolph, Democrat of Pennsylvania. The committee was hearing testimony about the conduct of the war in Vietnam and had expanded its investigation to look into certain "irregular" business practices of American businessmen operating in the Far East.

Whyte was not, at first, overly concerned. He had read in the American press about this committee's probing of black-marketing and other illegal financial dealings in Asia. It was started by a case involving certain amateurish Army sergeants in Japan who had built themselves a fortune out of skimming service club slot machines. It was not surprising that the name of Omega Chi would come up in any kind of investigation into recent American enterprise in the Orient. He had actually expected something like this sooner or later and was sure he had the necessary pull to get out of it: He was, after all, in secret partnership with the U.S. Government.

He sent Phillips to see Ambassador Stevens and ask him to personally intervene. But Stevens had only bad news to report. He had already made several calls back to the States, from which he learned that a group of dovish senators on this particular committee were eager to use any means at hand to turn public opinion against the war. "These are very powerful and very ruthless men," the ambassador told Phillips, "and are not to be underestimated. Randolph is their leader and we exercise no control over him."

Phillips felt his heart sink. "But why us? Why are they singling us out?"

The ambassador looked as grave as Phillips had ever seen him. "I suspect someone has been feeding Randolph a great deal of information about your activities. Maybe someone from your own organization. He seems to know a lot of details—about your relationship with King Lu, for instance. Frankly, this thing could explode in all our faces. I think they're after blood and I'm worried as hell about it!"

* * *

Rumors of the subpoena spread throughout the grapevine of Asia by the next day. The day after that Captain Floyd Harris flew in from Saigon to meet with Whyte.

During lunch at the U.S. Officers' Club, Harris said he had been on the phone to Washington about this matter for the last thirty-six hours. "We have a good source inside the Randolph Committee itself and we have a general idea of the information they have. It's mostly stuff that would be very difficult to substantiate."

Whyte did not touch the food before him. "Do you know how they might have come by this information?"

"Probably some disaffected insider."

"Who?"

Harris looked Whyte squarely in the eye. "We think it may be John Casy."

"I don't believe it."

"It figures."

"How?"

"We've had him under observation. He has close ties to numerous radical and anarchist groups at Berkeley."

"I don't care. I still don't believe it. I don't believe it for one second."

"Don't believe it then. But tell me who else you know in a position to be in contact with Randolph."

Whyte said nothing.

"How much does Casy know about . . . ?"

"Everything. He's a full member of the board."

There were several awkward moments of silence.

Harris broke them. "In any case, it looks like you're going to have to ride this one out. It could get rough. Under no circumstances are you to admit that you have any working relationship with the CIA or me or Ambassador Stevens or anyone in an official capacity. Don't acknowledge any ties to anyone in the Green Pang or any tong anywhere in the world. The important thing to remember is that they don't have anything concrete on you. But they can suggest enough to spook you if you let them. You have to play it very, very cool. Do you understand?"

* * *

The first member of the press corps to hear of the subpoena was David Butler, who still always tried to keep an eye and ear open to the goings on of China Gate. As soon as he heard the news, he verified it with his sources in Washington D.C. then called Whyte for an interview.

Whyte agreed to it. He knew Butler had been following his rise very closely and was probably preparing a major story on him. Such a story right now would make his position even more precarious. He had to convince Butler to back off once again.

Over the years, the two of them had developed a very curious relationship. In many ways, they found each other to be surprisingly alike. Both grew up in small, patriotic American communities. Both fundamentally believed in the American system and the American goal in Asia. Both were ambitious and driven by a sense of personal destiny.

But they violently disagreed about the role of the press in the society they both idealized. Butler believed that a vigorous, free press was the one element that protected America from the ever-present dangers of monopoly and fascism. Whyte, while he paid lip service to the theory of a free press, believed that in practice the press was actually more of a hindrance to the system because it so often served to block the course of capitalism and free enterprise, which he believed had its own built-in morality and a natural system of checks and balances. They argued about this many times over dinner at China Gate in late 1966; it was an important argument to them and it created a very subtle competition and a certain enmity.

Once more face to face with Whyte across the big desk in the den of China Gate, Butler could barely suppress his pleasure and excitement. "Why do you think Senator Randolph has called you at this particular time?" he asked.

"I suspect some vindictive business competitor has fed the senator false information about the Omega Chi."

Butler scribbled on his notepad. "Do you expect the

committee to ask you questions about your alleged association with the Chinese underworld?"

Whyte arched his eyebrow. "As you know, we have
no more association with the underworld than any other
company doing business in Asia."

Butler smirked at that. "Will you be able to comply
with the subpoena?"

"I can't answer that at the present time. There are
certain problems that might force me to seek a postpone-
ment. . . ."

Butler continued asking questions and scribbling into
the notepad.

Finally, Whyte said, "David, I want to ask you, as a
friend, not to write a story about this right now."

Butler stiffened in his chair. He was ready for this.
Whyte had gotten away with it once. It would never happen again. "No," he said.

Whyte took a deep breath and let it out slowly.
"David, if you persist in this, your press credentials will
be revoked by the Nationalist Chinese Government and
you will be detained on criminal libel charges as long as
I deem necessary."

Butler stopped writing. He glared indignantly at
Whyte. "You can't do that. Do you think for a minute that
my bureau . . ."

"I've already spoken to your bureau chief in Hong
Kong. He agrees with me that such a story would be
. . . inadvisable."

"You can't do this! There are some things that are
sacred, things that are immune from your crooked ma-
neuverings. Just who do you think you are?"

Whyte shoved the phone on the desk toward Butler.
"Call your bureau chief in Hong Kong."

Butler stared at the phone. He knew Whyte did not
bluff. He started to protest again but was so choked up he
could not speak. He stood up and stormed angrily from
the room.

Whyte sat at his desk for a long time after Butler left.
There were times when he enjoyed destroying a competi-

tor in a tense business negotiation. But he got no pleasure at all out of breaking an idealistic man like David Butler.

Old Whyte put in a worried call that evening to Washington D.C. He spoke to an old friend in the State Department who was sympathetic to the China lobby and Chiang Kai-shek but who also knew Randolph personally. The man was even more pessimistic than Stevens and Harris. He said that the Randolph Committee was gearing up for a full-scale investigation into the American black market in Asia and was out for more than just publicity. It was going to fish for an indictment against Bryan Whyte. "My advice to your son would be to find an excuse not to appear," he said. "Get a doctor to certify he can't make the trip. Anything. That committee will eat him alive!"

A parade of callers made the trip to China Gate over the next few days to show the support of the American Community. The Reverend Warner came with an ecumenical group from the missionaries. Crusty old Kurt Perkins, taipan of China Petroleum, came and denounced Senator Randolph as a "dung-eating Commie traitor." There were also visits from Captain Thomas, the Navy doctor who ran the Naval Medical Research Unit (NAMRU), his wife, who was principal of the American School, and Professor Eric Johnson, the Asian scholar who ran Princeton University's Taipei extension campus. So many people came with so many dour expressions that Su Ling—who did not understand anything of what was going on—became very frightened and stayed close to Whyte at all times.

King Lu and his entire entourage came several times to discuss the situation. The Green chieftain also seemed particularly worried by the subpoena; he didn't understand the workings of the U.S. Government and was flabbergasted that there was a faction within it openly working against the war effort. He walked arm in arm with Whyte around the gardens of China Gate for hours.

King's advice was succinct and firm: "Don't go. There is no way they can force you to go. The Kuomintang will protect you. No one can make you leave this island."

At the end of the week, the Omega Chi had a board meeting to make a final decision. They sat around the big table in the council room of China Gate trying to decide what the committee could know and what kind of threat it posed to them.

"We don't know what they know until we know who gave them the information," said Taylor. "I just can't believe it was Casy. Even if he has become that much of a bastard, why would he want to bite the hand that supports him? Anyway, he hasn't been directly involved with us since high school. He doesn't know anything that specific."

"Yes, he does," said Georgie Warner gravely. "John and I have never been out of letter communication. I've kept him fully informed of everything. I'm sorry, but I was specifically asked to do it."

By this time Phillips was near panic. "I knew there was trouble coming. It's going to be worse than we can imagine. There must be a way out of it. Take King's advice. Don't go. They're going to make us look like criminals!"

But Whyte was strangely fatalistic about the whole affair. In fact, as the warnings became more dire and pessimistic, he found himself becoming invigorated by the challenge of it all. Perhaps there was some hidden opportunity here to be taken advantage of. . . . "Let's not worry any more about it, Alan. I think I should testify. It's been three years since I've been to the States and maybe I need to see for myself what's happening over there. Send a telegram and say we are most eager to appear in front of the committee. Tell them it will be an honor and a privilege."

Ignoring the disapproving glare of the bell captain, John Casy stepped into an elevator of the St. Francis Hotel and pushed a button for the fourth floor. He glanced quickly at the piece of paper to make sure he had the right number then smiled again to himself. "MacArthur Suite," he said aloud. "Wouldn't you know it?"

Casy's life had taken him so far from Bryan Whyte and the old days on Taiwan that he wondered if they could possibly find anything in common to talk about anymore. Since they had last seen each other in 1964, Casy had quit school, moved with a group of other dropouts into an old Victorian house in the Haight-Ashbury district—paid for entirely out of his monthly Omega Chi stipend—and more or less became a full-time unemployed rock 'n' roll musician. He'd been dreading this meeting—and the disapproval he knew would come with it—for the past week, but there was no way to avoid it: Whyte was coming to San Francisco specifically to see him.

When Ah Chin opened the door and led him into the suite, Casy saw Whyte sitting in a chair behind an antique desk calmly giving orders into a telephone. It was the same scene he had witnessed a thousand times in high-school days. He looked very dynamic, very much in command— General MacArthur himself couldn't have looked any more so—and for a brief moment all of Casy's experience and revelations of the past three years vanished; he was in the presence of a leader for whom he would unquestioningly lay down his life.

Whyte noticed him and quickly begged off the phone. He was momentarily thrown by Casy's shoulder-length hair and ragged army fatigues but he recovered at the sight of Casy's familiar, gentle smile. "Jesus wept," he said cheerfully. "You look like an ugly girl."

Casy laughed. "Goddamn capitalist," he struck back. "I hear you own Asia now."

"That's a vicious lie. I only own half of Asia."

"Well, you're young yet."

Whyte reached over and pinched Casy's hair, as if to make sure it was real. "Has your old man seen you lately?"

"Not lately."

"Poor old Colonel Casy. He'd have a fucking coronary at the sight of you."

Casy kept smiling but his eyes saddened. "My old man is flying strategic bombers over Vietnam. He wrote me off a long time ago. Everyone from the old days has written me off except the Omega Chi. Thanks for the money, Bryan. It's been very generous of you to keep me on for doing nothing."

"You're entitled," Whyte said. "And there's a hell of a lot more where that came from. It's waiting for you anytime you want to come back and be part of us again."

Casy didn't react to this. He just kept smiling and looking at Whyte. "It's really good to see you again, Bryan."

"Look, I've only got one day. I want to see it all. I want to experience the whole crazy circus here and I want you to be my guide."

Casy did it. He showed him everything there was to see. He took him to Haight-Ashbury to sit on a street corner and watch the freaks go by. He took him to a large Victorian mansion on Golden Gate Park where the Grateful Dead were jamming. He took him to a be-in tribal gathering in the park, where they smoked *jin chu* and drank wine and went barefoot in the cool grass. That night they went to the Avalon Ballroom for a concert by the Jefferson Airplane and Country Joe and the Fish. When Casy saw that Whyte did not seem to disapprove of all this, he introduced him to his friends as a "powerful American capitalist in Asia"—which, of course, was taken as the most outrageous of put-ons.

After the concert, they smoked more *jin chu,* bought more wine and went back to the park to drink it. As they got progressively higher, Casy became obsessed with the idea of making his friend see the beauty of what was happening all around them, of making him understand the remarkable evolutionary changes that were taking place in his consciousness. He told Whyte he had been experimenting with a hallucinogenic drug called LSD and it was changing his life. He said it had given him a vision of peace and oneness and God that was within him and all mankind. "For the first time in my life I see things clearly, Bryan," he said. "I'm not floundering anymore. I'm finally ready to be an artist."

Golden Gate Park was now dark except for the light of the quarter moon and a hundred tips of a hundred *jin chu* sticks flickering like fireflies in the distance. Casy put his hands on Whyte's shoulders, as if to start shaking him to his senses. "I want you to drop acid with me, Bryan. I want you to see what I see, to understand what I understand. I want you to get out of yourself and see what's real."

Whyte recoiled from his touch. The tension of his body told Casy he was not really going along with this at all.

Casy removed his hands from Whyte, smiled and reached down for the wine bottle. "Bryan, there's a revolution going on here. A revolution of love and brotherhood. It's going to be as if the whole world is in the Omega Chi."

Casy offered him the bottle and he took a drink. Whyte thought of how he had always dreamed that Casy would use his gifts to chronicle and glorify the Omega Chi and its exploits. He was jealous. "And you're going to be the artist who captures this revolution in words and music?"

"No," he said and stared at Whyte in drunken seriousness. "The words and music are going to *lead* the revolution. That's why I wanted you to hear the Dead and Airplane today—so you could see for yourself the magic in the music. Bryan, I've got that kind of music in me. I swear I do. I've got these incredible rhythms—Chinese rhythms—in my head and I hear them all the time. I hear them right now. Someday I'm gonna get that sound together and when I do it's going to have more power and impact than any artist has ever had with mere words alone. . . ."

Whyte was truly uncomfortable now. He understood now what Phillips had been talking about. What Phillips had seen and what Whyte was now seeing was that vast postwar baby boom coming into maturity and creating its own culture—a culture of equal parts hedonism, idealism and rebellion. In a way he envied Casy for being swept up in the drama and pageantry of all this, but everything he saw filled him with doom. There was no way he could see this revolution except as an obstacle to the fulfillment of his own destiny.

The two friends walked to a big tree on the edge of a football field and sat at the base of it, passing the bottle back and forth. "For a recording career you'll need money. Lots of money. This would be a good investment for the Omega Chi."

"I've taken too much of your money already."

"I'm not talking about a handout, you goddamn beatnik. I'm talking about an investment. I have confidence in you. I always have."

"I don't think I can accept Omega Chi money anymore." Casy hesitated. "It's money squeezed out of the misery of the Asian people."

Whyte felt he had been hit in the stomach with a baseball bat. Up until now he had not taken any of this rebellion personally. Maybe it *was* Casy selling them out, after all.

"I'm sorry," Casy immediately said. "Christ, I'm drunk. I don't want to talk about the war or anything we're gonna fight about. Christ . . . I'm drunk as a skunk and I always say stupid things when I'm drunk."

Whyte said nothing for a long time. Then he shut his eyes and told Casy why he was there. "I have to tell you something straight out, John. I'm in the States because I've been called before a Senate subcommittee in Washington to answer some hard questions about the Omega Chi. It looks like someone has been feeding the committee information about us. Someone who has connections with us and with the doves in Congress. Some people think that person is you."

Casy took a slug off the wine bottle. He held it a moment and then swallowed. "It wasn't me, old buddy," he said seriously, evenly, with no rancor at being questioned. "I didn't sell you out. I was never approached by anyone and I wouldn't know who to approach on my own."

Whyte believed him and he was greatly relieved. "You have to admit you're a likely suspect."

Casy's manner was very cold now. "Yes, Bryan, you were right to suspect me. You can never really trust me again. Because I've come to believe that everything we are and have been in Asia is an expression of a sickness that's destroying this country."

Whyte knew there was no going back now—for either of them. "Is it sickness to want to fight Communism and help the people of Asia create a market economy that can lift them out of centuries of poverty?"

"It's sick to tell yourself that when what you're really doing is interfering in a civil war and helping right-wing dictators at the expense of the people—the real people."

"That's what you really believe?"

"That's what I know. That's what this whole generation knows. And we're not going to let you get away with it."

Whyte said nothing for several moments. Then he said, "One of these days you'll wake up and realize you're living in make-believe. And when you do finally wake up and want to come back, we'll be waiting for you."

Having said that, they drank the rest of the wine in silence. They smoked the rest of the *jin chu* and then, without a word, Whyte left Casy in the park. He spent the rest of the evening drinking by himself in a Chinatown bar owned by the Hop Sung Tong.

Depressed and badly hung over the next afternoon, Whyte sat in a suite of the Capitol Hilton in Washington D.C. trying to come up with a strategy. Positioned in a semicircle around him were his lawyer, a gloomy man from the prestigious Washington firm of Higgings, Higgins and Hoffsteader, a fat congressman from Illinois named Laughton and Harlan Bamcheck of the Central Intelligence Agency—all of whom were trying to impress upon him the seriousness and potential danger of his appearance tomorrow before the Randolph Committee.

Congressman Alfred J. Laughton was an old friend of Billy Whyte from the war years, a member of the unofficial China lobby that had long supported Nationalist China in Congress and a long-time political foe of Senator Randolph. He puffed on a cigar and filled the room with smoke and his analysis of the situation. "Randolph thinks the antiwar sentiment is going to be strong enough by next year for him to beat LBJ for the nomination within his own party. In the meantime he's using his committee to dig up all the petty scandals he can about the American involvement in Asia so he will be identified with the issue in the public mind. The Omega Chi must have seemed like a gift from the Almighty to him. He knows about your relationship to both the U.S. Government and the Chinese underworld. With this kind of ammunition, he's going to make a play for all the publicity he can get."

Taylor had called from Taipei an hour ago and said he was now convinced it was Randy Ortega of the Warlords who had been feeding antiwar congressmen with information about the Omega Chi. He said that his informers were reasonably certain that Ortega was in personal contact with Randolph himself. But who was feeding Ortega? There had to be a traitor somewhere in the organization—someone in Taipei. But who? And on what level?

Bamcheck wiped his brow and paced about the room. "Naturally, there will be areas in which you simply will not be able to answer their questions. Anything about the details of, uh, our relationship is top secret and cannot be revealed. However, since you don't have any security clearance, you can hardly plead that as a reason for not answering. It would be better if you simply pleaded the Fifth Amendment and said nothing at all."

"Can I do that?" Whyte asked his lawyer. "Can I plead the Fifth?"

"That's your privilege," the lawyer said. "Of course, that always implies a certain degree of guilt in the public's eyes and, as a businessman, you have a reputation to consider."

"Will there be press coverage?"

"Absolutely," said the lawyer. "Randolph will see to it."

He looked to Laughton. "Is it possible to pack the gallery with a sympathetic audience?"

"That's already been arranged."

"Well then I'm not going to take the Fifth," Whyte said firmly. "I intend to answer their questions. I'm not going to run from this thing. I have not done anything to be ashamed of."

"That would be a *serious* mistake," said Bamcheck, jabbing his finger almost at Whyte's chest. "Their questions will be worded to subtly link the Omega Chi with the U.S. Government and the Chinese underworld without actually presenting any evidence. If they can trick you into acknowledging that connection, they'll get all the publicity they need to bury us, kid."

Whyte had never liked Bamcheck, and he especially did not like being called "kid" by anyone. He abruptly stood up to terminate the meeting.

"Thank you for your advice," he said. "I'll consider what you've said very carefully." He smiled and shook hands with each of them individually. "One way or another this will all be over tomorrow. Let's get a good night's sleep. Tomorrow will take care of itself."

The next morning, he went to the huge congressional chamber with his attorney and took a seat. He watched the senators and their staffs and the press gradually file in and assemble for the session. He studied the faces of the spectators as they filled the gallery.

He saw Senator Robert Kennedy of New York enter the chamber and whisper something to Senator Randolph. Before he left, the famous senator paused to stare indignantly at Whyte for several moments. This was unsettling. Whyte had always thought of himself as a Kennedy Democrat and now a Kennedy was going out of his way to declare himself an enemy.

Senator Randolph finally pounded the proceeding into session and Whyte was sworn in. Randolph began by asking: "Mr. Whyte, will you please tell the committee how old you are?"

"I am nearly twenty-three years old, sir. I'll be twenty-three in August."

"You're very young for someone of your accomplishments."

"Thank you, Senator."

"You have lived in the Far East most of your life, is that correct?"

"All of my life, sir. I was born in Chungking in 1944 and my family moved to Taipei after we lost the Mainland in 1949."

"Your father was a very successful American businessman in China? Shanghai, I believe?"

"That's correct, Senator. He lost his entire fortune in the Communist takeover, however. He's now retired."

"And your mother . . ."

". . . was killed in the civil war by a Communist bomb planted in our house."

"I see. . . ." Randolph paused to shuffle through some papers. He was a short, chubby, inoffensive man with the detached air of a college professor. Whyte felt no hatred for the man nor did he fear him. His confidence was building.

"Can you tell us how you now earn your living, Mr. Whyte?"

"I'm a businessman, sir. I am chairman of the board of a privately held company that deals in light manufacturing, finance, export-import, consulting and the Chinese motion picture industry. This company is entirely American owned and it actually began as a fraternal organization many years ago in the Taipei American School. We saw a great many business opportunities in the Asian market and, in the best American tradition, we took advantage of them."

"Your organization—which calls itself, I believe . . . Om . . ."

"That's Omega Chi. They're Greek letters."

"Yes, Omega Chi. From what I can see, it doesn't seem to be structured like any business firm with which I am familiar. How would you characterize it?"

"It's structured like a Japanese *zaibatsu.* A *zaibatsu* is a family-owned corporation that operates on loyalty and a code of honor within the family unit. It's a very effective form of business organization, when it works."

"Would you characterize it as a gang?"

Whyte smiled thinly. "I suppose. Not in the Hollywood sense, of course. Not in the sense of acting illegally. But in the sense that a gang is a capitalistic unit. In the sense that General Motors is a gang, I suppose."

"Is it true that your organization, your gang, has been involved in numerous criminal activities of varying degrees since about 1960?"

"No sir, that is not true. That is ridiculous. We have never been criminals. Far from it, we are very close to the police."

"I suppose you are not at all involved in the international black market?"

"The international black market? Certainly not."

"You have nothing to do with the smuggling of Cambodian marijuana into this country?"

"Absolutely not. As far as I know, they do not even grow marijuana in Cambodia."

"You have not engaged in bribery of U.S. and Nationalist Chinese officials for illegal purposes?"

"Bribery? No, Senator."

Randolph glared at Whyte angrily. "Perhaps, then, you'd care to tell this committee something about the activities you *do* engage in."

"Besides the business activity previously described, we support several Taiwanese orphanages in the city of Taipei. We are the largest organization now dealing in relief for Vietnamese orphans. We support halfway houses in Taipei and Hong Kong for refugees who have fled Red China. We aid and support some of the many Chinese families who have emigrated to Chinese communities in the United States since the end of the Chinese Exclusion Acts. . . ."

"Is it true that you are allied with the Chinese underworld, with criminal secret societies or tongs?"

"The senator obviously knows little about traditional Chinese culture. These tongs and secret societies you're talking about are integral parts of the social order, respected elements of the community—like the American Legion or the Lion's Club in this country. Of course I do business with them on occasion. Any American doing business in China knows that he must sooner or later deal in some way with this element you incorrectly refer to as the 'underworld.' "

"Mr. Whyte, what is the Green Society?"

"The Green Society is an anti-Communist fraternal organization that has had close ties to the Nationalist Chinese Government since the twenties. In 1927, the Green Society single-handedly saved Shanghai from a Communist takeover. During the Second World War, it was the most effective resistance force against the Japanese occupation of Mainland China. In the civil war that followed, it fought valiantly against the Communists and kept China free for several years longer than it would have been otherwise. I do business with the Green Society and enjoy the friendship of King Lu, its *tai-lo* or president. I am not ashamed of it. I consider it the single greatest honor of my life."

"Is it true that the Omega Chi has used the Green Society to extort millions of dollars from various Chinese and Taiwanese firms doing business with the American Government?"

"That is a libelous fabrication, Senator. Certainly the Omega Chi has used its unique knowledge to help the American government do business with Asian firms that will not exploit the government's inexperience in doing business in Asia—and sometimes we have collected a consulting fee for this service—but to use the words 'extort' and 'millions' is ludicrous. I defy you to bring forward even one Asian businessman or U.S. Government official who will make this charge against us."

"You sit there and deny you are making a fortune off this war?"

"Certainly we do much business because of it—as do IBM and Dow Chemical and dozens of other corporations. The war happens to be taking place in Asia and we happen to be doing business in the Asian market. But that hardly classifies us as war profiteers. If you check your history, Senator, you'll find that more than half of the top twenty-five U.S. corporations got their start in time of war and most of them with military and war-related contracts."

Whyte went on to try and detail some examples of Omega Chi service to the war effort but Randolph interrupted him and steered the questioning back to the issue of criminal conduct over the years. The liberal senator hinted at every shady operation the Omega Chi had ever been involved in. He obviously had been very well briefed by Randy Ortega or someone. The grilling continued for three hours but Whyte never once lost his composure, patiently answering every question and calmly denying any wrongdoing on the part of the Omega Chi.

When the questioning was over, Whyte asked to make a brief statement. Without waiting for permission he proceeded. "Senators," he said, "you have brought me here around the world for absolutely nothing. You have presented no testimony against me. You have not produced a single supportable fact—substantiated by the CIA, MAAG or any other American authority in Asia—that even puts my organization in a dim light. Your single purpose was to make insinuations that embarrass the war effort and make headlines for yourselves. . . ."

Randolph banged on the table. "That's quite enough, young man. You're out of order."

"You want to slander me because you are determined

to undermine the American efforts to help the free peoples of Asia resist Communism. You have come to believe that these people would be no worse off under Communism and thus we simply have no business there. You ignore the fact that twenty million people were murdered when the Communists took over in China. You ignore the fact that we have worked an economic miracle in Japan. You ignore the fact that we have given Taiwan the second highest standard of living in Asia and it no longer even needs our economic aid at all. You ignore the fact that we have demonstrated our unselfishness by creating a functioning and stable democracy in the Philippines. You ignore the fact that we have proven beyond any doubt that the American dream *can* work in Asia if we stand up. But it's gotten rough now in Vietnam and instead of rallying around our President, you want to cut and run. You represent the contention that it is not worth American lives to save the freedom of a bunch of little yellow men in far-off Asia. Oh, if it were Europe, that'd be different! But not Vietnam. Not Taiwan. Not Thailand or Laos or Cambodia. Gentlemen, the fact is that you're weak and cowardly and worse, you're racists. . . ."

The applause began to echo in the chamber as he stood up and half-screamed, "I'm not ashamed of being a capitalist. That's not a dirty word in this country. . . . Not yet it isn't!" The applause drowned him out and continued for a full minute and a half as Randolph pounded furiously to suppress it.

As they were leaving, his lawyer turned to him and grinned. "You sure didn't need me. They didn't touch you. You made them look like complete fools. It was one of the most beautiful things I've ever seen."

But Whyte was in no mood to gloat. "Maybe I did," he said, "but I didn't make them understand anything. I didn't change anything. And I'm afraid this is only the beginning."

12

WHYTE RETAINED AN OMINOUS AND INSECURE FEELING all the rest of his stay in Washington and all the way back across the Pacific. He sat in the rear of the first-class section of the plane making copious notes and pondering everything he had experienced over the last three tumultuous days. The more he thought about it, the more he saw that Phillips was absolutely right—he had seriously, tragically underestimated the depth of the resentment against the Vietnam War in America and what its effect would be on them personally.

His angry defense before the committee had been carried in the morning newspaper and it made him an instant celebrity in Washington. He had presented the American policy position in the best possible light just when the administration was about to announce another major escalation of American ground troops. He received dozens of telegrams along with a flood of phone calls congratulating him and inviting him to weekend social functions and begging him to speak before various luncheons and youth conferences and women's service organizations.

The night before he left, he went with Congressman Laughton to a black-tie reception at the White House welcoming the new ambassador from South Vietnam. There he was introduced to the coterie of professors, admirals and State Department officials who were the real architects of American foreign policy. While the party was going on inside, several hundred demonstrators gathered outside the White House gates chanting slogans and screaming obscenities. Periodically pulling back the curtain to glance down on the spectacle below, he felt like some Versailles aristocrat on the eve of the French Revolution. It made for a very bizarre evening.

Whyte found himself very much the party's center of attention. Cabinet members crowded around to shake his hand while their wives flirted with him behind their backs. "You're the star of the show," said one aging coquette with a wink. "They think you're a gangster. Everyone loves a gangster. Especially when they happen to be as handsome as you."

"I'm not a gangster, ma'am."

"Senator Kennedy told my husband he thinks you're a gangster. I think it's very exciting."

He arched his eyebrow and looked for a way out. "Senator Kennedy is mistaken."

Whyte left the party as soon as he could. He ducked out on the meaningless flirtations and the idle banter about the war and the contemptuous jokes made about the demonstrators outside. He walked to the gate on Pennsylvania Avenue where the demonstration was taking place. As he passed through it, a demonstrator with an extraordinary mass of curly hair recognized him from his picture in the *Washington Post.* "Look, it's the self-righteous war profiteer!"

Whyte stopped and turned threateningly to the boy. "What'd you say?"

"Baby-killer!"

Their bodies were now separated by only a few inches and a thin police cord. "You don't know what you're talking about."

"I know they're burning children in Asia and you're getting rich off it, fuck-face."

Whyte restrained his impulse to pound the boy into hamburger. "If you believe that, you're an even bigger fool than you look."

"Why don't you get the Air Force to napalm me? Isn't that what you do when people get in your way?"

Whyte calmed himself and stood a moment face-to-face with the hostile crowd. These people were all about his own age and he decided he had to try and reason with them. Something in him made him feel he had to stand up to these accusations. They were not just questioning a government policy: They were questioning his very existence.

But it was a waste of time. They were so vehemently and irrationally opposed to anything he had to say that he barely got in a word. For five minutes they lectured him. They quoted statistics. They chanted slogans. They did not want to hear his defense of American Asian policy. They did not want to understand him. They wanted to destroy him.

Whyte gave up on the demonstrators and went back to his hotel. He was beyond depression now. He was in a state of barely restrained panic. Not only had he seen the weakness and lack of creative initiative at the highest level of government, he had seen a deep, powerful, all-consuming alienation in the young people of America—and in this alienation lay the potential to shake the confidence that was the heart and soul of the American mission in Asia.

Whyte had not understood this before but this trip made it more than clear. The curious thing was that Randy Ortega and the Warlords had understood it first. Ortega understood it and latched onto it and was in the process of riding it as far as it would carry him. Yes, he thought, this was the immediate and very crucial tactical priority. It was very clear now that if he were to keep the Warlords from using this alienation against the Omega Chi, he would have to eliminate finally and totally the power of the Warlords.

And the only way to do this was to eliminate Randy Ortega.

When the plane landed at Taipei's Sung Shan Airport, Mark Taylor, The Elephant and five of the most experienced Blue Shirts were waiting anxiously at the landing gate. Like a squad of football players, they swept through the crowd to surround Bryan Whyte and rush him to an airport conference room.

Taylor looked grim and serious as he closed the door. He was chewing gum—his one sign of nervous energy.

"We've got some big problems," he said. "It's the fucking Warlords again. They're back with the Tiger Eels and they've been moving against us all over town. If there was ever any doubt as to who was tipping off the Randolph Committee, you can forget it now. Ortega has been openly bragging about it."

"I never doubted it," Whyte said, straining to think. He was exhausted from the fourteen-hour trip. He didn't need this. "Now start from the beginning."

Taylor went through it, chewing furiously between sentences. "I got up this morning to a phone call that told me two of our spas in Peitou had been bombed in the early hours of morning. Then I got a call from Lee Min telling me that all the Taiwanese workers at our three pool cue factories in Keelung were walking off the job. I got another call from the air base commander at Taichung telling me a delegation of Warlords and Tiger Eels were putting a massive squeeze on him. It's been one thing or another like that all day. They're launching an all-out offensive against us, man."

"But why now?"

"Because of all the publicity over the Randolph Committee, of course. Ortega figured out that he's got us by the short-and-curlies now. He knows that with the national spotlight on us, we can't afford to get involved in a gang war with anyone. . . . The minute we retaliate, the bastard will be on the horn to Randolph and you'll find yourself in Washington having to explain it before that fucking committee again."

"What about the Greens? Does Ortega have no fear of the Greens?"

"The Greens are in the same position we are and Ortega knows it. They would never be able to get away with another big retaliation like '63. There are just too many unfriendly big-time journalists around Asia now who would put it on the front page of every newspaper in America. Chiang would have to break with King Lu completely. He'd have to put King in jail."

Whyte paced back and forth around the tiny room and tried to let this insanity sink in. He felt he had been checkmated. God, how he had underestimated Ortega. Ortega had figured everything, had brilliantly taken advantage of all his opportunities. Whyte needed time to think. Time to rest up. "How sure are you it's the real thing?"

"There's no question about it. It's high school all over again."

Whyte studied Taylor's poker face as it continued to chew furiously. "What do you recommend?"

"I don't know but whatever it is we better do it fast. There's something I didn't tell you."

Whyte had sensed an omission. "And what is that?"

"The word from all of our sources is that Ortega's top priority this time is an all-out effort to assassinate you."

The southeast chamber of the National Palace Museum was empty and quiet the next morning. Whyte entered the large room filled with T'ang Dynasty scrolls and sat on a centrally located circular bench. Guarding the door across the room, a statue of a Ming devil dog glared angrily at him.

In a moment, he heard numerous footsteps echoing in the stone chamber, then he saw the unmistakable figure of King Lu enter the room and head toward him. King was a lifelong student of Chinese art and he often used this great suburban repository of his country's greatest art treasures—most of which he had personally evacuated from the Mainland in 1948—as a favorite place of meeting. Bodyguards flanked the passageways and entrances, forming several layers of protection for them.

King took a moment to gaze admiringly at a scroll that struck him, then sat beside Whyte. The overlord

seemed more impassive and self-controlled than usual—
or perhaps it was just the quiet awe he always experienced
in the presence of his cultural heritage.

Whyte said in Mandarin, "I suppose you have heard
of my appearance before the committee?"

"I have heard, Little Brother. You conducted yourself very well. You are to be commended."

"It seems certain now that I have a traitor in my
midst. Someone close has been feeding this Randolph information through Randy Ortega. Do you know who this
might be?"

King paused a moment and then said, "I have been
working on this. I do not know for sure yet. But I do know
that your man Hong Shih-chi—Johnny Hong—does business with Ortega in secret."

Whyte was surprised. Since the demise of the black
market as a major business, he had given old Hong a
responsible position in the export business of the Omega
Chi. The Warlords had killed his youngest son back in '63.
The ungrateful old turtle. "Yes—that would make sense.
Hong once had a working relationship with Ortega and is
very greedy. Thank you. I will dismiss him this very day."

"This is distressing to you?"

"No, actually I'm relieved it wasn't someone closer."

"There are other troubles we face. Ortega . . ."

"Yes, I need to know the size of the threat he poses
to us."

"No one knows. But he has joined forces with the
Tiger Eels and the Taiwanese Independence Movement
and the other growing antiwar, anti-American, pro-Com-
munist factions in this society. These groups seem to be
forming a coalition against us. They smell our impotence
in the face of these strange new circumstances. . . ."

"They say he's out to assassinate me."

"I have heard this also."

"Is there any way you can help me prevent this?"

"I can give you a hundred Blue Shirt bodyguards—
a thousand, if you need them."

"Can you attack the Tiger Eels?"

"I will give you all the protection you need from the Tiger Eels."

"That's not what I asked."

King shook his head negatively. "I am powerless at this time. As you know, Chiang is very disturbed by the student demonstrations in your country and terrified by their growing congressional support. He stays awake nights worrying that this other Kennedy will become president. He knows that a scandal involving the Greens will cause him to lose more face and more congressional support. I am forbidden to act. You will have to think of a way without me."

Whyte felt anger and resolve bubbling over his fear. "Then I will assassinate Ortega myself."

The suddenness and cold-bloodedness of this surprised King Lu. "No, Little Brother."

"This is a war."

"Yes, but . . ."

"Ortega must join his ancestors."

"It will not solve the problem."

"Of course it will. Ortega is the mastermind behind all these problems. Ortega is the link to the Randolph Committee. Eliminate Ortega and we eliminate the problem."

"You are not suited for this. Let it pass for now."

"How can I let it pass? I will not let this man destroy me. I will not go into hiding for the rest of my life. To what authority can I go for justice? You? Ambassador Stevens? The Foreign Affairs Police? Don't make me laugh. I have never killed anyone and I don't want to kill anyone now, but what's my alternative? I can't stand idly by and let this man destroy everything we believe in—everything we have built."

King thought about this long and hard. Then he said, "Who would you have do it?"

"I will do it myself. It is my responsibility."

"If it must be done by one of you, let Taylor do it. He is better suited."

"No," Whyte said firmly. "It's my lack of foresight

that has permitted Ortega to get in such a threatening position. It is my mistake and I must correct it. Besides, they'll be watching the Soldier. They will be very nervous if they don't know what he's doing every minute. Me, they expect to be hiding. I can do it. Will you help me draw him out?"

"It will be very difficult. He is well protected."

"Will you at least try?" There was an unusual desperation in his voice.

King looked at his protégé and nodded his head softly. "I am sworn to help you in any way I can," he said. "But you must know that I consider this a dangerous and foolhardy course of action at this time. There are bad omens everywhere!"

Miles away, in the Sin Alley headquarters of the Warlords, Randy Ortega was monitoring the movements of Bryan Whyte very closely. He knew that Whyte was back on the Island, he knew that he had met with King Lu already and no doubt was fully aware that the Tiger Eels, the Warlords and all their new allies were on the march against him.

When the Tiger Eel soldier handed him the message that Whyte had returned to China Gate from the National Palace Museum, Ortega dismissed the man with a wave of his hand. He sat in his favorite chair a moment to have a cigar and think out his next move.

By now, Whyte would know that he had been completely outmaneuvered. He would know that assassination orders had been issued and he would be considering his options. He would see that his hands were tied. The knowledge of the agony and panic that Bryan Whyte must be feeling at this moment filled Randy Ortega with satisfaction; it almost made all the pain and humiliation he had suffered at the hands of the Omega Chi worthwhile.

He sat there a moment, savoring the cigar and reliving all the injustices they had heaped upon him over the years: the racist ostracization in high school, the bullying of Mark Taylor, the cutthroat, monopolistic business tactics, deportation, the hell of prison . . .

The period right after he was deported in 1963 had been the worst for him. His father disowned him and he had suddenly found himself, at eighteen, with no apparent skills and no means of support. He went to Manila and worked as a thug for the Sanchez gang, hating every minute of it. He hated Sanchez, hated taking orders, hated the petty jobs he was given, hated Manila where he felt alienated from the culture—no matter how much he looked Filipino, he was American to his bones. He had patiently saved every peso until he had enough to bribe his way back to Taipei, his home.

Within two months of that, Whyte had him on the infamous Green Island, where he suffered a year-long ordeal of torture and incomparable misery in a tiny open-air cell in the middle of a festering jungle. Green Island had almost ruined his health but it had not broken his spirit; in many ways it had been a positive, eye-opening experience for him. He had come into contact with hundreds of Taiwan Nationalists and other political prisoners and heard their stories again and again. He began to see that the oppression of his life by the Omega Chi was part of a greater oppression by the establishment of all minorities —and this realization was a great source of strength and comfort.

When he finally was released and got back to Taipei, he found that the Warlords were crushed, the Tiger Eels were in hiding and the only way he could support himself was by working as a common pimp in Sin Alley. But he had enthusiastically thrown himself back in the race. He secretly went about rebuilding his organization. He kept up his contacts with the Tiger Eels, the Taiwan Nationalists and the other disaffected groups on the Island. He knew that someday something would come along that would be his big opportunity.

And the Vietnam War was just that. The influx of money and opportunities was so great in 1965 that even the Omega Chi could not handle it all and it had given the

Tiger Eels and Warlords a whole new lease on life. Over the next two years, the failing fortunes of the American effort had brought about a condition that he could never have foreseen in a million years: that certain powerful American factions against the war would become the natural allies of the Warlords and would work with them to bring down the Omega Chi and Green Society.

Ortega was smart enough to pursue the link with this new force practically from the beginning. The gang war of 1963 and Ortega's prison sentence in 1964 had given the Tiger Eels and Warlords great credibility with the Taiwanese Independence Movement. This movement was headquartered in American universities and had strong ties with the growing American antiwar movement. As a student at the University of Minnesota, Clinton Chen—one of the original Warlords—used this connection and credibility to become involved with the peace movement and soon was admitted to its highest levels. It was Chen who had gone to Senator Randolph and presented him with the detailed information on the Omega Chi obtained from their prize informer.

Ortega had not expected Whyte to come out of the committee hearing a hero. This was a surprise. When Ortega had read the transcript that was published in the *China Post,* he was beside himself. But he quickly decided that, in the long run, it didn't matter. The publicity was all that mattered. Whyte was now a public figure. The U.S. media would be watching Taipei from here on out. Never again would the Green Gang be able to launch an all-out attack on anyone without the whole world knowing about it. Never again would the Greens and Bryan Whyte be able to strangle the growth of the Tiger Eels and Warlords. Now, at long last, the tide of history was flowing in his direction and he was about to have his terrible revenge.

The door opened and his brother Juan poked his head in. "It's time, Randy," he said. Ortega looked at his watch, snuffed out the cigar and went in to meet with his allies and coordinate the murder of Bryan Whyte.

*   *   *

Inside the council room of Warlord headquarters were assembled a number of Taiwanese and Chinese political radicals and tong figures from various overseas Chinese communities who had either anti-Kuomintang, anti-Green or anti-American leanings.

Also at the long polished table were five of the Warlords: Fatso Magaha, Ya Ki Loi, Little Juan Ortega, Amos Wong and Lefty O'Hara.

Ortega entered the room and took a seat. "Thank you for coming, my comrades," he said in Mandarin. "As you know, I have asked you here so that I might present my plan for the next important stage of our movement—the assassination of Bryan Whyte."

Loma, the leader of the Tiger Eels, looked troubled. He immediately said: "I fear this goal may be unattainable and unnecessarily reckless at this time. Things are going well for us. We are making money as never before. Why risk an action that might send King Lu down on us again and perhaps provoke a long and costly war?"

"King Lu cannot move against us," Ortega said calmly. "The Kuomintang has forbidden him from taking any action against us. They cannot risk any publicity that will give fuel to Chiang's enemies in the United States. That is why we can and must act now."

"But it is well known that King Lu loves this Whyte," Loma went on. "He thinks of him as his son and has always had him under his personal protection. He will not react rationally. Chiang will not be able to control him. He will reap a devastating vengeance. We must wait."

"There can be no waiting!" It was the voice of Little Ortega, which had become firmer and more daring in these meetings as he approached his twentieth birthday. "Whyte is not stupid. He knows by now of our connection with the Randolph Committee. He and Taylor are already planning a retaliation. We must get them both before they have a chance to carry it out."

The various overseas allies each had a say. Each was afraid of a furious retaliation from the Greens or Hop Sung Tong in their respective cities. Unlike the Greens in

Taipei, the hands of the overseas Greens and their ally, the Hop Sungs, would not be tied by fear of bad publicity. Each advised abandoning the assassination plan at the present time.

All eyes began to gravitate toward a magnetic young man with dark glasses, who had been listening quietly from the end of the table opposite Ortega. This was Ming Te, head of the underground Taiwanese Independence Movement. He was an American-educated Taiwanese whose lawyer parents had been executed in the '47 massacre. He hated the Kuomintang, the Green Society and the Omega Chi even more than Ortega did and he had dedicated his life to a Taiwan free of the Nationalists, the Communists and the Americans.

Ming Te had originally been leery of Randy Ortega and his coalition. He knew that the Tiger Eel gangs had participated in the massacre of his people and were not to be trusted. But Taiwan was an island of gangs and he finally decided that if the Kuomintang could have its gang connections—the "tang" in the word actually meant the same thing as "tong"—his movement could have one too.

Now, hearing how these despicable turtle eggs were only concerned about their profits and their personal safety, he decided that Ortega was the only other true revolutionary in the room. He further decided to throw his full support to Ortega in this daring enterprise and thereby cement the Filipino's leadership of the coalition. He waited until he had the full attention of everyone in the room, then he spoke forcefully: "We will support you in this action in any way possible, my brother. The assassination of the taipan Whyte must be carried out without further delay—no matter what the personal sacrifice. He is a symbol of American capitalism, the myth of American invincibility, and his death will stir the hearts and lift the heads of the exploited people of Asia more than a thousand battlefield victories. . . ."

As Ming Te spoke, the room suddenly felt the presence of that something greater than self-interest that was increasingly dominating their lives and that drowned out all opposing arguments. The heads around the table nodded thoughtfully. Beaten, Loma asked with resignation, "How will you do it?"

"It's been arranged for tonight," Ortega answered happily. "We have word from our informer that Whyte is having dinner with Taylor and The Elephant tonight in the Min Chuan R&R area to work out the details of my assassination tomorrow. They will be there at approximately 6 P.M., before the restaurant is crowded. Their bodyguards will be eating at a nearby table. I will walk in with an automatic weapon and get them all at once."

"Bang, bang, bang!" Ya Ki Loi giggled hilariously.

"Perhaps it is not wise for you to do it yourself," said Little Ortega, concerned for his brother's safety. "Perhaps Loma can provide a more experienced Tiger Eel assassin. . . ."

"The Min Chuan is Chinese territory. The minute a Tiger Eel gets anywhere near the block, word will reach Whyte. No, it has to be someone whose appearance would not be unusual in the Min Chuan—an American or a Filipino-American like myself. Also, I need the satisfaction of seeing the expression on Whyte's face when he dies."

"Where are you to find a fully automatic weapon?" Loma asked. "They are very hard to come by. We have nothing like this in our arsenal."

From down the table, Fatso Magaha said, "I have arranged to buy one from an American marine. He stole it from the Navy brig this morning. Randy will pick it up in the Min Chuan itself just minutes before he needs it—so he won't have to be walking around with it. It will be completely clean and untraceable to us."

"Are there any other questions?" Ortega asked.

He looked at the worried faces around the table.

"Don't trouble yourselves," he said, and then smiled cunningly and switched to English. "As the Chinese always say, *Mayo guanchi*—not to sweat. I have thought of everything. Tomorrow we will have cause to celebrate."

* * *

Ortega spent most of that afternoon in his Sin Alley apartment waiting. He went over the movements again and again in his mind. He imagined himself picking up the gun in the Suzie Wong bar, then walking the single block to the Yen Yang restaurant and ripping the place to pieces in a blaze of bullets and dancing bodies. Then, he would simply drop the weapon and vanish into the night.

The door opened and his current live-in girlfriend, Marilyn, came in. She was an American call girl, one of several he had imported from San Francisco this year to service wealthy Chinese customers. She had honey-blond hair, a *Playboy* magazine figure and, except for a slightly broken nose, the face of a movie star. She was returning from an important engagement he had set up for her—a high KMT official—and she was very drunk. She came in without looking at Ortega, stripped and turned on the shower. Then, nude, she came back in the living room and stood in front of him. "You cocksucker," she said.

"What?"

"You told that old gook I'd blow him."

"So!"

"Did you tell him that?"

"That's what I told him." Ortega was getting angry.

"Well, I don't blow gooks. You're the only gook I blow and even then I feel like throwing up afterward."

Ortega stood up and slapped her hard. She fell back against the couch and onto the floor. "You fucking nigger degenerate," she shrieked.

Ortega made a fist and punched her in the face. When he saw blood he punched her again, then again. When he had beaten her sufficiently senseless, he found he had an erection. He pulled down his pants and made love to her as she sobbed and gasped in his ear, "That's good, Randy honey. Oh, that's *sooooo* good."

"You love me, doncha baby?"

"Ooooooh yes."

Before he came, however, he withdrew from her,

pulled up his pants and left her moaning on the floor. Like an athlete-in-training, he did not want to expend all his sexual energy before the big event. He looked at his watch and picked up the phone to call Dave Magaha. "This is Randy," he said. "Tell me again how I'll know what this bozo looks like?"

Magaha laughed obscenely. "He'll be the only marine in the Suzie Wong with a grease gun on his lap for sale."

"Don't be cute, asshole. I'm gonna be late."

"He's a lance corporal in the Marines. He'll be in summer khakis and drinking at the bar. When you see him just tell him you're Ortega and you're here for the goods. He'll hand you the briefcase. He's already been paid so you can take it and leave immediately."

"If this guy doesn't show, I'm gonna ring your fat neck. I figure we only got one good chance at Whyte and then forget it."

Magaha was offended that his competence was being questioned. "Hey, *mayo guanchi,* man. No sweat. I set this thing up myself. It can't go wrong. The guy is completely trustworthy. He'll be there. Relax and enjoy yourself."

"I intend to," Ortega said. Then he hung up, stepped over Marilyn's body and left the apartment.

Whyte spent the afternoon in the garden of China Gate, mentally preparing himself for the meeting with Taylor and The Elephant later that evening at the Yen Yang restaurant. As he grew older and the responsibilities thrust upon him became more complex, he found himself craving periods of solitude in the garden of China Gate— its explosion of color, its incomparable view and its fresh, cool mountain breezes making it the perfect spring and early summer retreat.

His father came by later and the amahs set up a formal tea in the garden's Japanese tea house. Su Ling joined them and Old Whyte went into one of his standard rambling reminiscences about the days when he controlled

the Chinese film industry. Su Ling hung on his every word
—she genuinely adored Old Whyte—and, with an audience, the old man chattered on and on. Neither seemed to
notice Bryan's preoccupation.

As he was swallowing the last of his tea, Whyte
looked up and saw Alan Phillips coming up the pathway
from the main house. He had wanted to work out a response to this new crisis alone so he had purposely not
called Phillips on his return yesterday. Phillips was no
doubt here to find out why.

"Congratulations on your showing before Randolph.
You did us all proud."

"Thank you. Join us."

"No, I can't. I just dropped by to welcome you back.
Doris is getting near her time and I have to stay close by.
Can you walk me back to my car?"

They walked back down the path and through the
house to the gravel driveway, where two bodyguards stood
next to Phillips's car. Phillips appeared tense and worried,
as he always seemed to these days.

"Bryan," he said, his voice now very serious. "I want
to know what you intend to do about this new trouble with
the Warlords."

He shrugged helplessly. "Our hands are tied. What
can I do?"

"I understand from Georgie that you're going into
town tonight. That's not very smart, is it? Can't you stay
home for a while?"

"Mark and I are going to Min Chuan. Nothing will
happen to us in Min Chuan. Even Ortega is not stupid
enough to try something there."

"Promise me you won't take any retaliatory action
without consulting me."

Whyte did not want to make this promise.

"We're a partnership," Phillips stressed. "You don't
have the right to act alone in something this important."

"I agree."

"Then promise me."

"Promise you what?"

"Promise me you won't try to assassinate Ortega or anyone else without a full vote of the board."

"Alan, it may be necessary sometime. . . ."

"It can never be necessary. If we commit murder we're no different from them. For the love of God, Bryan!"

Whyte had never heard such desperation in Phillips's voice. He said nothing for several moments. "All right, Alan."

"Promise me."

He looked Phillips straight in the eye. "Okay, Alan. I promise I'll take no action without a meeting of the board. But I want you to call a meeting for tomorrow at noon."

As Phillips drove off satisfied, Whyte went into the house to shower. When he got out with a towel wrapped around his wet body, he found that Su Ling had left Old Whyte in the garden and was waiting in the master bedroom. She pulled off the towel and got on her knees before him. She had noticed his tension earlier and was offering to relieve it with oral sex.

He pulled her to her feet and smiled at her. "Not now, sweetness. I'm going to be late as it is."

She looked as worried as Phillips had. "Bwyn, plese you no go to Taipei tonight never mind. I gots many bad feeling."

But Whyte continued to get dressed. "Why is it," he asked, irritated, "that I am surrounded by worrisome old ladies?"

Randy Ortega walked the two blocks to Warlords headquarters. His brother was waiting for him there.

"It looks good," Little Ortega said. "He left Grass Mountain five minutes ago. That gives us about half an hour until he's sitting down to eat. Better get moving."

Ortega nodded. He was feeling slightly nauseated. His mouth had an odd coppery taste.

Little Ortega looked very uneasy as he handed his brother a .357 Magnum revolver. "Take this for extra protection. It's clean. But be careful. It has quite a kick."

Ortega smiled grimly. "You look nervous, Juanito. Try to relax. Hey, *mayo guanchi*. Everything is gonna be okay."

Little Ortega frowned. "I think the whole plan is crazy, very unlike your normal good judgment. I want you to know that I don't approve at all."

"My little brother doesn't approve, huh?" He reached over and slapped him affectionately with the back of his hand. "Oh, my God! What am I gonna do without my little brother's approval?"

"Just remember to wear your gloves. Get the hell out of there fast. And keep an eye out for Greens once you get clear of the restaurant."

"You just be sure to have that car waiting for me on Lin Sen Road."

"I still want to come along to cover you."

Ortega shook his head. "This is my party." He checked to make sure the magnum was loaded then put it under his jacket.

"Make lots of noise. Scare the shit outta people so they get outta your way, okay?"

"Okay."

"How do you feel?"

Ortega shrugged. "Good." He stuffed a piece of chewing gum in his mouth and smiled. "But I'll feel a helluva lot better when this is over."

The two brothers looked at each other without speaking, each suddenly grasping the enormity of what was about to happen. Then they embraced for a full minute and Little Ortega fought to hold back tears. "God go with you."

"*Mayo guanchi,* Juanito. No sweat."

Ortega left the building and began walking. He disappeared down a series of alleys to make sure he was not being followed, then began the half mile hike down Lin Sen Road. He had to walk slowly and it took him some time. His lungs ached after any exertion—a result of some lingering jungle malady he had picked up on Green Island

—and he had to pause and rest after every few blocks.

As he entered the Min Chuan district, he looked at his watch and found that his walk had taken him less time than he had anticipated. He stopped at a bar on the edge of the district, a smokey place, crowded with rowdy R&R Americans. Soldiers, sailors, marines. Most of them looked like children to Ortega. He had a Tom Collins to steady his nerves and listened a moment to a Taiwanese cabaret singer flawlessly singing the words to "Yesterday" without understanding a single one of them.

He left the bar and walked through the neon-lit alleys to the Suzie Wong bar. This was the only existing bar in this area from before the American R&R began in '65. The whole seedy district had grown up around it. The bar had been an old Warlords hangout when he and Ya Ki and Fatso were all just troublesome kids. When he was eleven, he had lost his virginity to a crazy bargirl who worked here and claimed to be the Suzie Wong the movie was named after. What had ever become of her? Upstairs, there used to be one of those restaurants that specialized in monkey's brains served warm out of the monkey's skull.

It was very strange, Ortega thought. Here he was about to kill someone he had known all his life and he did not feel the slightest qualm or fear or hesitation about it. In fact, he had never felt so completely sure about anything. He was filled with the same feeling that had finally dominated the meeting earlier today, that feeling of oneness with something greater than himself, that overwhelming sense of being carried forward by a force beyond self-interest. It was a good feeling—the best feeling he had ever known.

He entered the Suzie Wong and quickly scanned the crowded room. The jukebox was blaring the Zombies' "Time of the Season" so loud the walls seemed to shake. The marine was at the bar with the suitcase. Right on schedule—with time to spare before getting over to the Yen Yang.

As Ortega approached the bar, the marine turned and looked at him. "I'm here for the goods," Ortega said.

It wasn't until the marine stood up that Ortega realized he was talking to Bryan Whyte.

Whyte screamed at the top of his lungs: "This is the last time you'll ever cheat me, you son of a bitch."

Ortega's face dropped and he reached for the magnum, but Whyte already had his own pointed at Ortega's head. Within a microsecond he squeezed the trigger. The bullet hit the surprised Filipino in the temple, splattering his brains along the bar mirror, sending a shower of bone fragments flying across the room like confetti. The barmaid shrieked and Whyte pulled the trigger once more, sending another bullet into the dead body, forcing it into a grotesque, slumped position between the barstool and bar.

Whyte's animal eyes surveyed the room quickly and, seeing only terrified people cowering on the floor and behind tables, he stepped calmly out of the bar and down the alley to the waiting car that took him to a change of clothes and then a quiet dinner at the Yen Yang restaurant.

13

ONE DAY IN THE EARLY SPRING OF 1968, A TRIO OF THE American business community's most prominent *compradores*—the old Portuguese title given to important Chinese associates or agents of foreign businessmen—came to see Bryan Whyte. The three men sat on the wicker furniture on the patio before the great view of China Gate, nervously wringing their hands, hesitating to begin what was sure to be a most difficult and unpleasant conversation.

Whyte poured them tea and went through the required amenities as gracefully as possible. Then he sat back and with full attention waited for them to begin.

The first man to speak was Jonathan Wu, an officer of the Bank of Taiwan, the institution that had become increasingly responsible for financing the Omega Chi's expansion in recent months. Wu was young, Harvard-educated and a close, personal friend of Whyte's. Like the others, he spoke in flawless English. "You will forgive me for being indelicate, Bryan," he said, "but there has been great concern among all of us about our future together. Recent events both here and in the U.S. have created a disturbing loss in our investor confidence and it is becoming more and more difficult to ignore. We have the beginnings of a crisis . . . a crisis in confidence on our hands and it is already affecting the way we do business."

"Your troops have been bogged down in Khe Sanh for months with no end in sight," the second man, David Ward Kee of the Pan-Asian Oil Company, said more pointedly. "Your strategists are shattered by the Tet Offensive. The North Koreans take your ships in open acts of piracy and you do nothing. Your young people openly defy authority and rebel against the draft and desert your army in droves without shame. Your cities are aflame with race riots. Now there is even speculation that this Robert Kennedy will become president! This terrifies my people. *Ayee yo,* Kennedy is saying he will pull U.S. forces out of Asia entirely and leave us to the Communist wolves!"

"Please understand that we have everything at stake," said the third man, Lee How-sui, a noted Chinese financier and Kuomintang Party theorist who now ran the Omega Chi's export business interests. "We are making long-term investments and all the events tell us that this may be extremely foolish. Our futures depend on the continued U.S. presence and continued stability in Asia. We are eager for some good news, Taipan, some sign of assurance . . . and all we hear is that President Johnson has quit because America is tired of the struggle against Communism in Asia, that this second Kennedy is inevitable."

Whyte nodded thoughtfully as he listened to the three men. He was dressed in a spotless three-piece off-white cotton suit and he looked in every way the very picture of American confidence.

When he was sure they were finished, he paused a moment for dramatic effect and said: "Understand that I have everything at stake as well. My life and fortune are also on the line in Asia and I have no Swiss bank accounts for a rainy day. Yet I am not worried because I have assurance. And that assurance is history. The United States has never in history turned its back on an ally. Never. Our investments will always be safe because there will always be U.S. support for a free, business-oriented Asia. We are a Pacific nation and we will always remain a power in the Pacific. It is as simple as that."

He stood up and paced before them. "You don't understand our politics. In political campaigns we Americans make all sorts of statements and threats we have no intention of keeping—it's all look-see pidgin. Even if a peace candidate like Kennedy were to be elected—which will never happen—he would never get the Congress or the people to back a sellout of Asia. Face is almost as important to us as it is to your people. America could not retain its economic and moral leadership of the free world if it even contemplated such an action. We are not going to be engulfed by Communism now or anytime in the future."

The three men looked at each other blankly. They seemed to want something more.

"Gentlemen," Whyte said, his jaw slightly out, his eyes shining with certainty, "I absolutely stake my reputation on my faith that America will not elect a peace candidate this year. You have my chop on it."

This seemed to satisfy the three men. Whyte took the opportunity to change the subject to more pleasant business matters and soon walked them to their limousines. He smiled and made jokes and put his arm affectionately around Jonathan Wu, but as he waved good-by, his stomach was a tangle of knots. A year ago, none of these men would have dreamed of questioning the permanency of the American commitment to Asia.

The *compradores* were not the only ones to experience The Doubt in early 1968. In one way or another, it affected all the Omega Chi, everyone in the city of Taipei, anyone who had any stake at all in the continued existence of a non-Communist Asia. For the past year, it had slowly but steadily eaten its way into the American consciousness until it was now shaking the traditional confidence of the American Community of Taipei to its very foundations.

It had begun, as far as anyone could tell, in the academic community. Scholars at Princeton University's Taipei extension campus and Asian scholars on sabbatical from Yale, Harvard and other Far East departments suddenly began speaking of the war in less enthusiastic terms at their cocktail parties in 1967. They began to say that, yes, American foreign policy in China has always been based on ignorance and misconception—as the parade of academic witnesses had pointed out so clearly before the Randolph Committee. They passed around such KMT-banned volumes as T.H. White's *Thunder out of China* and André Malraux's *Man's Fate* and began to express a not-so-grudging admiration for the courage and dedication of the barefoot guerrillas in baggy pajamas who were humiliating the American war machine. The new students who flooded in for the summer quarter had all been glued to the ongoing Randolph Committee hearings on television and they infected more and more people with The Doubt, until by year's end it was spreading like a cancer to every level of this isolated American society.

In November and December of that year, long-haired American hippies in search of Oriental enlightenment began appearing in the city. They banded together in a poor quarter of Lung Shan, begged for coins on the streets and told stories of flag-burning and massive civil disobedience. During Christmas week of 1967, Mark Taylor became so incensed by their presence—and the loss of face they represented for America—that he took a squad of Blue Shirts and "cleaned up" Taipei's hippieville with forced haircuts and baths. It did no good at all. The hippies remained hippies and their very existence spoke of a social upheaval undreamed of by most Americans in Taipei. Soon even the *Stars and Stripes* and *China Post,* always very heavily censored sources of news, could no longer ignore the story and began to report accurately the social and political turmoil The Doubt was causing in the States.

By the first months of 1968, The Doubt was wreaking havoc on the traditional way of life in American Taipei. The basic assumptions by which these people had been living for the past twenty years were being openly questioned by housewives in the commissary line. The military command had more disciplinary problems in the first quarter of 1968 than in the five years before it. Businessmen became cautious and uncertain and delayed their investments for a better time. The missionary community became fractured between the Old China mission veterans who embodied the established order and the younger, post-1949 ministers who challenged everything about it.

Most disturbing of all was the effect The Doubt was having on the children of the American Community. With the families of hundreds of Vietnam fighting men now living in Taipei, the size of the Taipei American School had doubled in the mid-sixties. These new students brought The Doubt with them ingrained in every aspect of their culture. Soon, all the students were letting their hair grow long, listening to antiestablishment songs played on Armed Forces Radio and using words like "racist" and "fascist" to describe their bewildered elders. Incredibly, the horde of teenage gangs that had always been the plague of TAS died out in a single year, replaced by antiwar clubs and societies demanding to know why America was defending freedom in Asia by interfering in its civil wars and supporting right-wing military dictators like Chiang Kai-shek.

All of the emerging radical forces on the Island in

1968—the Taiwanese Independence Movement, the American Students Against the War, the Asian Scholars' Mobilization Committee and the handful of missionary intellectual societies—were given financial support by the Tiger Eels and their Warlord allies. Gradually recovering from the assassination of Randy Ortega, the Warlords once again began to seize on The Doubt and make it their own property. They were actually starting to see themselves as glamorous revolutionary heroes and were doing everything conceivable to cultivate that image. In the spring of 1968, while Bryan Whyte was busy reassuring his *compradores* of American constancy, Fatso Magaha and Juan Ortega were printing up thousands of copies of a manifesto in which they proclaimed the late Randy Ortega a revolutionary martyr and demanded the downfall of his four murderers, the oppressors of the Taiwanese people: the Kuomintang, the U.S. Government, the Green Society and the Omega Chi.

All of these things weighed especially heavily on the mind of Alan Phillips as he waited to meet Bryan Whyte for their informal weekly planning session.

He had been up since long before dawn in the den of his big house on Roosevelt Road, going over accounts and generally worrying about the way things had been progressing. Of all the Omega Chi, none was more distressed by The Doubt than Phillips. For nearly a year now, it had undermined the basis of his existence and all the good thoughts about himself and his family's years on the Island.

His wife, Doris, entered the room. There had been an argument the night before over some insignificant household matter; both were still feeling the tension. "How long have you been up?" she asked.

"I don't know. Not long." He didn't look at her.

"You're working too hard again."

He ignored the comment.

"I hope the taipan appreciates how hard you work for

him," she said with some bitterness. She no longer tried to disguise her resentment of Whyte. She deeply regretted the fact that Alan had talked her into naming their son after him.

"No one works harder than Bryan," he said dryly.

"I just wish you'd stick up for me the way you stick up for him."

He didn't want to get in another argument so he left the house. He ate breakfast at a local noodle stand, then walked the five blocks to Taipei New Park for his appointment with Whyte. The two men met at the park's east gate and strolled slowly through the dewy, early morning grounds while Phillips attempted to go over the financial problems that had recently started to pile up on them.

"We're expanding too fast," Phillips told Bryan. "It's finally all catching up with us. Most of these investments we've made in the last two years won't see any return for five to ten years or more. We've got almost no cash at all. I'm not even sure I can meet our Taipei payroll this month. This summer we're going to have to drop or drastically cut back every single charity program we support— maybe even the Ta Tung Orphanage."

"You're right, we've overextended ourselves. But these were all necessary investments. They'll pay off in the long run. The gamble will have been worth it in the end."

"I hope so."

Whyte had noticed the same icy testiness in Phillips's manner ever since the assassination of Randy Ortega the year before. Though the subject had never been brought up between them, Phillips knew Whyte had blatantly lied to him that day at China Gate and that had changed something fundamental in Phillips's feelings toward him. Whyte hated this and had made numerous attempts to patch things up but the distance was still there. Neither man wanted to face the problem head-on because each was sure that to do so would only increase the distance.

"Perhaps we should talk to Jonathan Wu about another loan," Whyte said.

"It's going to be hard to pay back what we already

owe them and interest rates are way up. Up to seven percent by the end of the year."

"If worst comes to worst, we can always borrow interest-free from King Lu. . . ."

"We're getting so dependent on the Greens, we're never going to be free of them," Phillips snapped.

"We both believe in the same future. It's only good business that we work toward it together."

"You still have a lot of confidence in the future here, do you?"

"I do."

"A lot of people don't these days."

"Yes, I've noticed."

Phillips noted an unusual wistfulness in Whyte's voice. "Do you know something that I don't?"

He told Phillips about his meeting with the *compradores.*

"God," Phillips cried, suddenly distraught. "The confidence in America is disappearing by the second! The resentment against us is unbelievable already! How much more can we take?"

They stopped and Whyte bought a black-market Baby Ruth candy bar from a park vendor. A group of uniformed grade-school children scampered past them, several pausing to stare back and giggle at the Americans. In the distance, the east sides of the huge government buildings of the city center were bathed in the golden light of the rising sun.

"This is why I wanted to see you," Whyte said. "It's time we took some action."

"What can we do? It's out of our hands completely. . . ."

"We can ride out the criticism. I'm convinced that part of it is only a fad. But there is a real danger staring us in the face. If Kennedy or McCarthy or Randolph were to be elected president this year, it could be a disaster."

"That's not likely to happen."

"Perhaps not. But I don't think we can just sit back and assume it won't. We have access to a great deal of money that can be donated to the campaigns of the right politicians if they make the right guarantees."

"Green money?"

"Yes. And perhaps Kuomintang and South Vietnamese and even South Korean money. They all have as much to lose by the election of a dove as we do. Furthermore, I think it's time we set up some sort of permanent lobbying apparatus that can make these kinds of contributions on a regular basis."

Phillips was uneasy with the idea. "I don't know, Bryan. It doesn't sound very ethical to me."

"Why the hell not? Our enemies are spending millions lobbying against us. Lobby money has paid for Senator Randolph's campaign. Why shouldn't there be a lobby to represent the Americans who live and work in Asia?"

Phillips felt his body stiffening. "And need I ask who this lobby will be?"

Whyte put his hand on Phillips's shoulder. "We both know that there's only one person who can handle a sensitive assignment like this. Surely Doris and the baby can do without you for a few months."

In her dressing room at the Omega Chi National Studios in Shih Lin, Su Ling was spreading a heavy layer of white theatrical make-up on her cheeks and forehead. The film she was now shooting was an adaptation of a Sung Dynasty folk legend and, since it would be staged in the stylized manner of Chinese opera, she had to go through the hated ordeal of making herself up for several hours every morning—disguising her beauty under a ghostly, surreal mask of clay and chemicals.

Su Ling was aware of her great beauty and—without being in the least vain about it—always anxious to showcase it properly. It was, she felt, the only asset she possessed, and thus she was very objective about it. No family connections, no education, no skill except prostitution, which was honorable enough but nothing that would see her through her old age. Without beauty I am nothing, she thought as she covered it up with more handfuls of pale make-up. The Acid-face was a crazy man for insisting on doing a classic.

Her first film, *The Plunder of Heaven,* had been the biggest domestic hit in Taipei in five years. It was not particularly good but it was the first film ever to play in Shihminting with any erotic content at all. Su Ling had been photographed to ooze sex appeal and the plot, although tame by American standards, actually hinted at perversion and illicit relationships. Whyte used his influence to get it by the notoriously puritanical Kuomintang censors, and, as Warner had predicted, the audiences returned again and again to see it.

Yet the film had not been distributed in Hong Kong or around the Mandarin circuit. Afraid of rising competition from the Taiwan film industry, the giant Hong Kong film factories and their head mogul, Sir Harvard Chan, had effectively blackballed it. There was also no way Whyte could use the Greens to force Chan into accepting it because Chan was under the protection of the Triads, who backed him up on this decision. And even though the Omega Chi did business with the Triads, Whyte could not push the matter without risking the breakup of his alliance with them. It was a problem because, without the use of the established Mandarin circuit of distribution that stretched throughout the overseas Chinese communities of Asia, there could never be any real profit for the Omega Chi in making films.

In the two years she had been with Whyte, Su Ling's life had been split equally between these concerns of the Shih Lin studio and the duties of China Gate—with little time left over for anything else. By far the least successful for her was the China Gate half of her life. As *tai tai* of the great house, she was the most miserable of cursed failures and she lost face every time she tried, so she had long since quit trying. She knew she could never be the charming, sociable other-half that the barbarian girl whose pictures were in the cigarette ads had been to Whyte. She knew he still longed for this woman (she had found a stack of her pictures torn from American magazines hidden in his desk drawer) and many times she wished that he and this dream-person would get married so she, Su Ling, could assume the more comfortable position of courtesan. Better the big-footed barbarian become the neglected wife than Su Ling.

She finished applying the foundation and began drawing on the exaggerated, pointed eyebrows. She sighed and thought of how much more satisfactory the movie half of her life was. After *The Plunder of Heaven* was released, she had been mobbed by fans while shopping for vegetables at the Grass Mountain outdoor market and she found to her amazement that she thrived on it. She got great pleasure out of knowing she was giving her master immense face and she took pride in doing a good job. She enjoyed the mood of make-believe and memorizing lines and working out movements and bantering with technicians. The only thing she did not like about this part of her life was that it kept her in constant close contact with Acid-face Warner.

This ugly man was the torment of her life and she detested him. At the studio, which was nominally under his control, he used her as his secret love slave. The day after Whyte rescued her from the Tiger Eels, Warner had appeared at the old Omega Chi House and forced himself on her. She had not resisted him. She did all the things he asked of her in sex. She felt he deserved this for bringing her to Whyte, and she had long ago developed the ability to turn off her mind so that carnal acts meant nothing. But he kept coming back over the past two years, each time seemingly more cruel and demanding. He took great delight in slapping and humiliating her and forcing her to use her tongue to lick that most offensive part of his body. Then he would always break down afterward and apologize profusely and profess his love for her in the most disgusting manner. When they were filming, the acid-faced monster appeared in her dressing room almost every day for this tribute. It was very wearisome.

She never really considered telling Whyte about

Warner's attentions. She was afraid he would think of her as a partner in a deception and throw her out to save face. He would also have to kill Warner, who had been his brother since childhood—a sacred relationship. Certainly more sacred, in Chinese eyes anyway, than the relationship between man and mistress. No, she thought, I can never tell the taipan. He has enough troubles these days. Bad enough he stays up all night worrying about what the madness in America and Vietnam is doing to his business.

The door to the dressing room opened. It was Warner. Oh no, she thought, what terrible timing. He locked the door and stepped over to her. "Do me," he said, unzipping his pants.

"I've just put this make-up on," she protested in Mandarin. "It's almost time for the next camera setup."

"Do me," he said again. "I'm already excited. See?"

She shrugged and took him into her mouth.

"Oh, you bitch, you beautiful bitch . . ." he moaned with pleasure as she fellated him expertly.

He finished within seconds. "On your face," he cried. "On your face!"

But she pulled back to preserve what she could of the make-up job.

He instantly fell to his knees beside her. "I'm sorry," he sobbed. "I'm so sorry. If you only knew how much I love you. If only Bryan knew. . . ."

One of the sound technicians handed John Casy the tiny white business card and vanished again behind the cork-lined wall of the recording studio. Casy took one look at it, immediately took off his earphones and put down his electric guitar.

In the past six months, Casy's musical career had finally taken off in a blaze of "overnight" success. He had left the Haight-Ashbury in 1966 and moved to Los Angeles to work as a studio-session musician. A year after that, he formed his own group, Omega. For months they barnstormed the country, playing taverns, high school dances and college keggers, until finally Casy found the thing he had been searching for since he left Taiwan. One night while playing a Beatles' song in a grubby miners' tavern in Wallace, Idaho, it suddenly came to him out of the blue—a way of successfully counterpointing a standard rhythm and blues melodic line with an Oriental melody and have it come out sounding like rock 'n' roll. Like some gift from heaven, the sound was just suddenly there. Suddenly he had a unique personal style he could apply to any song, a voice of his own—and everyone who heard it went ape shit.

Within a month of this revelation, he had a high-powered Hollywood agent, a hit single, a contract for an album with a major label and the promise of a lucrative tour of the country as the opening act for the Rolling Stones. For weeks now, Casy had been living in the recording studio day and night, gulping amphetamines and Gallo wine, obsessed with making an album that would showcase this new sound and tell the world everything he had come to feel about the Omega Chi and his old life on Taiwan—the album which he intended to call "Orient."

Normally, he would not allow himself to be disturbed by anyone or anything during this crucial creative period. But this was different. The card in his hand was from Alan Phillips.

He stepped out into the corridor and saw Phillips in the waiting room, dressed in a light blue three-button business suit, looking very out of place in the hip splendor of the Sunset Boulevard recording studio. Casy wore Levis and a tie-dyed tanktop and his wavy black hair dangled at his shoulders, creating an impression of freedom that Phillips, when he spotted him coming down the hall, immediately envied.

"I don't believe you," Phillips said as Casy grabbed and hugged him. "You look even more like a freak than the last time I saw you."

Casy was strangely delighted to see him—strange because he had never been as close to Phillips as he was to Whyte or Warner or even Soldier Taylor. "And you look more like my banker. How's Doris and the kid?"

"They're fine. We've got another little one on the way."

"That's terrific, man. I wish I could see your family sometime. I'm gonna get back to Taipei one of these days. Hey, I understand I wouldn't recognize the place."

Phillips looked around admiringly. "So this is where you make hit records."

"Let me show you around, introduce you to a few people. The Byrds are recording down the hall. So are The Doors. The Buffalo Springfield are due in tomorrow. This is really the big time."

Phillips didn't recognize any of these names but he tried to look impressed.

"Take off your tie and stay a while."

"Actually, I'm on my way to Washington to do some business."

"Oh wow, is Whyte going to buy this country too?"

Phillips smiled. "No, we're just doing a little lobbying."

Casy dropped his smile. "Wasn't that an awful thing about Kennedy?"

"Terrible. Just terrible. I don't know what's happening to this country."

Phillips had heard about the assassination of Robert Kennedy as he got off the airplane early the day before at Los Angeles International. For one wild, insane, utterly impossible moment he half-suspected Bryan Whyte of having engineered it. It was almost *too* incredible a stroke of luck for them.

"I read about Bryan's appearance before the Randolph Committee. It's nice to know he hasn't lost his touch. Christ, he made mincemeat of them. They didn't know what hit them."

"He sends his best, by the way, and he wants you to know you have a blank check on advertising and promotion of the album. We want to make sure the thing gets every possible break."

"Thanks, but if this album turns out to be as good as

I think it will be, I'm never going to have to take any money from you guys again."

Phillips had been prepared for this. "That's ridiculous. It's your money as much as it's ours."

"Still, I'd kinda like to do this completely on my own."

He said this in such a way that Phillips felt offended, although he was not sure why.

Phillips looked at him a moment and then said, "Are you trying to break with us completely, John?"

Casy's face took on a tormented look. "Did Bryan send you here to talk to me?"

Phillips ignored the question. "The Omega Chi has become a big business, true. But it's still the Omega Chi, still a brotherhood. It still does more good works than all the other charitable agencies in Asia combined. I've seen to that." His voice was hurt and defensive and without much conviction.

"Don't shit me, Alan. I know about Randy Ortega. Georgie wrote me all about it."

Phillips experienced a surge of anguish. "Bryan has a tough job. There have been many threats against his life. If he hadn't eliminated Ortega, Ortega would surely have eliminated him. There's no telling how many lives he saved by the assassination of Randy Ortega."

"The way I heard it Ortega had become a revolutionary whose only crime was that he threatened the business interests of the Omega Chi."

"That's bullshit, John! That's an awful lie. Ortega was a murderer. Ortega was the guy who nearly had you killed in 1963! Have you forgotten that?" He was shouting.

"Okay, okay, man. Loosen up."

"You don't really believe that, do you? Tell me the truth."

"I don't believe you can delude yourself forever. No one had more respect for Bryan Whyte than I did. I mean, I loved the guy and possibly still do. But I recognize the fact that he's become something evil. He kills people and he rationalizes it away."

"He has no choice. You have to understand that the Omega Chi is now essential to the American effort in the Far East. The stakes are high. The pressures on him are very great and the decisions he must make very difficult." Phillips seemed on the verge of tears.

"Alan, can't you see it yet? Don't you understand anything? The whole thing over there has turned into a nightmare. The values we had in the old days have become twisted and grotesque, the logic has become the logic of insanity. Jesus Christ! We're murdering babies for the benefit of Asian dictators and the profit of Asian capitalists like Bryan Whyte."

Phillips felt The Doubt rising so strongly in himself that he had to put his hand against the wall to remain steady. "No, we're fighting for a concept, a totally unselfish principle. It's difficult to see but it's there. Beneath all the confusion and evidence to the contrary, it's there. I know it is. We're in Asia for no other reason than to help those people. . . ."

"They don't want us, Alan. That's the plain and simple truth. They don't want us and we don't belong there. There's nothing we can do for them."

"I can't accept that, John. If I ever accepted that I would have to reject my whole life. My father's life too."

Casy reached for Phillips's hand, squeezed it gently, looked into Phillips's baby eyes with tenderness and great seriousness. He had never felt so close to his friend. "We all have to reject the past now. We have to completely kill it. That's what a revolution is. And there *is* a revolution going on out there—a revolution against everything Bryan Whyte is. It can't be stopped, Alan. Join us or we're going to grind you up and spit you out."

"But we have to keep the family together, John. We have to give it our loyalty. The Omega Chi has to be the most important thing to us."

"Not anymore. That's all over now."

"What else is there?"

"Our generation. Now we owe that loyalty to our whole generation."

"I'm leaving. I don't think we can talk about this. I don't understand you anymore."

Casy's lips formed a sweet smile. "I think we both understand a lot. Someday we'll talk again. Someday soon, I think."

Phillips moved uneasily toward the door. "Good-by."

Casy watched him half-running down the hallway. "Good-by, old friend."

Phillips stood in front of the Chicago Hilton, watching the crowd of demonstrators across the street in Grant Park. It was a bizarre sideshow of hippies, yippies, rock stars, Quakers, renegade college professors, student radicals and other antiwar activists—all holding signs, shouting slogans and posing for the television cameramen who hovered around them like so many gnats.

Mentally, he had been in a state of anguish and confusion for months. Ever since he saw Casy at the beginning of summer he had not been the same. He had gone on to Washington D.C. and worked weeks of sixteen-hour days setting up the Americans for a Free Asia but his heart had not been in it for one minute. The Doubt gnawed at his confidence and ravaged his sleep.

He went inside the hotel, checked into his suite and waited. Outside, the mob of demonstrators was getting larger and more threatening; he watched them for what must have been an hour from his window. These are my contemporaries, he thought, my generation, and they hate my guts. They hate everything I stand for. I am their enemy.

The doorbell rang and Phillips opened the door. Warren Stevens, departing this month from his ambassadorship and now considered a rising star in the party, appeared at the door with the Candidate. Phillips had seen the Candidate on the cover of *Time* and had read about him all his life. Yet the man's presence did not excite or awe him in the least.

The Candidate looked old and sallow and drained from his weeks of heavy campaigning. He nodded to Phillips then moaned as he fell into a chair. The sounds of the demonstrators were clearly audible and, as Stevens poured him a drink at the bar, he seemed to be listening to them. "I tell you," he said after a moment, "there is no joy in this campaign for me. First Bobby's murder and now this . . . this spectacle. I don't know what's happening to this country. . . ."

Phillips didn't know what to say. He was still waiting for Stevens to introduce him.

The Candidate suddenly looked up at Phillips. "Warren here tells me you want to make a very generous contribution to our campaign."

"Yes, sir," Phillips said. "That's why I'm here."

"That's wonderful," he said without much enthusiasm. "We're going to need all the help we can get come this November. Yessir. Every penny helps."

"As Ambassador Stevens may have told you, I represent a group of businessmen who have a great many financial, personal and charitable interests in the Far East."

"Yes, the Americans for a Free Asia. Warren has told me all about your organization. It's high time the media concentrated on *your* type of young person instead of those . . . those . . ." He couldn't quite find the word. "Outside."

"Thank you, sir."

"Now what can I do for you?"

"Frankly, sir, my organization is very concerned that America may be on the verge of throwing in the towel in Asia. We are all liberals by nature and we understand the frustration over the war, but we feel a unilateral pull-out —in Vietnam or anywhere else—would be a national disaster. Naturally, we don't pretend to want to dictate American foreign policy, but, to be completely honest, sir, we're looking for a sympathetic ear in this crucial election." He removed his glasses and wiped the lens with a handkerchief. He was vaguely aware that he had given this speech word for word as Whyte had given it to him.

The Candidate gulped from his drink. "I think I understand you," he said thoughtfully, "and I couldn't agree with you more. Our posture is going to have to change in Asia and we're going to have to end this terrible war somehow. But we have to do it with honor. And, as you point out, we have to remain a power in the Far East. . . . You have a sympathetic ear in me, Mr. Phillips. Yessir."

"Then I think I can offer you a sizeable contribution."

"How sizeable?" He gulped again from the drink.

"One million dollars. Maybe twice that much if you need it. As much as you need. Delivered in any form or denomination with which your election committee would feel comfortable."

The Candidate was clearly surprised. He had not expected even a tenth of that amount. "That's very generous," he said. "Most generous."

"Very generous," Stevens echoed. He too was surprised—and not altogether pleased.

The Candidate also looked vaguely troubled. "But tell me one thing. Why me instead of the Republicans?"

Phillips smiled stiffly. "Please. We're not fanatics. We're just old-fashioned, common-sense Americans."

Some weeks earlier in Miami, he had said the exact same thing to the Republican candidate.

When his business was concluded, Phillips stayed in his room. The meeting left him even more depressed and uncertain than before. All his life he had relished politics, avidly followed the national campaigns, been active in student government, *believed* in the process. Yet he had just participated in the total corruption of that process at its highest level. This cherished part of his life had been ruined forever. Thank you, Bryan Whyte. Thank you very much.

Angry at the world, he changed his clothes and impulsively decided to walk across Michigan Avenue to mingle inconspicuously with the demonstrators until it was time to leave for the airport.

Across from the hotel, the crowd was holding up signs and playing to the television cameras, but deeper into the park the atmosphere was considerably less intense, even relaxed. Here, the gathering seemed more of a social event. Phillips sat cross-legged on the grass beside a pretty, rosy-cheeked, frizzy-haired girl who told him she was from Mills College in California. She produced a stick of *jin chu.* "Wanna blow on this, man?"

When he refused, she shrugged and seemed to lose interest in him. She obviously thought he was a square. This amused him and he smiled to himself. If she only knew that it was likely the Omega Chi was responsible for getting that *jin chu* in her hand, he thought. The irony, the irony . . .

He continued to walk through the park in the gathering dusk. The people all around him seemed so different from him that they could have been creatures from an alien planet. He wondered if these could possibly be the same people he had started Cornell with five years ago. Could this much change possibly be packed into that short span of time? Could *he* have been part of this if Whyte had not talked him into staying on Taiwan?

It was not a completely abhorrent thought. Despite their carnival appearance, these people seemed to be banded together in an extraordinary sense of community, of belonging to something big, pure and earthshaking. They seemed to believe firmly that they knew what was right and what was wrong—the way he had once been able to feel about life. He envied them the harmony and simplicity of their vision.

From out of nowhere, a scrawny Oriental hippie approached him with a quizzical look. "Alan Phillips? I'll be damned!"

Phillips strained to identify the face under the scraggy beard. It was Clinton Chen of the Warlords. "What are *you* doing here?"

"I'm with the Asian Mobilization Against the War, for chrissakes," Chen said. He stuck out his hand.

Phillips took it. Here, a world away from Taipei, it seemed the thing to do, even though they had been enemies all their lives. "I'm lobbying too." Phillips suddenly knew who had been the Warlords' connection with the American antiwar movement. "Are you still with the Warlords?"

Chen shrugged. "I'm in and out. You know how it is. I stay in touch but I pretty much live in the States year round these days."

Phillips started to ask him more but there was a distracting shift in the crowd across from the hotel, then the sound of angry voices. From a distance, it looked as if there was a fight going on. As they moved closer to investigate, Phillips could see that a number of Chicago police had come into the crowd. He watched a policeman approach the hippie girl from Mills College, calmly lift his riot stick and bring it down on her head, splitting it like a ripe melon. Chen instantly disappeared but Phillips just stood there in horror and disbelief. Several busloads of riot police arrived on the scene now and charged into the crowd, indiscriminately swinging their clubs at the stunned demonstrators. Phillips couldn't fathom what was happening. The police had to be going crazy. They were his people—the frustrated, hard-cutting-edge of his side in this war—and they were attacking innocent people like Nazi storm troopers.

Two canisters of tear gas exploded on the ground near him. His eyes started to burn and he rushed away from the spewing smoke, coughing, crying out for help. Completely disoriented, he began running wildly through the park in terror alongside a hundred other young people who were doing the same thing. In the melee, he could make out a young policeman standing by a tree catching his breath. The man looked as pained and horrified by the scene as Phillips was, and the authority of his badge and uniform seemed to offer some faint hope of salvation.

Phillips ran to him. "Help me, please," he gasped. "I'm not part of . . ."

The policeman unhesitatingly hauled back and swung his stick. Phillips felt the impact, then his knees buckled and he slipped to the ground. He drifted in and out of consciousness as the policeman moved on to another victim. Then, his head covered with blood, his glasses cracked by the blow, he rose to his feet and somehow managed to make it to Michigan Avenue where several other wounded demonstrators helped him to a Quaker aid station.

He sat on the pavement with some of the more badly battered and tried to recover his senses. The people were comparing wounds and trying to comprehend what was happening. Oddly, the tone was happy. The mood was one of shared joy. The wounds were displayed like badges of honor, colors of some exclusive new fraternity.

Clinton Chen found him there. He examined Phillips's head and put a gauze pad on it to stop the bleeding. "The fuckers got you real good," he said. "You'd better come with us."

"No."

"Come on. We have doctors. I want to talk to you anyway."

"I can't."

"Why the hell not?"

"I'm not one of you."

"You are now."

And it was true. By the time the day was out he would come to realize with great relief and increasing joy that this new sense of generation was the most powerful force in his life. He knew he would have no peace until he gave himself over to it completely.

14

KING LU WAITED FOR WHYTE AT THE MAIN ENTRANCE of China Gate. He was dressed ominously in all black—black suit, black shirt and tie, black sunglasses—and for the first time in Whyte's memory of their association, he did not automatically smile in greeting.

The two men dismissed their bodyguards and walked into the big house together. A chilly wind, rustling the willow trees that snuggled the cobblestone walkway to the front door, signaled the coming of winter. "You have a troubled look on your face, Older Brother," Whyte said in Mandarin.

King nodded absently. "These are very troubled times. I have heard the news about Phillips. My heart goes out to you."

"Thank you."

"To Chinese people, the betrayal of a friend is the deepest of wounds and leaves the ugliest of scars."

"It's going to be hard to learn to get along without him. He was the man who made my organization run efficiently."

Alan Phillips had not returned from his lobbying trip to the States. He had sent for Doris and the baby and joined the antiwar movement, irrevocably renouncing all his ties to the Omega Chi. The subject was an agony to Whyte. He was still trying everything short of kidnapping to lure him back.

"To what do I owe the honor of this unexpected personal visit?"

King took out a handkerchief and wiped the corners of his mouth. "More trouble, I'm afraid."

Whyte did not permit himself to react. He led King into his study. It was a cosy corner room with a big stone fireplace, a Ching Dynasty carpet, a large globe, ceiling-high book shelves and Australian leather chairs. He shut the door. "Is it the Warlords?"

"Of course. What else? It is this Juan Ortega—who has clearly emerged as victor in all these power struggles that have occupied our enemies since the death of Randy Ortega. He is very smart, very cunning, very professional. He seems to have slipped very neatly into his brother's old position and he troubles me. More so, I think, than his brother ever did. . . ."

Whyte knew this and it was another agony to him. He had believed that the coalition would be broken without Randy Ortega. But it had recently regrouped under Ortega's brother and moved its headquarters to Japan, where the Omega Chi and Greens had no influence and could not touch it. This baby Ortega had grown up while no one was watching and their intelligence reports characterized him as an inspired leader who was driven to avenge his brother's death.

". . . And he is lucky. Every time I pick up a newspaper I read something that gives added strength to his side."

Whyte lit a thin Filipino cigar and blew the smoke thoughtfully into the air. He had only recently taken to smoking them—he enjoyed having something to hold during his many hours of business negotiations each week—and the taste was still harsh and unfamiliar. "What is your latest concern?"

"I have learned that David Magaha and Ya Ki Loi are in Saigon. They have been meeting secretly with our less-than-completely-loyal ally, 'Pockmarked' Hwang."

Whyte looked up sharply. "What about?"

"Drugs."

"God."

"It was inevitable. Hwang has wanted to use our facilities to transport hard drugs to the United States ever since he formed the alliance. He knows that if we can do it for *jin chu* we can do it for heroin or even raw opium, neither of which is nearly so cumbersome."

"Can't you talk to him?"

"I cannot. We have not spoken cordially since Shanghai. Anyway, it would do no good. He is a pig without a conscience, an evil man who can see no further than his own greed. He has always been this way and always will be. I am cursed because I did not kill him years ago."

Whyte put out the cigar and began pacing before the big fireplace, which still glowed with embers from the fire he had lit that morning while unsuccessfully trying to track down Phillips by transoceanic telephone.

"He's trying to make a deal with the Warlords," he finally said, as if accepting the enormity of the obvious.

"Yes. The Warlords have many U.S. military connections on their payroll these days. It is not a bit inconceivable that they could set up their own system."

"It would not be easy for them."

"But if they do, they will become unacceptably affluent off it. It will put them in a position to destroy us one day. You, me, all of us, everything we profess to believe in, everything we hope to do in the future for China. That is why we must get control of it ourselves before it is too late."

"I will not touch it. If I were to be anywhere near this despicable business I would lose all my support from the U.S. Government. And I wouldn't blame them."

This whole situation was painful to King Lu. He too loathed the thought of the hard-drug business. He had kept his branch of the Greens out of it for years. But this was a new age and it was becoming increasingly important. He had to be realistic. "Little Brother, it is simple economics. There is an unlimited supply of opium in Southeast Asia. There is an unlimited demand for it in the United States. There is already a complicated transportation system set up between the two regions by the U.S. military. There is going to be a trade. The profit margin from it is going to be greater than all the rest of our business combined. Even if we do not want to profit from it out of principle, we have to get in a position to exercise some control over it—for our self-defense. I absolutely believe that in the next decade, the organization that controls the drug trade is going to be the organization that controls Asia."

"Old friend, what can I say? I simply will have nothing to do with this filth. We have to have some principles or we will be no different from these common gangsters who threaten us. We have to draw the line somewhere and this is it. . . ." He intended to be very firm about this with King. He had to be. Even to contemplate giving in on this would be unconscionable.

But King Lu was also firm in a way that Whyte had never quite seen before. "You cannot ignore this in the name of principle. If you are to survive you must deal with it in some way. Believe me, this is the greatest threat that has ever faced us."

"I must talk . . ." He faded off midsentence and went to sit in one of the chairs.

"Yes . . . ?"

"Nothing. Let us think about this over sleep and meet again tomorrow."

Whyte had started to say that he wanted to talk it over with Alan Phillips. When there was a moral dilemma of any dimension facing the Omega Chi, he automatically thought to talk it over with Alan Phillips. But, as he started to say it, he realized with a sinking feeling of finality that Phillips had deserted him.

The alarming resurgence and increasing threat of the Warlords did not come as a surprise to Mark Taylor. He had watched it happening day by day throughout the troubled autumn of 1968 and he knew that the Warlords were continuing to capitalize psychologically on the failure of the American effort in Vietnam. Under the surprisingly effective leadership of Juan Ortega, the coalition of Tiger Eels, Warlords, Taiwanese Independence advocates, antiwar types of all nationalities, hippies, peaceniks, Maoists and anti-Green Chinese was grouping against the Omega Chi from a base in Tokyo. He knew that many of their traditional allies in the overseas Chinese communities were already defecting to this coalition. And he knew that if this coalition were ever to make the Southeast Asia connection with "Pockmarked" Hwang, it would surely mean the downfall of King Lu and the Omega Chi.

Taylor felt that, for all his brilliance and knowledge of the Orient, Bryan Whyte simply failed to comprehend the absolute necessity of neutralizing the drug business. Whyte had, from the beginning, ordered them to stay out of everything but *jin chu.* Taylor knew that this would be impossible in the long run. The hard-drug trade was now a fact of economic life in Asia. The best they could do would be to gain control of it, profit by it and try to keep it within moderate limits. From an economic standpoint, they desperately needed the money to solve their enormous cash-flow problems. From a military standpoint, it was insanity just to ignore it and leave it as an open springboard to power for their enemies. For the first time in his life, he was convinced that Bryan Whyte was acting unsoundly—he appeared to be so shaken by Phillips's cowardly defection that he could not think straight—and, amazingly, King Lu was going along with it.

As word of the possibility of Hwang's breaking away and joining their enemies spread in late 1968, Taylor began to hear stories that the Taipei Greens were also becoming increasingly dissatisfied with the orders to stay out of the lucrative drug business, especially in light of the threatened alliance that would very possibly end up overwhelming them. Soon he was hearing reports of open criticism of King Lu from the ranks of the Greens. The reports had it that most of this criticism was being instigated by a young Green warrior named Samuel Yin, who happened to be Taylor's counterpart and best friend in the Green Society.

Samuel Yin was a confident young man of twenty-eight, a long-time King Lu protégé and general of the elite Blue Shirt faction of the Greens. He had attended the University of Hawaii and the Kuomintang military academy, graduating at the top of his classes. He and Mark Taylor were virtual mirror images of one another in outlook and interest and had inevitably become close in the years of the Omega Chi-Green alliance. Both lived austere lives without a great deal of female companionship, both spent their spare time reading military strategy and working out in the martial arts, both enjoyed the exhilaration of battle, both were utterly dedicated to their respective leaders and organizations and the stoic code of the warrior class.

One morning in November, Taylor got a call from Yin inviting him to lunch. It was a bright, brisk autumn day and he walked all the way from his townhouse just off Chung Shan to the Mongolian Barbecue across from the Grand Hotel on the Tamsui River. As he neared the floating restaurant, he saw that it was surrounded by the largest detachment of bodyguards Taylor had ever seen in one place. There were bodyguards on the walkway, in the main entrance, on the street outside, even on the roof. There could be other explanations for this, but Taylor's instinct told him that Samuel Yin was about to force the issue of the hard-drug business.

Yin was waiting just inside the vestibule behind two huge Blue Shirts. "Who is winning?" he asked Taylor in English.

It was election eve in the States and, like most Taipei Americans this day, Taylor carried a transistor radio to keep up with the returns. "It's going to be very close," he answered.

Yin smiled thinly. "Does it really matter all that much who wins?"

"Not this time."

They walked to a small, private booth in the rear of the restaurant and took a seat. Waiters scurried up and Yin dismissed them with a quick, harsh demand to be left alone.

Yin then began to speak in a very confidential tone, his small hands nervously clenched into fists. "I have just returned from Saigon," he said. "I have spoken to Hwang. The stories are true. He intends to break with us and use the Warlords' influence to set up his own transportation network to smuggle processed heroin into the American market."

"That turtle egg!"

"Hwang does not want to do it. I am convinced of that. He does not want to deal with Taiwanese pirates and Communist sympathizers. But he feels he has no choice. It is an opportunity that must be taken advantage of and King Lu will have nothing to do with it."

"Have you spoken to King? Have you told him what Hwang has said to you?"

Yin shrugged. "It will do no good. It is your Whyte who has made the decision, not King. King has this unshakable belief in Whyte's infallibility. He will never go against his wishes. It is you who must speak to Whyte."

Taylor reached for a stick of gum. The pack was empty and he angrily wadded it up and threw it on the floor. "I *have* spoken to him. Many times. Everyone has spoken to him. He's adamant."

"If the Tiger Eels and Warlords and their allies take over the drug trade, they will be unstoppable. They will use that money to work their way into all our operations and businesses. They will take over our present position of dominance within a year. Hundreds, thousands will die in the process. Does Whyte understand this?"

Taylor hated being in this position, felt disloyal at even being in the conversation, but knew Yin was right. "Understand . . ." he said. "Understand that it is a *very* difficult thing for us to face. You are saying that in order to stay alive and maintain the security of the American effort in Asia we have to import hard drugs into our own country. It is not an easy concept to grasp—or live with once underway."

"The drugs will come into the country anyway! It is economics. Supply and demand. You have the opportunity to profit by it and keep it under control."

"I understand that. But I cannot make Bryan Whyte understand it."

"You must try again."

"And if I'm unsuccessful?"

"Then you must let me help you become the new taipan of the Omega Chi. With you in control, I am convinced that King Lu will cooperate with Hwang and we can avoid this tragedy."

Taylor was shocked. Such an idea had never entered his head. And yet, he knew it would appear as the obvious solution to many people.

"If not, there will be a civil war within the Green Society. It may already be starting."

One week later President-elect Nixon, a strong supporter of Nationalist China throughout his political career, dispatched a delegation of prominent Republican congressmen to the Island for a diplomatic courtesy call. Whyte decided to honor the dignitaries with a reception in the new mansion that had been built for Georgie Warner in the booming new Jen Ai residential district of East Taipei. The party was planned initially as an intimate private affair but Whyte soon seized upon the opportunity to make it an elegant show of confidence—the prelude, he hoped, to an inaugural season that would surpass even the Kennedy celebrations of eight years before. He invited all the leaders of the American Community, the entire diplomatic corps, hundreds of influential Chinese and even King Lu and his entourage.

Mark Taylor spent the day checking and rechecking security for the event. He took personal charge because this was the first major social gathering of its kind in many months and it would be like Juan Ortega to launch some sort of attack. So far, however, everything checked out. There was no unusual stirring among the Tiger Eel gangs. Everything seemed in order except for the fact that The Elephant had not yet made his latest call-in. This worried him somewhat. The Elephant was in charge of protecting Whyte and King and it was unlike him not to make his routine call-ins to Taylor as he moved from point to point during this important day.

As he waited by the telephone, Taylor realized that he had not slept for more than a few hours during the past week. He had stayed up every night thinking about the grim conversation with Samuel Yin. He was appalled, of course, by Yin's suggestion that he assume control of the Omega Chi. But he also knew that Yin was right about the catastrophe that faced them. He somehow had to convince Whyte that to continue to deny Hwang their services would mean starting a civil war within the Taipei Greens that would be disastrous for all concerned. He knew he had to do this and yet he had been hesitating. Why?

The phone rang. It was Warner. He wanted to know what time Whyte and King would be arriving.

Taylor glanced at his watch. "About an hour. Have you heard anything from The Elephant?"

"Nothing."

"Damn."

He put on his tuxedo, left his townhouse and had his driver take him to the Shih Lin apartment where The Elephant had been hiding out from his wife. It was a source of much amusement among the Greens that their most awesome enforcer was terrified of his shrewish ninety pound *tai tai* and would go to any lengths to avoid her when she went on one of her periodic rampages.

When the car pulled up in front of the apartment, Taylor observed that the front door was slightly ajar. He got out and approached it cautiously, sensing trouble. No, he thought. No professional assassin would be so sloppy as to leave this kind of signal. He pushed it open with his foot and peered inside. Nothing. The house amah was not there. The room hadn't been cleaned. He pulled out his pearl-handled revolver and stepped lightly into the parlor.

There was no sign of The Elephant. Surely he had already left. He went into the kitchen. There was a half-eaten bowl of rice on the counter with chopsticks still sticking in it. The amah's. She had left in a hurry. He went in the bedroom. The Elephant's huge, tentlike brown suit was lying neatly on the bed. Now he was really concerned. Taylor opened the bathroom door.

The great, nude body of The Elephant was crammed into the oversized bathtub. His throat had been cut from ear to ear and his blood was an inch deep in the tub. Five butterfly knives were sticking out of the corpse from various angles in what Taylor recognized as a traditional Green design of death for an honored victim.

He stood back and took in the scene. There was no sign of a struggle and no one could have struggled quite like The Elephant. This meant that the giant had been taken by surprise, most likely by a close associate. Who? It had to be another Green. Taylor's hand holding the revolver trembled. Samuel Yin!

He stepped into the parlor again and tried to think clearly. The Elephant was to command the limousine that would accompany Whyte and King Lu from King's townhouse to Warner's new house. Whyte and King would be assassinated somewhere on the way to Warner's house.

Taylor realized now that Samuel Yin had construed their conversation of a week ago as a conspiracy and his silence as support. Yin was going ahead and taking the steps to make him, Mark Taylor, taipan of the Omega Chi. All that was expected of him was to stand aside and do nothing.

He picked up the telephone and put it down again—he didn't know King's unlisted number. Then he ran out of the apartment screaming orders at the driver and they zoomed off into the night. Whyte would have already left China Gate by this time in his car to meet King at his townhouse, whence The Elephant's car would lead the cortege to Warner's house. Taylor had to get to King's house *before* he and Whyte left. He slapped the driver on the back of the head and cursed at him to hurry.

The car raced through the streets of Shih Lin, over the Chung Shan bridge, then turned off Chung Shan North Road to take a shortcut through the Min Chuan R&R bar area. They were immediately stalled in the early evening traffic. The driver kept his hand on the horn and dented and sideswiped several angry taxis as he forced his way through the traffic jam. He pulled down a side street to avoid the congestion but there was a sudden crash that stopped them again. They had hit a motorcycle.

Taylor jumped out. The driver and the motorcyclist stood screaming accusations at each other. Taylor could see that the left front wheel of his car was flat. King's townhouse was several miles away through the residential district along Canal Road. He started running. He ran through the narrow lanes, knocking people down and threatening them out of his path with his pistol. His heart pounded and his side ached from the running. How had he gotten himself into this situation? Why hadn't he gotten around to warning Whyte about Samuel Yin? Had he unconsciously wanted the death of the very person he loved most in this disgusting dungheap of a world? Was it possible that some part of him had become that corrupt? No. He didn't want it. He *didn't* want it.

A mile down the road he saw a Datsun heading down the street toward him. He blocked the road with his body and waved his arms. The driver, a prosperous-looking Taiwanese, rolled down the window and Taylor stuck the pistol in his face. "Get out, you son of a bitch!" he screamed in English.

The man did not understand so Taylor savagely slammed him against the side of the head three times with the pistol barrel. He pulled the unconscious body from the vehicle, got behind the wheel and roared off toward Canal Road.

He reached King's townhouse just as the parade of

limousines was starting to leave. Stepping furiously on the gas, Soldier Taylor drove the Datsun straight into the side of the limousine of Yin's traitors, his pistol blazing from the window.

The civil war among the Greens broke out at once. Even though the assassination plot failed, Samuel Yin had no choice but to play out his hand. For the next twenty-four hours, sporadic, indecisive fighting continued between the King Lu loyalists and the Samuel Yin rebels. The following day, the Kuomintang offered King a strong show of support by sending regular army troops into the city to suppress the rebel Greens. The day after that, Samuel Yin was hunted down and killed in the Yen Ping district by a squad of Chinese Army commandos. With Yin out of the way, King Lu immediately established a cease-fire and offered amnesty to Yin's troops.

King had temporarily triumphed but he knew that his support in this ideological dispute was not strong, that unless he changed his position he was merely prolonging the inevitable. The drug business was the wave of the future in Asia, and the pro-Hwang faction of the Green Society was not, finally, to be denied.

Bryan Whyte sat on the floor of his study with his face in his hands. Taylor sat beside him. Outside the closed door, Su Ling held a worried vigil. Bodyguards nervously paced the hallway.

Whyte had not slept more than a few hours during the three-day rebellion. He was edgy and exhausted and worn down by opposing arguments.

Taylor had come to report to him that Yin was dead and a shaky cease-fire had been arranged. He looked alert and invigorated by the scent of battle, not a bit perturbed by the demise of his former friend, Samuel Yin.

Ah Chin entered the room and brought them tea.

Whyte reached for one of the steaming hot glasses. "How is King doing?" he asked Taylor.

"About as well as anyone who must hold an impossible position.

"Can he hold out against the pro-Hwang people?"

"I seriously doubt it. Not in the long run anyway."

"What'll he do then?"

"He'll do anything you say. He still has that mystical confidence in your leadership. It's very strange."

Whyte laughed humorlessly. "Yes, very strange."

"I didn't mean that the way it came out."

"I know what you meant. What's Ortega doing meanwhile?"

"He's sitting on his ass over in Tokyo waiting to see what you do. Hoping you won't make a deal with Hwang so that he can."

"You think I'm making a terrible mistake, don't you?"

"Yes."

"I wish Alan were here."

Taylor bristled at the mention of the name. Phillips was an extremely sore point with him. He couldn't even think about Alan Phillips without getting upset. He was sure now that Phillips had been the long-suspected traitor in the Omega Chi organization. Still, he said, "Alan would tell you to make the deal and solve all the cash-flow problems that were driving him crazy."

Whyte shook his head ironically. "You believe that, do you?"

"Yes."

It was such an obvious lie that it embarrassed Taylor and he quickly added, "Militarily, we have to deny our enemies control of the drug business. The only way we can do that is to control it ourselves."

"How can we possibly justify that? How can we justify it morally? We will no longer be the Omega Chi if we do that. We will be something altogether different."

Taylor was struggling to hold back his desperation. He *had* to convince Whyte to change his mind. He had experienced a frightening temptation for the first time in his life—a temptation that had shaken him to his core—and he never wanted to be tested again. "The drug business is going to flourish no matter what we do," he went on. "Doesn't it make sense to get in a position to keep it under control? Rather than let Ortega run rampant with it and use it to destroy us?"

"I've heard that argument before."

"Hwang is only interested in our connections with the military transport system. We won't have to go near the stuff if we don't want to. We don't have to know anything about it."

Whyte just shook his head, stubbornly, sadly.

"Can't we just sit down and talk to Hwang about it?" Taylor pleaded.

"This is an evil thing, Mark."

"We're involved in other evil businesses. We've always been involved in evil businesses."

"We've profited indirectly from human vices, sure. This is much different."

"Be honest with yourself, Bryan. The taipans of China have always been involved in this business. What do you think the Opium Wars were fought about? Even your old man profited by it in one way or another at some time in his career—all the big foreign businessmen did. Ask King if you don't believe me."

"Mark, King once told me a story about 'Pock-marked' Hwang. It happened back in 1961 when the Thai Government was having one of its periodic crackdowns on the wholesale smuggling from Hwang's poppy fields in Burma and Laos. The UN and Interpol were pressuring them so hard that the Thais finally just closed Hwang down. But rather than lying low and losing profits for a few months, Hwang came up with an ingenious new method of smuggling that fooled even the most diligent authorities. Do you know what this new method was?"

"No, and I don't see that it pertains to the problem at hand."

"What Hwang did was purchase a number of infant

babies from several of the poorer border villages. Hwang had his men take these babies, suffocate them, gut them and cram plastic sacks of refined heroin into the holes where their little bellies had been. Then he sewed them up and, while they were still warm and still had their color, sent them over the border as babies sleeping in their mothers' arms. *This* is the kind of man and the kind of evil we're talking about."

Taylor's face turned an ash gray. He reached into his coat and pulled out his revolver and placed it on the rug between them as an offering. "Bryan, Hwang will never get away with anything like that again. If I ever hear another story like that, I swear to God that I'll take the next plane to Saigon and personally blow off the fucker's ugly head. . . . But, for chrissakes, Bryan, it's all the more reason to get some control over this horrible business before that kind of evil is turned against us."

Whyte could think of nothing else to say. He knew he was fighting a losing battle. He simply had no choice but to deal with Hwang. He closed his eyes and rubbed his temples. "Okay," he said. "Tell Hwang I'll meet with him. Call King and tell him to be there too."

"Pockmarked" Hwang arrived in Taipei several days before Christmas. Mark Taylor and Georgie Warner met his party at the airport and took them in a fleet of limousines behind a police escort to China Gate for the conference.

Hwang greeted Whyte like a relative, embracing him warmly and showering him with compliments and gifts, including a ruby ring so large it had—as Hwang openly bragged—a market value of a quarter of a million U.S. dollars.

As the round of greetings was made in the council room, the longstanding friction between Hwang and King Lu was immediately evident. They represented a split in the Green Society from twenty years before and they were opposites in every way—the Yin and Yang of the Greens,

Whyte thought. King shook hands with his old rival stiffly, bowed slightly and stepped to the rear of the room to indicate he would take no part in the negotiations.

Hwang made his pitch in Mandarin. "We are looking at the greatest single business opportunity of our careers," he told them. "The American presence in Asia has brought about a great network of communications and transportation that directly link the opium fields of the Golden Triangle of Asia with the untapped demand of American heroin addicts. If we can join together, we can profit in this enterprise beyond all precedent. . . ."

"But why do you come to us?" Whyte asked, also in Mandarin. "Why not do it yourself and make all the profit. Surely you could bribe your own military transports. Surely you could make a much more advantageous arrangement with the Warlords to do it for you."

Hwang gave them a crafty smile. "For small amounts, yes. But only the Omega Chi has the influence with the U.S. military to create a large-scale operation and keep it running on a regular schedule over a long period of time."

"And you want to run it from Saigon to Taipei to Travis Air Force Base?" Whyte asked.

"Yes. Just as we run the *jin chu.*"

"And how will the material be distributed once it gets into the States?"

"This has been arranged. It will be stored and cut by the Hop Sungs in San Francisco and then sold directly to the West Coast Mafia for distribution."

Whyte began to unwrap a cheroot. "I see." So Hwang had also made inroads into the Hop Sungs. Was there no end to this man's intrigue?

"For you, it will be only profit and no risk," the old man continued. "You have no overhead and you do not have to put up any financial backing. We want only your influence to make the system work. You merely sit back and take in a quarter of the profits. . . ."

Whyte lit the cheroot, puffed at it, mulled over Hwang's words. The irony of the situation was extraordinary, he thought. One hundred years ago, the taipans of China were smuggling opium into China at such a rate that it very nearly destroyed that society. Now, in this room, the plans were being made to reverse the flow and who knew what the consequences might be? Perhaps he was to be the instrument of a different kind of divine justice from the one he had anticipated. Maybe this was his destiny. He smiled at Hwang and thought of how much he loathed his obscene, pockmarked face.

"I think we can do business," Whyte said in English. "But only with certain conditions. First, I want to control the flow and keep it under reasonable limits. I will establish a strict quota that will be followed religiously. Second, I want your efforts in completely squeezing the Warlords and their allies out of the drug business and keeping them out. Third, I want a full third of the gross profits and I will not haggle."

"Accepted," Hwang said immediately.

They all shook hands.

"What will we call this operation?" Taylor asked as they all went in to dinner. "Surely anything this ambitious deserves a name of its own."

"I've got a name," Georgie Warner, walking behind him, said with a grin. "We'll call it the Orient Express."

When the last guest left China Gate that evening, Whyte went into the master bedroom and lay in the shadows by himself. Su Ling slipped into the dark room and sat on the bed beside him. When she began to gently rub his back, he rolled to his side, took her hand and kissed it.

"You sad?" she whispered.

"Some."

"Howcome so?"

"Because I'm being manipulated by forces I do not understand into making decisions I cannot justify."

Although he had never once mentioned it to her, she knew all about the pressure on him to capture the Asian-

American drug trade. Very little escaped her. "It is done. Do not think about it."

She continued rubbing his back and they remained there for several silent moments.

"What are you thinking?" she finally asked him.

"I was thinking about my friend, Phillips. I was thinking that in so many ways he was the morality of the Omega Chi. Maybe it's appropriate that he has left us."

"He you brother. He love you very much never mind. He come back, you see."

"No, I don't think so. He's gone forever. And I didn't know how important he was until tonight. Without him, the Omega Chi is a cripple."

It was, for Bryan Whyte, an unusual expression of vulnerability and it touched her. She was suddenly overcome with affection and tenderness and great fear for him, and she hugged him and sobbed into his chest. "You talkee now, plese. You tellee me what bother you."

He wanted to but he didn't know how. He didn't know how to begin to express this new feeling that the events determining his life were totally outside his control.

15

THE DAY AFTER THE AMERICAN NEW YEAR, 1969, Mark Taylor flew to Saigon to make the final arrangements for the establishment of the Orient Express.

According to the plan, raw opium grown in Hwang's Golden Triangle fields in Burma, Laos and Thailand would be smuggled through the war zone to Saigon, where it would be refined to heroin in Hwang's back-alley laboratories. The heroin would then travel the regular *jin chu* route from Saigon to Taipei via Nationalist Chinese transports and on to Travis Air Base outside San Francisco on U.S. Military Air Transport Service (MATS) cargo planes. From Travis, it would be delivered by Omega Chi employees (who, like everyone else along the route, would have no idea it was not the usual load of *jin chu*) to the Hop Sung Tong headquarters in Chinatown. The Omega Chi would never have direct contact with the merchandise and, in accordance with Whyte's wishes, the flow of product would be kept to a predetermined limit each month that would vary slightly with the demand, as determined by Chu Yung-liu of the Hop Sungs.

Taylor and Hwang ironed out the details of this in a series of cordial meetings at Hwang's mansion and quickly reached an agreement that would see the first shipment reach San Francisco in late February. Conscious that he lacked Whyte's great negotiating skill or Phillips's sense of organization, Taylor was very uncomfortable during these sessions. He was particularly suspicious of Hwang's willingness to give in on almost every point—the man was too eager. Yet this one business enterprise would not only deny the drug trade to their enemies, it would, by the end of the year 1969, net the Omega Chi somewhere between fifteen and twenty million U.S. dollars—enough to solve their cash problems five times over. What could he possibly find to complain about that? "*Hao*," he said as he finally formalized the agreement with a handshake. "*Ding hao.*"

As they left the council room, the old gangster's number one son was waiting for them in the parlor with a champagne toast.

"We real partners now," Hwang said with a grin that exposed all his gold teeth. "We get dirty rich together, hey."

"Together," Taylor said and clinked his glass with theirs uneasily.

"Now that business is done, what can I do to make your visit more enjoyable?" Hwang asked. "Is there some sight you have not seen in this inferior little country—or perhaps some pleasure you have not experienced?"

"Yes," Taylor said, without hesitation.

"Just name it, my friend."

"I want to see the war."

Hwang arranged with the Army of Vietnam Command for Taylor to take a quick inspection tour of the northern war zone. He caught a U.S. Army cargo plane to Da Nang then hopped an ARVN helicopter for the Central Highlands, where the fighting had been particularly intense that week and where he could be under the protection of a company of Nationalist Chinese Army volunteers operating in the area.

At the base camp, he discovered that the Chinese troops were being commanded by none other than Dennis Chou—former Taipei Ranger punk, former informer for the Omega Chi, former Taylor flunkie and now a Chinese Army captain.

"Good God, how long have *you* been down here, Dennis?"

"Two years, Soldier."

"That long?"

"I'm one of the originals here. I've killed over a hundred Cong so far and I'm going for a hundred fifty." He grinned, immediately falling into his old pattern of trying desperately to impress Taylor. "They don't mess with me, man."

The sight of little Dennis Chou actually leading men in combat was a devastating blow to Taylor. They had not seen one another for six years and Taylor still thought of him as the obnoxious boy who had idolized him all during high school. It was almost unendurable. It made Taylor feel that his whole life was slipping away without his doing any of the things that were really important to him.

The objective of Chou's unit this day was a Vietcong-controlled village some three kilometers away. "Normally, it's hard to surprise these guys," Chou explained as they force marched through the jungle. "But we're a lot better at it than the ARVNs. We've got our own intelligence network."

"How did you manage that?"

"All these little dungheap villages are served by Chinese traveling merchants. Most of them have been here for generations and are so established the Cong allow them free access. We've managed to convert some of them into informers. It's given us the jump on the Cong many times. We also never rely on Vietnamese guides or interpreters so there're no leaks to let the Cong get a jump on us."

The village of Boc Dung was situated around a Catholic church in a clearing along the Boyung River. Chou was attacking from the north so he had a soldier take Taylor around the rear of the village where he could have a panoramic view of the battle from the top of a bluff.

It took Taylor and his escort almost an hour to get into position. Taylor carried an M-16 rifle and the escort had a German sniper rifle with a gigantic scope sight. The sun came out from the clouds and it was suddenly a beautiful, autumnlike day. A perfect day for a battle, Taylor thought as he nervously waited for it to begin.

Some forty minutes later, the air support came into view from the west. A squadron of U.S. Navy jets made a wide circle and roared down over the village, releasing small bombs that made neat, orderly rows of fireballs over several square miles of green countryside. The planes circled again, repeated the operation, then flew off to the west. It took several minutes for the smoke to clear, then Taylor could see Chou's men come in from the north in a single wave, actually marching in formation like Napoleonic troops, firing in the direction of the village with no clear target.

The sheer spectacle of the scene below him was breathtaking. It was like one of the famous American Civil War battles he was forever studying, but without the impersonality of those dry, textbook cases. The village under attack was filled with Communists. The enemy who had killed his parents and forced him into exile, the enemy he had never seen but had spent his whole life hating. At last within his sight!

As the wave of Nationalist Chinese troops swept into the village, Taylor could see individual VC running out the back way, making a dash through the clearing for the safety of the jungle. The escort picked up the sniper rifle and Taylor understood finally why they had brought it— the man was a sharpshooter responsible for closing off the southern escape route. Unable to control himself, Taylor grabbed the rifle away from the sharpshooter and put one of the fleeing figures in the scope sight. He squeezed off a shot and the figure dropped. He lined up another figure and squeezed. It too dropped. He repeated this process again and again and soon he was caught up in a frenzy of killing. The soldier tried to take his rifle back and Taylor slammed him in the mouth with the butt of it. Even after Chou gave a flare signal that the village was secure, he stayed in position, hoping, praying to God for just one more figure to make a break across the clearing.

But none did and an hour later, he and his frightened companion—who was sure he was in the presence of a madman—climbed back down to what was left of the village. The scene had a horrific beauty about it. Small pocket fires burned here and there. Shrill cries of prisoners being interrogated filled the air. Mangled and already reeking corpses were being lined up along the riverbank for inspection.

Chou was waiting for him. He saw the sniper rifle in Taylor's hands and giggled hysterically. "It was you! I knew it! I *knew* it! You killed more than all the rest of us put together! Good old Soldier Taylor!"

Taylor went down to the river and inspected the bodies, noting from the wounds which kills were his. He felt fulfilled and invigorated. The satisfaction of a hunter inspecting his fallen prey. How many could he claim? Ten, fifteen? He had lost count. And to think that a few hours ago he had feared he might not have the guts to actually kill another human being. Why, it was easy! His whole life had been a preparation for it. This was his calling, as surely as business was the calling of Bryan Whyte. Everything now made sense.

Just before dusk, the big helicopter swooped down and took him and the wounded back to Da Nang. But as he watched the smoking village recede into the jungle darkness, he knew there was no force on earth powerful enough to prevent him from returning.

Back in Saigon, Taylor immediately went to see Floyd Harris, who was finishing up his second tour as chief of Naval Intelligence for the Saigon metropolitan area. Harris greeted him coolly and only after a long wait. The stumpy little man looked haggard, burnt-out, his eyes hollow and unfocused—as if he hadn't had a decent night's sleep since the Tet Offensive a year ago.

When the door closed and the two men were alone, Harris stared at the big city map on the wall a moment and then angrily threw a pencil at it. "It's hopeless," he said. "They're everywhere. They're behind every fucking noodle stand. They have sympathizers on my own staff. They grow stronger every day and nothing we do makes any difference at all! How do you fight this kind of enemy?"

Taylor had never seen Harris lose his composure before, much less display this kind of open defeatism. But he was still so high from his experience of the day before, it did not bother him. He lit a cigarette and waited for the red-faced Naval officer to cool off.

"Forgive me," Harris said, finally. "There was a bombing this morning at the Dien Hong bachelor officers' quarters. Five dead. Three of them Americans. I'm taking a lot of heat for it."

"I thought you had pretty much recovered from Tet," Taylor said.

"We're never going to recover from Tet. Not in this city. Not in a million years. Not if we bomb the rest of the country off the map. Tet finished us here. We're never going to have security again."

"I've just been upcountry and things are looking swell."

Harris looked irritated. "I know where you've been. You've been with the Chinese volunteers. Hell, they're the only troops left with any spirit and that's because they're all crazy. Hang around here for a couple days and watch how your perspective changes."

"C'mon, it can't be that bad."

"I go to the general staff briefings every morning and I'm telling you it's worse than you can possibly imagine."

Taylor decided it was time to come to the point of his visit. "I have an idea that might change everything."

Harris eyed him suspiciously. Although he had been genuinely fond of Phillips and had a grudging admiration for Whyte, he had never liked Taylor. There was a single-mindedness and quiet menace about him that made Harris extremely uncomfortable. In his twenty years in the military he had met a lot of people with this same threatening quality. "And what would that be?"

"How would it be if you had 'Pockmarked' Hwang and the Saigon underworld reporting directly to you? Nothing moves in this city that Hwang doesn't know about. If properly mobilized, the Saigon Greens could be the intelligence force that could make the difference for you. Not only in Saigon but in every village and hamlet in the country. They could act for you here in the same capacity they acted for the Allies during World War Two."

Harris shook his head. "The VC pay off Hwang. He takes squeeze from both sides. We could never trust a man like that."

"That can't be true!"

"No? To pull off Tet, the VC would have had to pay off Hwang. As you said, nothing moves here that he doesn't know about."

"But the Greens are more vehemently anti-Communist than we are. The Greens and the Communists have been blood enemies since 1927."

"This is not Taipei. Hwang is not King Lu. Haven't you found that out yet?"

"Listen. The Omega Chi does business with Hwang. Big business. He needs us. We can exercise control over him."

"No one controls Hwang."

"I can."

"It's too late. Nothing is going to help us make it here. I don't care what the politicians say, we're whipped. Beat. The sooner we get out the better for all concerned."

"Get out?" Taylor's euphoria completely vanished. He experienced an overwhelming contempt for Harris. He wanted to slap him to his senses.

"Of course."

"We can't get out. We have to win here. If we ever hope to retake the Mainland we . . ."

Harris exploded with sarcastic laughter. "Retake the Mainland? You mean you're actually still buying that old horse? Jesus, you people *do* live in a dream world up there on the Island of Fugitives. I can't believe that anyone ever seriously thought Vietnam was going to be some sort of step toward China. It was always intended to be a limited war—that's why we can't win the damn thing. Because we can't risk a war with China."

Harris stood up and laughed again. He seemed to be genuinely amused. "Well, in any case, you can forget it now, old buddy. We're leaving and the VC are going to gradually take over here. We know it and we're looking for a graceful way out the back door. It's that simple. If the Omega Chi has any sense, it'll close out its financial interests and leave before it has to do it in a big hurry."

Taylor was too stunned to argue. He had never dreamed that The Doubt was so great it reached the upper levels of the American Command, so virulent it could infect and immobilize a man who had been as strong and determined as Floyd Harris.

*   *   *

Because of its position high on Grass Mountain, China Gate was always several degrees cooler than the rest of the city. As Mark Taylor hiked the short distance from his car to the main house in the early winter twilight, his feet made little crunching noises on the frozen ground and his breath condensed before him.

He passed the Green sentry regularly stationed at the door and went into the parlor where Old Whyte and Su Ling were playing gin rummy and watching *The Real McCoys* on television. Old Whyte had moved into China Gate last month (Bryan thought he made too tempting a kidnap victim in the little house in Sung Shan) and he and Su Ling spent so much time together that the amahs suspected them of being lovers.

Taylor put his hand affectionately on the old man's shoulder and teased him gently about his losses to the girl. Then he went back to the makeshift editing room Whyte had set up in one of the unused amah's quarters. Whyte had been burying himself in there for months, going over and over rushes of Su Ling's new film on the Movieola to no particular end.

When he saw Taylor, he dismissed the editor and asked him to close the door on his way out. "How'd it go?" he asked.

"It's all set up for February. Hwang was very agreeable. Almost too agreeable."

Whyte nodded noncommittally and rather awkwardly changed the subject to the difficulties he was having with the new film. His manner said that he really did not want to know anything more about the Orient Express. He seemed to be withdrawing from the whole subject, withdrawing from everything.

This was very distressing to Taylor. All his life he had relied on his friend's utter confidence and belief in himself. Seeing him like this was like being handed evidence that there was no God. "Bryan, I had an unsettling talk with Floyd Harris while I was there."

"What's troubling the good captain now?"

"He's real pessimistic about the war. He says it's even

a lot worse than the papers make out. He told me confidentially that the American Command there knows it can't win and is looking for a way out."

"If he's openly talking like that we must really be in trouble."

"The man was distraught."

Whyte angrily flipped off the Movieola. "Does anyone down there know what the fuck they're doing? They got half a million men and they can't even protect the U.S. fucking Embassy!"

"It's time *we* did something drastic, Bryan. The Omega Chi should be doubling, tripling its efforts down there."

"Realistically, Mark, what more can be done?"

"I want to go back there and try to figure that out for myself."

Whyte raised his eyebrow suspiciously. "I think maybe you just want some action."

"That's not true and not fair."

"I've heard all about your exploits in the Highlands. You had no right to risk your life like that. You're too important to go sloshing around the mud with a rifle in your hands."

"You know, I don't believe you sometimes, Bryan. I'm telling you that America is running out on the war we waited for all our lives. Our world is coming to an end down there and you're sitting on your ass making a second-rate sex movie and telling me not to take any initiative. What's happening to you?"

"What can we do?"

"For one thing we can keep our thumb pressed a bit tighter on that slimy-assed bastard Hwang."

"We can do that from here."

"We're not doing a very good job of it. The guy is not helping the war effort at all. Harris says he may even be getting squeeze from the VC."

"That's not likely."

"But how do we know?"

"Exactly what are you suggesting?"

"Hwang has a communications network that links every village and rice paddy in Indochina. We've always known this but never taken any kind of advantage of it. I'm suggesting we find a way to use this network as an intelligence force against the enemy. I'm suggesting that I put it together and stay on top of it and make sure it runs smoothly and without corruption."

"But you'll be in alien territory. You'll be as lost as anyone else in the American Command. You'll only be able to go where others want you to go, see what they want you to see. . . ."

Taylor had been waiting for this objection. He drew closer to Whyte, his tone became more intimate, almost affectionate. "The Ministry of War is putting together another band of Nationalist Chinese volunteers to fight in Vietnam. They'll give me command if I want it."

"How can they do that?"

"They hire other mercenaries. Why not me? I could operate as a free agent between the Americans, the South Vietnamese and Hwang's Greens. I would be in a position to make a real difference, Bryan."

"What do you know about that kind of fighting? You've no training. . . ."

"I'm entering the Chinese Army commando school next week."

Whyte knew it was no use to argue further against it. He had always known that Taylor, being the man he was, would eventually find his way to that war. But the thought of risking Taylor in so precarious a mission filled him with dread. Taylor was the foundation of physical courage on which the power of the Omega Chi had always been based.

"Will you do me a favor and try to stay in one piece?" he said dryly. "I can't afford any more losses right now."

Within two months of this conversation, Mark Taylor was back in South Vietnam leading his own desperate operation to put some new life into the crumbling war effort.

His first order of business was to mobilize the Saigon Greens firmly behind him. As a huge Vietcong force was threatening the very gates of Saigon that March, an emergency council was held in Hong Kong with Hwang, King Lu, Whyte, Taylor and Floyd Harris attending. In this three-day meeting, it was decided that henceforth the extensive Green intelligence network in Vietnam would be at the disposal of Harris's office and Hwang himself would cooperate in every way with the American Command. Hwang obviously did not like this ruling, but in the face of the Vietcong push, the Greens' avowed anti-Communism, his dependence on the Omega Chi for the maintenance of the Orient Express and the united front against him at the meeting, there seemed no way he could reasonably object.

When this was arranged to Taylor's satisfaction, his next order of business was to actually get in the fighting, to demonstrate what could be done with an uncorruptible will to win and the proper intelligence. He carefully handpicked a company of Nationalist Chinese irregulars, all trained commandos and experienced Green warriors. He made sure each of them was fearless, thoroughly ruthless and personally loyal to him. He had them break all contact with the American and South Vietnamese authority and charged them up to the edge of fanaticism in an intense two-week training session. Then he led them into the backcountry and with great enthusiasm proceeded to do the thing he had been geared to do all his life—kill Communists.

While Taylor was experiencing the war as a guerrilla in north central South Vietnam in the first part of 1969, David Butler was experiencing it as a war correspondent in the Mekong Delta region south of Saigon.

Butler had been covering the war off and on since 1963; he had quit the Hong Kong AP bureau in 1966 to free-lance out of Saigon. Butler was one of those correspondents who found the war a grand adventure—the perfect arena for all his boyhood fantasies about the practice of journalism. He liked the men, he loved the freedom of operation free-lancing gave him, he risked his life constantly and he had developed a distinctive and very subjective journalistic style that seemed to fit the insane nature of the proceedings.

Above all else, he felt professionally liberated by the war, felt free to write whatever he wanted for the first time since he had come to Asia. Never again would a Bryan Whyte interfere in his quest for journalistic truth. *That* Asia was dying.

It was while he was doing a piece for *Esquire* on the war in the Delta that he began hearing stories about an American irregular who was making life hell for the VC in the north. When he heard that the American's name was Taylor and that he was leading Nationalist Chinese volunteers, he put two and two together and cabled Taipei. The AP bureau there confirmed that this guerrilla Taylor was indeed the Taylor of the Omega Chi, and Butler dropped everything he was doing and rushed north to seek out the story.

After considerable difficulty and numerous false leads, he reached Taylor's headquarters a week later. When he was finally escorted into the camp on the banks of some nameless river near the coast, he found the object of his search interrogating prisoners with a hot branding iron.

Butler barely recognized him. Taylor's dirty brown hair was long and tied into a ponytail, and his angular, inexpressive face had become skeletal, halfcovered with some scaly jungle rash. The eyes, always red and puffy from asthma, had taken on a demonic conviction the like of which Butler had not seen in all his years in Nam.

Taylor recognized the correspondent but did not immediately show it. He pressed the hot iron against the flesh of a terrified, bound VC prisoner and waited unemotionally for the screaming to subside. When it did, he asked, "What the fuck do you want here, Butler?"

Butler recovered quickly. "Is that any way to greet an old friend? I've tramped all over this stink-hole trying to find you."

"Why?"

"I want to do a story on you. Maybe follow you around for a while."

"We move fast. You'd never be able to keep up."

"Oh, yeah?" he tossed back. "I've been in this war four years running. I guess I can keep up with a couple of asshole newcomers."

Taylor half-smiled, thinking, strangely, of that night, centuries ago, when Butler had come hat in hand to ask the Omega Chi to get back his stolen briefcase. The ultimate greenhorn. Well, maybe he wasn't a greenhorn anymore. "I can't stop you from following me around but if you get in our way I'll personally waste you. Got it?"

In the days and weeks that followed, Butler did keep up. In the process he came very much under the spell of Mark Taylor. Taylor was the only man he had ever met in Vietnam who seemed to have no fear for his life or care for his health and safety. The compulsive ruthlessness Butler had seen in him as orphan-at-large of the Taipei American Community seemed to have grown to epic proportions in this environment. Butler had met many Americans who took to the killing and brutality of Vietnam, but never anyone who took to it quite like Mark Taylor. With Taylor it was a religious calling, the fulfillment of a boyhood dream, an obsessive revenge for the murder of the parents he had never known. There was something bigger than life about Taylor's mission here that Butler found irresistibly poetic even though he was sickened by just about everything Taylor did.

Butler began sending back stories and dispatches about the success of Taylor's renegades and, though he did not intentionally set out to do it, they all tended to glorify Mark Taylor. Taylor was the only positive news to come out of the war in 1969 and everything he did—including refusing a U.S. Army commission because he one day intended to "take the war into China"—made for wonderful, outrageous copy. Soon all the wire services and magazines were screaming for stories about the Boy General of the Highlands and Butler couldn't begin to supply them fast enough. By the time the monsoon of 1969 hit, Mark Taylor was a media event—the T.E. Lawrence of Southeast Asia.

It was a sweltering, rain-drenched Fourth of July. Taylor, Butler and several of the Chinese irregulars were headquartered in the shelter of an old rubber plantation fieldhouse some one hundred kilometers north of Saigon. A soldier was making a report to Taylor in Mandarin. As he spoke, Taylor interrupted him several times to ask questions. When the soldier was finally finished, Taylor dismissed him briskly. A flush of intense excitement came over the Boy General's face.

"What'd he say?" Butler demanded from the rear of the hut, where he was sitting on the floor and monitoring this conversation. The monsoon had kept them cooped up for weeks now and, like all of Taylor's troops, he was about to go out of his mind with boredom. He was desperate for some action and he picked up on Taylor's excitement at once.

"Chou's patrol has turned up something interesting," Taylor said as casually as he could.

"The arsenal?"

"Sounds like it."

"How far?"

"Three clicks."

"Lemme get my camera."

For months they had been hearing rumors of a giant arsenal in the district that was supplying the VC of three provinces. Finding it had been Taylor's foremost objective of the summer.

An hour later, they were there. As Taylor walked through the captured encampment in the steadily pouring rain, he could scarcely believe what he was seeing. Stored neatly in row upon row of thatched roof huts was every type of small-arms weaponry imaginable—all of it American-made, apparently stolen from U.S. Army supply depots up and down the country.

But the weapons took up only half the supply complex. The other half of the huts contained what appeared to be drugs. Hut after hut of *jin chu* and raw opium. Stacks of it. A supermarket! The largest drugstore in Asia.

"Take me to the prisoners," Taylor commanded Dennis Chou.

Chou took Taylor and Butler into one of the huts. Taylor saw at once that the prisoners were not Vietnamese but ethnic Chinese. Several of them bore the distinctive dragon tattoos of the Green Society. The prisoners grinned. The soldiers guarding them all grinned. Dennis Chou grinned.

"What the hell is everybody so happy about?" Butler demanded to know.

Taylor did not answer him. His mind was reeling under the impact of the realization that this was not a Vietcong arsenal at all but a "Pockmarked" Hwang arsenal—the exchange point between the drugs he bought from the VC to supply the Orient Express and the American weapons he used to pay for them.

The discovery of the arsenal had taken everything out of Taylor. As the monsoon rains intensified throughout July and early August, he lost all stomach for fighting. He stayed in his hut, refusing to see anyone.

He had spent one day brutally interrogating the arsenal guards, trying to determine exactly how this hideous system worked. Then he had Butler forcibly escorted out of the district—forcibly, because Butler could see there was a hot story here and did not want to leave—and withdrew into his command hut to be by himself and think.

It was unbearable! All along, from the very beginning of the first *jin chu* run, Hwang had been playing this game with them. All this time, the Omega Chi had profited by it and never once questioned where the drugs were coming from or how they were being paid for. It never occurred to them that the only conceivable way Hwang could secretly transport such a volume of drugs from his fields in

Burma and Laos was by making a deal with the Vietcong. It never occurred to them that Hwang would eventually find it cheaper to forget his own fields and buy opium from the Chinese fields in southern Yunnan. Why, the Red Chinese were probably giving the junk to him.

To Taylor, it made everything he was doing there a ridiculous sham, a cruel and meaningless joke. Here he was playing at being a soldier like some dumb junior high kid, while his other efforts were resulting in American weapons for America's enemies and Asian poison for the veins of America's youth.

The morality, the sense of high purpose he had felt every minute he'd been in Vietnam disappeared. It was drowned in the tidal wave of evil and corruption this war had engendered.

He himself was drowning in the same wave with no hope of salvation. But before he was completely swallowed he knew he somehow had to strike back. He had to muster the strength for one last effort to bottle up the evil at the wave's source. He had to atone for his crime with one last gesture worthy of Soldier Taylor of the Omega Chi.

Hwang was a happy man. The Orient Express was bringing in profits that would soon be measured in the tens of millions of U.S. dollars. He had brought off the masterwork of his career—the brilliant culmination of over sixty years in the business of crime. He could afford to relax now, to enjoy his remaining years on this earth. The only dark cloud on his horizon at all was the increasing American troop withdrawals—Nixon's laughable "Vietnamization" program—but even this was of no real concern. Hwang was convinced that it would be another five, perhaps ten years before the South Vietnamese could fight the war on their own, if ever. Plenty of time to make a fortune so vast that even his extravagant family would not be able to squander it in a century.

Hwang was pleased to welcome Mark Taylor into his home once more. All during their meal together at his mansion, the old man happily flattered Taylor, whom he had genuinely come to admire. "Everyone speaks of your exploits," the ancient gangster said as he poked at his shrimp with jade chopsticks. "They say you are the greatest tactician of the war, that the leaders in Hanoi have nightmares about you in their sleep. You are truly a remarkable young man. I am proud to call you my nephew."

Taylor had not touched his food. He just stared at Hwang with watery, vacant eyes and let him ramble on.

"But one thing I do not understand," Hwang said, looking disturbed now. "Why do you take such unnecessary personal risk? You have money enough to buy whole regiments to do your bidding. You have great influence with the military leaders and politicians in Washington and can make them accept your ideas. You have no need to endanger your life. Yet you do it. Why? Maybe you are one of those Americans who enjoy the adventure of killing, eh?" The old man broke into giggles.

Taylor did not smile. "Yes, I am one of those Americans. But there is more to it than that. There is something which you will never understand, Hwang. You are incapable of understanding. That is why you have never understood the Omega Chi. That is why you are not going to understand what it is I am about to ask you to do."

Hwang straightened in his chair. This was a signal that Taylor intended to conduct business. It was so uncustomary to do this during the meal that it irritated Hwang, a man who had little sense of propriety. "And what is that, Little Nephew?"

"End the squeeze. End it completely until the war is won. You are no longer to accept black-market business from ARVN troops. You are to eliminate anyone who does. You are to end all dealings with the VC. . . ."

"Dealings with . . . !"

"I found your exchange near Loc Nhon. I know all about your stinking operation."

Hwang was speechless. His ancient eyes darted obscenely in their sockets. "It is a part of my business that does not concern you."

"You are to end all business dealings with the Communists."

"That is not possible."

"You are to destroy all the drugs you have already stockpiled around the country."

"No."

"Loc Nhon has already been torched."

"*Ayee yo!* Son of a turtle egg! This is insanity itself! I am staring into the face of madness! The jungle has gotten to your reason!"

Taylor was enjoying this, enjoying watching the old man squirm, enjoying the incredible, suicidal recklessness of it all. "I will give you three hours to think about it," he said. "If you don't agree by then I am going to strike against you in any way I can. I will encourage King Lu to break with you. I will recommend to the taipan Whyte that we sever all relations with you and cooperate with the U.S. military to stamp out the Orient Express and destroy you."

Hwang sat stonefaced across the table and said nothing.

"The only thing that can save you from my wrath is an all-out, crash effort on your part to atone for your monumental evil."

Hwang still said nothing.

As he got up to leave, Taylor considered making a violent gesture—grabbing the old man and shaking him—but decided against it. The truth was he did not have the energy. Instead, strangely submissive now, he put his hand on Hwang's shoulder, and said in an eerie voice, almost begging for relief, "I will be in my quarters at the Majestic Hotel, Uncle. Do not make me wait long."

Taylor unlocked the door of the hotel room. Inside, it was an oven. He had automatically not turned on the air conditioner earlier because he had not wanted to have to suffer a reacclimatization to the jungle. Now it didn't matter. He flipped the switch and it hummed to life.

The radio was already on. The Saigon Armed Forces Network station was playing "I Am the Walrus" by the Beatles. What a strange cacophony of sounds to be a popular song, he thought. He lay on the bed and it occurred to him that he should call Bryan Whyte. Whyte would not understand what was about to happen. Well, that didn't really matter either. Because Whyte had failed him. All their lives together he had relied on Whyte, worshiped him, but when it came down to it, Whyte had not had the strength or the foresight to keep them out of this unspeakable evil.

Anyway, it was too late to call. It was too late for anything. He already heard the footsteps running down the bare wood floor of the hallway.

The door kicked open. A squad of Hwang's Blue Shirts carrying hatchets, butterfly knives and pistols flooded the room. Cold, merciless, animal eyes. One of them stepped over and turned the radio to full volume.

They hovered over him and began their terrible work. Soldier Taylor saw his outstretched hand severed at the wrist and fall to the bed beside him. Then blows to his arms, severing them as well. Then each of his legs and finally a powerful blow to the neck that severed his head. And the last sensation of his life was that he was not being hacked to death by axes at all, but drowning. Drowning in evil. Consumed by The Doubt.

━━━━━━ 16

THE NIGHT'S SILENCE WAS BROKEN BY THE SOUND OF a car coming up the gravel driveway of China Gate. Bryan Whyte, from the semidarkness of the master bedroom, heard the voices of his bodyguards questioning someone. Moments later, Ah Chin's voice drifted in from the front door, followed by a vaguely familiar voice speaking in English.

Careful not to wake Su Ling, Whyte slipped out of bed, put on his blue silk bathrobe and walked down the long hallway. As the voices came nearer he realized that the one he could not originally identify belonged to Floyd Harris.

He rounded the corner into the vestibule. Ah Chin and Captain Harris turned to stare at him.

"Bryan, I've come with bad news," Harris said quickly.

Only one thing would bring him all the way from Saigon in the middle of the night. "It's Mark, isn't it?"

"I'm afraid so."

Whyte put his hand on the wall to steady himself. "How?"

"They got him this afternoon in his Saigon hotel room. God only knows who did it or how they managed to catch him by surprise. But the VC had a big reward on his head."

"I'll get dressed and go back with you."

"That's not a good idea."

"I have to bring him home."

"The body's in about a dozen pieces, Bryan."

Harris said this with a certain cruel satisfaction. He found himself waiting for Whyte's reaction with perverse pleasure, waiting to see the great man break down and lose it all. Perhaps this was why he had insisted on coming all this way to deliver the news personally.

Whyte did not oblige him. He merely looked at Harris and said with an eerie, calm determination, "Then I will put him back together."

Whyte flew to Saigon to take the remains of Mark Taylor back to Taipei for cremation and burial. He picked up the body sack at the American Embassy and sat with it in stunned silence for the three-hour trip back across the South China Sea. As he unloaded it at Sung Shan, he was surprised to see that the news had already spread—a large crowd was gathered at the terminal to catch a glimpse of the fallen hero. The faces, mostly Oriental, were awe-struck, curious, curiously threatening.

Georgie Warner was also waiting in the terminal. He took one look at the khaki sack and suddenly, frantically embraced Whyte, sobbing uncontrollably. The depth and sincerity of this emotion shocked Whyte. He had not seen any kind of reaction out of Warner in years. It had not even occurred to him that Warner would be feeling a similar pain. It profoundly moved him, strangely com-forted him.

"What'll we do now, Bryan?" Warner sobbed, the tears streaming down the acid-scarred cheeks.

"We'll do what Mark would want us to do," he said, hugging Warner back. He started to say that "it will make us stronger" but it sounded so absurd in his mind that his lips would not form the words.

Then he broke away from Warner and looked into his eyes with great determination, seized by the thought that the only possible consolation for this tragedy was that it might erase the animosity Warner had so obviously felt toward him these last few years, that it would reform their bond of brotherhood. "It's just us now, Georgie."

Warner wiped the tears away with the back of his hand and nodded. "Yes," he said. "What can I do to help?"

"Have your father make funeral arrangements. Then cable Alan and John. Tell them their brother is dead!"

A memorial service for the American Community was held the next day at the Taipei Episcopal Church on Canal Road. The Reverend Clifton Warner tearfully eulo-gized their martyred son, finding numerous levels of meaning to his demise.

"What has Mark Taylor taught us?" the old mission-ary asked the rafters. "He has taught us that even in these bleak and cynical times there are still those among us whose love of country and love of his fellow man and love of God—yes, love of God—is so great that they will gladly sacrifice their lives. Mark Taylor has taught us in the only way he knew how that spirit has not yet vanished from this Community. . . ."

After the service, the KMT Minister of Public Information came to Whyte and insisted the casket be moved to the forecourt of the Presidential Palace so that the Chinese people could file by it and pay their respects. "Mark Taylor has come to stand for something greater than himself," the propaganda minister, a smooth-talking Cantonese, argued over Whyte's reluctance. "Since he was an orphan child, he has been a symbol of American courage, determination and anti-Communism on this island. The sight of his body will be a powerful unifying reminder of the purity of our great cause."

Spurred on by lavish obituaries in the Chinese press, they came to see him by the thousands, by the tens of thousands. Day and night, people filed by the waxy, hastily reconstructed corpse in a continuous, snakelike stream —mostly Taiwanese, all with the same remote, curious and oddly threatening expression. A parade of Taylor's old enemies came, as if to make absolutely sure their old scourge was really gone. Fatso Magaha and Juan Ortega came from Japan. Loma, Ya Ki Loi, Lefty O'Hara and Amos Wong. It was rumored that even Ming Te, head of the underground Taiwanese Independence Movement, had come out of hiding long enough to sneak a look.

As Whyte and Georgie Warner studied the faces watching the body of their brother, Whyte gradually sensed through his shock and numbness that this sideshow was a serious mistake. It was going to have the opposite effect from the one intended. These people were not here to pay tribute, but rather to witness the destruction of a legend. They were there to see for themselves the corpse of American invulnerability in Asia and, far from unifying the various factions, the sight of the body was bound to unleash terrible, long-suppressed ambitions.

It did so within twenty-four hours. Without a word

from a leader or a shadow of a thought-out plan, the Warlords and Tiger Eels, with their alliance of Taiwanese independence groups, antiwar activists, Maoists and anti-Green Chinese, began to harass and challenge Omega Chi and Green authority. Not only in Taipei but all over the Island. Through some mysterious process of subliminal communication, these forces all knew at once that the time to move, the time of maximum American vulnerability, had finally arrived. The death of Mark Taylor was the spark that finally ignited a full-scale, long-dreaded, open rebellion against the order of the Omega Chi.

King Lu paced the rear patio of China Gate. Sweat streaked his blue dress shirt and a distinct edginess broke his characteristic evenness and air of imperturbability.

"I think you must return to the United States until this threat is over," he said very pointedly in Mandarin. "The ultimate object of this rebellion will be to assassinate you."

Whyte, seated behind him at the tea table, shielded his eyes from the blazing August sun. He had been feverishly figuring his options. "I can't do that," he said. "This situation has come about because of a crisis in confidence, because of a fundamental doubt about American determination here. For me to leave Asia would only reinforce that doubt and further weaken our position. I have to stay right here and make a show of confidence."

"My foremost consideration has to be your safety," King said. "And I can't properly protect you here. Our ranks are riddled with traitors and antiwar sympathizers. I have moved two hundred Triads into the city to bolster our defenses but it is still not enough to guarantee your safety. If the rebellion spreads to Hong Kong and Singapore and Manila—and I think it will—I'll lose even these men."

"Is there no way we can end this crisis by quickly eliminating Juan Ortega?"

"Juan Ortega is safely back in Japan, where he is protected by Yakuza gangsters. He at least is smart enough to know when to leave the field of battle."

"Let's ask for negotiations and stall them until we can figure out a suitable course of action."

King stopped pacing and looked as grave and worried as Whyte had ever seen him. "I have already asked for negotiations. Loma refuses to even sit down with us. They are obviously set to go all the way with this rebellion until they get exactly what they want."

Whyte shook his head helplessly. He was thinking of how lost he felt in this kind of situation without Mark Taylor whispering military advice in his ear. He experienced an irrational flash of anger at his friend for getting himself killed, for leaving him to face the consequences alone. "But what do they want?"

"They want our destruction. But they will accept three major concessions. First, they want the Greens to leave the new growing eastern section of Taipei solely to them. Second, they want half of the Min Chuan R&R area to be their exclusive territory. Third, and most important, they want a cut of the Orient Express. A sizeable cut, I might add."

Whyte sipped thoughtfully from his tea. "We can't allow it. Any of it. It would be the beginning of the end."

King looked at him sternly. "It may be that we will have to compromise on some of it. The alternative is a long war which we don't have the luxury of fighting. If this business is not settled in a week, if it breaks out in serious violence, you'll be in front of the Randolph Committee and I will be in front of a wrathful Generalissimo."

"Surely the Generalissimo . . ."

"The Generalissimo cannot afford a war. The publicity will undermine his congressional support. He will not tolerate it."

Whyte did not know what to say, what to do. He did not even have an idea. Once again, he was paralyzed by that sensation of impotence, of powerful forces closing in on him and offering no rational escape. Everything was out of control. Completely out of control. . . .

* * *

In the early hours of morning, China Gate was bright with lights and alive with people. King Lu and Georgie Warner came and went with their entourages for a hectic midnight strategy session. A steady succession of Green couriers brought up-to-the-minute reports on enemy activity. Squads of Blue Shirts methodically patrolled the grounds and monitored everything that moved on the upper half of Grass Mountain.

At dawn, Whyte was still at his desk in his office drafting a cable to Harlan Bamcheck of the CIA telling him about the evolving situation in Taipei. Whyte had not slept for well over twenty-four hours. He always worked hard but now he needed that work, had to keep mentally occupied. If he didn't, he would think about everything that had happened to the Omega Chi over the past five years. If he didn't work, he would experience that creeping, crippling new awareness that he now recognized as The Doubt.

The wall he had mentally erected was being bombarded every second by terrible, agonizing thoughts. Thoughts that Senator Randolph had found indisputable evidence last week that the Gulf of Tonkin incident was contrived by the U.S. Navy. Thoughts that Vietnam and Czechoslovakia and Rumania were proving that Communism was not the monolithic monster of his nightmares so much as a vague political concept that was often identified with nationalism. Thoughts that all his capitalistic values, his faith in the American Dream and his sense of destiny had led him straight into a role as the world's number one smuggler of drugs. He struggled to keep these thoughts out. If he didn't, they would kill him, kill the thing that had been Bryan Whyte. . . .

Su Ling quietly entered the room and sat on the floor beside his desk. Since the latest troubles started, he refused to let her leave the estate grounds. She had little to do but hang around the hallways and try to stay out of everyone's way. "When you comie bed?" she nagged gently.

"Soon," he said without looking at her. It would do no good to go to bed. He would not be able to sleep.

Su Ling was pregnant. She had made the announcement yesterday and it was the only good news he had heard in months. He had always wanted a son. The prospect of his being Eurasian did not bother him; he considered Eurasians the smartest and most beautiful people on earth.

The announcement was greeted with such approval that Su Ling almost felt secure enough to tell him what she had been trying to work up the courage to tell him for the past year—that his brother Warner was using her in a sexual manner. She felt that she *had* to tell him if she was to be the honored mother of his first born. But how would she find the words? And what would the knowledge that his last friend was disloyal do to him?

"Comie bed now," she said again, a little more insistently.

Whyte looked up at her and smiled. She looked very maternal tonight, he thought. It occurred to him—almost as a shock—that he loved her a great deal. Not with the same passion he originally felt for her and not with the bittersweet longing some instinctive part of him still felt for the perfect Americanness of Shelley Spencer. But love nonetheless. He had come to accept her limitations as a *tai tai* and they were comfortable together. The last few years would have been unendurable without her. A baby was good, he thought. Perhaps even an omen of a new beginning. "In a while."

"You needee lovings," she said, pouting. "Not good to go whole week without lovings."

He sighed and put down the pencil. "All right, Su Ling." He smiled at her tenderly. "Time for lovings."

"Bout time," she said with a note of triumph.

He stood up and kissed her and she rubbed his crotch through his jeans. He pulled her toward him and they walked arm-in-arm into the bedroom. When they reached their bed, she kissed him hungrily and fell back on the mattress, triggering the bomb that blew the room apart.

* * *

Su Ling was buried in the Catholic cemetery near Tamsui in an elaborate ceremony two days after the explosion. The U.S. ambassador, half the American Community and a mob of her fans came to mourn. A Chinese musical ensemble sent her soul to heaven in a cacophony of gongs and cymbals. Stacks of fake cemetery money, placed on her grave for the afterlife, scattered in the wind.

Bryan Whyte was not there. He had undergone three operations in forty-eight hours for removal of shrapnel and was in the most critical of conditions. The doctors at the U.S. Navy Hospital offered little hope that he would ever regain consciousness.

King Lu was the first informed of the explosion; he made it to the hospital just minutes after the ambulances. He sent escorts back to China Gate for Old Whyte and to Jen Ai for Georgie Warner, who rushed to form a waiting-room vigil.

Old Whyte was so stunned at the ghastly, eerie repeat of his own tragedy in 1947 that he fell into catatonia and would not utter a word. Warner, the heir to all the responsibility of the Omega Chi should Whyte die, seemed almost as distraught. Only King kept his confidence and an unshakable belief that Bryan Whyte would not die.

The Navy surgeon came out after the third operation. "I've taken thirty-seven pieces of metal out of that man's body. Extensive damage has been done to several of his vital organs and his brain has suffered a massive concussion. I don't see that he has much of a chance."

"No, Doctor, you are mistaken," King said. "He will not die."

Over the protests of the hospital staff, King had Old Whyte sign his son out. They took him back to China Gate under an armed guard the size of an army. A hospital room was set up as King brought in medical specialists and Taoist folk magicians from all over Asia—many enlisted at gunpoint and all terrified of King's wrath should their treatments fail.

"He is not to die," King told each one of them.

A liver specialist from Hong Kong was the most pessimistic. "The damage seems irreparable. He is very weak and seems to have no strong will to live. I think he will die soon."

"He will not die."

"There is nothing that can be done, my *tai-lo.*"

"He will not die," King said firmly. "He cannot die. He still has a destiny to fulfill."

Bryan Whyte did not die. Two weeks later he suddenly blinked awake. The first thing he saw was King Lu sitting beside him, looking blurry-eyed from lack of sleep.

As Whyte's vision cleared, he strained to focus his consciousness. "Su . . . Ling?"

"She is gone."

"And my father?"

"He is in the next room. The bomb didn't touch him."

Whyte closed his eyes for a few moments, then opened them and looked to King for an explanation.

"I do not know how it happened," King said, his voice breaking, unable to disguise the anguish and humiliation he felt. "The entire squad charged with your protection has been put to death. There are other traitors among us and I promise I will root them out and hand you their hearts."

"I believe you."

King's black eyes looked down in shame as he continued to speak. "Bryan, I have made a peace with our enemies. I could not hold out any longer. There was no other way to avoid a war or guarantee your safety. I have granted them concessions in the Min Chuan area and the share they wanted of the Orient Express. I am sorry."

"I understand, Elder Brother."

When he was able to get out of bed to start his physical therapy a month later, Whyte immediately tried to take back the reins of the Omega Chi—a company that was now in serious financial difficulty.

Racked by fears of an American pull-out in Vietnam,

by bad management, by the death of Mark Taylor, the near-death of Bryan Whyte and concessions granted to the Warlords-Tiger Eels, the business empire that Whyte had painstakingly constructed on American confidence in Asia was disintegrating before his eyes.

After the bombing at China Gate, all the traditional sources of credit instantly dried up. Financial managers in Omega Chi branch offices in Manila and Singapore and Penang found bank doors closed to them. Omega Chi expansion was halted in its tracks and then, almost immediately, Omega Chi businesses all over Asia began to fold. One by one, the little blue pins began to be removed from the map in the council room of China Gate.

A run started. *Compradores* besieged China Gate demanding payments, calling in loans and canceling contracts. Whyte closed his doors to them. Soon, even Whyte's friend, David Ward Kee, knowing his career was tied to Whyte and therefore ruined, had no choice but to call in his notes for the Bank of Taiwan. The doors of China Gate closed to him as well.

Despite the peace negotiations by King Lu, the anti-Omega Chi coalition began encroaching on every operation in every city of the world where the Omega Chi did business. Once inside, they quickly took over the Orient Express for themselves. They proceeded to squeeze the U.S. installations and their Chinese and Taiwanese contractors. The Taiwanese Independence Movement was riding so high it tried to assassinate Chiang's son and heir apparent, Chiang Ching-kuo, on the streets of New York City—further dirtying the face of the Omega Chi, the Green Society and the Kuomintang.

Still bedridden except for brief periods, Whyte realized that the only way to keep the organization alive until he got on his feet was to somehow convince Alan Phillips to come back and run it. Warner was trying hard to fill in during the convalescence, but he was hopelessly incompetent as a leader or businessman. Phillips was the only person besides himself who really knew how the Omega Chi functioned, who had the skill to be everywhere at once, who could restore confidence with his sincerity and charm, and oversee the thousands of daily business details.

Finally, he had no choice but to swallow his pride and write Phillips a long letter, explaining everything that had happened, reminding him he was still an equal partner, telling him how the Omega Chi desperately needed him, begging him to return. He sent this letter by special courier. Three days later the courier brought the letter back with its answer rudely scrawled across it in red ink:

"Have you learned nothing?!!!"

Ah Chin slipped into the dim bedroom and whispered to Whyte that David Butler was there to see him.

"Tell him I'm asleep."

"He says he's leaving for the States in the morning."

Whyte's dislike for David Butler had grown over the last few years. He loathed the stories Butler wrote about Taylor, stories that seemed to celebrate him as a warrior but were actually slyly written, Whyte felt, to denigrate the war effort. He blamed much of The Doubt and the failure of the war on journalists like Butler. Even at the mention of his name, he felt a rising tide of frustration over the impossibility of controlling them.

But Butler was the last person to see Mark Taylor alive and it occurred to Whyte that he should question the journalist about Soldier's death while he had the chance. "Okay," he said to Ah Chin. "But rescue me after a few minutes with doctor's orders or something." Butler was led into the room. He had come for no other reason than the pleasure of seeing the great man on the floor and Whyte knew this. The reporter reached over the bed to offer his hand.

"I wanted to say good-by before I took off."

Whyte said nothing.

"I wanted to tell you how sorry I am about your present troubles—and about Mark."

"Thank you."

"I feel privileged to be the one who let the whole world know about him."

Uninvited, he pulled up a chair beside the bed and sat on it.

"How—exactly—did it happen?" Whyte asked.

"What?"

"His death."

Butler made a nervous half-laugh. "Didn't Taylor write you before he died?"

"We hadn't heard anything from him for months."

"Oh, Christ," Butler said. "I thought you knew."

"Knew what?"

"Taylor found out that Hwang and the Saigon Greens were buying opium and *jin chu* from the VC by the truckload—and paying for it with stolen American arms." He shook his head disgustedly. "I'm doing a whole series of stories about it for AP this month."

Whyte's entire body seemed to turn to stone.

"Finding that out seemed to absolutely destroy him. My guess is he went to Saigon to try and stop it at the source."

"How . . . did . . . he . . . die?"

"I don't know exactly, but it sure as hell wasn't the VC. Those boys don't go in for ritualistic killings. No, most likely he was chopped down by your old friend, 'Pockmarked' Hwang of the Green Society."

"Better hustle your buns, man, that crowd's been waitin' an hour."

John Casy scrambled out of the helicopter with the rest of his band and followed the nervous, stoned promoter to the backstage area of the huge outdoor rock concert in Woodstock, New York. His body was still tingling from the view coming in. The crowd was staggering; it just went on for miles with no end in sight. The pilot told him they were already estimating it at more than half a million—the greatest gathering of its kind in American history.

Casy had spent the last twenty-four hours in deep depression. Phillips had called yesterday to tell him about the death of Mark Taylor, the breakup of the Omega Chi empire and the bomb attack on Bryan Whyte. The image of Whyte as a broken invalid profoundly affected him, filled him with sadness and guilt and a compulsion to drop everything and run back to Taipei. It was a last bittersweet nostalgia for a past he had given up long ago, and no amount of coke or grass or speed or wine would get rid of it.

But when the promoter introduced his band, the depression instantly vanished. Several hundred thousand people roared and Casy was consumed in glory and power. From the stage, it was an even more extraordinary sight than it had been from the air. A whole American generation—the biggest and best this country had ever produced—had turned out to celebrate itself. Its culture, its idealism, its unity, its determination to build a future based on love and peace and justice. And he, John Casy, was a voice of that generation, a leader of a cultural revolution, a prophet of a whole new state of consciousness. . . .

Casy stood center stage and waved to the crowd. As he made a V for peace sign with two fingers, a photographer snapped a picture of him. A week later Bryan Whyte, lying in his bed at China Gate, saw it in *Newsweek* under a headline that read: "We Are All One."

After Butler's visit, Bryan Whyte underwent a startling change of personality. He dismissed his physical therapists, went back to bed and told Ah Chin he would not see anyone—not his father or King Lu or Georgie Warner or any of the hundred staff members who desperately wanted a decision out of him about a thousand vital matters.

As the new decade of the seventies began, Whyte's problems were mounting at a devastating rate. The Omega Chi business empire continued to disintegrate in direct proportion to the growing acceptance in Free Asia that the war was lost. Reports flowed in from his congressional supporters in the States that he would likely be called before a grand jury investigation or a reconvened session of the Randolph Committee. Doctors sent him stern warnings that if he didn't get out of bed and start a serious physical therapy program soon, he might never walk again.

But he could not deal with any of it. The Doubt that had nagged at the edges of his security all these months finally engulfed and immobilized him. Throughout the opening months of 1970, he lay in his bed, no longer struggling, letting it all wash him away like a toothpick caught in a storm drain.

He looked unflinchingly at all those things he had been so afraid to see. He let himself understand how the American Dream he embraced all his life had been twisted and compromised, rationalized away in this unchecked Asian environment until it had turned into something unconscionable, a kind of monster that operated on the logic of insanity. He let himself see all the darkness in the crevices of that Dream—just as Casy and Phillips and Taylor had seen it before him.

And when he faced it, squarely, unemotionally, an extraordinary thing happened. He realized that what he saw was not strong enough to kill him. Even at full flood, The Doubt was not powerful enough to completely eradicate the Dream. He still had something to hang on to— and it was enough.

One morning he stared up at the shafts of white winter light streaming through his bedroom window and realized he had just survived the ordeal of his life. He had survived and was ready now to get out of bed, to get well and face all the terrible consequences that awaited him.

His life was in ruins but Bryan Whyte's sense of destiny was intact. He was ready to start over.

BOOK THREE
1971–1979

17

EARLY IN THE YEAR 1971, SHELLEY SPENCER AND PRACtically every other free-lance journalist in New York City became obsessed with the idea of experiencing the war in Southeast Asia before it was too late. With the advent of massive troop withdrawals and increased "Vietnamization," it finally looked as if that epic conflict might actually have an end somewhere in sight for America. The panicky realization hit Shelley that she might actually miss the single most traumatic, most formative event of her generation.

A few years ago, it would not have occurred to her to feel bad about missing Vietnam. She was not a journalist then and had never been very politically oriented or particularly interested in Asia. She had dropped out of college in 1965 and became a reasonably successful, second-level photographer's model in New York, living an extremely frivolous existence surrounded by silly and useless people who never spoke of anything more serious than eyeliner and lip-gloss.

She soon became dissatisfied with this life and discovered she did not like modeling. The inactivity of it all drove her straight up the wall, as did the mindlessly vain people associated with it. Nor could she see any real future in it as a career. The lifespan of even the top models was a few years at best and she had no interest in using the profession as a stepping-stone to acting or television commercials. Furthermore, every time she picked up a newspaper or magazine she felt she was missing out on the most exciting college days any American generation had ever experienced—and she deeply regretted leaving school before it had started.

In 1967, she enrolled at NYU and began to hang around the emerging hippie crowd in the East Village, continuing to model only often enough to pay the rent. There, she met and fell in love with a fiery, movie-star handsome, totally radicalized Columbia University student who was organizing state chapters of the Students for a Democratic Society. She devoted herself to him and his cause, moved into his bachelor apartment on Mac-Dougal Street, became pregnant, had an abortion (she had long since drifted away from the Catholic Church), married him (at her horrified parents' insistence) and divorced him after the third time she came home from work early and caught him in bed with another man (an expression of his radicalism she was not, at that point, prepared to accept).

After the divorce, she moved back in with her parents, trying to sort out her life. As part of her soul-searching, she began seeing a psychiatrist in nearby St. Louis. In the course of her therapy, she and the psychiatrist fell in love and had an affair. This too ended badly—the doctor turned out to be the prototypical mama's boy and Shelley lost interest fast. But before she did, she learned from him an important thing about herself: She was fatally attracted to strong, dominant, dangerous men whom she used her beauty to attract and on whom she relied for her feelings of self-esteem. These men invariably fell from their macho pedestals and disappointed her. It became clear to her that she would never have a successful, mature relationship until she developed a sense of self-worth. And she would never feel good about herself until she found a profession or job at which she could excel without relying on her looks—preferably a profession at which she could make a social contribution yet one with some hint of glamor to keep her attracted to it.

Journalism proved to be that profession. She always had a knack for writing, though she never dared to aspire to be a real honest-to-goodness writer. Using several oblique references and all the charm she could muster, she conned herself a job on a small weekly in upstate New York for six months. She then went on a dedicated campaign to teach herself the Norman Mailer–style New Journalism. After another year of struggle, she sold a piece on the American Nazi Party in New England to the *New York Times Magazine* and then a bitchy show business profile to *Esquire*. Soon after, she managed to become a regular contributor to the rising counterculture tabloid, *New World*.

The past year had been the most eventful and utterly insane of her whole life. She began to specialize in stories about Hollywood and rock music and she found herself constantly jet-setting between New York and L.A. She began to move in the trendiest circles and went to parties where the guest list always seemed to include Mick Jagger, Roman Polanski or Warren Beatty. She had a brief affair with a famous black rock star, who later died of a drug overdose, and she hung out with some of the Chicago Seven. She even went to several chic sex orgies in Beverly Hills and Bel Air. As the glamorous star reporter for *New World* magazine, all doors were open to her—and once inside she did her best to experience everything.

By the second year of the new decade, she had tried just about everything and was growing very weary of it all —weary and disillusioned. She still had not come close to forming a happy, workable relationship with a man. The closer she came to the bold outlaw figures that always intrigued her, the more conventional and shallow they all seemed. The more famous she became as a journalist, the more she despised herself because she felt she still owed most of her success to her looks rather than any real talent. Gradually, she began to thirst for something that would take her out of her glamorous rut, something with more seriousness and relevance, something that would challenge every fiber of her journalistic being and make her feel good about herself. Something like a trip to face the dark jungle horror of Vietnam.

On this particular morning, she flew into the editorial

offices of *New World* magazine to try once again to badger herself into a Vietnam assignment.

Jim Hallowell, the assistant editor, was examining color transparencies in his tiny office overlooking Madison Avenue. He was a pudgy, consciously hip young Bostonian who had been editor of the *Harvard Lampoon* and who had been trying to get into her pants for over a year now. "Well," he said, "looks like I've got an Asian assignment for you if you still want it."

She moved very close to him, close enough so that he could smell her, close enough to promise even greater intimacy. "I love you, Jimbo," she said, beaming. "I knew you'd come through for me. When do I leave?"

"Hold on," he said coyly. "It's not Vietnam."

"Not Vietnam? What're you talking about?"

She moved abruptly away from him, and he swiveled in his chair to keep his eyes on her body. "We have all the stories on Vietnam we need right now. We want something different. I want you to go somewhere else in Southeast Asia—to the place where our policy really started . . . Formosa."

She moaned and flopped back in a chair. "Tell me you're kidding. Please tell me."

"Come on, you used to live there. There must be a hell of a story going on. These people are going to be drastically affected by the coming pull-out from Southeast Asia. How do they feel about it? What are their worries about America's will to protect them? What is this decade going to be like? Talk to as many people as you can. American, Chinese, whatever. Give me something on 'Asia After Vietnam' or 'Asia in the Seventies' or some damn thing like that. And a great sidebar would be an interview with this tycoon they're calling a gangster and war profiteer. The guy you used to know. . . ." He picked up a piece of paper with a name scrawled on it. "Yeah, get me an interview with this William Bryan Whyte."

The one place in the world that Shelley Spencer was convinced she did *not* want to go was Taiwan. She had

been through a very difficult metamorphosis in her thinking about the place. She still cherished her memories of the
colonial way of life she had enjoyed there at the height of
America's confidence in Asia. It was simply a magical way
to grow up. But she had come to realize—as did her entire
generation—that that life was based on arrogance and
racism and a paranoid fallacy about an international Communist conspiracy. Because of that way of life and that
thinking, Americans and Asians were dying by the thousands every day in the jungles of Southeast Asia. She had
come to accept this about her past life but she did not want
to go back and stare it in the face.

She particularly did not want to see Bryan Whyte.
Since she left him on that Missouri airfield nearly seven
years ago, she had heard many things about him—all of
them bad. She knew vaguely that he had carved himself
a business empire in Asia, that he lived in a palace on
Grass Mountain and that he served the reactionary military dictators who were strangling the people of Asia. She
also supposed he was somehow still connected with Oriental gangsters who were making fortunes off the war. It was
just that his world was now being destroyed and she felt
only pity and contempt for this man who was so utterly
out of step with the course of history.

But, despite her reservations, she went to her apartment, packed her bags and left the next morning. She got
a connection in San Francisco on China Airlines and flew
to Taipei in one marathon day.

Shelley landed at Sung Shan in the middle of the
night. A Government Information Office guide picked her
up and took her to the Grand Hotel, the very hotel where
she and her family stayed when they first arrived there in
1960. The cool air and the familiar pungent odor of the city
stirred her memory. She strolled out on the bluff overlooking the Tamsui River and thought of the night she and
Bryan Whyte had watched the fireworks celebrating the
Kennedy inaugural from the same spot.

For a brief instant, Shelley relived that night, felt
exactly the way she felt over a decade ago when Bryan told
her they were heading into a "great adventure" together.

The memory, the experience, was so sweet and so vivid that it unsettled her. When she finally went into the great, gaudy lobby of the Grand Hotel, there were tears in her eyes.

The next day, she went out to begin her interviews. She decided to narrow her story to the effect of the war on the American Community—a personal view of then and now. She had her guide take her around to the various American military, business and missionary leaders and she asked them all the same question: How had Vietnam changed the sensibility of this tiny, self-contained community of Americans? They all had windy, evasive answers but she could see for herself that that sensibility had been devastated. These people all knew that an American pull-out from Asia was coming—in some form or another. For all essential purposes, the Taipei American Community no longer even existed. It represented an idea of what America could do for Asia that no one really believed any longer. It was a state of confidence that had passed into history as surely as the confidence that created the British raj.

She next went to the Taipei American School, which had moved out to Shih Lin in 1964. The principal there was still Carla Thomas—wife of Captain Thomas, head of the Naval Medical Research Unit in Taipei since the early fifties.

Mrs. Thomas served as the American Community's unofficial historian and was able to give Shelley a rundown on the fate of most of the people who had graduated with her in the TAS class of 1963.

"Of course, you know about Mark Taylor . . . ?" The principal asked carefully. She was a warm, pretty and unusually fair-minded woman who was adored by all her former students.

"Yes, I read about it."

"He's our authentic hero. But we've lost many others to the war. More than our share, certainly. Probably because we've had so many military families through here. I received word yesterday that little Dennis

Chou was killed near Da Nang. Do you remember him?"

Shelley couldn't place the name. She shook her head sadly and said, "I also know about John Casy. Would anyone have ever dreamed that serious, sensitive John Casy would turn out to be a rock 'n' roll star?"

"Do you know about Alan Phillips?"

"No."

The woman smiled gently. "Alan Phillips left here several years ago and is now a professional war protester. He's been in jail a good deal."

This floored Shelley. She couldn't even imagine Phillips in such a role. What all this must have done to poor Bryan Whyte. Whyte and his precious Omega Chi. "What about Georgie Warner?"

"He still lives in Taipei. He manages a movie studio not far from here. He's rather a strange case, though. He rarely goes out in public and I haven't seen him in years."

She thought a moment about the merry prankster who used to be her special friend. He had probably never gotten over his scarred face. "What about Randy Ortega?"

"He's dead. Murdered in a barroom brawl in 1967."

No loss there, she thought. "What about his friends, the Warlords?"

"Oh, most of them are around in some business or another. Amos Wong went on to college in the States. He's now in graduate school. Remember Tim Cutler? He left the Warlords in 1965 and is now head of the Hari Krishna for the State of Ohio."

Shelley laughed. She thought of the arrogant bully who used to chase around the younger kids at school with a bicycle chain. "Unbelievable!"

As the woman continued to reel off the names and fates, Shelley began to get excited. It was apparent that, in one way or another, all of her class had been caught up or revolutionized or destroyed in the drama and change of the sixties. It occurred to her in a thunderbolt of inspiration that the story of this class—which came from a prototypical American community yet provided an international cross section, which was the first graduating class of the great postwar baby boom, which was the first class to experience the social revolution of Vietnam—was simply an extraordinary story, the story of her generation, perhaps the one big story of her life.

She took a deep breath. "And what do you know about Bryan Whyte?"

Mrs. Thomas smiled again, suddenly remembering for the first time the girl's relationship to Whyte. "Oh, he's still very much an enigma. He's the one who has changed the most and at the same time not changed at all. He's a very strong man who has been very hurt by the events of the last few years. . . ."

Shelley's heart was inexplicably pounding. "I want to see him . . . to . . . interview him. . . ."

"Now that might be difficult. He's been inaccessible for nearly a year now. I understand he sees no one—not even his closest friends."

Shelley had the guide take her directly to China Gate, high on Grass Mountain. Stepping out of the car, she gazed up in surprise and awe at what looked like a storybook castle looming above its great outer wall. Her image of the kind of man who would live in such a house evoked a deep, long-buried romantic excitement in her. Standing there before China Gate, she was swept away by an emotion so intense that it engendered her second thunderbolt of insight for the day, an even more startling moment of truth.

She suddenly realized that she had been deluding herself. She saw, with amazing clarity, that she had been lying to herself all along about wanting to see Vietnam. She had subconsciously engineered this trip to Taiwan by telling her editor irresistible stories about the Island for the past year. She had never stopped being obsessed by Bryan Whyte, even for a minute, even if everything she had become told her she must despise him. She had spent her whole adult life vainly searching for his equal and denying it to herself. She had spent the last year trying to get to this spot, to be in a position to satisfy her burning female curiosity about this strange, powerful, larger-than-life figure of her youth, to see if he could possibly have turned out to be even a fraction of his former self.

Trembling with this revelation, she took a deep breath and approached the gate.

But the armed sentry refused them entry. Her guide chattered back and forth with him for several minutes, then turned to her. "This man, he say the taipan is gone. He doesn't know where exactly. No one is being admitted on the grounds while he's away."

Shelley was undaunted. She reached into her purse. "Never mind," she said to the sentry. "Give Mr. Whyte this card when he returns. Tell him I'll be back tomorrow. And as many days after that as it takes until he'll see me."

Shelley had dinner alone that evening at the Taipei Press Club near Shihminting, the old city center. She went into the lounge for an after-dinner drink and noticed David Butler nursing a gin and tonic at the bar.

She was a great admirer of Butler, who, with Michael Herr and John Sacks, was probably the best-known correspondent to come out of the war. She had read and reread all his stuff in *Esquire*, even consciously copying his style on occasion.

As she walked toward him, Butler eyed her lustfully, vaguely startled at seeing such a beautiful American woman alone in a bar in this part of the world. "A goddess in our midst," he said, a bit suspiciously, as she joined him.

"I'm Shelley Spencer. You don't remember me but I used to live here in the early sixties. I used to go with Bryan Whyte and we met once a long time ago." She offered her hand.

"Sure I remember you, Shelley," he said, taking her hand and holding it a moment, noticing the unusually long, slender fingers. He didn't actually remember her at all. "What brings you back this way?"

"I'm doing a story for *New World* magazine."

"Ah, a fellow journalist."

"And a big fan of yours." Her big green eyes were brimming with admiration.

He acknowledged the compliment with a slight bow of his head.

"The piece you did in the Chicago *Tribune* on Mark Taylor was one of the best things I've ever read about Vietnam. You really captured something."

Butler smiled awkwardly, embarrassed. "Tell me, Shelley, why are you here instead of Saigon with the rest of the pack?"

"I'm doing a piece on the effect of the war on the American Community here."

"That's an interesting angle. How're you doing with it so far?"

"Terrific. I'm very excited about the whole project. I may even get a book out of it."

Butler laughed scornfully. "Is there any journalist out there who isn't writing a book?"

Shelley just smiled.

Butler finished his drink with a gulp then signaled the bartender for another round for each of them. With any luck he might not have to hit the whorehouses tonight.

"I'm going to interview everyone I went to high school with here. The Omega Chi. The Warlords. All of the old gangs, their girlfriends, their hangers-on and everyone else in the TAS class of '63. I'm going to tell the story of how the sixties changed them and changed the world that used to exist on this island."

Butler nodded thoughtfully. "Sounds great, only . . ."

"Only what?"

"Only you're a bit premature. We haven't even begun to see the changes that will take place around here because of the war."

"You think so?"

"I know so. We've had our ass kicked down in Nam. Nothing will ever be the same again for Americans in Asia. The postwar period here will be as radical as Reconstruction was in the South after the Civil War."

Butler moved closer and his knee now touched hers. His breath was an alcoholic abomination and he was making her very uncomfortable, but she did not move away. There was still information she wanted from him.

Butler kept right on talking. "All these Americans who have dedicated themselves to the old order are going to end up disgraced and empty-handed. And believe me, none of them will be more disgraced than your old sweetheart, Bryan Whyte."

"I . . . I understand he's in seclusion and won't see anyone."

"He was badly hurt—crippled—in a bombing at China Gate last year. The bomb killed his mistress."

"Mistress?"

"Yeah, Chinese mistress. A real looker. He's been taking it hard. I understand it took him a full year just to get out of bed."

She reached in her purse for a cigarette and let Butler light it. "Any idea what he'll do now?"

"Maybe he'll go back to the States. He's crazy if he doesn't. He can't last long here. It's only a matter of time till one of his enemies gets lucky and shoots him dead."

"He'll never live in the States," Shelley said, "no matter what."

Butler chuckled. "You may be right. A guy like Whyte wouldn't even know *how* to live in the States."

Shelley said nothing for several moments. A reservoir of old feelings broke loose and flooded her body. The realization of Bryan Whyte's impossible situation made her feel both very protective of him and deeply excited. "I'm going to try and interview him. Do you have any idea how I can get into China Gate?"

"He's not there. He's in Washington D.C. I understand he's in some big trouble with the government again. He's back there trying to talk his way out of it."

Shelley put out her cigarette and picked up her purse.

Butler placed his hand on her knee. "Hey, how about coming over to my hotel room for another drink?"

She smiled knowingly. "I'd love to—expect that I intend to be on the next plane for the States."

Whyte stared into the cold, killer eyes of the presidential aide. The man was young, Whyte thought, too young—a hotshot. All these years he had been accustomed to being the youngest party of every business transaction, but now at age twenty-seven, others were finally catching up with him. He was actually dealing with someone his own age and didn't much like it.

The presidential aide, whose name was Caryer, put his feet on his desk and shoved a stick of gum in his mouth. The man knew Whyte was down and he had deliberately humiliated him further by having him wait forty minutes before seeing him. "I have to be frank with you, Bryan," he said. "The Justice Department has been getting a hell of a lot of pressure to make a full inquiry into your career. There are certain elements even within this administration that are pushing for an indictment against you."

This came as no surprise to Whyte. His attorneys had been warning him of this possibility for the past year. The liberal press was after him with a vengeance and he had become so controversial that even Congressman Laughton and the China lobby—his staunchest political supporters —were afraid to speak up for him. Why else would he be in Washington talking to this irritating all-American boy?

Caryer smacked the gum and looked at the ceiling as he spoke. "Now this administration realizes the invaluable contribution you and the Omega Chi have made to our efforts in the Far East. We don't intend to see our friends harassed because of legal technicalities which don't really apply to doing business in Asia. We intend to put a lid on any such indictment as long as we're in a position to do so. However, I must tell you that should our mutual enemies win the election next time around . . ."

Whyte had to restrain himself from laughing outloud. This Princeton punk was putting the squeeze on him for a campaign contribution! He had come halfway around the world to offer them big money to quiet a Justice Department investigation and this amateur was trying to crudely hustle him for peanuts. He thought he much preferred doing business with Democrats, who observed the subtleties of the game. "I fully realize that, Mr. Caryer. I know that it is vital for this country and its interests in Asia that the President be reelected in 1972. That's why I'm prepared to offer a substantial campaign contribution. In fact, I'm prepared to offer a *very* substantial sum and more."

The eyes of the presidential aide widened perceptibly. "More?" he asked.

"Speaking for the business communities of the free countries of Asia, I can promise substantial contributions to the majority of the friendly members of your party who are up for reelection."

"Really?" Caryer picked up a letter opener and played with it. His tone became noticeably more respectful. "And where will this money come from?"

"It will come from various friendly governments of Asia that feel they have a stake in this election. Anti-Communist governments and financial interests who fear being sold out by a Democratic appeaser like Randolph or this McGovern character. Beyond that I can say no more. This will be totally unofficial, of course, and your only connection will be the Americans for a Free Asia office here in town."

"How much money?" the aide asked bluntly.

"As much as you want," Whyte answered, just as bluntly.

The aide calmly put down the letter opener. "This is a very intriguing proposal," he said. "I will relay it to the chairman of the President's reelection committee. I'm sure he'll find it a very friendly gesture on your part."

"This is all contingent, of course, on your assurances that certain disturbing rumors now circulating are unfounded."

"Rumors?"

"Rumors that Mr. Kissinger has entered into some

sort of secret negotiations with the Chinese Communists."

Caryer took his feet off the desk and faced Whyte for the first time during their conversation. "Where did you hear this?"

"The story was originally overheard at a Georgetown cocktail party by a younger staffer from the Nationalist Chinese Embassy. Since then, it's been cabled back to Taipei from several other sources."

"Extraordinary. How *do* these things get started?"

"I need your assurances that the rumors are false. You can't, after all, expect these governments to finance their own sellout."

Caryer appeared distraught for a moment. "Yes, of course. The President is the oldest and strongest supporter Nationalist China has ever had. There are no circumstances under which he would sell out his old friend and ally."

"Good."

Whyte stood up to leave as the phone rang. Caryer picked it up, listened, cupped it and looked panic-stricken. "There's a reporter outside to see you. Who knows you're here?"

"No idea."

He growled into the phone. "Send him away. Mr. Whyte is not here. This office has no connection with Bryan Whyte or the Omega Chi."

"Screw it, I'll talk to him," Whyte said and he opened the door to see Shelley Spencer waiting for him.

He recognized her immediately. Her hair was longer, her body slimmer, more desirable, and her face without make-up was somehow more youthful and wholesome. The sight of her stabbed him with wistful memories of prewar days when his life was simple and his responsibility clear.

Unhesitatingly, she ran to him and threw her arms around him. He hugged back, inhaling her still familiar, exciting scent, then forced himself to break away. "A long time," he said.

"Only seven years."

"Why now?"

"I'm a journalist now."

"I heard that."

"I've been assigned by *New World* to interview you."

"Oh, I see," he said, not hiding his disappointment. "How did you find me?"

"It wasn't easy. I started in Taipei and followed your trail from there."

"What kind of story are you doing?"

"Something on the Taipei American Community—how it's been devastated by the war."

He jerked slightly. There was an icy moment of silence in which they each glimpsed the gulf between them.

"I want to interview as many of our old classmates as I can find," she quickly added, feeling suddenly stupid and awkward.

"Really? Have you seen any of the others yet?"

"I spoke to Alan yesterday on the phone. Do you realize that he practically runs the antiwar movement in New York State."

"He has a way of making himself indispensable to an organization."

"He seems to be very happy. He says he's found something to believe in. I guess he's the kind of person who needs that."

"How about Casy?"

"I interviewed John for *New World* a few months ago."

"And how is old Casy these days?"

"Surrounded by groupies and yes-men and spaced out beyond belief. He wears cartridge belts now. Can you imagine that? Very radical chic."

Whyte grinned. He thought of the time Casy had been too frightened to walk down Sin Alley. "No, I can't imagine it."

"He's been very hot these last two years but I think his career is peaking. People are starting to listen to mellower stuff these days."

"I suppose I'm an embarrassment to those guys."

"They both asked about you. I think they both . . ."

"Feel sorry for me." He smiled good-naturedly.

"No. Care about you very much."

He kept smiling. "They have a funny way of showing it."

They walked out of the old Executive Office Building and down a snow-covered Pennsylvania Avenue. She did not comment on the obvious fact that he needed a cane to walk. The conversation was difficult and very awkward. He strangely could not think of anything to say; even though the only thing on his mind was that, after everything that had happened, he still wanted to possess this woman in that same unrestrained way he had once wanted to possess all of America.

Finally, he stopped and turned to her. "I have to run," he said. "I have an appointment in Georgetown."

He was pleased to see the disappointment register on her face. "What about the interview?" she asked.

"Why not? Let's meet for lunch tomorrow. I'm staying at the Hilton."

She was already waiting in the hotel café, a tape recorder on the table before her, when he came down five minutes early for the interview. She smiled her most radiant smile as he approached.

Whyte smiled back stiffly and sat down and stared at the recorder, his manner suspicious and guarded. "Now why is it that you want to interview me?" he asked.

"Actually, it was a direct assignment. My editor said, 'Get me an interview with this William Bryan Whyte.' "

"Amazing coincidence."

Her eyes lowered. "Well, I suppose I did plant the idea in his mind."

"Why?"

"Curiosity."

"Curiosity as to whether or not I've really become all the things you've heard about me?"

"I never believe anything I read in the papers. I was curious to see if the image of you I've been carrying around for the last seven years was real or not."

"Well, is it?"

"I'm not sure." She was lying. She was sure. Ever since she laid eyes on him yesterday she had been under his spell as surely as if she were a high-school senior again. Every minute with him only served to reinforce the great moment of truth she'd experienced standing before China Gate.

"Well, let's get this thing over," he said.

"You don't really want to do an interview, do you?"

"No."

"Are you hungry?"

"No."

"What *were* you going to do today?"

"I was going to do a little sightseeing. Would you care to join me?"

They took a taxi to the Capitol building. On the way, Bryan took it upon himself to point out various historical places of interest. His mood changed; he was lighter, playful, very charming and fully appreciative of the gift of their being together again.

They toured the Capitol, then walked down the Mall and through some of the buildings of the Smithsonian. They happily reminisced about the old days, carefully avoiding any subject that might break the magical mood, until finally, standing before the enormous Francis Scott Key flag in the Museum of American History, Shelley risked it by taking his hand and saying, "Bryan, I'm sorry about your tragedies. About your . . . girlfriend . . . and about Mark. I can imagine how his death particularly must have affected you."

"I'm afraid I have a difficult time talking about that subject," he said, tensing up.

She pressed his hand. "I just wanted you to know how I feel."

Bryan had to leave for another appointment but they met again later that evening at his hotel. Over dinner, she told him about her life since 1964, about modeling and journalism, about meeting Bob Dylan and smoking *jin chu* with the Rolling Stones, about her failed marriage and failed romances, about her dissatisfaction with herself and ambitions for the future.

"It wasn't until I went back to Taipei that I fully realized how empty and fatuous my life has been. I've spent seven years chasing after glamorous, insipid people who aren't even a fraction as interesting as the people I knew in high school. It's all been for nothing. And you knew, didn't you? You knew that day in 1964 that I was making a mistake. You tried to tell me and I wouldn't listen."

He shook his head. "I didn't know anything."

"But, Bryan, I feel I can save myself by doing a book. If I can use my journalism experience and the sixties experience to capture the incredible story of what happened to our class . . . well, then, it will all have been for *something.*"

He thought for a long time about what she was saying, very impressed with her. He was proud of her. Proud of the kind of woman she had become.

"You know," he finally said, "we're alike, aren't we? We've been up and down and now we're rebuilding our lives. We always were . . ." He suddenly stopped when he noticed she was crying. "What's the matter?"

"I love you," she sobbed. "I've always loved you. I've never stopped loving you."

Without another word, he took her up to his room, where they made love with a special passion and tenderness that neither had known since high school.

They snuggled in blissful repose in the darkness of the bedroom. Shelley desperately wanted to light a cigarette but she remembered how her smoking irritated him so she resisted the temptation.

"The scars didn't bother you?" he asked.

"They turned me on. Couldn't you tell?"

"What a pervert."

"Am I still the only American girl you've ever been with?"

He smiled. "Yes."

"That really turns me on."

He tenderly played with her hair, delighting in its softness. "You haven't chosen the most opportune time to come back into my life again," he said. "Things have not exactly been going swell for me."

She looked up and made a mock smile. "I've researched you, don't forget. You're fabulously wealthy. I know you can afford me."

"That's not nearly as true as you think. Ask my accountants if you don't believe me."

"You have a business empire."

"A crumbling empire."

"Three hundred separate businesses spread the length of Asia."

"Most of them totally dependent on influence I can no longer exert."

"And property . . ."

"Most of it on the Island, which, given Taiwan's less-than-auspicious future, is not worth a whole lot."

"Well, you can walk away any time you like and still live like a king for the rest of your life."

"I can't walk away. I can't even limp away. Too many people depend on me."

She kissed his chest and snuggled closer. They drifted off for a few moments until Shelley said, "Bryan, are you asleep?"

"Nearly."

"Can I ask you something?"

"Sure."

"These stories about your being the overlord of the Orient Express. Are they true?"

"Am I speaking to a journalist or a lover?"

"A lover, of course."

"Then they're true."

"Oh, Bryan . . ."

"But it's all over. The Omega Chi is out of the business entirely."

"I hate drugs," she said. "I've never understood why all my friends thought drugs would liberate our generation. Everything I've seen over the last few years has convinced me they're going to do just the opposite. I hate to think you were involved."

"It was a terrible mistake. I agreed to it in a moment of weakness and defeat. I'll spend the rest of my life making up for it. Does it make you hate me?"

"No, we're all responsible. My side created the demand, your side supplied it."

Neither spoke for some time. Then Bryan noticed she was crying. "See—you do hate me," he said.

"No. I'm crying because I'm happy. What you've told me makes me love you even more. And I've never, ever loved anyone for being weak. It's wonderful."

She convinced him to come to New York with her for a getaway visit. They taxied into the snow-covered city from Kennedy Airport, moved into her Village apartment on Cornelia Street, unplugged the phone and lost themselves in the anonymity of the city for two glorious weeks.

It was, he confessed to her, the first vacation he had ever taken in his life. And he proved to be very good at it. He seemed relaxed, carefree, funny. He was a dedicated tourist. She took him to plays, concerts and museums and he enjoyed everything. He loved sightseeing and was particularly fascinated by the historical places. They lingered for hours around Wall Street, Ellis Island, the Statue of Liberty. These things seemed to invigorate him, renew his strength and vision.

They had sex every day, often two and three times in succession. They were never able to get enough of one another. They were thoroughly, happily, hopelessly in love again.

One early morning as they lay in bed, she woke him

up with a kiss and impulsively said, "Why don't we get married?"

He yawned. "I tried to marry you seven years ago and you wouldn't have me. Remember?"

"I wasn't ready then. Neither were you."

"Are you serious?"

"I'm completely serious."

"What makes you think you're ready for marriage now?"

"I've changed. I've got a man I love. I've got a book I want to write. As my shrink would say, I have my goals in place and priorities in order and I am now ready to enter into a mature, equal relationship. I'll even quit smoking."

"I can't marry you."

"And why not?"

He sighed. "Because I'm in a very dangerous position. Because there're people out there gunning for me. People like our old friends, the Warlords. People like half the U.S. Congress. Everyone who gets close to me ends up getting hurt in one way or another. You don't need that."

"You can always move back to the States. Is there any reason why you can't run your businesses from San Francisco?"

"I can't run out, Shelley."

"There's no law that says you have to go down with the flag, you know? Certainly you can't still entirely believe in what America is doing over there."

"I still entirely believe in what we started out *trying* to do. I still believe in what capitalism can do for Asia. There's no reason why we can't go on with our mission."

"What mission? I don't know what you mean by that word. I never have. Do you still believe that you're going to restore the Mainland someday?"

"Yes. I believe that. I believe it with all my heart."

She smiled ironically. "You must be the only one. Not even Chiang Kai-shek believes that anymore, I'll bet."

"I don't care. I believe it."

"How are you going to do this?"

"I'm not sure. I have a vague plan but it's uncertain and extremely difficult. And it will take all of my time and energy for years to come."

"You do have a plan?"

"Maybe not a plan exactly. But a faith, a confidence, a . . . certainty that things are going to work out my way. Do you understand?"

She laid her head on his shoulder. "No, I guess I don't. But I don't need to. I don't care about anything except being with you for the rest of my life."

18

THEY WERE MARRIED BY A JUSTICE OF THE PEACE three days later and flew back to Taipei the same morning. Shelley realized that it was hardly a well-thought-out decision on her part but she had never felt quite so sure about anything. She abandoned herself to the idea with a zeal and finally convinced Bryan that she would make a proper taipan's wife, that she could be the person she had been to him in high school, that marrying her was a bold, positive thing to do, an expression of confidence in the future that in no way would interfere with his sacred "mission."

When she called her parents to tell them she was marrying Bryan Whyte and moving to Taiwan, they were aghast. They remembered Whyte as a juvenile delinquent, a criminal, and nothing they had read in the newspapers contradicted this image. Her father, Col. Spencer, refused even to come to the phone. Her mother bitterly castigated her in a snippy, upper-class British accent. But nothing she said could deflate Shelley's joy.

Old Whyte met the couple at Sung Shan and he was ecstatic at the news. He barely remembered Shelley Spencer from the old days but he treated her as his long lost daughter, smothering her with fatherly affection and hopeful hints about grandchildren. She, in turn, instantly adored him.

In fact, she was quite ebullient about her return to Taiwan right up until the moment they drove into China Gate. Then, as the limousine passed through the main entrance, she was seized with a mild panic. From the inside, the estate did not look like a storybook castle at all. She took one look at the barbed wire, the guard dogs, the milling Green bodyguards and the huge, forbidding, institution of a house and Shelley Spencer had the distinct impression she was entering a prison.

The wedding reception was held at the British Consulate at Tamsui on the northwestern coast, some fifteen miles from Taipei. Everyone of any importance in Taipei was invited and most everyone who was invited showed up to witness the reemergence of Bryan Whyte from almost two years of seclusion.

The guests arrived in a fleet of American cars that blocked the narrow streets around the old sixteenth-century Spanish fortress. They were soon all crowding around the consulate ballroom in stiff formal attire as a small orchestra played dance music and a battalion of servants dispensed champagne and trays of Szechwan delicacies.

The official best man, Georgie Warner, met the Whyte limousine at the main gate and escorted the newlyweds into the building. Shelley had not seen Warner since high school and she couldn't keep from staring at him. He was a shocking sight. It was not just his horribly scarred face. In the intervening years, everything about him had come to reflect his not-so-secret life of drink and debauchery. He could pass for twice his twenty-six years and was starting to go badly to fat. There was no trace of the eager-to-please high-school comedian. As they walked up the ancient stone walkway together, she tried to reminisce with him but he rejected her overtures with an uneasy shrug, then disappeared into the crowd.

Old Whyte took her around, introducing her to the assembled guests. As he rattled off their names and positions, it occurred to Shelley that these were the very people whom she, as a New Left journalist, was supposed to despise. They were businessmen whose companies had been exploiting the Asian market for generations, Bible-thumping missionaries of every denomination, American generals and admirals, two visiting right-wing, China lobby congressmen, Kuomintang officials and leaders of the notorious Green Pang Society—all of whom were somewhat uncomfortable at being together in one spot and noticeably preoccupied with some bit of political gossip that she could not quite overhear.

David Butler was there with a swarm of other journalists and he quickly grabbed Shelley for a dance. He maneuvered her out into the middle of the dance floor and then looked her over with an irritating smirk. "I see you managed to find your old boyfriend after all."

She ignored the sarcasm of the remark and smiled back. "Looks like it, doesn't it?"

Butler held her tightly. He had been drinking heavily. "How about a personal interview sometime? You could tell me all about life with the great man."

"I'm afraid you'd find it pretty dull."

"You could come over to my apartment and if we got tired of talking about him . . ."

"You're drunk." She stopped dancing and broke from him.

"Of course I'm drunk. I'm celebrating the end of this world. My prediction is coming true even faster than I thought possible."

"What are you talking about?"

"You mean you don't know?"

"What *is* going on around here?"

"Nixon is selling them all out. All of them—including your husband, despite all the bribes he's paid. The place is buzzing with it. You've married into a doomed race, my dear."

"I don't believe you."

"I told you once that there was a new order coming, didn't I? Well, this is the beginning of it."

She left Butler standing in the dance area and ran to her new husband. She kissed him on the cheek and pulled him away from a congressman.

"What's the matter, honey?"

"Bryan, I was talking to David Butler. He's mumbling something about the Nixon administration abandoning you."

Whyte arched his eyebrow in Butler's direction. "That sounds like a typical, half-assed David Butler analysis of the situation. Who let all these journalists in here, anyway?"

"Is it true?"

"The President announced this morning that there may be cultural exchanges with Communist China sometime in the distant future. The rest is just bullshit speculation. Don't let Butler get under your skin."

He kissed her, winked and returned to the congressman. She stood and watched him a moment, admiring the bold, romantic figure he made, brimming with love for him and confident he could handle any situation.

Later in the evening, Butler approached her again. This time he was more sober and apologetic. "Sorry if I offended you, Mrs. Whyte. I have had a few too many. I'm serious about the interview, though. Your views on the meaning of the cultural exchanges could be very enlightening. Also, I'm hoping we can be friends while we're both living in Taipei. We have a lot in common. . . ."

Her eyes burned holes in him. "If you want to interview anyone, interview my husband. He speaks for both of us. He has my *complete* loyalty. Is that clear, Mr. Butler?"

"Too clear," he said and smiled his irritating smile.

* * *

For their honeymoon, the bride and groom traveled to the famous Hung Mon Temple in the mountains of Central Taiwan. There they consummated their marriage with the sacred Taoist Union of Breaths ritual.

The Union of Breaths was one of several sexual rites developed in the first century A.D. by the Taoist philosopher, Yung Chung. All of the rites were later discredited by Neo-Taoist philosophy but they continued to be practiced over the centuries by certain obscure sects and several of the secret societies, including the Green Pang. The Union was the most famous of these rites and was occasionally used as part of the marriage ceremony by adventurous members of the Greens. In her high school days, Shelley had heard countless stories about it—how it could be used to attain the highest level of physical and spiritual love—and had long been fascinated by the idea. The minute they were officially married, she began working on her new husband to arrange it for them.

Bryan was shocked that she would even consider it. Shocked but aroused. "You're talking about an orgy!"

"It can't be that bad. It's a religious ceremony, isn't it?"

"So's the burning of witches."

"Are you afraid?"

"Of course not. It's just . . . Look, are you sure you want to get into something like this?"

"I want to do anything that will make our marriage more perfect," she purred.

He pulled the necessary strings to set up the ritual for them. They went to Taichung and met with a young priest of the *Fang Chung* sect for an orientation. The priest told them that the rite would consist of two parts. In the first part, which went on for six to ten hours, the body was carefully guided to its highest possible level of sexual excitement without orgasm, thereby storing up the maximum amount of sexual *chee* energy. In the second part, which lasted for an equal amount of time, this *chee* energy was released and exchanged between the participants in a union of ecstacy, creating a perfect balance and subsequent physical and mental harmony. In essense, he said, the idea was to get to that level of communion that was beyond the physical. But to get there, one had to go to the absolute limits of the physical, then slightly beyond.

A two-day fast prior to the event was required to purge the body of all poisons that might retard the storage of *chee* energy. He warned them that the experience was very intense and people were known to keel over and die in the midst of it.

The next morning they entered the Hung Mon Temple.

The first half of the rite was a blur of sensation that Shelley would never be able to completely recall. She was separated from her husband and led to a warm tatami room lit by a single red candle. There she was stripped by two nuns and asked to meditate on the candle for the next hour. Sixty minutes later, three male priests entered the dim room and placed her in a spread-eagle position. They massaged her muscles for another hour. When she was finally, wonderfully, relaxed, she felt something wet moving on her toes. It was a tongue. Two more tongues joined it and continued licking, moving from her feet to her head, slithering over every inch in between and meeting again at her vagina, culminating, as the lips were gently separated, on the clitoris. As she lost herself in this ecstacy and approached orgasm, the tongues stopped. Instantly. There was a long period of inactivity. Just as she began to recover herself, she began to feel a long, curved ceremonial dildo, a *lu-tang*, entering her, expertly masturbating her as a finger plunged into her exposed anus and moved in rhythm with the instrument. This continued, off and on, for a considerable time, hours. But each time she approached orgasm, all movement ceased. The cumulative effect was extraordinary and Shelley soon lost all sense of modesty or shame. She screamed, begged for, demanded relief from the strangers.

During this time, she could not see her husband and had no idea he was having a similar experience just a few feet away in an adjoining room. He too had been stripped and laid bare on the tatami. Two nuns took turns with their mouths, tongues and hands to bring him to a full erection, then jointly licked and sucked him until he was about to come. When the tumescence began to subside, they rubbed the shaft with an odd-smelling oil that numbed it and gave him a remarkable staying power. They would then repeat this process—stopping so he would not reach orgasm—each time with a little more intensity, each time bringing him to a higher plateau of pleasure and lust.

At the end of some six hours of this, Bryan was led into his wife's room. In her sexual drunkenness, she noticed that he was kneeling before her and entering her at last, at last filling her with pleasure and sweet relief. They had ten minutes of exquisite intercourse, then a mutual climax of such shattering satisfaction and intensity that it seemed only a breath away from real physical death. They lay exhausted until the priests entered and slowly began massaging and masturbating them. Remarkably quickly, Bryan entered her again from a side position and the sensation was only slightly less rapturous than before. They exploded into another great climax, like the first carefully modulated to occur at exactly the same time. Bryan felt himself losing consciousness now but the nuns kept him awake, massaging him with the numbing oils until he was ready again. This time they helped him into position to enter her from the rear. The intercourse, now aided by the fingers and tongues of the attendants, went on for an even longer time and ended in a staggeringly satisfying mutual orgasm. Over the next two hours, the process was repeated three more times in three more positions. After the fifth orgasm, they both passed out.

Bryan and Shelley slept for twenty-four hours. When they awoke, the union was complete, a balance of *chee* had been achieved and, according to the teachings of Yung Chung, their communion had surpassed all things physical to that perfect union of souls that lay on the other side.

*   *   *

Shelley returned from her Hung Mon experience deeply in love, ready to start her new life, determined to be a good taipan wife.

She moved into China Gate and took over the running of the house with an iron hand. Since the death of Su Ling, the big house had not had any kind of *tai tai* and the horde of servants had fallen into anarchy. The new Mrs. Whyte started out by firing a third of the existing staff and reorganizing the duties of all the others. She called in Ah Chin and Old Whyte and told them in no uncertain terms who was the new boss of China Gate. Then she flew to Hong Kong and bought enough Ch'ing Dynasty antiques to redecorate the house and erase any trace of the taste of its former mistress (toward whose memory she frequently felt an irrational, shameful jealousy).

This done, she closed herself off in her study and began researching her book, which she intended to call *Change is Now: The Story of One High School Class.* Her idea was to profile a dozen of her old TAS classmates—Randy Ortega, Alan Phillips, Mark Taylor and John Casy among them. It would be a book about the revolution in consciousness of the sixties and what it did to a unique overseas American community that was the physical embodiment of the American foreign policy that had set off the revolution.

Bryan turned out to be surprisingly helpful to her, though she often had the feeling she was being patronized. She doubted he had any real confidence in her literary ability but he listened patiently while she rattled off her ideas to him. He didn't object when she called all over the world and taped long interviews that ran up astronomical phone bills. He never once complained when she stayed up all night writing, filling the air of China Gate with cigarette smoke.

On the other hand, she was perfectly willing to drop her work at a moment's notice whenever he needed her. And he needed her a great deal. She acted as hostess to an endless parade of visitors: Warner, King Lu, various mysterious Chinese underworld characters, businessmen from America and Japan, KMT figures and touring American congressmen. Despite the doubts about their whole position that continued to plague her quiet moments, she was the ever-gracious mistress of the great house and a faithful ally in Bryan Whyte's battle to keep the threads of his financial empire together.

In mid-1971, that battle was not going well for him. The influence and financial stability of the Omega Chi continued to shrink by the day. The Warlords–Tiger Eels coalition gained strength and credibility in direct proportion to this decline; the threat of another assassination attempt was ever-present. His face was also badly damaged by the U.S. ping-pong team's visit to Mainland China. That strange event instigated a flurry of rumors of soon-to-follow diplomatic overtures and drove investor confidence in Free Asia—and particularly Nationalist China—to its lowest point since the early fifties.

Whyte explained to Shelley at one point that he was hurriedly moving what Omega Chi capital was left—and whatever he could still borrow from his few remaining sources of credit—into light manufacturing industries on the Island itself. He believed that the only way to survive in his present circumstances was to do what Japan had done in the initial stages of its economic rebirth. He wanted to build a dependence in the U.S. market on cheap imports which he could produce with low-cost, unskilled labor. Since 1970, Omega Chi had constructed or bought up hundreds of tiny plants downisland that manufactured toys, rubber items, plastic souvenirs, textiles and other products that were making the term "made in Taiwan" synonymous with "cheap" all over the world.

As he had done all his business life, he invested most of the money he made right back into his business and thus back into the economy of the Island. He steadfastly refused to hoard capital in foreign bank accounts or make safe investments in Europe or America. He took every opportunity to reaffirm to all the world his stubborn confidence in the future of capitalism in Asia.

*   *   *

It was a splendid morning at the end of her fifth month at China Gate and Shelley was sitting at a table on the patio, feverishly typing away on her manuscript. Bryan and Ah Chin were in Tokyo for several days so she had sent Old Whyte to Hong Kong and given most of the staff the week off. She wanted to work undisturbed.

One of the remaining amahs interrupted her to say that an American was at the door asking for her. She looked at the calling card. It was Harlan Bamcheck of the Central Intelligence Agency.

She went to the door and greeted Bamcheck as cordially as possible, given the fact that she hated his guts. She could not forget the way this crude man had called in and harassed all the kids close to the Omega Chi back during the gang troubles of '62–'63. This, of course, was before the Vietnam War had made him an ally of the Omega Chi.

"I'm afraid Bryan is out," she told him.

Bamcheck smiled shrewdly. "I came here to see you, Miss Spencer. Or should I call you Mrs. Whyte now?"

"See me? What on earth for?"

"May I sit down a moment?"

"I suppose."

She uneasily led the man into the parlor. He sat down and glanced around the room admiringly. "You have a magnificent home. This is the first time I've actually been inside, you know. Your husband, for some reason, never saw fit to invite me up here."

"Mr. Bamcheck, I'm in the middle of something. Perhaps you can tell me what this is all about."

He looked at her evenly and blinked several times. "Mrs. Whyte, my office knows quite a bit about your past of the last five years. About your . . . political loyalties and . . . social preferences . . . and how you feel about world affairs. With this knowledge, we thought you might want to help us in a difficult situation in which, strangely, we find ourselves on the same side."

"And what side is that?"

"Mrs. Whyte, there is a new reality shaping up in America's relations in Asia. You've probably been getting wind of it over the past few months. The ping-pong business is part of it, though only a small part. Now, however, a truly major development is in the works. . . ."

"You really should be talking to my husband."

"Oh, we intend to. But we also want to talk to you. You see, this development is absolutely essential for the United States but it will represent a setback for Nationalist China. Your husband has a great influence with the Kuomintang, and how he reacts to the development will be very important to how they accept it. We believe your husband could be the key."

"And you want me to influence my husband?" She laughed with distaste. "You don't know him very well, do you?"

"We know him extremely well. And we think your influence on him could be considerable."

A rush of anger flushed her cheeks. "I think you'd better leave. I don't want to know what your major development is. Even having you here is a betrayal of his confidence."

"Mrs. Whyte, how he reacts is going to be very important to your husband's future. Please don't let him do or say anything foolish. I'm afraid he could very easily wind up in jail."

She stood up abruptly. "I said get out."

Bamcheck's face grew hard. "Little lady, there are certain things about your past that you probably wouldn't want to be made public in a conservative community like this one. Things like your relationship with a certain Negro musician? Like a certain party you attended with him in Los Angeles in 1969 at which photographs were taken? Think about it carefully before you completely refuse to help us."

"Get the fuck out!" she screamed. And at the angry sound of her voice, two of her regular Green bodyguards appeared out of nowhere. "Do I have to have you thrown out?"

"No, I'll be leaving. But just think about what I told you. Think about it long and hard and I'm sure you'll do the right thing—by your husband and your country."

When Whyte returned on Friday afternoon, Shelley was still distraught over the incident with Bamcheck.

Her husband came back to town in a bit of a triumphant mood. He had actually managed to talk a major Japanese bank into financing a new electronics plant for him downisland—a small victory in a season of defeat. He was ready to celebrate but, taking one look at the icy face that met him in the doorway, he knew there would be no celebrating tonight.

"What is it?"

"Your old friend Bamcheck stopped by to pay me a visit."

"Pay *you* a visit?"

She angrily wiped a wayward strand of hair from her eyes. "He wanted me to use my influence on you. He wanted me to conspire with them behind your back."

He motioned to one of the amahs to take his bags to the bedroom.

"When I refused, he tried to blackmail me into it. They know everything about me! They know who the hell I slept with on any given night in 1967! Christ, how do they know those things?"

Whyte knew all about her sexually active past and was not concerned with it. Especially since the Union of Breaths. "Influence me to do what?"

"He says some drastic new development is about to take place in our relations with Communist China. He wants your help in keeping the Nationalist Chinese in line when the story breaks."

"What did you tell him?"

"I told him to get out."

"Good for you."

"What could this big development be?"

"I don't know, but I'm going to find out." He yelled down the hallway for the amah not to unpack his bags.

"What are you doing?"

"I'm going to the States and get some answers."

"I'll come too."

"No. I need you to stay here and run the house."

"Bryan, I'm frightened. These men are stupid and unbelievably ruthless and they're obviously very much afraid of you. What will they do if you don't go along with them?"

"We may soon have to find out."

Caryer, the presidential aide, led Whyte into a modest White House office overlooking Pennsylvania Avenue. His manner was serious and respectful, much more so than in their meeting the previous year.

"Good to see you, Bryan," he began. "Actually, we were getting ready to send for you."

"I couldn't wait."

"You've been hearing rumors, I suppose."

"You suppose correctly."

"Yes, there are just too many leaks in this administration for its own good. We're going to have to do something about that. Can I get you anything? Cup of coffee—or are all you Old China hands confirmed tea drinkers?"

"Nothing for me." He took a seat.

"Yes, well I'm afraid I have to confirm those rumors. The President is going to Peking next February. It's his first step toward establishing some sort of meaningful relations with the People's Republic of China."

Whyte's face remained impassive but his stomach squeezed into a tiny, hard knot. Not even in his most pessimistic moment had he dreamed of such a possibility. It was so bizarre he thought for a moment that this man was having grotesque fun at his expense.

"Kissinger has already been there and made all the arrangements. Secretly, of course."

"So it's true," Whyte said. "You're selling us out."

"No, that's not the case," Caryer quickly said. "In fact, that's why we wanted to see you first. We wanted to express the President's determination to honor our commitment to Taiwan and the Nationalist Chinese Government personally."

"That's bullshit," Whyte spat angrily. "Neither the Communists or the Nationalists will accept a two-China policy from us. If we go with the Mainland we'll eventually have to sell out the Nationalists. That's always been the one condition for any kind of relations. The Communists have been very specific about that."

Caryer looked sheepish a moment, like a child caught in a lie, and then proceeded cautiously. "The President feels it is time to start the process of bringing the people of Mainland China back into the world arena."

"What about all the promises we've been making to the people of Taiwan for the past twenty years? Doesn't our word count for anything anymore?"

"There are certain realities that have to be faced, Bryan. One of those realities is that Peking rules the largest population in the world and rules it damn efficiently. We may not like that reality but we have to accept it. More importantly, America and China have realized that they have a common enemy in the Soviet Union and it is in our interests to . . ."

Whyte could no longer hear the words. It was a struggle to keep control of himself. He was thinking of all the campaign contributions the AFFA had made to Nixon to ensure that something like this would never happen. What a naive fool he had been. Tricked by Tricky Dick . . .

"We want you to be the one to tell President Chiang the . . . uh, the news . . ." Caryer stammered on.

"My friend, you've got some nerve." Bryan's outrage was growing.

"Governor Reagan is going to Taipei later this week to officially inform the Generalissimo."

Reagan too. This was even worse. Reagan was the staunchest supporter of Taiwan. "I assume that means the governor is behind you?"

"He—and some of the others of the conservative

wing of the party—have qualms, naturally. But, yes, they are behind the President all the way."

"I don't know what to say."

"We would like you to prepare the way for Reagan. Tell Chiang we intend to honor our mutual defense treaty and this will in no way affect our good relations."

"He's not going to buy that. The man is not a complete idiot."

"You're the most influential American businessman in Taiwan and have longstanding family connections with the KMT. You can convince him. He trusts you."

"He never will again."

Caryer stood up to end the meeting. "We're counting on you, Bryan. Your country needs you and you've got to carry the ball for it." He put his arm on Whyte's shoulder and walked him to the door. "If you don't, I guess I don't have to tell you that the consequences could be very grave for you. I don't need to remind you how many people in this town want to see you behind bars."

Whyte went directly from the White House to Dulles Airport. He caught a plane to San Francisco and made the connection with the Wednesday morning China Airlines flight to Taipei. He did not sleep on the plane. He sat in a stunned silence and thought about how he was going to tell his friends what he had to tell them.

There was, of course, no possible way he would be able to explain it satisfactorily to them. The Chinese, for all their reputation for pragmatism, were a highly emotional and visceral people. Friendship was a sacred trust. Loyalty was loyalty. There was no possibility he could get them to accept Nixon's betrayal with some half-assed explanation of new foreign policy priorities. All the speeches and assurances he practiced in his mind sounded ludicrous in light of the simple and obvious fact: America had begun the process of selling out Nationalist China. This was the new reality of post-Vietnam Asia.

Shelley met him at the airport and she guessed from

his strained expression how it had gone. "Butler was right, wasn't he?"

"Yes. I never thought it would go this far or come this fast. I've been caught completely off guard."

"What will you do?"

"I have no idea."

She took his hand and kissed it. "Bryan, I'm so sorry for you."

Forgoing his customary day of catch-up sleep, he had Shelley take him directly to Chiang Kai-shek's fortresslike Grass Mountain home a few miles from China Gate. She waited in the car while he walked up the long flight of stone steps to the main guard station. She watched him ascend awkwardly, pathetically, having to balance himself with the cane as he took one step at a time. Above him, the sky was nearly black. As on nearly every afternoon in early summer, it would soon pour rain.

As he was escorted into the large imperial chamber by two guards, he could see Chiang and King Lu waiting for him. King was helping the old man into a throne of a chair in the center of the receiving room. They looked like father and son, Whyte thought, the old emperor and the middle-aged prince. All the obligations of filial piety still held between them, just as they held between Whyte and King. How could any people who lived by such a code ever understand this kind of treachery?

King had guessed the seriousness of what was about to transpire when Whyte cabled ahead and requested this special audience. "I think perhaps you have some important news for us, Little Brother," he said.

Whyte nodded gravely.

King introduced Whyte as the son of Chiang's old friend Billy Whyte.

"*Hao,*" Chiang said and offered his hand. Whyte took the hand and made an obedient bow. He had met the Generalissimo before but not in some time and never in a private audience. He was alarmed by the weakness of the old man's handshake and the feebleness of his manner.

King explained to Chiang that Whyte was acting as a personal emissary of the President of the United States. Chiang acknowledged this with an uneasy smile, then looked at Whyte eagerly.

There was no way to make this painless so he merely layed it out before them in his clearest and bluntest Mandarin. "The President has asked me to extend to you his personal greetings and best wishes. He wants me to tell you he is planning to accept an invitation to visit the bandit government in Peiping in the early part of the coming year."

There was a moment of panic in Chiang's ancient eyes and then a blankness.

"The President wants you to know that this acceptance of their invitation in no way implies a recognition of that outlaw government and is in no way an abrogation of the 1954 Treaty between our two countries. He urges me to assure you in every possible way that nothing has changed in our traditional relationship."

"Do you believe that?" Chiang asked.

"No."

"You are telling me that your government is lying? That it has every intention of pursuing relations with the bandits on the Mainland?"

"Yes, sir. That is what I am saying."

The Generalissimo asked King to help him up. He walked slowly out of the enormous room without another word.

King and Whyte were left looking at each other. The enormity of the moment rendered them speechless. For all these many years they had been bound by the belief that they would one day see a U.S.-backed restoration of Mainland China. They had believed it was their personal destiny to oversee that restoration. It was the justification for all their actions. Now those beliefs and that destiny seemed a cruel hoax.

Whyte wanted to say something but there was nothing to say. King just stared sadly at him a moment, then followed his president out of the chamber.

* * *

The news of Nixon's upcoming China trip was announced to the world two days later. The Island of Taiwan responded by going into a state of profound shock followed by raging indignation. A mob gathered in front of the U.S. Embassy to protest as soon as the announcement was made. Whyte watched it calmly as his limousine passed by, noting the usual Green Gang agitators at the forefront.

The automobile continued up to Chung Shan North Road, made a left turn and stopped before an office building. Ah Chin hopped out and opened the door for Whyte, Shelley and Georgie Warner. The party went through the lobby and took the elevator to a large fifth-story conference room where the American Chamber of Commerce was holding an emergency session.

The room was already packed with angry, sweating American businessmen. Whyte went directly to the front and held his arms into the air to quiet them. They all looked at him sourly. The mood was tense and pessimistic.

"I've asked you all here because I've just returned from a meeting with the Nixon administration. Maybe I can shed some light on the bombshell that was dropped on us this morning."

"What we all want to know is whether or not this trip signals the beginning of a major shift in American Asian policy," said crusty old Kurt Perkins, the taipan of China Petroleum.

"The Nixon people want me to tell you that it does not. They say they intend to continue recognizing the Republic of China as the only legitimate government of China. They say they intend to stand by their treaty obligations to their old friend and ally."

"And you believe that?" Perkins challenged.

Whyte paused a few moments for dramatic emphasis. "Not for a minute. Not for a second. I promise you that this is only the beginning of a long process in which the U.S. will eventually break all relations with Taiwan. It has set itself on a course with one inevitable destination. It is pulling back from Asia—both physically and psychologically—and it needs a friendly Communist China as an ally to keep the Soviet Union out of the area. There is no place for a Nationalist China in this plan."

"I'm not going to sit around waiting for the ax to fall," said another businessman. "I'm getting out now."

"We can do that," said Whyte sharply. "We can turn tail and give up everything we've built here over the past twenty years, or we can join together and fight."

Warner, standing beside Whyte, gave a little chuckle. "Fight the U.S. Government?"

"Yes."

There were disbelieving cries of "How?" and "What can we do?"

"We can make this island such a successful bastion of free enterprise and capitalism that there'll be no way in hell the U.S. Government can ever dump it without being a traitor to all the principles for which America has supposedly stood for the past two hundred years."

"But how is Taiwan going to do this without the support of the United States?" someone yelled from the back.

"I'm telling you that we don't need the United States. We already have a sound economy and the second largest standing army in Asia here. To hell with Nixon! To hell with all of them! We can form the machinery to attract foreign investment on a grand scale. We can reach out to the other free, capitalistic countries of Asia for mutual protection—particularly Japan, which should become our best friend and role model. We can demonstrate to the world that capitalism is the best future for China even if the United States Government has given up on the idea."

"You want this business community, in effect, to secede from the United States?" asked Kurt Perkins incredulously.

"Yes. In effect and in spirit. At least until America comes to its senses."

There was a good deal of buzzing in the crowd.

"This has been a terrible blow for us but we can survive it," Whyte continued. "We can survive it by getting off our duffs and forcing the KMT to do a lot of things it has never done before to restore business confidence."

The crowd was genuinely excited now. It had been desperate for optimistic leadership and Whyte was giving it to them with all his old power and charisma. He had masterfully turned the mood around. He could see Shelley smiling at him proudly. There were cries of "What?" and "Tell us, Bryan."

"First, the KMT is going to have to set up a package of tax incentives that will be irresistible to foreign investors—no matter how shaky the political situation. Second, it is going to have to join with the Chinese underworld to put an end to the bureaucratic corruption—the squeeze— that has always been taken for granted and has always hampered the free conduct of business. Third, it is going to have to recognize this Chamber of Commerce as its chief lobbying arm in the United States and, toward that end, I would like to offer my services as president. If you give me the legitimacy of the office, if you let me represent all of you, I'll give this fight every ounce of my strength and every second of my time."

He waited a moment for the applause to die down and then he outlined in detail his plans for the future of Taiwan.

19

THE YEAR BETWEEN THE SUMMERS OF 1971 AND 1972 was the year that ended an era in Asia. The people of Nationalist China watched with mounting heartbreak as the United States did all the things it promised it would never do. They watched as President Nixon journeyed to Mainland China and signed an agreement that began the process of "normalizing" their relations. They watched as the U.S. delegation at the United Nations let Peking's bid for entry pass and thus sent Taiwan's delegation walking out of that world body forever. They watched as an American liaison office opened in Peking and a quarter century of American trade embargoes were lifted and all prohibition on American travel in China was rescinded.

During all this, State Department officials came to Taipei by the hundreds with briefcases full of assurances of continued support and friendship. But no one was fooled. The winds of the future were blowing in only one direction.

The economy of the Island went into an immediate slump and stayed there all year. Most of the big foreign companies that had been on the verge of major investment before the announcement backed off completely. The American R&R money dried to a mere trickle and the end was in sight for all the big American military money. Even many of the foreign companies that were already well established in Taipei saw the handwriting on the wall and quietly began to move their offices and assets to Hong Kong and Singapore and Manila. Business reflected confidence and, since there was no confidence in the future of Taiwan, there was no business.

Bryan Whyte spent most of that traumatic year trying to restore this ever-dwindling confidence. As president of the American Chamber of Commerce and the voice of the Taipei business community, he was true to his promise and worked tirelessly to turn the dismal situation around. He seemed to enjoy the work and relish the fight, seemed actually to have found himself in it. As the overall dilemma became more hopeless and impossible, he became more optimistic and sure of himself. The overwhelming boyish confidence in himself and his mission seemed to be returning in some new form which he did not yet fully understand but which he could feel growing within himself almost daily.

He did have some success implementing his master plan, especially in the beginning. He was able to talk the KMT into giving sweeping tax incentives to encourage foreign investment. He mobilized King Lu into effectively ending any corruption that might hamper business growth. He took dozens of expeditions to New York and San Francisco and Tokyo to lobby with corporations and banks and try to convince them of the investment potential of Taiwan. But, in the end, it was simply not enough. The massive capital did not come.

There were many reasons for this, but the most obvious one to Whyte was that the Nixon administration was working against him. The U.S. Government did not want a heavily capitalized and industrialized Taiwan because it did not fit into its new picture of Asia—and might even cause problems in the future. Whenever Whyte collared a banker or corporation executive, he knew that Caryer or Bamcheck or one of their flunkies would be right behind him. It was a campaign. They went so far as to spread stories in the world financial community that he was an outlaw and would soon be indicted by the Justice Department—a threat he considered fairly empty since there was no way the administration could charge him with anything without finding itself incriminated in a payoff scandal.

He knew exactly what he needed to counteract this campaign. He needed something glamorous and exciting. He needed something new and dramatic to catch investor imagination and lead the way. He needed a dynamic, runaway growth industry to rejuvenate faith in the economy overnight. In short, he needed a miracle.

After a year of trying, he finally found one in a Taiwan business he had long held in his back pocket—the movies.

It all began one insufferably humid afternoon in the early summer of 1972 when Georgie Warner dragged Whyte to the Shen Shen Theater in Shihminting to see a Hong Kong-made Chinese-language feature. The movie was called *Seven Dragons of Shensi* and what made it different from all the other historical epics that were annually cranked out for the Mandarin circuit was that the hero vanquished the villains not in the usual flurry of swordplay but by means of the ancient Chinese martial art of kung fu.

Whyte immediately understood why Warner was so excited. The small Hong Kong studio that made the film had gone to great lengths to capture the savage beauty of the Chinese martial arts in the context of an adventure story; the highly choreographed fighting sequences were rousing and compelling to watch. The crowd went berserk over it with an enthusiasm he had never seen in an Asian audience.

The movie industry had never been a moneymaker for the Omega Chi. The Asian market was heavily dominated by Hollywood films and the Hong Kong output of Run Run Shaw, Golden Harvest and particularly Harvard Chan, an ex-Shanghai movie exhibitor who had once worked for Whyte's father. Even at the height of his power, Whyte had been unable to loosen these moguls' near-monopoly on the market; and after the death of Su Ling two years before, he had stopped trying. The Shih Lin Studios had been largely inactive ever since, turning out only an occasional low-budget Chinese opera, romance or sword epic for the Taiwan domestic market.

Seeing the kung fu movie made him think again. There was a unique magic and beauty in the fighting sequences that seemed to hypnotize an audience. For the first time, his instinct told him there was real money in this business. Warner—who was his resident expert on movies and the movie business—was so insistent about the worldwide financial possibilities of the kung fu movie that Whyte went with him that very day to seek out the counsel of King Lu.

King received them at his townhouse, looking extremely tired. To a great extent, the fortunes of the Greens were tied to the legitimacy of the Nationalist Government. The setbacks the KMT had suffered in the last year had brought about many little rebellions in his overseas empire and King was weary of putting them down. Strangely, his attitude had not changed a bit toward Whyte since the crushing American betrayal. Even though all evidence was to the contrary, he had not lost any of his faith in Bryan Whyte's special destiny.

He was, however, appalled by the idea of investing heavily in kung fu movies. "Kung fu is a sacred subject to the Chinese people," he lectured them sternly. "It is an art that has been preserved and passed down within the secret societies for hundreds of years. It is not a thing that is to be exploited for frivolous entertainment."

"We are not talking about real kung fu," Warner said. "This is just faked ballet stuff—not the sacred routines. No secrets will be given away, for chrissake."

King was still not enthusiastic. "The returns of the movie business are very small," he said. "It's hardly worth our time."

"But suppose," Whyte said, "suppose these kung fu movies could be the first Chinese movies to appeal to an international audience . . . to Americans even. I've never seen a response like the one at the Shen Shen this afternoon. This may be the opportunity we have been waiting for. This may be something that can capture the world's attention."

"If these movies have such potential, why have not the Hong Kong factories latched onto them in a big way?" King asked dryly.

"Because," Warner answered quickly, "they're big and slow and resistant to change. Because they don't really know what they have with this movie and won't figure it out for several months. Because they will never dream that any Chinese movie could appeal to a Western mass audience."

"What makes you think it will?"

"Because it appealed to me," said Warner.

King thought about this a moment and then said, "Still, it would be unwise for us to attempt to compete too strongly with someone like Harvard Chan at this time. He has the protection of the Triads and the Triads' alliance with us is very shaky right now. It could bring about a war that we cannot afford to wage."

"I don't think we should try to compete with him at all," said Whyte. "It would be better to use his superior facilities and give him a cut. Let's go to Chan and tell him we want to increase our film production in a big way. Tell him we want to rent his equipment and technicians— maybe even his studios in Hong Kong—and try to make films that can play the American market. Tell him he has the exclusive right to distribute these films in Asia, exclusive of Taiwan, if he should desire to. It will offer him no threat and he can't fail to make money."

King was still skeptical, but he gave in when he saw his apathy was no match for the excitement of the two Americans. "Then, I suppose it is worth a try."

Whyte turned to Warner. "Georgie, I want you to take personal charge. Get a print of *Seven Dragons* and send it to San Francisco to be tested on an urban American audience. Hire one of the more reputable public-opinion pollsters to do the test. Tell them we want the results and a complete interpretation right away. If the results are positive, pay them a premium to keep their mouths shut about it."

Warner nodded eagerly. He seemed to be caught up in something for the first time in years, maybe the first time ever. "I'll get on it," he said.

"Then the most important order of business is to find a star. Someone who has the right charisma and the necessary knowledge of martial arts. Someone to be a face for this style of film. If we can be the first to establish a star, it'll give us the edge over Chan and the others, who'll surely jump on the bandwagon once it takes off."

"What about Johnny Yen?" asked Warner. "He's an actor."

It was so obvious that Whyte broke into an excited grin. Of course. But he had not seen or heard from the handsome Green warrior since he moved to the States in the mid-sixties. "Where is Johnny now?"

"He's teaching martial arts in Los Angeles," said King Lu. "He's acted in several television commercials but he's been discouraged in his career and has asked for a new position within the Greens."

"Tell him to get back here as soon as possible," said Whyte. "Tell him we want to make him a star."

The plan hammered out by Whyte and Warner that afternoon came to fruition so quickly and easily—and so spectacularly—that it left them and most everyone else in the Asian movie business stunned and breathless.

Warner immediately outlined a script called *Fury of the Tiger* about a young secret-society member seeking revenge against the Manchus for killing his family in 1900 Peking. Johnny Yen flew over from Los Angeles, tested successfully and was offered the part. Surprisingly, the thirty-year-old failed actor did not seem to want it. Whyte and Warner had to speak to him for three hours to convince him it would not cheapen the sacred Chinese martial arts or break the code of the Green Society. Even then he refused to budge until King Lu personally gave him the nod and Whyte promised he would burn the negative if Johnny wasn't one hundred percent satisfied with the finished product.

Finally convinced, Johnny threw himself into the part with an enthusiasm that was infectious to everyone involved in the project. He cast all the fighting extras and choreographed all the kung fu sequences himself. Whyte and Warner sealed off the huge Kong Kong sound stage rented from Harvard Chan and, in a frantic rush to beat any competitors to the theaters, worked day and night as a kind of family enterprise. Even Shelley put aside her book for a few days to do script rewrites. The picture was finished in two grueling weeks and quickly edited at the Omega Chi National Studios in Shih Lin. It was exhibited in a test run at the Shen Shen Theater in Taipei a month later. It was an immediate, undisputed, monster hit.

The Shihminting crowds went crazy for Johnny Yen

in a way they never had for another Asian star. He had an animal magnetism and cocky arrogance that was irresistible; the audience also saw something else in his performance, something subtle and intangible and totally new in the Asian cinema—an unmistakable pride in being Chinese. He so filled the screen with his physical presence and air of confidence that no one noticed the amateurish quality of the writing and editing. When the film opened in Hong Kong, the lines wound three times around the block of the Victoria Theater. The following day they were twice as long and every television station and fan magazine in the Colony was screaming for an interview with Johnny Yen, the kung fu superstar.

When the box office receipts from the first week were counted, it looked as if Whyte might just have the economic miracle he had been seeking. The negative cost of *Fury* was less than one hundred thousand U.S. dollars. If the crowds held up even two more weeks, they would clear in excess of five million U.S. in Taiwan and Hong Kong alone. They could expect to do at least half that well on the three Johnny Yen sequels that were already in various stages of preproduction. By the time these films went around the entire Mandarin circuit, there was no telling how much money could be earned on them. If the San Francisco test results were accurate and the dubbed version took off in America, Bryan Whyte had the splashy success he needed to throw in the face of the international financial community and everyone else who had given up on Taiwan.

Sir Harvard Chan was a cagey old ex-Shanghai movie exhibitor who had fled to Hong Kong in the early days of the Japanese occupation of North China in the thirties. Beginning with a single movie theater on Nathan Road, and thanks largely to Triad support and financing, Chan became the most successful movie mogul in the Crown Colony. He carved himself an empire of Chinese-language cinemas that stretched from the Chinatowns of Kuala

Lumpur to Amsterdam and London. He now owned a gargantuan movie factory in the Hong Kong New Territories that rivaled the size of MGM in its heyday and he lived in a palatial estate on Hong Kong Island that would have been the envy of a Ming emperor.

Chan was successful mainly because he always managed to stay one step ahead of his competition in figuring out what the public wanted to see on the screen. When romantic musicals became the vogue in the fifties, Harvard Chan was the first to have them in his theaters. When the public suddenly tired of them in the early sixties and wanted historical sword epics, Harvard Chan had guessed it six months earlier and had already changed his production schedule accordingly. He was famous for his uncanny ability to predict public taste. Therefore, the fact that he had totally missed this kung fu craze severely shook him. He quickly rushed out his own version of the genre but it was not doing a fraction of the business of *Fury of the Tiger,* even though his film cost five times as much. The public clearly did not want just any kung fu star. It wanted Johnny Yen.

When this became obvious to him, Chan felt he had no choice but to make a continuing deal with the Omega Chi to distribute the Yen films around the Mandarin circuit. But Harvard Chan did not like the idea of merely being the distributor of other men's films—especially those of a turtle-egg Taiwan company that had lost virtually all of its power and prestige over the last few years. Every waking hour of his day was spent thinking of a way to get Yen away from the Omega Chi without instigating a war between his protectors, the Triads, and their protectors, the Green Pang.

One day during the second month of the Hong Kong run of *Fury of the Tiger,* Whyte and Warner sat across from Chan in the immense, auditorium-sized sitting room of Chan's estate. The mogul wore a conservative, American-made pin-striped suit and horn-rimmed glasses that made him look like a jolly old owl. His fingernails were manicured to a high gloss that reflected the sunlight flooding the room from the great picture window overlooking the harbor. Between interruptions by phone calls and whispered messages from his secretaries, the old showman was entertaining his guests with anecdotes about the old days of the Shanghai movie business.

"Do you know that I once worked for your father?" he was saying to Whyte. "I managed a theater for him in Pootung in 1931. He was one of the smartest businessmen I have ever known. I am only sorry his career had to end so tragically."

"Well, he's quite happy now," Whyte answered.

"You know, the thing that made him so smart was that he had the good sense to let *compradores* like myself actually run the business and make the decisions for him. He knew that only a Chinese can know what will appeal to a Chinese audience. That was his genius."

Whyte's sensitive negotiating antennae picked up the beginnings of a play for advantage. He arched his eyebrow and made a faint smile. Warner sensed it too and he looked at Whyte worriedly. "Do you really think so?" Whyte said.

"Absolutely. And there is a valuable lesson here for you."

"A lesson?"

"Yes, this is not a good business for you to be directly involved in. This is a silly, childish business run by silly, inconsequential people. The Omega Chi has more important things to do, surely. You would be much better off to let me buy into your contract with Johnny Yen and handle these affairs. After all, I have a lifetime of experience and we are all brothers who trust one another."

"We do not have a contract with Johnny Yen," Whyte said. "He works for us out of personal loyalty."

"Yes, of course. He is a loyal Green. But if you were to convince him to work for me I would be happy to pay you a percentage of the profits for your friendship. Better to let me handle the business of movies and make us all richer, what?"

Whyte nodded respectfully. "Thank you for this generous offer. However, we will continue by our unworthy selves for the time being. . . ."

Unable to control his rising temper and emboldened by the newfound esteem that came from his recent business success, Georgie Warner did a very uncharacteristic thing. He suddenly lunged forward in his chair and cut in sharply on the conversation. "We want nothing from you but your distribution system in Asia and the rental of your studios and technicians. That's all!"

Chan's old face contorted into a smile. He could be tough too. "And if I choose to deny these services to you?"

"Then," Warner went on fearlessly, "you will be cutting your own throat. Because we will make the films in Hollywood and distribute them ourselves with American studio money and expertise."

The smile left Chan's face. One of his greatest fears was that someday Hollywood would begin to make Chinese-language films and raid the lucrative Mandarin market. Warner knew this and it was an effective bluff.

"Do I make myself clear?" Warner said.

"Of course," Chan said. "But that will never happen because we are friends and we will continue to do business together as before."

Harvard Chan's easy capitulation seemed to satisfy Warner but it troubled Whyte. Harvard Chan did not rise to his preeminent position in this cutthroat business by giving in so easily. The old devil was up to something.

Whyte flew back to Taipei that night. Despite his apprehension about Chan, he felt completely at ease about leaving everything in Warner's hands. This was one of the great pleasant surprises of his life. All these years he had carried Warner—because he wanted to keep the old Omega Chi together, because he felt guilty about Warner's acid face, because of a dozen other reasons. Now the investment was paying off. Warner was finally coming through like a champ.

On the plane, his mind buzzed with thoughts of his

next move. He would go to the States the following week. He would go around to all the corporations and big private investors who had been scared off by the Nixon trip. He would show them his balance sheet on the Yen movies. He would argue that this was the beginning of a whole new economic boom on the Island. He would convince them that Taiwan was not dead, not by a long shot, and, no matter what Nixon's people told them, they had better think again before completely abandoning this territory.

He stepped out of the limo and hurried into China Gate, eager as always to see Shelley and tell her everything that had happened. He went back to her workroom and found it empty. He looked around the room a moment. It was crowded with books, magazines, notes, interview tapes, pages of manuscript, file cabinets crammed with paper. The walls were covered with inspirational photos (Woodstock, the Tet Offensive, the two Kennedy assassinations) and an extensive outline was chalked on a large stand-up blackboard. God, she was lost in all this, he thought.

He went back and found her sitting on a couch before the big stone fireplace in the parlor. She was burning something. Her eyes were vacant and red from crying. An ashtray beside her was filled with butts.

"What's the matter?"

She didn't answer.

"What are you burning?"

"My book."

"Your book? I don't understand."

She took another handful of manuscript and reached toward the roaring fire.

He grabbed her arm. "Stop it!"

"Leave me alone," she cried, and pulled her arm free.

"But *why?*"

"Because I can't do it! Because I've been kidding myself all along. I don't know how to write a . . . book."

"You heard from your agent."

"This morning. The proposal was rejected by twenty-five publishers. They all loved the idea but considered the writing *hopelessly* amateurish."

"We'll publish the book ourselves. We'll spend a fortune advertising it."

"No one will buy it. And I'll be a laughingstock."

He sat beside her. He placed his arm around her and let her cry into his shoulder. Oddly, he wasn't disappointed. He secretly considered the book an invasion of his privacy and an unnecessary drain on her energy that would probably lead to no good end. Now she could spend all of her time being his wife. "I know you're disappointed," he said gently. "But it's not the end of the world. In the great scheme of things, it's not that big a deal."

She sobbed. "What am I going to do now? What am I going to do with myself?"

He kissed her on the cheek and wiped away a tear with his thumb. "You can get yourself pregnant," he said. "It's high time I had a son."

Georgie Warner sat with his feet propped on the desk of his Hong Kong office. He wore a stylish, double-breasted Samtani-tailored suit, a hundred-dollar silk tie and snakeskin shoes. His right hand played with a coin as he barked across the Pacific, "Forget it, jerk. For that kind of money, you can kiss my ass! So can your board of directors, all your flunky brothers-in-law and all the starlets you fuck on your coffee breaks." He slammed down the receiver and smiled, vaguely aware that in this outburst he was imitating a scene from some Sam Fuller movie he had seen years ago.

Warner could afford to be tough. He had already been offered a distribution deal with another American studio that was several times more lucrative. He knew and they knew that the American inner-city audiences were starting to go crazy for *Fury of the Tiger.* Johnny Yen was a ticket to movie immortality and he was not about to let anyone steal that ticket from him. Not some shark in a

Hollywood studio. Not Harvard Chan on his mountaintop place. Not even Bryan Whyte.

Warner loved playing mogul. He had moved over to Hong Kong a month ago and now spent all his time in his office on the Chan lot making deals, being flattered, refusing people access to Johnny Yen. He thrived on the frantic activity, the power struggles, the willing starlets around every corner, the devious back room maneuvering, the daily rush from the glamor and excitement of being associated with the movies—the single greatest attraction of his life.

He was also relishing being completely in charge of an important segment of the Omega Chi business for the first time. Ever since high school, ever since he was a child really, he had languished uneasily in the shadows of the brothers of Omega Chi, secretly envying and sometimes even hating them. He had always been the goat, the comic relief, and the knowledge of this had made him miserable in a way that no amount of money could compensate. Now, at last, he had found his niche and he was happy and alive. He had been miraculously rescued from the long, dark tunnel of dissolution and despair in which he had been hiding since 1963. He had recently stopped drinking entirely and had already shed some fifty pounds. He was finally his own man and what he was accomplishing here was single-handedly going to save the postwar Omega Chi from oblivion.

He walked through the big Harvard Chan studio sound stage where they were choreographing a fight sequence from Johnny's new movie, *Revenge of the Tiger*. An American gangster movie called *The Godfather* was sweeping the Chinatowns of Asia and Warner wanted to capitalize on this phenomenon with a tong movie of his own, one that glamorized an early episode of Green Society history. Johnny was playing a fictional tong leader who battles the nefarious Red Gang and its British allies for control of the Yangtze basin in the 1850s.

Warner watched the action on the set, occasionally shouting out to the young hotshot director his own suggestions for how to shoot the scene or giving an encouraging word to Johnny, who had come to trust his judgment implicitly. Next movie, he thought, I'll direct myself. Yes indeed, Georgie Warner was made for this business.

He went back to his office, put his feet on the desk and felt enormously pleased with himself. Then Juan Ortega walked through the door and ruined everything.

The lean, ominous figure of Juan Ortega made a shadow over Warner's desk. He wore a navy blue blazer that made him look like a malevolent preppy and he smoked the same kind of long Filipino cigar his brother once regularly smoked. He looked older, somewhat less sure of himself than the last time Warner had seen him in 1969. Behind him, guarding the door, was Dave Magaha, who looked just as fat and deadly as ever. Both seemed amused at the image of Georgie Warner as movie mogul.

Warner turned pale at the sight of them. Willing himself not to panic, he leaned back in his swivel chair and thought about the .38 caliber revolver in his desk drawer. He wondered how long it would take him to get to it. "What's this all about?" he demanded.

Ortega sat in a wicker chair across from him and gazed about the office admiringly. "I have to hand it to you, Georgie. You've done a hell of a job with this Johnny Yen thing. One hell of a job. Who would have figured there'd be money in Chinese movies? This is a real breakthrough for all of us. An inspiration. And you did it all yourself. You can be proud of that."

"This is crazy. What if someone recognizes you? Are you trying to get me killed?"

"Just relax, Georgie."

"What do you want?"

"Part of the action. What else?"

"Forget it."

"I can't forget it, Georgie. We're hungry."

"I thought you assholes were on top of the world."

Ortega smiled thinly. "Everything is changing, Georgie. The R&R has dried up for us just like it has for you. The old Orient Express doesn't run anymore. There's no money at all in revolution these days. We've got to get in some other lines of business and this movie deal looks real good."

Warner stood up to leave. "I'm busy and I don't have time for you shitbirds."

Magaha unbuttoned his coat to expose a shoulder holster and then locked the door. "You're busy and you don't got time for us?" the fat man said. "That's a helluva way to treat your old friends."

Ortega nodded. "He's got a point, Georgie. We've been friends for a long time. Please don't get high-handed with us now."

Warner was trembling. "That's all over!" he screamed. "That was years ago and I didn't know what I was doing. Now I *do* know and I'm not going to let you blackmail me into helping you again. So you can just haul ass outa here!"

Ortega's almond eyes showed no emotion but inside he was not enjoying this. He had little of his brother's relish for dispensing pain; he only wanted to get on with his business. He looked at Warner evenly. "We want another favor from you. If you don't oblige I'm going to have a little talk with Mr. Whyte. It's that simple."

Warner sat back down. Just like that, he was defeated. "What do you want this time?"

"We want to see Johnny Yen."

"What for?"

Ortega shrugged. "We've begun an association with Harvard Chan and the Triads. We're going into the kung fu movie business with them—so is Johnny Yen."

Warner violently shook his head. "Absolutely no way."

"We want to talk to Johnny about doing a few pictures with us. We would like for you to give him a little encouragement to the effect that it might be a good idea."

"He'll never work for you."

"He might if you tell him to."

"It would mean deserting the Green Society. It would mean certain death for him."

"I doubt it. Let's face it, the Greens don't have that kind of power anymore. Why else would the Triads be willing to break their longtime alliance with them over this issue?"

"Please don't do this. I'll do anything else. This is just too important to me." Tears filled his eyes and spilled down the scarred cheeks.

Ortega looked back at him with distaste. "Do I talk to Johnny Yen or do I talk to Bryan Whyte? You decide, my friend."

Warner knew there was no way out for him. And he knew he would do anything to keep from having Whyte know about his years of treachery. Anything. "All right, you can talk to him, but it won't do you any good."

He picked up the phone and dialed Johnny's dressing room.

Two months later, Johnny Yen completed his third picture, *Furious Fists.* In the meantime, the first two had become the show business phenomenon of the year in America. His name was a household word and his face was fast becoming a merchandising industry: Already Omega Chi was franchising the sale of Johnny Yen tee-shirts, Johnny Yen hero posters, Johnny Yen calendars, Johnny Yen pencils, Johnny Yen school-lunch boxes, Johnny Yen girl's panties.

In the course of these lightning months, Johnny had, with the knowledge and permission of Georgie Warner, been secretly besieged by Juan Ortega and the representatives of Harvard Chan with offers of a picture contract. The deal was for three times what Omega Chi National was paying him and would, with one stroke of his pen, ensure his financial security for the rest of his life.

Ortega had been particularly persuasive. "The American interest will not last," he argued. "It's merely this year's fad over there. White America will never accept a

Chinese star and a year from now you'll be playing Paul Newman's houseboy. But Harvard Chan can make your star burn bright for the rest of your life—here, in Asia, among your own people. And think of this. If you don't work for him, he will simply cut you off from his distribution system and promote his own kung fu star. You will lose out on everything! Georgie understands this and this is why he urges you to accept even though it is contrary to his own financial interest."

Out of respect for Warner, Johnny Yen listened to their offer very courteously on several occasions and each time firmly refused it.

The day *Furious Fists* wrapped, Georgie Warner went to his dressing room trailer for one last try. Desperation was written all over his face. He knew that if he could not convince him this time, the Warlords would move against Johnny with all their muscle. And if he, Warner, refused to help them, they would expose him as a traitor to the Omega Chi.

Johnny was, by this time, angry, confused and tired of being pressured. He could not understand why Warner would even consider talking him into signing with a competitor. Yet it was Warner who had brought him out of obscurity. Warner had made him what he was. He still trusted Warner implicitly.

"Johnny, I want you to reconsider your decision about doing a picture with Chan Studios."

"Why are you working with our enemies in this manner?" Johnny screamed. "You know what you suggest is unthinkable!"

"It's just that I'm convinced that something terrible is going to happen if you don't. I'm begging you, Johnny. Please change your mind. Do one picture, for chrissake."

"That's insanity. I have the protection of the Green Society and the Omega Chi. I'm better guarded than the President of the United States. How could an enemy possibly get to me?"

"The Greens and Omega Chi are *not* what they once

were," Warner cried. "There's a different wave of the future. You must ride it."

All at once, Johnny seemed to understand what was happening. "They have something on you, don't they? Something very big."

Warner did not answer but his pleading eyes confessed everything.

"I'm sorry, Georgie. I can't sell out my brothers when they are depending on me the most." He abruptly got up and left the trailer.

Six days later he was dead.

The death of Johnny Yen shocked Asia and much of the rest of the world. The newspapers reported that he died of a massive coronary while taking a shower at the Hong Kong home of his producer, George Warner. In reality, Johnny's heart stopped from a lethal dose of a potent Chinese herb poison administered through his coffee. Bryan Whyte paid a fortune to keep that information out of the official report, thereby avoiding a scandalous press inquiry that might bring out the star's connections with the Chinese underworld.

The funeral service was held at St. John's Cathedral on Garden Road in Hong Kong. The police were not prepared for the mourners who turned out by the thousands and quickly transformed the event into a free-for-all. They wept openly and carried huge, crudely painted pictures of Johnny high in the air. They chanted his name like a political slogan. The emotion was genuine. Clearly Johnny Yen was more than a movie star to these people. He was a symbol of their nationalism.

The scene was so frantic that Whyte—especially concerned with Shelley, who was several months pregnant—had his party wait for two hours for the mob to clear before venturing out of the cathedral. As they were finally walking down the church steps, Whyte sent his wife and father ahead in the first limousine and asked Warner to wait with him. Warner's eyes were red and swollen from weeping all through the ceremony. Whyte put his arm around his old friend and sat down with him on a street bench. "I know all about it, Georgie," he said.

Warner assumed Whyte was offering sympathy. "Thank you," he sniffed.

"I know everything."

"Everything?"

"I know that it was you who put the Warlords onto Johnny Yen. I know it was you who supplied them with information over the years and indirectly supplied the Randolph Committee. I know it was you who helped them plant the bomb in China Gate. I know all about it and I guess I've known for some time."

Warner was so stunned he didn't even think to deny it. "How . . . ?"

"There was no one else left."

"Why didn't you say something?"

"I'm not sure. Maybe I was hoping it wasn't true. Maybe I was forcing myself not to believe it until this last thing made that no longer possible."

"They owned me, Bryan."

"What did you ever do to give them that kind of hold?"

Warner felt exquisitely relieved. He was tired of fighting it, eager to confess, eager to get it all out in the open at last no matter what the consequences. "I killed a whore one night in the old Lung Shan. It was an accident but who would believe that? The Tiger Eels knew right away and the Ortegas used it to blackmail me into feeding them information. Once I got started there was no way out."

"You should have come to me. Didn't you know you could come to me and I would try to help you? We were brothers. Brothers! All our lives. Did that mean nothing to you?"

Warner began to sob. "I didn't know Su Ling would be killed."

"No?"

"I loved Su Ling. She loved me too. We were lovers but we were afraid to tell you. . . ."

Whyte's eyes hardened and his body tightened, but the outrage soon passed and he resumed his sad, resigned tone. "And Johnny?"

"The Warlords were in it with Harvard Chan and the Triads. They wanted him to work for them. When he refused they killed him so they could build their own star to fill the vacuum."

"I hope you know you've accomplished nothing. The movie industry boom has already served its purpose for the Omega Chi. All you've done is create a cult for Johnny Yen. Now his films will always be in demand. You've murdered your friend for nothing."

"I didn't want to hurt Johnny," he cried. "I never wanted to hurt Johnny."

"Who did you want to hurt?"

"I wanted to hurt *you.*"

"But why?"

"Because I hate you. Hate you for what you've done to me."

"What have I ever done to hurt you?"

"Jesus, Bryan. Look at me. Take a good look at me."

"You could have had plastic surgery. We tried to get you to have surgery."

"I don't mean my face. I mean *me.* Look at me!"

Whyte looked at him. He said nothing.

"You really don't see anything, do you? I think you really are crazy—just like people say."

Whyte did see. He saw the wreck of his old friend. He saw the overwhelming hatred and bitterness of the man. He saw what his own belief in the family of Omega Chi had done to him, to all of them. Whyte reached into his coat pocket and pulled out Taylor's pearl-handled revolver, placing it on his lap.

Warner's fear overcame his bitterness, his instinct for survival reasserted itself. "Oh, Jesus, what are you going to do to me?"

"Nothing," Whyte said. "I've stopped passing judgment on people. But King Lu will surely kill you when he recovers from the shock of Johnny's death and puts two and two together."

"You have to help me, Bryan. I don't want to fall into King's hands."

"The limo is waiting for you. It will take you to Kai Tak where you can get a plane for the States. I don't know what the hell you'll do once you get there. That's your problem. But you're not to take anything with you."

"I'm entitled to some of the Omega Chi treasury."

"No you're not."

"But I'm an equal partner in the corporation. I have an equal vote and an equal share to all profits. That's the rule you made. I could go to court against you."

"You have rights only if you're physically on the Island of Taiwan. That's the rule we all agreed to live by."

"I deserve something!"

"I said nothing."

"I have to go back to Taipei for at least a day. I have to get my things, say good-by to my folks!"

"No."

"What will I do? What am I trained for? I've never even been to the States."

"I don't know, Georgie. But don't ever come back to Asia or step into a Chinatown or go anywhere you might see a Chinese ever again. I can't protect you. I don't even want to. Better hurry and catch that plane."

Warner got in the car. As it slowly drove up Garden Road he looked back through the tinted window at the figure of Bryan Whyte standing in front of the church. The taipan looked curiously alone, more alone than he had ever been in his life.

20

ALAN PHILLIPS SWITCHED ON THE LIVING ROOM
lights of his East Greenwich Village apartment and looked
at his watch. It was just after 2 A.M. The buzzing continued. He pressed the intercom. "Who is it?" he asked.

"It's Georgie. Georgie Warner."

"I don't believe it!"

"You might if you'd open the goddamn door."

He pushed a button and stood at the top of the stair-
well as Warner climbed the five flights. They embraced,
awkwardly, then moved into the light of the apartment to
take stock of over five years of startling physical change.
Warner must have gained a hundred pounds in that time,
Phillips thought. And he clearly was a heavy drinker.

"What're you doing here?" Phillips asked, still in-
credulous.

"I've been kicked out."

"What?"

"Bryan let me build up his movie business for him.
He let me save the fucking Island for him. Then he kicks
me out. He says that if I ever set foot in Asia again, he'll
have me killed."

Phillips sat back on the arm of an overstuffed chair.
Warner's angry voice woke up the baby, and he heard
Doris scurry back to see to him. The oldest Phillips boy
peered curiously around the doorway of another bedroom.
"Why would he do that to you? You're the only friend the
man has left in the world."

"He's become a monster, that's why. He's so corrupt
and power-mad, he's no longer sane. He's like a Roman

emperor at the end of his reign—isolated and jealous of everyone around him. I was lucky to escape with my life. I'm telling you he's not the same person we grew up with, Alan. . . ."

"You must have done something specific. I can't believe Bryan . . ."

"He blames me for the death of Johnny Yen, for chrissakes. He holds me personally responsible because the guy happened to have a heart attack while he was in *my* shower."

Phillips yawned into the back of his hand. "Why would he care more about Johnny Yen than you? He considers you his brother."

"Johnny Yen was very important to him. He was using the success of the Yen pictures as his wedge to begin restoring confidence in the economy of the Island—you know, to catch the attention of the international business community and show them we still had the moxie."

"Are you serious? That sounds like a real act of desperation."

"It was. But it worked and it worked because I put my blood in it. Foreign investment in the Island during the first quarter of 1973 has been booming. You can read all about it in *Fortune* magazine."

Phillips experienced a wave of something like nausea. "Wait a minute. I've been told the Omega Chi is on the verge of financial collapse."

"It was—a year ago. But in the last three months Whyte's managed to turn everything around. Taiwan's economy is suddenly going crazy and the Omega Chi is making big money again."

"In *what?*"

"Movies, sporting goods, tea, toys—you name it. He's expanding all the Omega Chi's old legitimate businesses and branching out into new ones. He's making deals all over the world and stomping on anyone who gets in his way."

"But how can that be possible? I know what the Omega Chi's financial position was like when I left it in late '68. It's only gotten worse since then. No American bank will loan him a penny."

"That's not true. The American banks are giving way because he's got the support of some of the more powerful right-wing conservatives. He's got considerable Japanese financing. He's also invested all his Orient Express money into the Island and *that's* beginning to pay off for him."

The mention of the Orient Express was a knife to Phillips's stomach. He had heard that the Omega Chi had gone into the hard-drug business after he left the Island. He hadn't wanted to believe it. "Bryan was sending heroin through the Express, wasn't he?"

"Of course. He started the minute you left us."

"Is he still?"

"No. But not on moral grounds. He was squeezed out of most of the business by the Warlords. Then the Express was gradually shut down by the American troop withdrawals."

Phillips said nothing for several moments and then he looked at Warner and asked, "What are you going to do now?"

"Good question. I've been bumming around this wonderful country of ours for the past few months trying to figure that one out. I didn't get off the Island with a cent and I've been living off a handout from John Casy. I'm thirty fucking years old and I've never had a fucking job. You tell me. What am I supposed to do with my life now?"

Phillips couldn't answer him. He knew that Warner was helpless in the real world. He knew Warner had been ruined by the American disaster in Asia as surely as if he had stepped on a Vietcong land mine. He knew that in one way or another all the Omega Chi were casualties of a social order and economic system that they had perpetuated in Asia and that had rightly died in the jungles of Vietnam. He had accepted all this long ago.

But what he could not accept was the fact that Bryan Whyte was still insanely struggling to rebuild that order and that system—and was apparently succeeding. This was intolerable to him. Truly, Bryan Whyte had become a monster and the time had finally come to put a stop to him once and for all.

In the past five years, Alan Phillips had been an integral part of seemingly every significant antiwar and people-oriented activity in the counterculture. He had organized sit-ins, peace marches and political rallies with enormous drive and monklike dedication. He had served time in jail and watched his family go without the necessities while he wandered from state to state raising money. He had fought bitter power struggles with the Weathermen and all the others who wanted to "bring the war home" and thereby destroy the credibility and effectiveness of the resistance. He had given every inch of himself —right up until the last American soldier was withdrawn and the last prisoner of war returned this very month— and this total commitment had earned him a very special place in the upper echelon of the Movement.

But in all of this time, he had never once spoken out against his past association with the Omega Chi and American capitalism in Asia. Many times, he had been approached by those who knew of his connection to write a piece for *Ramparts* or *Rolling Stone* about the Chinese underworld and its intimate relationship with the U.S. Government and the war. Each time he had firmly refused. Despite his commitment to the antiwar movement, the bond of the Omega Chi had always held— somewhere deep within his psyche, his love for and loyalty to Bryan Whyte had always been intact.

Now the bond was broken. Warner had convinced him that Bryan Whyte had finally gone over the edge. The war was over. The old American Community of Taipei was in psychological ruins. The whole philosophy that had built it and the Omega Chi was thoroughly repudiated and America was at last reaching out to Mainland China as it should have thirty years ago. The very idea that, after all they had learned and experienced, Whyte—crippled and probably as crazy as his father—was still in the ball game with drug money and right-wing support, still ruthlessly struggling to save the old capitalistic order, still fighting Taiwanese independence, still holding onto his ties with Asian gangsters and Asian dictators, was absolutely mind-boggling to Phillips. He saw clearly now that Whyte had to be finished for good or everything this country had gone through would be meaningless. The Omega Chi had to be crushed and he, Alan Jeffrey Phillips, was the only person in the world with sufficient inside knowledge to do the job.

This was why he had flown to Washington D.C. and why he was sitting in the office of Senator Randolph, the liberal Democrat from Pennsylvania, and why he was now prepared to offer testimony against Bryan Whyte, taipan of the Omega Chi.

Randolph peered across the desk at Alan Phillips and puffed philosophically on his pipe. Phillips was getting very frustrated with the conversation. He had told the senator every scandalous thing he could remember about the activities of the Omega Chi between 1964 and 1968 and the man still did not seem at all impressed.

"These things are ancient history and almost impossible to prove without records," Randolph finally said. "The war is over for America and public attention is focused on this Watergate business. For me to reconvene the special committee and go after Whyte in this climate, I'm going to need something very substantial and a good deal more current."

"But surely just establishing the underworld connection to the Omega Chi and establishing the Omega Chi's connection to the last two administrations will be enough to destroy Whyte's credibility, to prevent him from ever doing any kind of major business again. I don't really want to send him to jail."

"If you don't want to send him to jail, why don't you and Warner and Casy go to Taipei and take the company away from him. You're all equal partners once you set foot on the Island. Gang up on him. Throw him out. Disband the company."

"That was my first thought. But what chance do you think we would have in Taiwan against Bryan Whyte? Besides, I don't want to be tempted by the money and power . . ."

"Then the only way to stop Whyte is to send him to jail. And that will be very difficult unless you know something you're not telling me." As Randolph spoke these words he noticed Phillips's eyes fall to the floor.

"How about drugs? Can we get him on drugs?"

"I can't help you there. That all happened after I left him."

"Warner would know all about it."

"Warner is a coward. You'd never get him on the stand."

"Perhaps he could be persuaded."

"He says Whyte's not involved anymore."

"With Europe closed off, Southeast Asia is the primary source for this country's heroin supply. Do you believe . . ."

"It's all handled by the Hong Kong Triads and their allies—"Pockmarked" Hwang in Saigon and the *Chiu Chao* gangs of Vancouver, British Columbia."

Phillips stood up and walked to the window. He pulled back the curtain and looked through the budding dogwood branches at the Capitol dome gleaming in the April sunshine. "No, Senator, you're not going to do it with drugs. You're going to need something else."

"There is something else, isn't there? Something you're not telling me."

Phillips removed his rimless glasses and rubbed his tired eyes, continuing to stare out the window. "Yes," he said.

Randolph strained not to give away his eagerness. After all these years of trying, he now felt himself close enough to nailing Bryan Whyte to taste the experience. As Phillips agonized in silence, Randolph puffed on the pipe and anxiously crossed and recrossed his legs beneath the desk. "This is no time to get cold feet, son."

Phillips hesitated for another full minute, then he

said: "Whyte has illegally paid out millions of dollars from the Nationalist Chinese, South Korean and Green Society treasuries into the accounts of American legislators. This program was getting started just when I left the organization and peaked in '69 and '70. It probably still exists to a lesser extent and involves some of the biggest names in Washington, Republican and Democrat. . . ."

"Jesus!"

"The majority of the money paid out was tong money, gathered by the Chinese underworld from drugs, prostitution, American supply rip-offs, squeeze and every other dirty business you can imagine."

"Can you prove this?"

"I set it up."

"Will you testify to that effect?"

"Why not?"

Randolph pushed his intercom and told his secretary to find the committee's legal counsel at once. "Now we're in business," he said to Phillips. "And we'd better have a twenty-four-hour guard on you."

"That won't be necessary," Phillips said. "Unless he's gone completely mad, he's not about to have me killed. The guy still believes in the brotherhood of the Omega Chi."

Bryan Whyte proudly picked up his new son and cradled him against his body. The infant opened his eyes, stared at his father blankly and made an impromptu bubble on tiny blue lips.

Below them, propped up on a pillow and looking extremely tired, Shelley watched the tender scene. "The nurse told me she thinks he looks just like you," she said. "She says he has the same single-minded look in his eyes."

Whyte kissed the baby. He felt very proud, very emotional. "You bet he does. This kid knows exactly where he's going."

They were in the maternity ward of St. Louis General Hospital. Shelley had wanted the baby to be born in the

States and had also wanted to be near her parents. The Whytes had flown back over a month ago and were living with the Spencers in their suburban St. Louis home. It had been most uncomfortable. Mrs. Spencer tried to be hospitable in a snippy way, but the retired colonel made it clear every day of the stay that he still considered Bryan a juvenile delinquent and the marriage a criminal abduction.

Seeing his wife in her family situation was very enlightening for him. On the one hand they spoiled her rotten and on the other they were very hard on her, very disapproving and forever letting her know they had little confidence in her ability to do anything right. If she had a poor image of herself—and he had come to believe that she did—it was easy to see where it originated. Better to have a nonparent like Old Whyte than this, he thought.

He spent the month avoiding conversation with them and trying to get something educational out of his trip. He read magazines and newspapers in his room. He watched a good deal of television. He took the bus into St. Louis, walked the streets and observed the people. He looked closely at the country and what he saw scared him more than anything he had seen in his previous trips. Something very dark and sinister was happening to the spirit here. . . .

"You still want to call him James?" he asked Shelley with a grin. "He doesn't look much like a James to me."

"There are enough William Bryan Whytes running around the world, thank you."

"Two are enough?"

"Bryan, I want to name this one after *my* side of the family. Your father won't be insulted. He'll just be so happy it was a boy that he won't be able to think of anything else."

"Well, at this point you can have whatever you want. You've done a nice night's work. James Bryan Whyte he will be. Maybe your old man will be so honored he'll start thinking of me as a human being."

Her eyes glazed wistfully a moment as she looked at

her baby and husband. "Sometimes I wish we could stay here. I hate to think of the poor little thing growing up surrounded by armed guards."

It was an uncharacteristic and very threatening comment. He reminded himself that she was exhausted and depressed. He made himself smile and kissed the baby again.

She pressed on. "What kind of life will that be for him? We'll live in constant fear of kidnapping or bombing. Couldn't we stay, at least for a while? You'd learn to love it."

Whyte looked kindly at Shelley a moment, then spoke very slowly and surely so there could be no mistaking his meaning. "There's no way this child is going to be raised in the States. He has a heritage and a destiny. No matter how bleak it may seem right now, his future is in China."

These words filled Shelley with new and tangled emotions. Bryan's heroic determination was one of the things she loved so much in him and it stirred her affection—part of her was still willing to follow him anywhere, even if it meant her own destruction. But some new part resisted the words. Ever since her failure with the book, she had begun to feel neglected and inadequate in her marriage— almost as if the book had been her symbol of equality and self-esteem. Its absence made her need Bryan more, made her resent his time away from her, made her see the Island of Taiwan as a rival for his attentions and affection—and as a potential danger to her new baby's life.

"When do you want to go back?" she asked with resignation.

"As soon as you feel up to it."

"I feel up to it now."

Bryan was conscious of the change that had come over her since she had given up her book project. She was less communicative and less interested in the running of China Gate. She spent hours reading self-help psychology books. She began going to mass again for the first time since their marriage. She was not happy. Well, perhaps the baby would give her life the focus she obviously desperately needed.

He handed the baby back to her and kissed her on the forehead. "Get some rest," he said.

As he left the ward, he thought of how tiring it was to have to keep up a front of optimism. No matter how much success he had with his plan of making Taiwan a self-sufficient bastion of capitalism, he could not really offer his family a future. With every day that passed, there seemed to be another U.S. overture to the Mainland; with every passing hour he became more isolated and his ultimate dream became more hopeless. Yet he had to hang on and keep plugging away. He had to. There was nothing else.

As he stepped into the maternity corridor, his feelings of hopelessness were about to become even more overwhelming. A federal marshal was waiting for him with a subpoena.

Bryan went into the waiting room, sat between two expectant fathers and read over the document. It demanded his presence in Washington D.C. the following week to appear before a special reconvening of the Randolph Committee's ongoing inquiry into U.S. Asia policy.

He went to a pay phone and made several calls, trying to find out exactly what was behind it. His sources close to the committee told him that the senator was out for his blood again. The man was going for a media event that would lead to criminal indictments and this time he had the ammunition to do it. He had a star witness named Alan Phillips.

Whyte had long feared that Phillips's alienation might someday lead to this. He also knew that Phillips was in a position to do real damage and that he had the moral courage to carry it out. But why had he chosen to act now? The war was over, the Omega Chi was struggling for survival, the antiwar movement was largely disbanded. It didn't make any sense! He only wished he had gone with his instincts and insisted on staying in Taipei for the birth of the baby. There, he could have stalled off an appearance for a year or more. Here, there was no way he could get out of it. They were no doubt watching his every movement and would grab him the minute he tried to leave the country.

He flew to Washington D.C. A large meeting of the Omega Chi's Washington attorneys as well as Caryer representing the Nixon administration, and Bamcheck of the CIA gathered in his suite at the Capitol Hilton that evening. The conversation was grim, the atmosphere tense and unpleasant. No one in the room seemed to trust anyone else but they were all drawn together in a spirit of self-preservation.

Caryer made it immediately clear to Whyte that the Nixon people were washing their hands of him. "If this thing becomes a circus, don't expect us to go out on any limbs for you," he said. "We have our hands full till this Watergate thing blows over. Besides, our interests no longer coincide—even on China policy. Particularly on China policy. You've been working against us in that area, as everyone in this room knows. We no longer have any connection with you whatsoever. We don't even know you exist."

Whyte was thinking that his friends in the conservative wing of the Republican party had not bothered to send a representative to this meeting. No doubt they were waiting to see how deep he would be incriminated before offering him any support. Smart of them.

The head Omega Chi lawyer asked, "How much does Phillips really know about your current affairs? He hasn't been directly involved for five years, after all."

"He knows everything there is to know about the Omega Chi's operations," Whyte said. "He organized most of them himself. What he didn't know a month ago, Warner has probably filled in. He can do terrific damage —not only to me but to everyone in this room and a great many congressmen in both houses. He knows about the campaign contributions and payoffs from Asian governments. He knows all about the involvement of the Chinese underworld with those governments and, through us, with the U.S. Government—names, dates, places, everything. I've never known anyone with such an uncanny memory for details."

"This is a disaster," said Caryer. "We have to find a way to shut him up."

Bamcheck asked, "Can you reach him, threaten him, buy him off, scare him off, change his mind?"

"No. He's not the kind of man to go into something like this without a lot of thought. Now that he's made up his mind, there's probably nothing anyone can do to change it."

Bamcheck tried again. "Is there anything in his past that you know of that would destroy his credibility as a witness? Homosexuality? Drugs?"

"Nothing. I've known him all his life. Alan has absolutely no vices at all. Except morality."

Caryer gave a disgusted half-laugh. "You almost sound like you admire him."

"I do admire him. I have nothing but respect for him. He's a man of real principle."

"That's the most dangerous kind," said Bamcheck.

Senator Randolph and his colleagues on the committee took their places and the milling crowd began to gravitate toward the gallery to wait for the session to begin.

Whyte sat in the front row with his attorney, his view of Randolph obscured by the open briefcases and bobbing heads around the long conference table. He waited stoically, not knowing exactly when he would be called and trying not to think about the bank of television cameras that would be trained on him. He thought back on his last appearance before this committee in 1967. This time he was not likely to come out a hero. This was a different era and this time even the one or two conservatives on the committee were not likely to stick their necks out for him.

After another moment, Alan Phillips was escorted

into the room. Whyte had not seen him for over five years. He looked heavy around the middle and his long hair was noticeably thinning on top. There was also a bitterness about the mouth and lines around the eyes that had not been there before. He was barely thirty, but, like Whyte, he looked a good ten years older.

Randolph rapped his gavel to call the session to order and then made a short statement about the nature of the proceeding. Then he called Phillips to the witness stand and swore him in. "Please state your name and occupation," he said.

"My name is Alan Jeffrey Phillips. I am a salaried employee of the American Friends' Service Committee. For the past five years I have been a salaried employee of the New York Mobilization to End the War. I am also a former executive officer and board member of Omega Chi Enterprises."

"Do you have a prepared statement to read?"

He read the statement. Slowly and methodically he told of how he had become personally involved in criminal activities in Asia. He told of how he and his childhood friends formed the Omega Chi as a fraternity of enterprise and good works and how they were able to serve the U.S. authority by acting as its communication link to the powerful Chinese underworld. He told of how he had served the organization during its years of growth and how he became disillusioned with it and quit in late 1968.

"When did you first realize that the Omega Chi was turning into something you found unconscionable?" Randolph asked.

"With the war in Vietnam. When the war went bad and began to change the consciousness of the world, to severely threaten us, we fought back. We stopped doing good works because we no longer had the time or money. As our troubles mounted, we rationalized all sorts of actions that once would have appalled us. We became . . ." His voice trailed off.

"You became what?"

"Evil."

"Evil in what way?"

"We became involved in marijuana smuggling. We suppressed minority groups like the Taiwanese Independence Movement. We assassinated the leader of a coalition of anti-American and anticapitalistic groups that had formed to oppose us. We used tong money to corrupt the American political process. We did all of this very logically and with the best of intentions under the assumptions by which we had been living since 1949. We were protecting freedom in Asia by protecting corrupt dictatorships, capitalistic gangsters and our own greed."

"And your leader during all this was the man sitting at the right end of the front row of the gallery?"

"Yes, William Bryan Whyte."

"What kind of man is Mr. Whyte?"

"A man of great intelligence and leadership ability. A brilliant, enterprising man with a peculiarly American kind of genius for getting things done in the face of great obstacles. A very unselfish, patriotic man who started out wanting to do nothing but good. It just . . . got out of hand for him. Before the war I considered him my closest friend. I named my oldest son after him and I don't regret that for a moment."

"Why then do you come forward with testimony against him? At this late date?"

"Because, even though the war is over, even though our brothers are dead and forever maimed, even though our country is in psychological ruins, the Omega Chi goes on and threatens to rebuild its corrupt power. This can never be allowed to happen. I see now that the Omega Chi and the principles it stands for must be destroyed. Bryan Whyte has to be discredited so thoroughly he can never rise again."

Phillips continued responding to Randolph's questions for the next three hours. He spoke about the history of the Green Pang Society, the conduct of the gang war with the Taiwanese Tiger Eels in 1963, the murder of Randy Ortega in 1967 and his own job as bagman at the 1968 conventions.

Throughout the testimony, Whyte showed no emotion. He doodled on a note pad, studied the press gallery, and occasionally whispered to the attorney beside him. Finally, the session adjourned until the next day.

As the chamber was clearing, Phillips walked up to Whyte. He stood before his old comrade, a man who, despite everything, still held a powerful attraction for him. "I have to do this, Bryan."

Whyte stared back at him with great calm and not a hint of bitterness. "I know, Alan."

"It was the drugs. If it hadn't been for that I never would have done it. I swear. But I have to do something to make up for that."

"I needed you, Alan. It wouldn't have happened if you'd been there."

"Bryan, do you understand what happened to us? I mean, do you really see?"

"I think I do, Alan," he said and then added, "We just don't agree on what it all means and how we recover from it."

"I'm so sorry it's come to this," Phillips said. "So very sorry."

Whyte smiled ironically, his big, wide eyes full of warmth and approval. "You're doing what you have to do and I'm doing what I have to do," he said. Then he picked up his cane and followed his lawyer out of the room.

The next morning the gallery was packed. The media had finally gotten itself hyped on the story late the day before; both CBS and NBC had given it a full thirty seconds on the national news. By later that same evening, every news-gathering service in the world knew that a major scandal was brewing, that a former American bagman was going to name influential congressmen who had received payoffs and illegal contributions from Asian gangs and Asian government sources.

Phillips did not sleep that night. The image of Bryan Whyte calmly sitting there listening to the testimony burned in his mind like a fever. He knew now that Warner had been lying, or at least not telling the entire truth. Whyte was not a monster. Perhaps he really did understand after all. Perhaps he *had* learned from the tragedies that had befallen him and was trying to extricate himself in a dignified way that he, Phillips, knew nothing about. No matter what arguments he gave himself, he could not get rid of the feeling that he was making a terrible mistake. And he wasn't sure he could continue with the testimony.

Early that morning, he woke Senator Randolph with a phone call. "I'm not sure I can go on," Phillips said. "I'm very confused."

Randolph suppressed his panic and tried to sound unperturbed. "You can't back out now, son."

"I know that intellectually . . ."

"This is the most important part of your testimony. This is going to get us indictments."

"I know . . ."

"You also know in your heart that this is the right thing to do."

"That's just it. For the first time I *don't* know that it's the right thing to do."

"What's happened?"

"Nothing has really happened."

"Who got to you?"

"No one has gotten to me."

"Then what's the matter?"

"Being face-to-face with Whyte has somehow shaken me up."

"Then I feel sorry for you. But I'm not going to let you quit on me." Randolph hung up the phone.

Later in the morning, Phillips called his wife at the apartment the American Friends rented for him in New York. He wanted to tell her his doubts, but she told him about the many calls of encouragement and support from their comrades in the Movement and he couldn't find the words. Then he spoke a moment to his son—the son who was named after Bryan Whyte—and hung up.

God, it was so confusing.

An hour later, he climbed into the limousine and was driven once again to the congressional hearing room. When the vehicle pulled up to the front steps, there was a press contingent waiting for him that would have embarrassed a presidential candidate. Phillips swallowed hard and tried to get a grip on himself. He knew in that instant that he would not be able to do it. He could not do it, at least until he had spoken to Whyte again. He would tell Randolph this the minute he was inside.

He stepped out of the car and started making his way toward the crowd. He had taken no more than three steps when a young Korean man darted out from behind one of the NBC cameramen. The wild-eyed Oriental pointed something at him and Phillips instinctively raised his hands for protection. There were explosions, spits of fire and an impact that took his breath away. As he fell back against the limousine and slid to the pavement, he barely sensed the police guards shooting back or the panic of the crowd as it ran for cover.

Then he lay dead.

Whyte was inside when he heard the shots. He fought his way through the crowd and frantic newsmen and saw Phillips sprawled in a pool of blood at the base of the steps, his face half shot away. A few feet beyond he could see the dead assassin, whom he immediately recognized as a freelance operative often employed by Bamcheck in the sixties. He forced his way to Phillips's body and lifted the mangled head to his lap, futilely checking for signs of life until two security men quickly pulled him away.

He began to perceive through his haze of shock and horror just what had happened. Bamcheck had obviously arranged it. There were just too many important people who stood to lose from Alan's testimony. Get rid of Phillips and there would be no indictments. Blame Whyte because he had the most obvious motive. Kill Whyte while he was trying to escape and that would be the end of Phillips *and* Whyte. Two problems removed with one bold stroke.

He backed out of the crowd and ran as fast as he could from the Capitol area to the safety of the crowded city streets.

He didn't know what to do or where to go. There was no one he could trust. They were no doubt watching his hotel room. He was covered with Phillips's blood and it was only a matter of seconds before his absence was noticed and they would come after him to finish the job.

The only thing he could think of was to go to a pay phone and call the one Washington figure who might have some sympathy for him. His hand trembled as he dialed the number.

Warren Stevens picked up the phone on the first ring. "Don't tell me where you are," he said immediately. "I believe my phone is tapped."

A nightmare, Whyte suddenly thought. This had to be a nightmare. It couldn't really be happening.

"I saw it all on television," Stevens said. "I was half expecting you to call. They'll be after you next and you can bet they don't want a trial so you best leave the country. Get back to Taiwan. Go by way of Canada."

"Can you help me get there?"

"They'll be watching me. The only thing you can do at this point is go to the Nationalist Chinese Embassy and ask for asylum. Go quickly before Bamcheck thinks of it and heads you off."

"I'm not about to spend the rest of my life in that building."

"Then get them to hide you in Chinatown. Bryan, listen to me. This is your only chance."

He noticed a patrol car casing the street and he hung up at once. He walked hurriedly around a corner and ran down a block of bars and pawnshops. He saw two patrolmen enter a bar across the street. They seemed to be searching the area, building by building.

He darted into a small movie theater—apparently a porno. He paid five dollars to a fat lady in the lobby who did not look back at him and stepped inside the auditorium. It was pitch black. No house lights at all.

Whyte fumbled his way to a seat. On the screen a pretty blonde was performing fellatio on a black man as three other men held her. Even in his present state of mind he was shocked. This would not have been legal and open in Taipei even at the height of the R&R.

Within a few minutes, two D.C. policemen entered the little auditorium. Whyte crouched on the floor, trying to get as far under the row of seats as he could. The cops stood at the entrance curtain a moment, watching the action on screen, letting their eyes adjust to the light. Then they walked down the aisle, shining their flashlights into the faces of the three or four traumatized patrons. The cops stood watching the movie for a while longer. Then they left.

Whyte stayed flat on the floor. It was almost too much for him, all of it. A few blocks away, Alan Phillips lay dead, murdered. And he was hiding on the floor of a pornographic movie theater that was in the very shadow of the Capitol building. Well, he could think about it now. He had to survive. Don't think! he commanded himself. Survive!

He waited for half an hour, then went to a pay phone in the lobby. He dialed a number from a piece of paper in his wallet. The phone rang several times before a voice answered. It was John Casy in Los Angeles.

"John, this is Whyte."

There was a suspicious pause. "Bryan?"

"Have you been following this thing with Alan?"

"I haven't had the stomach."

"Then listen carefully because I don't have much time. Something terrible has happened and you're going to hear all about it very soon. I want you to know that I didn't have anything to do with it and I'm being set up to take the blame."

"Something's happened to Alan."

"You'll know the minute you turn on a radio or TV. But first listen. I desperately need your help."

"What's happened to Alan?"

"John, he's dead. . . ."

"You had him killed."

"No . . ."

"You corrupt, dirty fuck. . . ."

Whyte fought back a wave of anger at the injustice of the accusation. "I didn't have him killed! They killed him! The United States of America killed him! As an official act of policy!"

There was a long pause on the other end of the line.

"John . . . ?"

"Do you see? Do you see what this country has become? Do you see what your war has done to this country? Your fucking destiny?"

"Yes, I see." He noticed the fat ticket-seller looking at him suspiciously now. He had to get out of there quickly.

"Oh God," Casy sobbed. "I can't stand it anymore. I don't have the strength."

"John, get a hold of yourself. I need your help. They're going to kill me next. Do you understand that? They have to kill me to close the case. I've got to get out of the country."

"I can't help you. . . ."

"You have a private plane. A jet. I need you to fly me to Canada. If the Omega Chi still means anything to you, come to Washington and go to Ambassador Lin at the Chinese Embassy. He'll tell you where I am."

There was another long pause.

"Will you come, John?"

The voice that answered was in agony. "I guess I have no choice."

"And John . . ."

"What?"

"You may be under surveillance. For God's sake, make sure no one follows you."

21

WHYTE TOOK STEVENS'S ADVICE AND CALLED THE Nationalist Chinese Embassy. The ambassador there—another old friend of his father's from Shanghai days—picked him up and took him to an apartment in southeast Washington where he stayed the night while the District police continued to comb the city for him. The next morning John Casy appeared. They drove to a small airfield near Alexandria, Virginia, where a Lear jet Casy had borrowed from his record company—Casy himself had not owned one since his glory days in the late sixties—took them to New York and then across the border to Montreal.

For most of their flight together on the plush jet, Casy barely spoke. He appeared to be under the influence of some narcotic; he just stared into space with scary determination. But as they were preparing to land in Montreal, he suddenly screamed at Whyte, "Alan's dead! Alan's dead! Alan's dead!" and burst into tears.

"I didn't do it," Whyte said, placing his hand on the sobbing man's shoulder.

"You did it. *You* did it. Even if you had nothing to do with it, you did it."

"I know how it looks," Whyte said, struggling to maintain his calm will to survive at all costs, "but it's not that way at all. I know it's very hard for you, but try not to judge me right now. . . ."

When they landed in Montreal, Casy wouldn't even say good-by. "You're not my brother anymore," he spit at him. "I never want to see you again."

* * *

From Montreal, Whyte flew on to Vancouver, where the Hop Sungs were waiting with a phony passport. Then he took a series of commercial liners to Tokyo, Manila and finally Taipei.

When he got to Sung Shan, he made no calls to announce his arrival. He took a taxi directly to the safety of China Gate, where he could hole up in privacy for a few days to recover his wits and regroup his thoughts on how to continue the struggle. He vaguely realized that he was now officially in exile. If he returned to the States for any reason, he would be arrested for interstate flight and conspiracy in the murder of a government witness. And he would surely be assassinated long before he had a chance to tell his side of the story.

He knew he would be safe remaining on the Island under the protection of the Green Society for a time, but there was no telling how long that safety would last. The power of the Greens and their ability to offer him total security seemed to shrink with each passing day. The U.S. Government would put enormous pressure on Chiang to extradite him, would use threats of further concessions to Red China to force the old Generalissimo and his people to go along. CIA hit men and his other enemies would be waiting to kill him every time he ventured beyond the entrance of China Gate. Possibly Shelley and the baby would even be prevented from leaving the States and would be used as a standing bait to lure him back. Yes, his future seemed very dark, but he couldn't allow himself to despair. He had to stay in control of himself. He had to survive. So many people were depending on him. . . .

King Lu appeared at China Gate early the next morning. The assassination of Alan Phillips was all over the news and King's spies had informed him the moment Whyte arrived back in Taipei. His eyes searched Whyte's face keenly to measure the damage done by the ordeal. The face betrayed some of the anguish behind it. Was the young taipan finally reaching the limits of his endurance?

"Why have you not called me?"

"I wanted to be alone. I needed a few hours to mourn the death of my friend."

"Did you think I would not be concerned? Did you not know that I would be suffering with you?"

"I am sorry, Older Brother. I was thoughtless."

King sat beside him on the wicker couch in the shade of the China Gate patio. "What will you do now?"

"The only thing I can do is stay here as long as the KMT lets me. I can never go back to the States again. I have been repudiated by my own people. I'm a criminal on the run and the Isle of Fugitives is the only place I can find refuge."

"You will be under my protection for as long as you remain on the Island. It will be my personal responsibility. I will stand outside your door myself, if necessary."

"They'll exert great diplomatic pressure to have me extradited."

"It doesn't matter. The Generalissimo will never turn you over to them no matter how much pressure is exerted. He is very loyal to his friends and you and your father are his closest American friends—the only Americans he completely trusts."

"But the Generalissimo is old and sick. When he dies, what then? How deep will my support run in the government?"

"We will worry about that when it happens."

"I am a grave liability to you now. And to the cause we have long served."

"You must not talk like this. The day of your destiny is still to come. You will see."

Weakened by these empty words and King's fatherly presence, his defenses suddenly came crashing down. All the dark thoughts he had willed himself not to think suddenly came rushing in on him. His voice was shrill with agony. "Oh, my elder brother! Have we not been the victim of some cruel cosmic trick? Is there any use in deluding ourselves any longer?"

King, looking more frantic than Whyte had ever seen

him, grabbed him and shook him violently. "No," he cried.

"We have failed."

"We have not failed. We will continue to fight them. We will continue the work we have started. We will fight everyone and we will free China, you and I. It is written. The prophecy never varies."

Whyte sank deep into the wicker. He was mentally and physically exhausted, sick to death of his "destiny." He wanted only to be left alone. He wanted his wife and child. He wanted a normal life.

"Promise me."

Whyte thought he had never felt quite so tired. He barely noticed the tears rolling down his cheeks.

"Promise me you will fight on."

"What can I do?"

"Say it."

"I . . . I promise."

"Promise me you will never allow those thoughts to enter your head again."

"I promise. I promise!"

"Good. Now get some rest. Tomorrow we will talk again." King stood up to leave.

Whyte looked up at him and their eyes met for the first time in this visit. "The American business community will not want a fugitive as head of their chamber of commerce. Surely they'll try to depose me at the first opportunity."

"Let them just try," said King.

Shelley and the baby made it back to Taipei two weeks later. After Whyte fled, she was detained by the St. Louis FBI office and interrogated by Bamcheck himself for two full days. Then he piled so much red tape and harassment on her that it was another two weeks before she could finally get on a plane.

Three limousines filled with heavily armed Blue Shirts picked them up and took them to China Gate.

When she was at last alone with her husband, she fell apart in his arms. Bamcheck and the publicity ordeal and the long trip with a screaming baby had made her mind a disaster area. She was also ravaged by doubt as to what had actually happened—exactly what part her husband had played in the assassination. Certainly he *was* capable of committing such an act if he thought it necessary for his cause.

"It was so awful," she cried.

"Were Bamcheck's men rough?"

"They told me you were a murderer."

"Do I have to tell you I had nothing to do with it?"

"No . . . of course not." She searched his eyes for sincerity. It was there. With great relief, she decided he was telling the truth.

"I've been trying to get through to his wife for days. She won't talk to me."

"I called her right after it happened. She believes you were behind it somehow. I offered her our financial support and she spit at it."

"She'll change her mind when she finds out what really happened. I'll see that those kids never want for anything."

"Bryan, what's going to happen to *us* now?"

"I don't know. I really don't. But we can't allow this thing to destroy us. We have to think positively. We have to keep going."

He felt her body tense and she pulled away from him. "Why do we have to keep going, Bryan? What law says we have to stay here?"

"It's the only place we're safe."

"We have money. Why don't we just leave the Orient and move to Europe or somewhere else where we can have a little peace?"

"I'd be arrested the minute I stepped off the Island."

"There must be dozens of countries that wouldn't extradite you. Countries where we'd be much safer. Argentina. Maybe Switzerland. South Africa for sure. Why couldn't we go to South Africa?"

"I can't leave. I have a big responsibility here. These are my people and this is my fight."

"Surely your responsibility doesn't include getting yourself killed."

"If it's my destiny to be killed, it will happen no matter where I am."

She could see that she was wasting her breath. She broke from his arms.

"Shelley, the simple truth is that we don't have enough money that we could live indefinitely in another country."

"We have millions."

"What I have is interests in a lot of different Taiwan companies that are just starting to take off. The cash in our personal bank account wouldn't even be enough to grease the right foreign palms to get the asylum."

"I don't understand. We made millions on the Johnny Yen films."

"I've put all that money and all the money I've made since then back into the Island. Into real estate and other ventures and investments that can't be liquidated for years."

"All of it?"

"Almost every penny."

She sat down in a chair. "Then I guess it's just you and me and Taiwan against the world."

She smiled bravely but inside she was thinking that something had changed in her. In another time she would have found this situation wildly romantic. But she did not feel romantic at all. She felt trapped.

Old Whyte had a heart attack a month after his son returned from the States as a fugitive. It was a mild one, but he was very old and dangerously frail. To make sure he recuperated properly, Bryan put him in the Franciscan Hospital in Shih Lin for a long stay.

When the old man regained his strength and was able

to get around somewhat, Bryan came to visit him as often as possible. This particular morning he found him in the hospital garden surrounded by the full bloom of the Taiwan spring. As he stood and watched the old man in this setting, Bryan thought he had never seen his father look so old or so distinguished. Somehow, despite everything, his presence was always a comfort.

They sat together on ancient, threadbare wicker in the coolness of the shade made by the hospital building. A smiling Filipino nun brought them a pitcher of lemonade and two glasses.

Bryan looked weary from overwork and Old Whyte noticed for the first time that his son's hair was beginning to turn as gray as his own.

"Shelley sends her love."

"She brings the baby by to see me most every afternoon. Oh, Sonny, he's a clever little thing. He reminds me so much of you at that age."

Bryan smiled. He was enormously proud of the little boy, even though he was unable to find much time to spend with him.

"I worry about Shelley, though. It's not normal for a young woman like her to be so cooped up all the time."

"Don't. She's tough. And she understands that she's always in danger outside the house."

"I suppose."

"I'm sorry I can't come as often as they do. I've been very busy."

"I know that, boy." Old Whyte stared a moment at the Green bodyguards standing sentry across the garden and seemed to drift off and lose himself in some thought.

Bryan had never gotten over being alarmed at his father's inability to keep a serious train of thought for more than a few minutes' time. He tried, in that moment, to imagine him as one of the most powerful men in the old China but it was impossible. What must he have been like?

"I suppose I'm never going to live to see the Mainland again," he finally said. "There was a time when I really believed I would walk along the Bund in Shanghai once again. Maybe see our old villa, if it's still there. I really believed Chiang was going to do it."

"He might have had it not been for Vietnam."

"Sonny, I'm sorry."

"Sorry for what?"

"For giving you such a hopeless cause."

He smiled lovingly at his father. "Nothing is hopeless. And I chose this life myself."

"Were we wrong?"

"Wrong?"

"Yes. Wrong about everything?"

"Well," he smiled gently, "we were wrong about some things."

"I don't have much to do with my time so I spend a lot of it thinking. I look back over all those years and all those people and it's damned confusing. Sometimes I get to thinking I was wrong about everything from the beginning—and it scares me."

"I don't think you were wrong about everything. I still think that what we had to offer is better than what they've got in China. And what they're going to get in Indochina. I'm not ashamed of believing in capitalism for Asia. I still think it's worth fighting for . . . worth trying to salvage."

Old Billy Whyte reached over and squeezed his son's hand. There was pain and desperation in his eyes that had never been there before. "Sonny, it's too late for me to do anything else. But it's not too late for you. You're a young man. Take Shelley and the baby and get out of here. Get out for my sake."

Bryan squeezed back. "It's too late for me too, Father. There's no turning back now. Our fate is tied to this Island. We have to make a stand here whether we like it or not."

After Bryan Whyte's return in disgrace from the United States, there was a drastic change in the life at

China Gate. As the months wore on and he fully comprehended the implications of permanent exile, he withdrew deeper into himself and worked harder at his goal. He drove himself mercilessly. He seemed to have little time for his wife and even less for his new son. There was no time for fun, no time for sex, no time to relax at all. Work was a therapy, an obsession and a shield against the reality that constantly threatened to crush him.

Outside of China Gate, the Whytes had no social life whatsoever. He found himself a kind of pariah in the American Community. Because he was a fugitive wanted for murder, the military and diplomatic people would not be seen in public with him and his ever-present battalion of Green bodyguards. Even old friends like the Perkinses, the Thomases and the Clifton Warners soon stopped inviting them over. It was beginning to be openly said that Bryan Whyte was a gangster, a dangerous, possibly imbalanced character. He quickly lost all of the social standing and respectability he had acquired in the Vietnam years, though an even greater mystique now surrounded his name. In private, people bragged of his friendship and praised his accomplishments. Ironically, he had returned to the same kind of outlaw position he had held as a high-school gang chieftain.

Yet, as in high school, he was a necessary ingredient of the Community—perhaps *the* most necessary ingredient of its composition. He went unchallenged for his position as president of the American Chamber of Commerce and remained the behind-the-scenes taipan of the business community. Heads of major U.S. corporations investing in the Island secretly made trips to China Gate to seek his advice. The Chinese Council on Economic Planning and Development hardly made a decision without consulting him. Under his leadership, the Omega Chi fearlessly pushed ahead, expanding its operations, leading the way for all the other companies. He continued to use his connections with the underworld and the Kuomintang to facilitate the flow of business in general. He continued to be committed to his goal of making Taiwan into a showcase of capitalism that would be a thorn in that hideous, ever-growing rapprochement between the United States of America and the People's Republic of China.

As the months of exile wore on, Shelley Whyte began to fear that she was going quietly but completely insane.

Desperate, negative thoughts crept into the corners of her mind and threatened to overwhelm her. They disrupted her sleep and destroyed her peace of mind. Every waking moment was a struggle to keep them down and thereby they obsessed her.

She simply could no longer delude herself into seeing anything grand or heroic about their stand on Taiwan. She felt she had been trapped into defending a position that, in her heart of hearts, she knew was indefensible. Everything about her life now seemed wrong, stupid, hopeless. . . .

These thoughts had begun, of course, with the murder of Alan Phillips. This cataclysmic event had deeply affected her and continued to obsess her. Sometimes, she took out the file of press clippings on the murder and read them again and again, comparing them to her husband's story. She did not want to believe he had anything to do with it, but how could he not have had some small part in it? Why else would it have changed him so much, made him so remote to her?

When she was not thinking about Alan or the hopelessness of Taiwan, her mind was filled with other destructive thoughts. She found she was not a natural mother: She hated the feedings and diapers, yet she felt tremendous guilt about letting the amahs do all the dirty work of raising the child. She was haunted by the memory of Su Ling and Su Ling's death and feared a similar attack that might harm her baby. She resented Bryan's many absences, his constant late work nights, and recently had taken to imagining him in torrid affairs with various Oriental women.

In her less anxious moments, she realized what she

was doing to herself. Her problem was that she basically had nothing to do but think bad thoughts. There was absolutely nothing in her life except a husband who would not communicate with her and a baby, both of whom she could not help herself from resenting.

She finally reached a point where she had to do something to preserve her sanity. It was the morning of the day Bryan was leaving for his third business trip to Tokyo that month. He was on the floor of the nursery playing with the baby as two amahs looked happily on.

She entered the room quietly and watched the scene a moment. It was obvious that he adored his son. He seemed to have transferred all his affection from her to him.

"How long will you be gone this time?" she asked.

He looked over at her and smiled. "Oh, just the weekend."

"I think I need to get out of China Gate for a while. Maybe I'll go to Sun Moon Lake or the beach while you're gone."

His smile vanished. The mask of remoteness returned to his face. "It's too dangerous, Shelley."

She took a deep breath. "Bryan, I think maybe I need to go to the States for a while. My parents are very worried about me. They really want to see their grandson again."

He handed the baby to one of the amahs and stood up. "You know I can't allow that," he said. "You know they'd probably never let you leave. Why do you ask me?"

"Why don't you let me go with you then?" Her voice cracked. "Maybe I can . . . help you or something."

"I need you right here."

She put her palm over her eyes and fought back the urge to break down and cry. "I just thought maybe I could help you."

"You're helping me just by being my wife."

As more and more months of exile passed, her sense of isolation became unbearable.

The thing that made her life so intolerable, she knew, was that she had no friends. There was no confidant, no one person to whom she could express her complicated feelings. She wrote her mother for this purpose for a time but her mother only wrote back stern and disapproving lectures. She tried to make friends with some of the other taipan wives but they tended to avoid her because of Bryan's notoriety. Even the amahs avoided her because she tried to draw them into deep conversations and it embarrassed them.

She was about to despair of ever having such a friend again when one suddenly appeared in the unexpected form of David Butler.

Butler maintained a very curious relationship to China Gate. Bryan clearly did not like him but for some reason continued to tolerate him, even seemed drawn to him. Butler obviously represented some sort of challenge to her husband—there always seemed to be some strange competition going on between them—and he was the only journalist who could regularly gain admittance to the estate.

Butler saw her desperation at once and, what's more, he understood it. He changed his tone toward her and became very respectful. He began dropping by on various excuses and spoke to her about writing, loaned her some of his favorite books to read. Later, as she lowered her guard, she let him read some of her discarded manuscript. He praised it, encouraged her and softened the sense of humiliating defeat that had never left her. Finally, he suggested they work together to expand her chapters on Mark Taylor into a major book about Vietnam. She accepted and it saved her life.

As they began working closely together, she saw him in a totally different light—saw him as the frustrated idealist that he was—and warmed to him. The only thing that continued to bother her about him was his cutting cynicism about her husband, which never let up.

"You really do hate him, don't you?" she asked him one day after a particularly caustic remark.

"Yes, I do," he said unashamedly.

"Why?"

"Because he's a hypocrite."

"Hypocrite?"

"Sure, he likes to think of himself as a great defender of Americanism and personal freedom, but we both know it's all bullshit. He only exists because people like me can't touch him, question him, make him account . . . expose him. It's funny. I came here to nail people like Bryan Whyte and I can't because people like Bryan Whyte own people like me. That's what Asia is all about. For a while, I thought Vietnam would change that. But things seem to be going right back to the way they were before."

This time, Shelley did not rise to defend her husband. Seeing the depth of her friend's feeling, she instead took his hand and squeezed it with affection and understanding.

But Butler hardly noticed. He was lost in his bitterness. "My mission is to destroy that man," he said. "One way or the other."

22

WITHIN TWO YEARS OF HIS DAY OF EXILE, BRYAN Whyte's vision for Taiwan became a reality.

When the Board of Foreign Trade released its statistics for the year 1973, it was apparent that a miracle had been worked. Foreign investment that year was an astonishing $248 million, almost doubling the figure for the year before. Even though the U.S. Government had unofficially done everything in its power to prevent it, the confidence of the international business community in the future of Taiwan had been fully restored—and then some.

In the following months of 1974, the OPEC oil embargo sparked a worldwide recession. But the boom that began the year before in Taiwan could not be stopped. American and Japanese businessmen came to Taiwan by the planeloads to take advantage of the cheap labor and government incentives. The lobby of the Grand Hotel began to look like the floor of the New York Stock Exchange, with hundreds of sweating traders frantically making deals at any time of the day or night. The skyline of Taipei blossomed with new construction. The economy was on fire.

Of the thousands of companies that profited by this unprecedented boom, none profited quite as much as the Omega Chi. Its lean-year investments in Taiwan real estate and small industry turned into gold overnight. Under the directorship of Whyte and an aggressive executive team that included David Ward Kee, Jonathan Wu and old Lee Min, the company was working toward becoming one of the largest *zaibatsu*-style trading conglomerates in the Orient, already a tough competitor in this part of the world to Mitsubishi, Mitsui and the other Japanese giants. Its interests on the Island included textiles, sporting goods, pleasure-boat manufacturing, motion pictures, tea-growing, toys, chemicals, food processing and footwear. It acquired a fleet of containerized cargo ships. It gobbled up a controlling interest in the Hong Kong and Taipei Banking Corporation and offered full financial services to any U.S. corporation interested in investing in the Island. It entered into a joint venture with Japan's Nissan Motors to begin manufacturing automobiles on the Island by the end of the decade. It moved heavily into electronics and the fledgling computer industry. It maneuvered its way into tourism, hotels, supermarkets, fast-food franchises and department stores.

The stunning success of Taiwan and the Omega Chi between 1973 and 1975 gave Whyte an international reputation as a financial genius. Still a fugitive from justice, a shadowy figure surrounded by gangster bodyguards and veils of mystery and rumor, he was the subject of boundless curiosity from the world press and the financial community. *Fortune* called him "the exiled prince of American business" and China Gate "the court to which the leaders of the great multinationals invariably pay homage if they want to do business in the Far East." *Barron's* frequently referred to Taiwan as "the Isle of Whyte." Other, less kind writers hinted at eccentricity and even brain damage from the 1969 bombing attempt on his life.

To his close business associates, he was even more of an enigma. Except for King Lu, he never confided his personal feelings to anyone; no one ever knew for sure what he was thinking. He did not seem at all surprised by his enormous success nor did he particularly delight in it. Everything was just going according to plan and he accepted it calmly with more plans, more work, more audacious ventures.

Then one day in February, 1975, something happened which did actually surprise him and was not according to plan.

He was in the council room of China Gate with several executives from the top American oil companies, speculating upon how the worsening situation in South Vietnam might affect their plans to form a consortium to drill for offshore Indonesian oil. Ah Chin came into the room looking very pale and shaken.

"Sir," he whispered urgently, "a courier has delivered a special diplomatic message for you."

"Is it not apparent that I am in conference, Ah Chin?" he snapped in Mandarin.

"Sir, I think you may want to give this your immediate attention."

"What is it?"

"It's very confidential, sir. If . . ."

"Tell me now. These men do not speak Chinese."

"Sir, if you will just excuse yourself for one moment."

Irritated, he got up and stepped into the hallway. Ah Chin handed him the dispatch.

"Who is it from?"

"Peking."

"Great God!" It was impossible. Unthinkable.

"They want to have a meeting with you on some neutral ground."

Whyte was as dazed as if he had been hit in the head with a rock. "Why?"

"They don't say."

Whyte stood looking at the message for several moments. Then he shook his head and smiled ironically. "Do you know, Ah Chin, that just the possession of this dispatch would buy us a death sentence under Taiwan law?"

"Will you do it, sir? Meet with them?"

Bryan Whyte didn't answer. He started back into his meeting, then stopped and turned to Ah Chin. "Call King Lu. Tell him I need to see him at once."

On the other side of the world, also in the late winter of 1975, Warren Stevens stepped uneasily past a Marine guard and into a White House conference room.

Staring at him from around the table were the somber faces of the Republican enemy. There was Caryer, of the White House staff (a clever young fellow, Stevens thought —one of the few insiders to weather the Nixon resignation). There was Harlan Bamcheck, head of Far East operations of the Central Intelligence Agency (an evil fellow, Stevens thought—the man responsible for the assassination of Alan Phillips). There was even the globe-trotting, celebrity Secretary of State of the new administration, whom Stevens had never met.

Stevens had no idea why he had been summoned here. He had not held a government post since 1968. In all that time, the Republicans had never once consulted him about Far Eastern affairs. He sat down at the table and waited.

Caryer was spokesman for the group. "Thank you for coming, Ambassador Stevens," he said. "We have asked you here to inform you that the fall of Saigon is imminent. The last American should be evacuated within the month."

Stevens was surprised but not greatly. It was just a bit

sooner than expected. "I'm sorry to hear it. But, of course, if was inevitable. Maybe it's even a positive thing to get it over and behind us."

"It has caught us somewhat off guard, Mr. Stevens. We expected Saigon to hold out for another year, even longer. It's forcing us to rather hastily reexamine our Asian policy. Our future is coming at us faster than anticipated and, of course, our future in Asia is China. As you know, with America out of the picture in Southeast Asia we desperately need a strong ally to block the ambitions of the Soviet Union in the area. . . ."

"And the ambitions of the North Vietnamese," Bamcheck added. "The Chinese are more afraid of the Vietnamese than we are. We're natural allies in that respect."

"For these reasons," Caryer went on, "it is imperative that we establish full diplomatic relations with Peking as soon as possible."

Stevens was beginning to understand what he was doing here. "I quite agree with your analysis. But we have a small problem, don't we?"

"Yes," Caryer said. "The problem is Taiwan. We have a pissant island off the coast of China that's standing between us and the future."

Stevens shifted the weight of his long body in the chair. He was beginning to enjoy this. "Yes, I'd say it was a problem all right. China will never establish relations with us until we break relations with Taiwan. Oh, they're very touchy about that subject—a two-China policy is unthinkable to any Chinese. And how do we break relations with a country we created? A country that nominally espouses all our principles? A country that has received twenty-five years of our sacred promises of protection? A country that is now a roaring capitalistic success? Probably our single greatest success in Asia, not excluding Japan? The economic miracle of the seventies? Yes," he smiled, "that's a tough one." He looked directly at Bamcheck. "I'd say our old friend Bryan Whyte has us by the balls on this one. Wouldn't you say so, Harlan?"

The men looked at one another. They were surprised

by Stevens's obvious pleasure at their predicament. Caryer said, "Well, we *are* going to break relations with Taiwan. We have no choice. The security of our country in the 1980s demands it. Our challenge is to make that move as smoothly as possible. Toward that end, there are certain things we can do. First, we can take steps to slow down the pace of the Taiwanese economy—to make it appear to the world as something other than our greatest success. Second, we can give secret support to some of the Taiwanese resistance groups—to give Chiang Kai-shek such nasty internal problems that he won't have time to worry about his foreign policy problems. Third and most important, we can neutralize the influence of Bryan Whyte. We can prevent that madman from orchestrating the Island's reaction against us."

"Yes," Stevens said with sarcastic seriousness. "I'd say the third is the most important. Whyte can be very dangerous to us now. Very dangerous indeed."

"This is why we want your help. Whyte trusts you. You can get to him. Do it and you'll be the first American ambassador to the People's Republic of China."

The pleasure left Stevens's eyes. "You must be completely out of your mind. I *admire* that madman. There's no way you can bribe me into setting him up for slaughter!"

The Secretary of State spoke up for the first time. He was a controlled, reasonable-sounding man who spoke with a slight German accent. "Mr. Stevens, there is going to be an election next year. Suppose for a moment that the Democrats win. Given Watergate, this is even likely. Suppose also you were to find yourself in my chair. Given your prominence in East Asian affairs, that is not impossible. You would be faced with this same situation. Would your options be any different from mine? Would you be able to come up with a different solution? Can you think of a way to be fair to Taiwan and still build a necessary relationship with the real China? I think not and I think you know it. Please consider this a moment and then help us close the book on this painful chapter of our history forever."

* * *

In the first week of April, 1975, it became increasingly obvious to the world that Saigon would fall to the Communists within a matter of weeks. In Taipei, American businessmen who still foolishly had interests there waited in line at Sung Shan for transportation to get what they could out of the city before the inevitable took place. Whyte stayed at China Gate and watched the cables around the clock, stubbornly refusing to pull out his remaining people until the last possible moment.

Within another few days, however, that moment arrived. The city was completely encircled by the advancing Communist troops. The American Embassy was closed and the last American evacuated. Communications with the outside world were expected to be severed at any time.

Whyte cabled his people to be ready and took the Omega Chi company jet to Saigon to pick them up.

On the long flight down, he sat in the back of the luxurious executive jet nursing a gin and tonic, thinking not about the fall of Saigon but about his wife. For the past year, Shelley had been rebelling against him in numerous small, irritating ways. She started smoking in front of him again and refused to act as hostess to many important China Gate social functions. She spent almost every afternoon assisting David Butler on some writing project about Vietnam, even though she knew this particularly disturbed him.

That morning he discovered that she had left their child with the amahs *every* day for the past two weeks. He exploded. "What kind of mother are you, anyway?"

"What kind of father are you," she yelled back. "You haven't spent more than five minutes at a time with him since he was born."

"You don't do a damn thing constructive. You can damn well spend some time with your child."

"I'm going into town today. *You* spend the day with him."

"I've got to go to Saigon. I've got important business to attend to."

The word "business" was like a red flag to her. "Well, I've got important business of my own."

She gave in, of course. But just barely. And he was very troubled by the change in her. The unnatural strain of her life was obviously beginning to get to her. She was becoming a different person and he didn't know what he could do about it, how he could stop this creeping deterioration—short of abandoning the Island with her.

The plane landed at Tan Son Nhut and Whyte was immediately jarred out of his thoughts of domestic turmoil. He could see that it was much later in the game than anyone in Taipei had imagined. The Communists were just miles away from the airport; the roads leading to it were clogged with refugees scrambling to escape the city.

The three Omega Chi employees were anxiously waiting in the crowded terminal area and Whyte quickly put them on the plane. Then he told the pilot, "I have to pick up someone else in the city. If I'm not back within ninety minutes leave without me."

The pilot, an American, looked at Whyte incredulously. "Not to worry, boss. In ninety minutes or the first sight of a VC, I'm gone."

Whyte found a solitary taxi driver who agreed to take him into the city for his gold watch and two hundred U.S. dollars. They drove out of the teeming terminal area and sped through the deserted countryside, past burnt-out automobiles, looted businesses and an occasional body left behind in the rush. In the far distance, Whyte could hear the sounds of mortar barrages falling on the southern outskirts of the city like thunder on a summer night.

"Why are you staying?" he asked the driver.

"No place to go. Anyhow, I figure Charlie, he gonna need a taxi too sometimes." He turned around and grinned happily at Whyte. "Maybe he need to know where to catchee nice girl too, eh?"

Whyte grinned back. The capitalistic instinct dies hard, he thought.

Saigon was a ghost town. The boulevards were empty. Most of the inhabitants had already fled and the remaining ones were staying out of sight. It was that same eerie stillness that descends on an Asian city just before a typhoon hits. Whyte was thinking, strangely, about the first time he and Mark Taylor had driven down these streets in 1966. The sense of adventure they had had. God, how he missed those days.

He had the driver stop at the new modern building on Tran Hung Dao Boulevard where the Omega Chi had its Saigon offices. The security door was open and the building appeared abandoned. Deciding to have a quick look, he patted the driver on the shoulder. "You wait here a minute, okay?"

He climbed the stairs to the second-story office suite. The hallway was empty. No sign of life at all. Inside the office, the files were turned over on the floor. The executive offices had been ransacked and the safe blown open. In some incomprehensible act of defiance, someone had defecated on the manager's desk.

He pulled out a chair and sat a moment in the silence of the vandalized office, morbidly enjoying it. So this was what the end looked like, he thought. The end of the American Dream in Asia. A vision of what all his empire might be someday in the not-so-distant future. Somehow, actually seeing it wasn't all that bad. Not nearly as bad as the fear of it.

He sat for a few more moments, then hurriedly left the office and drove three miles to the villa of "Pock-marked" Hwang. He paid the driver and dismissed him.

Old Hwang had not suffered since the demise of the Orient Express. With the unprecedented demand for Oriental heroin shooting prices to the sky, he had merely reorganized his pipeline to send his Golden Triangle merchandise in smaller quantities—but with almost equal profits—through Bangkok to the various overseas Chinese communities of the world, principally Amsterdam, London and Vancouver. He now had the full support of the Hong Kong Triad and an army of smugglers under his command.

Hwang regarded the impending fall of Saigon as little more than a minor inconvenience. It was not until his spies told him that the VC had ordered his execution the minute the city was taken that he got worried. Then he hastily requested asylum in Hong Kong, Bangkok and Singapore, but was denied it in all three cities. Only Taipei —whose authorities gave sanctuary to any Oriental gangster on the run—would accept him. Whyte had personally made the arrangements.

Hwang and his youngest son were frantically waiting for him in Hwang's living room amidst mountains of cardboard boxes. These boxes contained the large part of the old gangster's fortune that had not already been moved to Hong Kong and Taipei banks or hand-carried by the rest of his family to the estate he had bought in England last year. A look of immense relief came over his old face. "You are *very* late," he barked in Mandarin.

"I'm sorry, Uncle."

"Where is the helicopter?"

"Again I'm sorry. I couldn't get one."

Hwang let loose a tirade of profanity. Whyte had assured him several times that there would be a helicopter to transport his valuables to the airport.

"I am humiliated, my uncle," Whyte said.

"It is inconceivable that we could carry all this by automobile!" He furiously motioned toward the boxes of priceless antiques, jewelry and cash of various currencies. Spit drooled from the corners of his mouth.

"Even if we could, there is no time. We have waited too long."

"*You* waited too long. Every day you have sent us a cable saying you would be here the following day. Every day for a week you have deceived us."

"I take full responsibility. I will reimburse you for all losses."

"You don't have that much money, you little turtle egg."

Whyte let this vilest of Chinese insults pass. "Surely King Lu will honor any losses you may have suffered through my inexcusable incompetence."

"Bah!"

"We can talk about it later. The route to the airport could be cut off at any moment. My pilot has orders to leave within the half hour. It may be too late as it is."

Hwang's black eyes darted rapidly in their sockets. The will to survive overcame his outrage and he recovered from his loss. "All right, we go."

Hwang's Mercedes raced toward the airport through wet, empty streets. Beside Whyte, Hwang's son drove recklessly; the sound of the exploding artillery shells, just blocks away, frightened him to suicidal speeds.

At the main entrance to the airport, the road was blocked by a crowd of Vietnamese fighting each other to climb over the locked, six-foot-high wood and barbed-wire gate—apparently trying to get to the runway and the last hope of evacuation. When this crowd refused to make way for the honking automobile, Hwang hurriedly rolled down the back window and pointed his pistol at the people nearest him.

Before Whyte could deflect his arm, Hwang fired three shots, dispersing the crowd at once and leaving two lifeless bodies in its wake.

The car roared through the gate and broke it into a hundred splintery pieces. Up ahead, Whyte saw the jet waiting for him. The other evacuation planes had all left and his was the only plane remaining on the field. They drove to the terminal parking lot and stopped.

Behind them, the crowd had quickly regrouped and was rampaging through the broken gate, toward the field and the lone airplane. Whyte knew that he had only a second to finish his business. Now, he told himself. Now, now, now.

He reached under his shirt and pulled out a .38 special. While Hwang and his son were still watching the crowd and the plane, he pointed the revolver at Hwang. The old gangster instinctively turned and stared at him in disbelief. "What is this?"

"This is for Mark Taylor," Whyte said, reaching over

and removing the pistol from Hwang's hand, throwing it out the open window.

Hwang spat at him angrily. "Taylor was a fool. So are you. The plane is leaving!"

"For every Yin there is a Yang. You are the dark side of all my boyhood dreams. You are my nightmare."

"You clazy boy. We gotta hurry. Look!" He pointed at the crowd.

Whyte squeezed off two shots into Hwang's brain. He turned quickly and fired a third bullet that hit Hwang's astonished son in the forehead. They were both instantly dead.

Whyte's unfinished business in Saigon was now completed.

He came around front and pulled Hwang's son's body out of the driver's seat, onto the pavement. He drove the vehicle over a hundred feet of lawn to the runway.

The crowd was getting so close to the jet that the pilot was now taxiing out to make a takeoff. Whyte drove as if to cut the plane off, then slammed on the breaks and ran for it, leaving Hwang's body slumped in the back of the car. A hand reached out to pull him in just as the crowd was beginning to gain on him.

"This is what I call cutting it close," the pilot yelled back. "You wanted the honor of being the last American out of Saigon, didja?"

Whyte did not answer him. The plane took off and made a wide circle. Bryan Whyte watched the advancing Communist troops marching unopposed into the southern section of the city.

Three weeks before the fall of Saigon, Generalissimo Chiang Kai-shek passed away. It had been expected. He was eighty-one and very ill from assorted ailments of advanced age. But it was still a shock to the people of Taiwan, a loss of the personification of Nationalist China that seemed all the more painful and portentous in conjunction with the final loss of Vietnam.

The city of Taipei went on a binge of mourning that continued throughout April and early May. The streets were draped in black. Ground was broken on hundreds of memorials. An epic funeral was held at which Old Whyte, looking deathly weak, came from his hospital bed to serve with King Lu as an honorary pallbearer. Hundreds of thousands of genuinely grief-stricken Chinese and Taiwanese filed by the casket as it lay in state.

Two days after the surrender of Saigon, the old Gimo was finally moved into his resting place—a mausoleum on Grass Mountain that would serve until a suitable sanctuary was built. He had finally passed into history alongside his old mentors, Sun Yat-sen and Tu Yueh-sen.

The political pundits of the world speculated on what the effect of that passing would be on the divided people whose history he had so dominated for the greater part of the twentieth century.

One day after the death of Chiang Kai-shek, Juan Ortega stepped out of his limousine and entered one of the many new glass office buildings on Jen Ai Road—a street that just a few years ago was lined by paddy fields but which now had so many grand, modernistic structures that it resembled Wilshire Boulevard in Los Angeles.

He took an elevator to the top floor, then walked down the highly polished linoleum hallway to a door beside a small, dignified sign that read: "War Tiger Products Ltd."

Behind the door was a suite of offices. Ortega nodded good morning to the receptionist and several office workers, continuing on into a large executive office. He sat at his desk as his secretary brought in a stack of newspaper clippings. She also handed him a glass of steaming hot tea which he placed beside a framed photograph of his Taiwanese wife and their two children. Above the desk was a large oil painting of his late beloved brother, Randy.

The secretary closed the door and Ortega laid the accounts of the Generalissimo's death over the desk. He shook his head disbelievingly. It seemed almost inconceivable that this day had finally come, that the last precondition for his master plan had finally moved into place.

He continued to study them a moment, then he buzzed his secretary and told her there would be a special executive conference today. He told her to call Ya Ki Loi, Amos Wong, Lefty O'Hara, Loma, Dave Magaha and Mr. Gordon—the code name for Ming Te, leader of the underground Taiwanese Independence Movement. She was to tell them to be there at eleven that morning.

"Sir, you have an eleven o'clock with Mr. Hiro of the Osaka Satsui Bank."

"Cancel it. Cancel all my appointments for the rest of the day."

"Yes, sir."

Almost six years had passed since Ortega made peace with King Lu after the abortive 1969 bombing of China Gate. During this time he had been under constant pressure from the coalition he headed to move against the Omega Chi, to unleash an all-out, once-and-for-all, open rebellion against them. But Ortega had always refused. Instead, he counseled caution and moderation and the necessity of waiting for the right time. Even when Whyte had returned from the United States an outcast and a fugitive, he knew that the time was still not right, that the KMT would still fiercely protect Whyte and such a rebellion would fail. Wait, Juan had insisted. Wait until the conditions were perfect. Time is on our side.

Waiting had proved to be a dangerous game. The events of the last few years had in many ways strengthened Bryan Whyte's organization and weakened the anti-Omega Chi coalition. The major financial concessions of the 1969 peace—the Orient Express and the R&R—had soon become worthless to the Warlords. The antiwar groups fell apart; the Maoist sympathizers and Taiwanese Independence advocates began to realize they had totally opposite ideas about the future of the Island.

The thing that had most weakened the links of the coalition was the economic boom they were having. It had taken Ortega by surprise and it was creating a social revolution all around him. The businessmen who were most profiting by the boom were Taiwanese—and they were slowly but surely taking over economic control from the Chinese minority. The Tiger Eels organization was losing men left and right because its more enterprising members realized they could make more money by going into legal business for themselves. The ironic fact of life was that there was more money in owning a small appliance store these days in Taipei than there was in owning a whorehouse. Everyone was getting in on the bonanza.

The year before, the Warlords themselves succumbed to this economic mania. Ortega had incorporated and invested all their remaining assets into various legitimate businesses. In one year, they had become a mini-conglomerate with thriving interests in textiles, construction, export-import, labor-intensive manufacturing and real estate. Ortega was even considering going public and selling stock on the Taipei Exchange to finance his new ventures. In one week, they had sold two parcels of Sin Alley real estate to an American luxury hotel chain for more money than they had made in a year at the height of their economic power in the sixties. The only clearly illegal business left in the Warlords' portfolio was their connection with the Triad drug trade—and the only thing that kept Ortega in this ugly business was his fear that forsaking it would give his rival, Dave "Fatso" Magaha, the excuse he was seeking to depose him as president.

But none of this mattered now. What mattered was that the coalition *had* held together through these years and these events. It still had the manpower and the will to wage war against the Omega Chi and Greens when Ortega was ready to call for it.

And he was ready to call for it now.

With the death of Chiang, the right time had finally come. The thing that had made the Greens invincible was that they had always had the power of government behind them: As a member of the Greens, Chiang had always kept the Society at the highest level of his council. But with Chiang now out of the way and his son, Chiang Ching-kuo, in power, the influence of the Greens was bound to wane. Ching-kuo had no such automatic loyalty to the Greens. In fact, it was strongly rumored that he had always resented their influence in government, that he personally saw King Lu as a rival for his father's affections and succession to ultimate power. He was also said to be a political realist in regard to the Taiwanese question and had carefully constructed a working relationship with Taiwanese leaders throughout his career in government.

Yes, Ortega thought with tremendous excitement and satisfaction, the time had finally come to set his long-held plan in motion. He would continue to infiltrate the Green Society and the vast Omega Chi business organization with his own people. He would continue to bribe the weaker members of the Kuomintang and build a network of support in the new government of Chiang Ching-kuo. He would continue to talk to Bamcheck of the CIA. Then, when he was sure that Whyte was isolated, without governmental support and at his point of maximum vulnerability, Juan Ortega would simply march into China Gate and destroy him.

23

WHEN ADMIRAL FLOYD HARRIS RETURNED TO TAIPEI in June of 1976 to assume command of all U.S. forces in Taiwan, he was stunned by the sights that greeted him.

In his State Department briefing, he had been warned that there had been an economic boom—that there had been changes that would surprise him—but he was in no way prepared for this. The city had nearly doubled in size since he had last seen it in the mid-sixties. Construction was underway on a new island-long freeway, a modern new airport and dozens of major new industrial complexes, harbors, dams and railways. Thousands of new office buildings and apartments and hundreds of new tourist hotels had risen where there had once been only rice paddies.

Giant department stores, supermarkets and luxurious specialty shops had replaced the haggler's alleys. Somehow, the old China of pedicabs, amahs, poverty, rank smells, dirt streets and sweating coolies had vanished in the years he was away.

It was a startling visual transformation and an extraordinary accomplishment! The American Dream had been a failure in Vietnam; Harris could certainly attest to that, had benefited greatly in his career by recognizing it earlier than most. But it was also just as certainly working here. Bryan Whyte and the Nationalists were making it work.

That afternoon, Harris stepped down the long corridor of the Taiwan Defense Command headquarters and into the office of the commander. Closing the door softly behind him, he stood for a moment in the middle of the big, airy room. He remembered all the times he had been on this carpet during his time as executive provost marshal. Now it was his office, his responsibility—though he did not want it and had accepted it only after voicing the loudest possible protest.

It had all happened very quickly. Harris had spent the last three years in the Pentagon, working diligently in fleet logistics, trying to gather the political connections he hoped would get him a promotion. The promotion had suddenly, unexpectedly, come through on Monday. His transfer papers reached him on Tuesday. On Wednesday he went to the State Department to be briefed on his assignment. When he got there, he discovered he was to be briefed by Warren Stevens—who was not in the government and not even a Republican.

Stevens told him right off that he would likely be the last American commander to serve on the Island. "America is moving toward complete recognition of Communist China and complete military withdrawal from Taiwan sometime in the next three years," he said. "Your mission is to make that difficult transition, when it comes, as painless as possible."

Harris was angry. He realized the minute he saw Stevens that he was about to be handed another impossible task by another thick-headed politician. His whole career had been a series of no-win, impossible political tasks— Korea, the American gangs of Taipei, Saigon, now this mess. "Do you have any suggestions as to how I might do that?"

"You're going to have to do something about Bryan Whyte," Stevens said uncomfortably.

It was all clear now. Why they had chosen him. Why he was being bribed with admiral's boards. "Haven't we done enough to the poor guy already?"

"Our policy in Taiwan is to see the old order die as quickly as possible so the Island can someday peacefully rejoin the Mainland. Whyte has been the greatest single obstacle to the working out of that policy. Now he may even be the cause of a civil war."

At the words "civil war," some of Harris's resistance subsided. He sat back to hear Stevens's formal briefing.

"Since the death of Chiang Kai-shek last year and the continuing loss of American support, the old ruling triumvirate of Omega Chi–Green Society–Kuomintang has steadily lost its grip on the Island. The Taiwanese majority has been just as steadily gaining social, political and especially economic power—mainly as a by-product of the economic progress that has been going on there for the last few years.

"For the most part this transition has been orderly. But, as you know, there are great hatreds and blood feuds against the old power that go back for decades, particularly from some of the old gang elements—the Tiger Eels and Warlords. Now that their old enemies are without overwhelming government support, they want blood. They particularly want the head of Bryan Whyte—which is not without its irony, since he is the prime architect of the economic success story that has given them all of their new, legitimate power.

"We have reports that Juan Ortega, leader of the Warlords, has spent the last year building up arms, supplies and political support for a move against Whyte. He believes—perhaps rightly—that the Generalissimo's son will not support King Lu and Whyte as the Generalissimo did. Now, it's very tempting for us just to sit back and see what happens, to hope that Ortega takes care of the Whyte problem for us. But if Ortega is wrong—if Whyte does still have the support of the KMT, if Chiang Ching-kuo feels he has to go along with Whyte or lose the support of his right wing, if a dozen other things—it could get very nasty. The Nationalist Government and Nationalist Army could split right down the middle over it. The old gang squabble could turn into a genuine civil war."

"I see."

"We can't let it happen, Floyd. We've got to convince Whyte to get off the Island."

"But he can't, can he? There's a warrant out for his arrest. He did, after all, mastermind the murder of Alan Phillips, didn't he?"

Stevens said nothing.

"Didn't he?"

"Between you and me, no he didn't. We did. The Government."

Harris shook his head and closed his eyes. Massaging his brow, he said softly, "What a business we're in."

"In any event, you must convince Whyte to leave. South Africa has agreed to take him. We won't attempt to extradite him from there. You can promise him that in my name."

Harris's eyes opened.

"And if he refuses?"

"If he refuses, you're to put your office, your old friendship and your inside knowledge of the man at the disposal of Juan Ortega. You're to do whatever is necessary to get rid of Whyte and prevent a civil war."

"If the Democrats win the presidential election this year? Will this, uh . . . policy remain the same?"

"Exactly the same. That's precisely why I'm the one telling you all this. We're a united front."

"You know, of course, there's talk that Whyte has strong support in the Goldwater-Reagan wing of the Republican party?"

"They pay lip service to him. They love the intellectual idea of Taiwan. But they know the future is with the Mainland. Believe me, Whyte is all alone."

Harris stopped his daydreaming and pushed down on the buzzer on his new desk. "Get in touch with Bryan Whyte. Tell him I'm back in town and I want to see him."

The female voice hesitated. "I don't think I have Mr. Whyte's unlisted number, Admiral. He hasn't exactly been . . . in contact with this office for many years. It may take a few hours. . . ."

"Get the number but never mind the call," he said. "I'll go up to China Gate myself."

Harris sat back in the chair and sighed. What bizarre twist of events it was that had brought him back to this island and into this chair. He had been made an admiral —he had achieved the goal that had driven him all his life —for the express purpose of overseeing the disposal of his old ally, William Bryan Whyte.

After Harris got through several layers of armed Green bodyguards stationed around the estate grounds, Ah Chin let him in the front door of China Gate. The Admiral was escorted through several more layers of guards to the small, elegant greeting room where the taipan had come and received him after hastily leaving a business meeting in the council room. As the burly little admiral walked down the main hallway, he glanced in the rooms and out the windows he passed, and caught a quick glimpse of Whyte's three-year-old son playing with his mother in the garden. He remembered the girl, Shelley something or other. He wondered what their life must be like year after year in this magnificent prison as they stoically lived out a great American tragedy.

"Welcome home," Whyte said as he rose and offered his hand. "It's about time we got an American commander who knows something about the Island. Congratulations on your star. It's richly deserved."

Harris took his hand and smiled. He thought he saw in Whyte's great eyes a recognition of just how empty he felt at finally attaining this goal. Perhaps it was just his imagination.

They sat uneasily opposite each other. Harris noticed how much Whyte had aged in the ten years since they had last met. What was he? Thirty-two? Thirty-three? He looked almost as old as Harris himself did—approaching middle age.

"Well," Whyte said happily, "you've come a long way since the days you used to chase high school kids around Haggler's Alley for black-marketing."

"Bryan," the admiral began awkwardly, "I better make my pitch quickly and let you get back to your meeting. I've come here to ask you to help me prevent what will almost certainly be a disaster."

"Disaster? What disaster?" There was a coy playfulness to his tone.

"Disaster with the Warlords."

Whyte smiled thinly. "Ah, yes. My old friends the Warlords. Haven't we had this conversation before?"

"Bryan, you've done some wondrous things on this island the last few years. I can see it all around me. But that fact is not going to spare you from the final retribution of history. Surely you know the Warlords and all their allies are building for an all-out rebellion against you—a rebellion which, this time, you can't begin to put down. The end is near."

"What is it you want me to do?"

"I want you to leave. Get off the Island. Walk away from all this while you still can. Go somewhere and start over. You have the money to do it now."

Whyte kept his thin smile. "How can I possibly do that? You're well aware that the minute I set foot off this island I'll be arrested. Unless, of course, you're here to offer me immunity from prosecution."

"I can't do that," Harris said quickly. "But surely with all the money you've made you can go to South Africa. Or maybe Switzerland. There are certain arrangements that can be made. In fact, if you can give me a guarantee you'll leave Taiwan I think I can get the Ford administration to agree not to initiate extradition proceedings against you no matter where the hell you choose to go."

Whyte tapped his fingers on his knees nervously. He was through playing with Harris. "I'm sorry. I can't walk away from this fight."

"It's the only logical thing you *can* do. Man, the game is over here. Why stick around for the ax to fall?"

"I've got a large organization under me. A corporation. What happens to it if I leave? I've got people who've worked for me and trusted me to protect them for more than fifteen years. What do you think Ortega will do to these people—particularly the Taiwanese—when they no longer have my protection? I can't just run out on them. We did that in Vietnam and I won't do it here!"

"What if I get Ortega to agree to make no reprisals? Would you leave if I got his word on that?"

"No. Because that's not the bottom line. The bottom line is that I'm not going to run out on the . . ." He searched a moment for the right words and then looked defiantly at Harris. ". . . the idea of a free China."

"A free China! You dare to call this society a *free* China?"

"Yes, I do. It's stable and it's free for people to conduct business and invest capital. That's as free as you get in this imperfect world."

Harris lost the battle to control his temper. "You know, fella, you're as crazy and self-destructive as people say you are. You're going to commit suicide for a false principle and you want all your people to go down with you."

Whyte rang for Ah Chin to show Harris out. But first he put his hand on the admiral's shoulder. "I'm not leaving, Floyd. And you don't have the power to make me leave. You don't have any influence with the Kuomintang anymore, you know."

Harris just stared at him angrily. "Neither do you, I'm told."

Juan Ortega was not as easy to find. Harris spent several frustrating days calling the office of War Tiger Products Ltd., trying to convince them that it was vital he see their president at once. When he finally got word that Ortega would meet with him, he was picked up by two Tiger Eels, blindfolded, driven deep into the city, taken through three car switches and then walked to the Warlords' secret headquarters in the old Lung Shan area.

Ever since he had begun the preparations for his final campaign one year ago, Ortega had been in deep hiding. He did not underestimate Bryan Whyte and he was taking no chances on a repeat of what had happened to his brother in 1967.

When the blindfold was removed, Harris saw that he was in a small, windowless kitchen at a table directly opposite Ortega. The Filipino stared at the admiral for a few moments, then used one finger to shove a pack of American cigarettes toward him. "Smoke?"

Harris held a grudging respect for Ortega. The man had started out as the prototypical early sixties punk and had shrewdly ridden the antiwar, anti-American, anti-Kuomintang sentiment through many hard times to a position of real economic and political power in the new postwar Taiwan. And somewhere along the way he seemed to have been genuinely changed by those sentiments. He was now the most powerful liberal force on the Island—the one aboveground spokesman for the Taiwan Nationalists and other oppressed peoples. Harris did not know whether to approach him as a greedy gangster or a selfless revolutionary. He shoved the cigarettes back. "No thanks. I've quit."

"I was told this meeting was urgent."

"I was told you're planning a big push against Bryan Whyte."

"Really?" Ortega sounded already bored with the conversation. "Who told you that?"

"I'm here to convince you that this is not in your best interests."

"And what are my best interests?"

"The same as ours. To see an orderly transition of power to the Taiwanese majority. To maintain stability on the Island as the old order gradually dies out."

"The United States is now committed to Taiwanese control of the Island, I suppose?"

"Yes," he lied. "Absolutely."

"A Taiwan free of the KMT and the Communist Chinese?"

"Yes. Ultimately."

Ortega smiled disbelievingly.

"We have to trust one another, Juan."

"I'm listening. Warily."

Harris moved a bit closer. "Right now everything is going your way. The Taiwanese have more political, social and economic power than at any time in their history and they're getting more every day that goes by. Ching-kuo is committed to that. Whyte and the Greens are on the ropes. But they're still strong enough to fight back. If you take them on now you're risking a civil war that could go on for years and cancel out all the progress that's been made on the Island. You're a reasonable man. Surely you understand this."

Ortega's tiny eyes grew hard as stones. "I am a reasonable man—even if you don't really think so—and I know that Bryan Whyte must be destroyed completely. The coalition of Omega Chi, Kuomintang and the Greens has been strangling the people of this island for over twenty years. During all these years we have been patiently waiting for our time to come. Now that it has, now that we finally are in a position to remove the hand from our throats, do you seriously think we are going to hesitate?"

"I'm disappointed," Harris said, unintimidated. "I had heard such good things about you. I had heard that you were a far-sighted revolutionary, a statesman even. I heard you had come to actually care about the welfare of the Taiwanese people. But no! You haven't changed a bit. You're just another bloodthirsty hatchet man. You need a blood bath before you can be satisfied."

"I want nothing more than to see Bryan Whyte stripped of all power. Get him off the Island and I will even forget that he brutally murdered my brother in 1967. This is as big a concession as you're going to get from me."

"He won't go. I've already tried that."

"Then he must die."

Harris's eyes blinked nervously. He reached for the cigarettes.

"And I think you understand that," Ortega said. "I think that is why you are really here. Am I right?"

Harris lit a cigarette, wrinkled his nose at the bitter taste, blew smoke into the air. "Yes, I suppose you are."

"I can count on your assistance then?"

"Only if you give me your word there will be no reprisals or acts of war of any kind after he is gone."

An eagerness swept over Ortega's face. "But can you get him away from the Blue Shirts? Can anyone?"

"It will be difficult. But I think it can be done—with patience and the proper planning. I think he still trusts me somewhat."

"Then I give you my word on the reprisals. We will cooperate in every way possible. We will be the closest of allies."

As he reached over and shook Juan Ortega's outstretched hand, Harris was thinking that he had just killed Bryan Whyte as surely as if he had put a pistol to his temple and personally pulled the trigger.

* * *

Ortega remained at the table for a long time after Admiral Harris was gone. He took out a long Filipino cigar from a silver carrying case and smoked it slowly as he played thoughtfully with the wrapper. He was experiencing a wonderfully triumphant and cathartic moment. He wanted to cherish it as long as possible.

But it did not last. No sooner had he mentally celebrated the demise of Bryan Whyte than his mind was flooded with concerns for the future. He well knew that the coalition he headed all these years had been held together by its hatred for Bryan Whyte and Chiang Kai-shek and all the things they represented. Chiang was now with his ancestors and the moment Whyte joined him it would become obvious that the interests of the coalition no longer coincided. It would break up—and Ortega had to prepare himself so that he would emerge unscathed.

He left the apartment and walked out into the Lung Shang to get some fresh air, to think.

The Lung Shan was the oldest and poorest part of the city, a traditional Tiger Eel stronghold. Last year, the government had come in here and eradicated prostitution, replacing all the slum dwellings with high-rise, low-cost housing, as it had done in Sin Alley, the Yin Ping and all the other poorer areas. As a result, Ortega no longer felt totally secure here. Strolling through the open-air shops that surrounded the Lung Shan temple, he continuously glanced back to make sure his bodyguards were following.

The first order of business, he thought, would be to somehow get rid of Fatso Magaha. Magaha had fought the Warlords' move into legitimate business every step of the way. He had been conducting the Warlords' drug business as his separate fief and had been subtly challenging Ortega's leadership for years. The pig was a constant irritant. Once Whyte was gone, there was bound to be a showdown.

Second, he would quickly have to purge the Maoist

and other politically radical elements of his organization. Despite his early flirtation with radicalism—despite the fact that his brother was considered a revolutionary martyr and young Chinese radicals all over the world called themselves "Randy Boys"—Ortega was not a Communist or a socialist or anything close to it; he had, in fact, been moving steadily away from the left for some time. Revolution no longer had a place in his investment portfolio. Anyone who thought otherwise would have to be eliminated from his ranks.

Ortega well knew that his best interest—as well as the best interest of Taiwan—was to see the gradual transfer of power on the Island to the Taiwanese majority while maintaining a growing economy. And in order for this to take place, he would need both the continued presence of the American business community and even the presence of the Omega Chi organization, which he now intended to keep intact with his own puppet in charge. He also needed the continued presence of the U.S. Armed Forces for security.

But how long could he count on indefinite U.S. military support? Like most businessmen on the Island, he lived with the lingering fear that if the KMT was gone, the United States could simply draw back, leave the Island to the Red Chinese with a clear conscience and no violation of the Mutual Defense Treaty of 1954—the perfect solution to America's two China's problem. The fear nagged at the back of all Ortega's plans. It was not alleviated by the blank insincerity he had seen in the eyes of Admiral Floyd Harris.

Whyte stared at the tormented face of Ah Chin, not wanting to believe him, knowing now that he must.

On the desk between them was the evidence: two months' worth of tape recordings painstakingly gathered by a special Blue Shirt intelligence team. There was no way to keep deluding himself: Shelley was having an affair with David Butler.

How could he have been so stupid not to have guessed it? The signs had been all around him: the new "writing project" on which she and Butler were supposedly collaborating; her flat refusal the past few months to have sex of any kind with him; her demand for a separate bedroom. Her sudden lack of interest in their son. . . .

And Butler! Butler of all people. That smug, hateful, pseudointellectual fraud. Butler, who had always hated him, who was doing this to get at him, he was sure of it.

"How many times?"

"There are at least three times clearly on tape, sir."

Ah Chin knew how humiliated the taipan had to feel in this situation and he ached for him. There was no greater loss of face for a man. He himself had heard the tapes and there was no question about it. His ears were still sizzling at what he had heard. The Missy swearing obscenities at Butler, asking for degradation, instructing him in which orifice to place his foul instrument, muttering obscenities as he slammed into her, the sounds of the vile fornication clearly audible on the tape. *Ayee yo!*

"Where?"

"Twice in his apartment. Once in his automobile."

"His automobile?"

"She did . . . to him . . . with . . . her . . . er . . . mouth."

"Where were her bodyguards during all this?"

"Never more than a few feet outside the closed door."

"She seems to have been very careless."

"Perhaps she wanted to be caught, sir."

"Perhaps."

"Do you want to hear the tape, sir?"

"No." Whyte was outwardly calm but inside he was dying. His senses were reeling under the impact of the blow. He was experiencing an overwhelming pain and outrage and sense of loss.

Yet he loved her in that moment more than any time in his life. And he pitied her. He knew it wasn't her fault. She had not been strong enough for this kind of life after all. She was not Jessica Wainright Whyte.

"Do you have any orders, sir?"

"Only that you may call off all surveillance on her as of this moment."

That afternoon, there was a meeting of the full Green Pang council at China Gate. It was the first council meeting of the Greens Whyte had ever attended. Present were King Lu, "Terrible" Ding Tze, a number of the younger Green lieutenants who had climbed the ranks since the Samuel Yin rebellion of 1968, and representatives from Chinese communities all over the world.

King skipped all the usual formalities and ceremonies. "I would like a full report on the situation as it now stands," he barked in Mandarin.

"The situation is most grave, *tai-lo,*" said Terrible Ding immediately. "Armed Tiger Eel units are poised to attack us at any moment. We are outnumbered five to one."

"And if we call in all our overseas forces and hire mercenary troops from Japan and Korea?"

"It won't be enough. They will still outnumber us three to one. Is there no possibility of Triad support?"

"None at all. If the Triads support anyone it will be their drug-running partners, the Tiger Eels."

"The numbers are even worse than I have indicated," Ding went on pessimistically. "There is no telling how many amateur Taiwanese zealots Ming Te will be able to muster. It is likely that some of the all-Taiwanese units of the army and municipal police will break away and join them. We also have many, many traitors in our midst. . . ."

Whyte interrupted to ask King: "How far will Chiang Ching-kuo support us? Can we count on the support of the army and police, as in the past?"

"He will not support us," said King.

The faces around the table dropped.

"You're sure?" Whyte asked.

"I spoke to him this morning. It is final."

"But surely we can count on some of the units of the Taiwan Garrison Command. . . ."

"I count on none of them."

There was a deathly silence.

"Then it is hopeless," said Terrible Ding. "My figures are based on army support. Without that, we cannot even put up a decent face-saving fight."

"Why do they not attack us now?" asked one of the younger Greens.

"Because they are winning a war of attrition," said King. "And because they do not know for sure that Ching-kuo has deserted us."

"Then what do we do?" asked Ding.

"There is nothing to be done," said King. "It is in the hands of destiny."

After a working dinner with King that evening, Whyte closed himself off in his study and put in a trans-Pacific call to Congressman Laughton, the last member of the old China lobby still remaining in Congress, and still an influential conservative who had recently switched to the Republican Party.

Laughton was expecting the call and picked up the phone on the first ring. "Hello, Bryan. Good to hear from you."

The voice was somewhat hesitant. It was a tone that Whyte had grown accustomed to since becoming a fugitive.

"Congressman, I called because I need some information."

"Shoot, son."

"I'm afraid I'm in a bit of a pickle over here."

"I've heard something about it."

"The fact is that I'm being threatened by armed Taiwanese insurgents. As a U.S. citizen I'm entitled to protection from the U.S. authority here."

"But not, of course, as a fugitive with a murder warrant hanging over your head."

"Yes. What I want to know is do I have any political support left over there and is there any way I can use it to get protection from the U.S. military here?"

It was an act of desperation but he had to try everything.

Laughton hesitated a moment and then said, "You have the support of the true conservatives. Goldwater. Reagan. Myself. Unfortunately, we're not in a position right now to exert any influence whatsoever. . . ."

"Any chance Reagan will take the nomination away from Ford at the convention next week?"

"No. We've decided to wait until '8o."

"Is there any chance I can get to Ford? Talk to him? Plead with him?" His desperation was really showing now.

"Bryan, there's something you should know. The word is out that the Ford administration is going for recognition of the PRC and soon."

"That's all I needed to hear."

"I'm sorry."

"What if the Democrats win this time?"

"They'll go for recognition too. It's a bipartisan thing. That's why Stevens and Harris were chosen to close down the shop there. Both parties feel that they have to get you out of the way."

"Stevens is behind Harris?"

"You didn't know that?"

"No."

"It's true."

"Then it's hopeless for me."

"Unless you can hold out for four more years. We're going for the White House in '8o and, if things go our way, we're going to take it. Reagan will support you and Taiwan to the bitter end. It's not in the man's nature to forget his friends."

"Congressman, I'll be lucky if I can hold out four more months."

* * *

Shelley blinked awake. The bedside clock said 3 A.M. exactly. She was overcome with a sense of doom: a leftover of a nightmare she couldn't quite remember.

Suddenly afraid of being alone, she rolled out of bed, slipped on a nightgown and stepped into the hallway. It was quiet, dark.

She walked the twenty feet or so to the open door of her husband's den. That room was also dark but she could make out his figure sitting in a chair by the window.

She stood there for a moment. Though they never discussed such things, she knew he had been working late every night, obsessed with this current dilemma, which, for reasons she did not understand, was worse than all his past dilemmas. Now, as she watched him in the darkness, she suddenly realized just how serious it was. The aura of total defeat was unmistakable. It both frightened her and filled her with pity for him.

She entered the room and knelt by the chair. Then she took his hand and kissed it. This was the first sign of affection she had given him in months and it clearly surprised him. "What do you want?" he asked uneasily.

"Come to bed, Bryan."

"With you?" There was an unpleasant sarcasm in his voice.

She ignored it. "Yes."

"If this is an attempt at a reconciliation, it's a little late. Everything is over for me."

"How can it be that bad?"

"I know all about Butler."

She dropped his hand. For an instant, she thought of denying it. But his words somehow filled her with a relief that was almost joy. She said nothing.

"You knew I'd find out."

"Yes, I suppose I did."

"Please don't insult me with an explanation."

"It's something I had to do. I'm not sure why. But I think it's over now. I know now that I was being used by him to get at you. I'm coming out of the darkness. . . ."

"Well," Bryan cut her off bitterly, "next time you see your lover you can tell him he can start writing the story of the fall of Bryan Whyte now. Maybe you two can collaborate."

"Bryan, I want you to understand . . ."

"I heard the tapes, Shelley. The fucking tapes. I was in the room with you."

"But you weren't in my mind."

"Don't say any more."

"Bryan . . ."

He suddenly seized her by the arms and shook her with all his might. *"Don't . . . say . . . anything!"*

She ran from the room.

Three weeks after Floyd Harris assumed command of all U.S. forces in Taiwan, the U.S. Embassy announced to the English-language press that it was contributing a new wing to the Taipei American School in Shih Lin. The construction would commence immediately and was scheduled to be completed sometime in early 1977.

The statement further announced a gala groundbreaking ceremony for the Bicentennial Fourth of July a week away. The program would feature a series of speakers and dramatic sketches on various patriotic American themes. There would be fireworks and hot dogs and an old-fashioned brass band. It would be the one official Bicentennial event of the Community—a celebration of thirty years of American endeavor on Taiwan.

Four days before the event, Admiral Harris called China Gate. He asked Bryan Whyte to attend the ceremony and, in fact, to give the dedication speech.

Whyte was surprised by the invitation. It was years since he had been asked to any social function in the Community. "Wouldn't that be a little awkward?" he wondered. "Considering my position, considering the current state of affairs in the city?"

"To hell with your position. To hell with the current state of affairs in the city. You are the single most important member of this community and, by God, it wouldn't be right for you not to be there. I want you to get out of that prison, to forget all your problems for one day. How often do we have a Bicentennial Fourth?"

"Admiral, thanks for the thought but I don't see how I could possibly be there."

Harris's voice grew slightly more serious. "Bryan, there's another reason I want you to be on hand. We've decided to name the new wing in honor of Mark Taylor. A plaque honoring him and all the TAS war dead will be dedicated. If you don't make the memorial speech, we're going to have to ask David Butler to do it—and I don't think I could stand that."

Whyte hesitated for a full minute. "You're not easy to refuse, Admiral," he finally said.

"You'll do it then?"

"I will. Actually, there are some things I'd like to say about America on the occasion of her two hundredth birthday."

"Wonderful. And listen, I know you're concerned about security so I'll have a platoon of Marine guards there to ensure your safety. You can leave your Blue Shirts at the gate and really relax for a change."

"You can personally guarantee my safety?"

"Absolutely. I give you my word and the word of the U.S. Government."

"Then I'll look forward to it."

When Harris hung up, he sat a moment, breathing easily. What he had not told Whyte was that, besides the Marines, the entourage would contain a Tiger Eel assassin who had been personally trained by Harlan Bamcheck. After Whyte made his speech, fireworks would go off that would sound very much like gunfire. In the noise and confusion Whyte would be assassinated. It would occur so smoothly that the ceremony would not even be disrupted.

Harris had orchestrated a trap which Bryan Whyte could not resist and from which there was no escape.

* * *

Ah Chin gently shook his taipan from sleep. Whyte jerked up in his bed groggily and looked at his watch. Then he quickly shot out of bed, not bothering to cover his nude body. He slipped on his underpants and bathrobe and left the room.

In the bathroom, Ah Chin asked him what time he would need the limousine that morning.

"I won't be needing it."

"But sir, this is the Fourth. You're supposed to be at the American School this morning."

"I've changed my mind. I'm not going."

"But sir, they're expecting you at ten o'clock. That's only two hours from now."

"I'm not going, Ah Chin."

"Yes, sir. I will call them and let them know."

"Do no such thing. If they call, tell them I am on my way."

Ah Chin was thoroughly confused. "If I may ask, sir. What *is* going on this morning?"

"Armageddon."

24

IN THE EARLY HOURS OF MORNING, SAN FRANCISCO'S Chinatown was alive with late-night diners, night club tour groups and shopkeepers still decorating the streets for the next day's Bicentennial Fourth of July celebration. Bobby Sun waited under a street light at the end of Ross Alley, just off Waverly Place, trying to look inconspicuous. Every few minutes he checked the expensive Rolex watch on his wrist. His stomach was a flight of butterflies.

Soon he saw his two comrades, Jo-jo and Tiger, walking up the street, each carrying a department store shopping bag. Inside the bags was a small arsenal of weapons —a .45 caliber Army model Colt revolver, a Beretta X-5 model submachine gun and a sawed-off Browning double-barreled shotgun.

"We got them," Jo-jo said excitedly. Gleefully he took out the pistol and waved it in the air.

"Put that fucking thing away!" Bobby Sun ordered sharply.

Jo-jo put it away instantly.

"Are you crazy?"

The boy looked very hurt. Bobby had never yelled at him before.

"Now let's go. And don't fuck this thing up or I'll have your balls. Got it?"

Bobby Sun was born in Fukien Province in 1961, the year of the Kennedy inauguration. His family left Red China during the great famine of 1962 and emigrated to San Francisco in 1965 to live with his mother's cousin's family in a one-room apartment above a grocery on Grant Avenue. There he grew to adolescence during the Vietnam War years and became both Americanized and radicalized in the process. In 1974 he became a member of the local Randy Ortega Society and—a natural, charismatic leader —in 1977, its president.

As in many overseas Chinese communities around the world, the Randy Ortega Society (or "Randy Boys") was a politically minded group of toughs who served as the enforcement arm of the anti-Kuomintang faction of the Chinese underworld. They were financially supported by the Warlords coalition in Taipei and for the past decade their mission had been to steadily muscle in on the activities of the Hop Sung Tong and harass it with daring acts of violence. Tonight they would make their most daring attack ever—the raid that would go down in the history books.

Bobby Sun had never personally met the leaders of

the anti-KMT underworld. He was merely handed orders through a hierarchy of underlings, and he carried them out without question. Two days ago he received orders for a great bodywash, the greatest bodywash of his career. He was told the orders had come from the lips of the Sacred Brother, the great Juan Ortega himself, and that all the important people within the Warlords organization would be watching how he performed.

"Where are the Maoists?" Tiger asked.

"They didn't show—the chickenshits. But we don't need them. Why share the glory, eh?"

"Do we know for sure that all the FOB leaders will be there?"

"Every one. Our informer guarantees that they will be celebrating there way into the morning."

"There will be bodyguards, surely? Maybe even Greens?"

"Yes. This is why our surprise must be total. We can't give them time to think."

The three Randy Boys selected their weapons in a corner of Ross Alley, then proceeded up Waverly Place, past the row of tong headquarters buildings, past the site where Little Pete Fong had been assassinated by similar assassins in the 1890s, to Washington Street.

They stood a moment outside the Summer Winds restaurant to steady their nerves and say a prayer to the God of All Wars. Then Bobby Sun nodded and they went inside. The place was about half-filled with diners, tourists and their deadliest enemies, the FOBs (for "Fresh Off the Boat")—the gang of young Chinese newly arrived from Taipei and Hong Kong that was used as the enforcement arm of the Hop Sung Tong and the Green Society.

When the Randy Boys took out their weapons, a waitress screamed. Bobby Sun took several steps forward and opened up with the submachine gun.

Diners in the rear of the restaurant thought someone had lit a string of firecrackers. The building exploded with noise. As bodies began to fall and blood splattered the walls, people dove for the floor in horror and panic. Bobby

Sun continued firing. Jo-jo stood at the entranceway methodically picking off diners with the forty-five. Tiger ran to the other side of the room and let loose two quick bursts from the shotgun into the crowd.

Then the moment of truth came to Bobby Sun!

There were no FOBs among these diners! They had been tricked! They had been set up to massacre a dozen innocent people.

Even in that instant Bobby Sun realized that it would create a wave of outrage and revulsion in San Francisco that would put an end to the Randy Boys there forever.

At that very moment, on the other side of the world, Fatso Dave Magaha stepped out of a business meeting in the penthouse suite of Hong Kong's Dynasty hotel.

Feeling unusually jovial about the conclusion of this latest of many meetings this week, he accepted salutations for a happy Bicentennial Fourth from two visiting American businessmen who saw him to the door. He shook hands with each of them and stepped into the elevator.

This meeting had finalized a very lucrative agreement to set up a bold new drug pipeline from Bangkok to Vancouver using Chiu Chao Triads and Taiwanese Tiger Eels as couriers and American Mafia as distributors. It was nothing as grand as the old Orient Express—but almost as profitable. He had seen to that.

While Magaha had grown into a very skilled negotiator over the years, it did not take much skill to make a good deal for himself these days. With Europe and South America all but closed off, Asia was the sole source of heroin for the U.S. and Magaha controlled it all. He could afford to pick and choose his partners and be as demanding in his deal-making as he deemed necessary.

As the elevator sped to the lower-level parking garage, Magaha experienced a rush of excitement. He was thinking now of his own future. By the time this morning was over, Bryan Whyte would be dead, the Omega Chi business empire would be absorbed by the Warlords and the mighty grip of the Green Society would be publicly broken. And, just as the Warlords were taking over in Asia, so Dave Magaha was going to take over the Warlords. He was going to correct the injustice that had taken place when Juan Ortega succeeded Randy in 1967. Little Ortega had done well, admittedly, but he was too conservative to guide them into this exciting new era. He was a fine businessman and a better organizer but he lacked the cold-bloodedness and killer instinct required to take control of the worldwide Asian heroin trade, to ride it to an undreamed of position of power and wealth. Already Magaha had gathered considerable support in this dispute. Soon, either by election or assassination, he would be taipan of the Warlords.

The elevator door opened and Magaha walked to the big Cadillac he had rented from the local American car rental agency. He maneuvered his near three hundred pounds into the vehicle and started the engine. He did not have time to realize that all his planning and good feeling were for nothing or that his meeting had been a setup or that his life was over. The instant the spark plug ignited, a bomb went off and spread Dave Magaha over the parking garage in ten thousand pieces.

In Taipei, the bell rang at the sumptuous new Ho Ping East Road apartment of Loma, the aging but still-much-feared leader of the Tiger Eels. He was in the kitchen eating a bowl of lechi nuts, reading a newspaper announcement of the day's events celebrating the Bicentennial holiday in the American Community. He didn't bother to look up when the bodyguards went to answer the door.

Loma had spent most of the past week in constant consultation with Juan Ortega and he was worn out. They were in the process of beginning their expansion into the former Green Gang strongholds of Shihminting and Peitou; he was gearing himself up for the grand takeover of all Green territory that would follow today's assassination of Bryan Whyte. Loma was amazed at just how weak the empire of King Lu had become in the past year, how easily it was already disintegrating at his initial inroads. He had not met a trace of resistance as he moved his forces into position all over Taipei. Still, he was getting old and he did not enjoy these victories as he would have as a younger man. Every day he found himself dreaming of the time he would retire and move his family to the peaceful shores of Sun Moon Lake.

Loma heard some stirring and arguing and then one of the bodyguards came back to see him. The bodyguard shrugged apologetically and handed him a piece of official-looking paper. "It's the police," the bodyguard said. "They say this is a warrant for your arrest."

Loma spit a mouthful of lechi nuts in the air and jumped out of his chair, livid with rage. For the past twenty years he had been paying the dungheap Taipei Municipal Police force its regular squeeze plus generous bonuses. The force was almost entirely Taiwanese these days and owed him a loyalty beyond mere money. It was unthinkable that a new officer would try to shake him down. Probably an arrogant, turtle egg of a Chinese, he thought, or a new man fresh out of the police academy who had not yet learned the ropes. Loma would have the man's badge—maybe even his head—for this insult. He hawked and spit on the arrest warrant and stormed to the door.

The two officers were nervously waiting for him. Loma launched into a head-on verbal attack, screaming at them, shaking his fist in an obscene gesture and cursing their ancestors all the way back to the Stone Age. The police glanced at each other quickly, then drew their revolvers and fired, hitting Loma in the cheek and throat, sending the bodyguards scurrying for cover in the rear of the apartment. As the gangster fell to the floor, the officers stood over him and continued firing bullets into his head until it was a ghastly nothingness. Then they put their guns away and began an official investigation into the murder of Loma, leader of the Tiger Eels.

* * *

Across town, Georgie Warner stepped out of a taxi at a busy intersection in the Yén Ping district. He paid the driver and walked toward an obscure Japanese bar–brothel—one of his favorite haunts in the old days—where he would wait until the assassination of Bryan Whyte was successfully carried out.

Ortega had absolutely forbidden him to leave his hiding place but Warner could stand it no longer. The pressure and anticipation were unbearable. He had been near panic when he finally just climbed out a bathroom window and took off. Now he wanted nothing more than to get pleasantly drunk, enjoy a nice girl and forget all about what was happening this Fourth of July morning at the Taipei American School.

He walked a block down Yen Ping North Road and came to the spot only to discover the bar no longer existed. The building now housed a fancy French restaurant and a pet store. A pet store, for chrissake! Three years ago you couldn't keep a pet in Taipei because someone would invariably steal it and eat it for dinner. Now they had pet stores replacing their whorehouses. Well, what was he supposed to do now? It was a pretty sad state of affairs when an American couldn't find a whorehouse in Taipei anymore.

Though he had not contacted his parents or anyone from the old days, Warner had secretly been back on the Island for well over a month. Ortega had tracked him down at his uncle's house in Los Angeles and offered to make him taipan of an Omega Chi without Bryan Whyte. Warner was destitute and without prospects so he had accepted outright—even though he fully realized it would mean a lifetime of being Ortega's puppet. Ortega smuggled him back and intended to spring him the minute Whyte was dead. As the sole remaining voting member of the Omega Chi board, he could simply move into China Gate and take over the reins of the organization without disrupting a day of business.

As he stood on the traffic-clogged street looking for a taxi, an official government car pulled up alongside him. Bad luck! It was the Foreign Affairs Police and he did not have the I.D. papers required of all foreigners.

The vehicle stopped. Two helmeted officers got out and asked to see his identification. In Chinese, he explained that he had left it at home and offered them each a hundred U.S. dollars to excuse his carelessness.

This seemed to make the officers very suspicious. One of them went to the car and radioed in some information. Warner knew now that he was about to be arrested. His only thought was somehow to get to a phone and tell Ortega. "Listen, I need to make a quick phone call. It's an emergency."

But the officers held him there. Again he tried to bribe them and again they did not react one way or the other. Five minutes later, a black Mercedes drove down the street toward them. An incredible sinking feeling came over him. He thought of making a break for it until he noticed a submachine gun trained on him from the back window.

"Please get in, Meestah Wawnah," a voice said to him.

Warner got in. He knew that if he hesitated even a second he would be dead. These were Blue Shirts, and Blue Shirts did not make idle threats. The ball game was over, for now.

As the car drove away, Warner's heart was pounding in his throat. I'll be all right, he told himself. They won't dare touch me. They'll take me to China Gate until they get word from Bryan Whyte and that word will never come because Bryan Whyte will be dead. That will make me taipan of the Omega Chi. I'm as safe as a baby. . . .

But, as usual, Warner was wrong.

Five hours later his body was found on a lonely stretch of the North Coast Highway. It was hacked almost beyond recognition by hand axes—the death traditionally reserved for the most despised enemies of the Green Pang Society.

* * *

For the next few hours, the streets of Taipei and the streets, alleys and warrens of Chinese communities of dozens of cities from Singapore to Vancouver B.C. exploded into violence. The attacks and assassinations continued with the cold-blooded precision of a long-planned military maneuver. They carried the element of surprise and for the most part they were brilliantly executed and overwhelmingly effective.

Floyd Harris only gradually got wind of what was happening all around him. First Whyte failed to show up for the TAS groundbreaking ceremony. Then there was the report of the Loma killing in Ho Ping. Then came cables of the Magaha murder in Hong Kong and the shocking massacre in San Francisco which the newspapers were calling the bloodiest gangland slaying in U.S. history. Then Georgie Warner's body was found near the ocean and Harris was handed reports of the assassinations of Ming Te, Ya Ki Loi and Amos Wong. Only then did it dawn on Harris that a major military campaign was underway, that Bryan Whyte had decided to go down with a fight, even if it was insanely futile and would cost thousands of lives.

When the magnitude of the operation finally became clear to Harris, he rushed up to China Gate to see Bryan Whyte. He found him in the garden, calmly having his late afternoon tea by himself.

"What are you doing to me?" Harris shrieked. "We had an understanding."

Whyte glared at Harris savagely. "You sold me out to the Warlords. You set me up for assassination. That's my understanding."

This caught Harris off guard. For a moment he was speechless. He had no idea that Whyte knew anything about his dealings with Ortega. He quickly recovered. "You're going to damage the whole American position in the Far East. You're starting a war that could go on for years. . . .

"With any luck, it will be over by tomorrow morning. I have the full support of the KMT, the Taipei Municipal Police, the Taiwan Garrison Command and the Chinese Army."

"That's impossible. Everyone knows the KMT has abandoned you. The rumors are everywhere and all our intelligence reports confirm them."

Whyte smiled thinly.

"*You* started the rumors."

"Of course."

Harris's mind raced to take it all in. "Even so, you're still outnumbered. The police and army are overwhelmingly Taiwanese and many of them are bound to break away and support Ortega when they realize what is happening. You're starting a civil war, goddammit!"

"True. But I have an ace to play. And, for all our sakes, you'd better pray it's successful."

"You'll never get away with this. Give it up, man! Can't you understand that you're finished, that your era is over? Can't you move on gracefully without causing any more bloodshed?"

Whyte reached for the teapot. "Excuse me. I didn't offer you any tea."

"I can stop it!" Harris screamed frantically. "I can move the Marines up here! I can have you arrested!"

"Then you'll really have a disaster on your hands, won't you? I'm the only one who can bring this thing to a successful conclusion now. I'm the only person who can bring stability to Asia again. If you even try to interfere, I'll have *you* arrested and thrown off the Island."

The air left Harris's body. He realized that Whyte had outmaneuvered everyone. He was in control of the situation—at least for now.

A Blue Shirt squad captured Juan Ortega that same afternoon. The Blue Shirts had known the location of his secret headquarters for over a week and, with the help of the Maoist contingent of Ortega's personal bodyguards, they merely marched in and took him prisoner without firing a shot.

Whyte had him taken to China Gate and placed under guard in the council room. He let the little Filipino simmer there for over an hour, then went in to see him.

Surprise and bitter hatred registered in Ortega's dazed black eyes. He sat in a corner of the room, broken and helpless and frightened, yet trying to maintain an air of dignity. He glared at Whyte a moment and then spit at him.

Whyte ignored the insult. He sat in a chair next to Ortega and asked the guards to leave them alone.

"How did you do it? How did you get the Maoists to turn on me? What possible bribe could you offer them?"

Whyte did not answer.

"Go ahead and kill me. . . . It won't matter. . . . You still have no future."

"I don't want to kill you. I want to talk to you."

Ortega continued to glare at him. "There's nothing to talk about."

"We could talk about the last twenty years. That's how long we've been fighting each other, you know. Twenty years. The world has changed all around us but we're still brawling like a couple of street gangs. We're still operating on ideas and prejudices and personal grudges that don't mean jack shit in this new world."

"And what *does* matter?" Ortega snapped.

"What matters is that capitalism is working here. For both of us. Beyond our wildest expectations. What matters is that this island continues to survive and that we continue to survive on this island. But the only way to do that is together . . . as allies."

Ortega was dumbfounded. It was so unthinkable as to be sheer lunacy. "You can't be serious?"

"I'm completely serious. America is going to dump Taiwan sometime in the next year or two. Squabbling like this, we're both going to be easy pickings for the wolves at the door. But united! United we can put up a fight. United we can bargain with them, demand concessions, make a good deal for ourselves. . . ."

"What exactly are you proposing?"

"I want to merge our two organizations. I want you to be my partner and my strong right arm. I want to use our combined business skill to survive and profit in the next decade, to make the best life possible for our families and the people who trust and believe in us. I want to do this within the political framework that now exists."

Ortega still couldn't accept what he was hearing. But it had to be true. It was too bizarre to be a trick. And it was also obvious and logical. It would solve all his own internal problems. "But there are those within my organization who will never go along even if I . . ."

"They are no longer a problem for either of us."

Ortega knew what this meant. It meant that Magaha and Ya Ki and Ming Te were dead and the Maoist faction had somehow gone over to Whyte's side. But how had he managed all this? How did he manage to get total Kuomintang support despite all the evidence that it was through with him? There was obviously so much he, Ortega, did not know and which Whyte was not about to tell him. "And if I refuse?"

"If you refuse . . . nothing. You will leave here unharmed and we will fight out the remainder of this . . . this civil war. We will fight until it destroys us both. And, believe me, it will destroy us both." Whyte offered his hand. "Take it. The time has finally come to give up the past and look toward the future together."

Ortega's mind was reeling. "It's too much for me to take in at one sitting. I need time to think about it."

"No, you don't. You know right now that it's the only possible solution for us."

Ortega stared at Whyte's outstretched hand a moment. "But my brother Randy . . ."

"Your brother was a casualty of war. No one can be held responsible."

Ortega continued to stare at the outstretched hand.

"Take my hand."

"I can't . . ."

"Take it."

"I . . . can't . . ."

"*Take it.*"

Juan Ortega took it.

Whyte walked down the hallway and entered the formal greeting room. King was waiting for him there.

"He accepted," Whyte said.

"Thank all gods." King half collapsed with relief.

"Yes, thank all gods." Whyte's hand was trembling. He made a fist to hide it.

"Then you have won the biggest gamble of your career."

"Apparently."

"It was . . . it was brilliant."

"No. I had no choice but to make the gamble. It was an act of desperation."

King smiled. "Maybe. But a brilliant act of desperation nonetheless. So skillfully done . . ."

Whyte had decided over a year ago that he had no choice but to make a grand play and risk everything on the faith that the economic miracle of the last six years had made Juan Ortega into a true capitalist, that, when backed to the wall and offered a way out, Ortega would make the practical business decision to *not* enter a civil war. Army and police support for the Omega Chi had been Whyte's secret trump card to ensure that Ortega's back was firmly against the wall. Actually, it had never been in question —but not even the members of the Green council had been allowed to know this. There was no possibility of a leak that would spoil the surprise.

"Are we meeting much Tiger Eel resistance?"

"Some in the Yen Ping. About what we expected in Lung Shan. But it is scattered and disorganized and Ding Tze will soon have it under control."

"Good."

"Are you convinced that Ortega will follow through?"

"Yes, I believe he will."

"Then I suppose we are now ready for the next step of the plan."

"Yes, my uncle. Now the real gamble begins."

Whyte left China Gate and raced to the airport under police escort. He took the Omega Chi company jet to Hong Kong. A limousine was waiting for him when he landed at Kai Tak ninety minutes later and rushed him across town to one of the new glass office buildings that were shooting up all over central Kowloon.

Ah Chin was there to open the car door and hand him his briefcase. They stood together a moment on the busy street. Whyte took a deep breath. "Are they already here?" he asked.

"They've been waiting, sir."

"How do they look?"

"Hard to tell, sir. Nervous, I'd say."

"Nervous? That's a good sign."

"Yes, sir."

"You look a bit nervous yourself, Ah Chin."

"Not nervous, sir. Terrified. If you don't mind, sir, I'll wait outside."

"You'll miss an historic event."

"Still and all, sir . . ."

"Suit yourself."

He entered the building and took an elevator to the twentieth-floor penthouse suite. On the way up, he thought of all the steps leading up to this moment. He felt good. Confident. He had done everything right. He had taken advantage of all the right opportunities.

He opened the door and saw the five representatives of the government of the People's Republic of China seated around the conference table. Hard-bitten old revolutionaries in Mao jackets, they were all peering at him sternly. He had studied their intelligence files thoroughly, had memorized every line of each of their weathered old faces. He nodded pleasantly to them and took his seat at the table.

"Please excuse my tardiness, gentlemen," he said in Mandarin. "But I am happy to report that the internal situation on Taiwan is now very much under control. We can now finally begin these long-delayed and very necessary negotiations."

25

DAVID BUTLER HEARD THE NEWS MIDMORNING. HE was having his third cup of coffee when his secretary brought in the wire and laid it on his desk without comment. He took one long look at it and ran out of his office to look for Bryan Whyte.

He found the taipan standing on a corner of Jen Ai Road about to cross the street and enter the magnificent new glass and steel building that had been constructed last year to house the corporate offices of the Omega Chi Trading Company. It was three years since Whyte had made the big peace in the Taipei underworld, but it still surprised Butler to see him alone, without a contingent of Green Gang bodyguards flanking his every move.

"Have you heard the big news?" Butler asked breathlessly.

Whyte had been watching the great rush of traffic absently. He turned in the direction of Butler's voice and arched his eyebrow. "No."

"Carter is officially recognizing Mainland China. It just came over the wire."

He did not react. He merely looked to Butler for further explanation.

"He's breaking relations with Taiwan and renouncing the Mutual Defense Treaty. It's the end."

"Yes, I guess it is the end—of one era, anyway."

"You don't even look surprised."

"Should I be, after all that's happened?"

"Well, they did say they'd never do this. They were making assurances to the Kuomintang right up until yesterday afternoon."

Whyte smiled ironically. "Surely you're used to being lied to by now."

"You knew, didn't you?"

Whyte didn't answer. The light changed and they crossed the boulevard together. Whyte's limp was now barely noticeable and he no longer used a cane. He was enjoying this interview, even though he still hated Butler, hated him so much that he often regretted his last minute decision not to have him eliminated back in 1976.

"How do you think the Nationalists will react?" Butler asked cagily.

"Off the record?"

"Off the record."

"They'll scream once again that they've been betrayed. There'll be a lot of anti-American sentiment. Riots even. I wouldn't be on the streets when this story breaks if I were you."

"Then?"

"Then they'll go on as before. They don't have much choice, do they?"

"Do you see war as an inevitability? After all, the U.S. will have to withdraw all its troops and renounce all its vows of protection."

"I don't see war."

Butler was annoyed by the confident and philosophical way Whyte was taking the news. It only confirmed the long-held suspicions of many China watchers that the Omega Chi had somehow established secret ties to the Mainland over the past three years. Whyte was obviously ready for this day and felt he had nothing to fear. "The Communists have sworn to reunite China—it's been the number one item on their foreign policy agenda for over thirty years. They have enough men to overwhelm the Island a thousand times. What do you know that I don't know?"

Whyte smiled triumphantly. "I know that China needs Taiwan intact," he said. "She needs what Taiwan has become and she finally knows it."

King Lu stepped into Whyte's penthouse office in the new Omega Chi Building and saw his friend sitting behind a huge antique mandarin's desk, dictating a letter into a machine.

Whyte put down the microphone and stood up to greet the *tai-lo.*

"Is everything done?" King asked.

"Almost. I'm finishing up now."

King looked vaguely troubled. "You still intend to leave everything here in the hands of Juan Ortega?"

"He's the best man we have—we've discussed this again and again." It bothered Whyte that, even after all this time, King was never quite able to accept Ortega's presence in their organization, never quite able to trust him fully.

"Why do you suppose they insist on our coming at this particular time?" King asked.

"The momentum of the recognition, perhaps. Perhaps also they just feel there is much to be done and they are tired of waiting now that the negotiations are completed."

The two men strolled over to a lounge area of the big office to take tea. A floor-to-ceiling window looked over the smog-shrouded, bustling city; the other walls were decorated with large photographs depicting various facets of the Omega Chi business empire, an empire that had almost doubled in the past three years and which now included interests in banking, mining, manufacturing, heavy construction, export-import, shipping, retailing, electronics, computers, transportation and communications.

"Are you sure they want *me* to go with you?" King asked.

"They specifically asked for you."

"They have had a price on my head for most of my adult life."

"Not anymore. They know that they need us, Elder Brother. The lesson of Taiwan has not been lost on them. China is truly making a commitment to return to a more traditional society. It is going to be reaching out for business and capital investment and economic development in the 1980s like never before in its history."

"That explains why they want you—not me."

"With a more traditional society comes many new problems, among them the renewed presence of secret societies. They need a mechanism for gaining control of this element before it gets out of hand for them, a means of controlling all organized crime and squeeze, an organizational structure that is strongly nationalist and oriented toward commerce, with which they can deal at the top. You *are* needed in the new China—just as you were needed in the China of Chiang Kai-shek."

The two friends sipped their tea in silence for a few moments, each with his own thoughts. Then King said, with uncharacteristic emotion in his voice, "Have you stopped to consider how this has all worked out? Chuangtzu's vision of thirty years ago *is* coming true—even if it is happening in a way that no one could have anticipated. China *is* being restored from an evil, anti-Chinese philosophy and it is being done by the example of Taiwan and your belief in capitalism. Your destiny *is* being fulfilled and my faith in you is being fully vindicated."

Whyte looked at King warmly and thought of their thirty-year journey together. His hand involuntarily clasped the *fu* that he still wore around his neck and he enjoyed the moment of victory. "We have been through a great deal, old friend," he said.

"Yes, my little brother, we have indeed."

"But it will be worth it. We will see Shanghai soon."

"Yes."

"The face of the Green Pang will be fully restored."

"Yes."

"There will be a whole new world waiting for us there."

"Yes, Bryan Whyte, and you will be taipan of it all."

Warren Stevens, acting as President Carter's special envoy to Taiwan, held the U.S. accreditation papers that Whyte would carry with him on his trip to the People's Republic of China. The two men stood in the lobby of what had been the old American Embassy, now eerily abandoned in the wake of the sudden end of U.S. Nationalist Chinese relations.

The craggy-faced diplomat shuffled through the file quickly to make sure everything was in order, then handed it to Whyte with a sigh. "I must say I still can't completely fathom why the Communists should be insisting on doing business with you of all people. By all rights they should despise you. You *do* stand for everything they profess to hate about the West, after all."

Whyte accepted the file and smiled. "The Chinese are a curious people, Mr. Ambassador. They respect strength and often end up trusting their enemies more than those who curry their favor. That's why they waited to deal with Nixon in '72. They think they understand the taipan-capitalist mentality. They feel comfortable with it, in fact."

"In any case, you're going to find yourself in the middle of a crossfire. There's fifty years of bad blood between the Communists and Nationalists and don't think you're going to erase it overnight."

"It'll be tough. But not nearly as tough as you might think. Already the two have unofficially agreed to resume trade—and that's the first big step. The fact is they're both being very accommodating, despite the hard language and look-see pidgin coming out of their propaganda machines. Chinese nationalism is a very ancient and very powerful force. Much stronger than anything in the European tradition of nationalism. Peking is proud of Taiwan and in its heart of hearts it wants all of China to be some version of what Taiwan is today. It'll take time—five, ten years down the road and much screaming and name calling—but it'll happen. They'll join together."

"And how do the native Taiwanese figure into this scheme?"

"There'll be some bitterness, of course. But the majority of them have too big a financial stake in the success of a peaceful merger to create any real problems. Ortega has been very successful in making them understand this."

Stevens watched Whyte leaf through the papers a moment and thought back to the first time they had met in this embassy, nearly twenty years before. Whyte was only a child then; even so he was manipulating whole governments and foreign policies. He had never stopped doing that in all the years since. He had consistently outsmarted all his enemies, including Stevens himself. "Will you insist on a restoration of your family property as a condition for Omega Chi investment in China?"

"Yes. And I've had an advance guarantee they'll accept it. They seem to be very accommodating on this point. Surprisingly so. Strange, isn't it?"

"That means your father will get all the holdings he lost in 1949. He'll be a rich man again in his own right. Does he know yet?"

"Not yet. I was planning on telling him this afternoon. He's in very bad shape, I'm afraid. They really don't know what's keeping him alive."

The two men started out the door together. Outside, the embassy building showed scars of the anti-American riots of the week before. They paused at the gate and shook hands.

"What's going to happen with the outstanding arrest warrant on me?" Whyte asked, almost as an afterthought.

"All charges have been dropped. You've become necessary to the United States again—you're the man who may just solve the two Chinas problem for us. The Carter administration will do anything it can to maintain your credibility—and keep your favor. You're welcome to return to the States any time you want."

"I'm not sure I'll ever want to," he said without bitterness. "Not until a lot of things change. But, of course, it's nice to know I have the option."

"One more thing, Bryan."

"Yes?"

"I want you to know that I'm sorry about the plot against you three years ago. I'm very ashamed of my part in it."

Whyte smiled generously. "Don't trouble yourself, Mr. Ambassador. Like everyone else in this little drama, you were only doing what you thought was right."

When Shelley Spencer Whyte returned from church, she found her husband packing for his trip to Mainland China. She walked into the bedroom and stood quietly watching him. Finally, he felt her presence, turned and looked at her. "Are you back already?" he asked absently.

"A first communion doesn't take long. I only wish you could have spared the time to be there."

He ignored the bitter tone. "I do too. But Ambassador Stevens was only going to be in town this one morning and I had to see him. How did Jimmy do?"

"Fine. He looked very sweet."

"Where is he?"

"I had one of the amahs take him to the Kiddyland Zoo."

Whyte went back to packing his bag.

"He'll be back before you leave," she added.

"Good."

"Bryan, there's something we have to talk about."

"I'm listening. Where are my blue dress shirts?"

"Bryan, I'm going back to the States while you're gone."

He stopped packing and turned to face her. "Oh?"

She began to play nervously with the ruffles of her blouse. "I'm going to New York to see some of my old friends and try to get a job in journalism again."

Whyte was not surprised. The past three years had been hell for their marriage; he could not even remember their last pleasant, loving moment together. Still, in the back of his mind, he had always intended to straighten everything out after he finally reached his goal—and he had finally reached his goal.

"I see," he said, at a loss.

"I'll be wanting a divorce. It might be easier to have your lawyers handle it here."

Whyte shook his head sadly. "So you're running out on me again. Just when I'm on the verge of coming through."

"You ran out on me a long time ago."

This made him angry. "Did I? I remember it differently."

She smiled grimly. "You've never been able to forgive me my one indiscretion, have you?"

"I've tried."

"But you can't. And it's not your fault. You weren't raised to forgive and forget."

"Shelley, I've tried to understand."

"It doesn't matter. It wouldn't solve anything if you did. I can never be the kind of woman you want. We both know that."

He sat on the edge of the bed beside her and realized she was right—that she had never been what he thought she was back in high school, that some part of him was even relieved by her decision to leave. It would relieve him of the single greatest source of stress in his life. Stress that he could not afford in the months and years of work ahead of him on the Mainland. "You know, of course, that I can't allow you to take my son off this island?"

"Yes, I've reconciled myself to that."

They sat in silence for several moments. His mind wandered back to the days when she was the prettiest American girl in the Taipei American School. Yes, it was certainly true. He had fallen in love with a Pepsi commercial. But understanding this somehow did not really lessen the still-powerful hold that image had on him.

He was suddenly afraid of what the loss of that fantasy might do to him. "You can change your mind, you know."

"I can't."

"You can come to China with me right now."

"No, I can't."

"How can you be so final?"

"Because the one thing I know for certain about myself is that I was not born to be the wife of a taipan."

Old Whyte lay in his hospital bed staring blankly at the ceiling. In his lucid moments—and this was one of them—he knew that the end was near. The doctors had told him that the cancer had spread throughout his tired old body. He could barely move now and when he did the pain was excruciating. The only thing keeping him going was an iron determination to hold out until Bryan left on his historic trip.

At that moment, his son entered the darkened room quietly and pulled up a chair beside the bed. "I'm going to the airport now," he whispered. "I'm going . . . home. For both of us."

"It's a miracle." The voice was very weak.

"Think of it, Father. I'm going to walk along the Bund in Shanghai. I'm going to be standing in the villa where you and Mama used to live. I'm going to see that restitution is made for every penny that was stolen from us. It's all *really* happening."

Tears filled the old man's eyes and his face twisted into an ugly mask of pain and emotion. "You've done so much, Sonny, and I gave you so little."

"You gave me a dream. That's much more than most people get from their parents."

"And you fulfilled it."

"Only because of your help and love."

"King Lu knew. He knew all along."

"Yes."

Old Whyte began to sob silently.

"Are you in pain, Father?"

"I'm feeling a terrible guilt. I'm thinking of the cost, the terrible personal cost."

"Yes, there was a price. . . ."

"Was it too great?"

"Too great?" Images of Shelley and Phillips and Taylor and Warner and Randy Ortega flooded his mind; for a moment, he did not answer.

For a fleeting instant, he experienced The Doubt. But he quickly suppressed it. He could not allow himself to feel guilty. Everything had been out of his hands from the beginning. He and all the others had been merely the instruments of history working toward this great end. This is what he had to believe.

"No," he said, "it was not too great, Father. It was worth it. Of course it was worth it. Now listen, you have to get some rest and I have to go."

"I never thought it would happen like this. Never in my wildest dreams. I thought there would have to be a war or a revolution or . . ."

Whyte smiled lovingly. "King Lu used to say that Communism in China was just another foreign dynasty—a dynasty of foreign thought. Like all foreign dynasties—like the Manchus and the Mongols—it has become assimilated by China. The traditional Chinese nature is reasserting itself again and that nature is very capitalistic and business-oriented."

A light came to the old man's eyes and he looked happy for the first time in months. "And so they need taipans again. What a time to be young, what a land of opportunities is waiting for you."

"It's a whole new beginning."

"You must always remember to take advantage of your opportunities, son. Always remember that."

Whyte moved closer and held his father's hand.

"I will, Father."

The story of John Casy's downfall was not unique among the great rock stars of the late sixties. His group had disbanded years before, their manager and record company were awarded most of their joint assets and future royalties after a lengthy court battle. After that, Casy's solo efforts never quite got off the ground. He began playing smaller and smaller arenas to smaller and smaller audiences until eventually he was on the tavern circuit again. Finally, he woke up one morning in a dingy Cleveland motel and found himself without a job or an agent or a prospect, up to his ears in debt and surrounded by a younger world that wanted to hear nothing but disco.

Worse, he was deep in trouble with a drug problem. A heavy cocaine user throughout the seventies, he succumbed to the drug the more his career fell apart, and the more the drug took over his life, the less he could afford to pay for it. By 1976, he was injecting the substance directly into his veins—often in week-long binges in which he would have to shoot up every fifteen minutes just to stay even. By 1977, he graduated to heroin. To pay for the increasingly demanding habit he had to sell off all his personal property—the cars, the house in Marin County, all his instruments and song copyrights, everything. When this ran out and he was completely destitute, he had no choice but to leave America and go to the one part of the world where drugs were plentiful and cheap and where he conceivably had a source of income. In 1978, John Casy returned to Taipei.

He took out a tourist visa and borrowed enough money for a plane ticket. When he landed at Sung Shan, he found a different world from the one he had left in 1964. The Taipei he had known as a boy had simply vanished into history. In its place was a city of uncontrollable traffic, cars, motorcycles, freeways, high-rise apartments, hustling businessmen, department stores, Shakey's pizza parlors, supermarkets, air conditioning and bustling middle-class prosperity. For weeks, he aimlessly wandered the streets of this foreign city, trying to adjust to it all, loathing its ugliness and cultural deformity.

Whyte heard of Casy's return through the Tiger Eels. They told him about a strange, emaciated American who lived in an alley down by the river and shoplifted from the downtown department stores to pay for drugs. Whyte somehow knew at once that it was Casy. He had him picked up, moved him into China Gate and brought in medical specialists from all over Asia to help him kick his habit. Whyte himself spent weeks of his time personally supervising the therapy, talking Casy through the hard times, trying to get him interested in life again, vowing to restore him to his rightful full partnership in the vast, multinational Omega Chi Trading Company.

Whyte was tireless in his determination to save John Casy. He felt that this last remaining link to the old brotherhood of Omega Chi had been given back to him for a purpose. He still believed in Casy's talent, still believed that Casy was the only person capable of truly understanding him, capable of even someday capturing and explaining his life in art. He desperately wanted to restore their old high-school relationship of artist and patron, of man of intellect and man of action.

When Casy had been clean for a full three months, Whyte hosted a special celebration dinner. Lee Min, David Ward Kee, Jonathan Wu and all the other *compradores,* Juan Ortega, King Lu and members of the Green Pang council all came to formally welcome the new half-owner of the Omega Chi. After everyone left, Whyte and Casy drew up chairs to the majestic fireplace in the huge living room of China Gate and had a Grand Marnier as they watched the lapping flames.

Casy was depressed, as the doctors warned he often would be during the first months of his recovery. He stared into the fire, hypnotized, for some time and finally Whyte asked him what he was thinking.

"I was thinking about the time we met in San Francisco in 1966. Do you remember?"

"Yes."

"Those were great times for me. I was thinking of the excitement. The hope I had then of building a better world. A new state of consciousness. Remember? It sounds silly now. Silly and naive. Everything turned out so badly. Badly for everyone. And I don't really know why."

The fire crackled and hissed. Whyte sipped his drink, savored it a moment and said, "I think what happened in the sixties was that we—we, the great baby boom generation—renounced or gave up on all the things that made America work. All those corny old values—the work ethic, religion, the importance of the family, social order, a confidence in an always-better tomorrow—were the fuel that made that beautiful and intricate system work. . . ."

"You really think it's that simple?"

"Yes, I do. Because of Vietnam, we questioned the system too strenuously, tampered with it, rebelled against it on such a scale and with such glamor that it fell apart. Fell into spiritual disarray, pornography, hedonism, drugs, crime and the lack of confidence that always brings about economic disorder."

Casy smiled for the first time in months. "Bryan, you've given a new meaning to the word conservative."

He smiled back, his big eyes confident and seductive. "I'm not ashamed of that, John. I do believe in conserving all the values that nurture capitalistic growth. If there is one thing I completely believe in, it is the perfection of capitalism."

"Perfection?"

"Yes, perfection. Capitalism works, John. Look around you. Look at what we're doing here and in Japan and South Korea." He sat up in his chair, growing excited by what he was saying. "We're showing America how well capitalism works—just as we showed China. If there is any hope for America, it's going to come from our example right here and a return to the old values we've managed to keep alive."

"And do you see this return coming?"

"Yes. It's there now. Just below the surface. A few more years of runaway inflation and Arab arrogance ought to do it. When they see their economic system about to collapse, your baby boom generation will embrace conservatism and capitalism like they were hula hoops and Beatles records. It's already happening—all those ex-radicals are getting into real estate! The 1980s will be the decade of capitalism. I believe that, John."

"What difference will any of that make? America is already run by big business."

"America is run by big government. It *should* be run by big business."

"But business wants order at any cost. It creates right-wing dictators. It doesn't care about political freedom or human rights."

Whyte smiled. "It doesn't have to care. That's the perfection of the system. Political freedom inevitably follows capitalistic success—not the other way around. That's the story of Western civilization, John. Look at what's happened here. The Taiwanese have gained political freedom in direct proportion to the Island's economic success. You can chart it on a graph. They've acquired more in the last three years than in the twenty years before 1975. How long do you think it will take Communist Vietnam to get this kind of prosperity and political freedom. Ten years? Twenty? A hundred? *Ever?*"

"But what about countries like the Philippines or Thailand or almost anywhere in South America? Your capitalistic altruism hasn't worked there. No middle class has emerged. Wealth has become concentrated in the hands of a few corrupt, upper-class families."

"Those countries are going through the same feudal stage that Japan and Taiwan went through. They're just going through it more slowly because of a lot of cultural reasons."

"And on the other side of Taiwan's current boom is where America is now—hedonism, drugs, spiritual disarray?"

"Not necessarily. Not inevitably. America has merely gone through a traumatic crisis and lost its confidence and purpose. It can be restored."

"Who will restore it? Ronald Reagan?"

"Or someone like him."

"I assume you've been in close contact with these people."

"Yes."

"To do it—to restore the conditions for capitalism—

you're going to try and turn around the social revolution of the sixties. All the advances in civil rights, sexual freedom, personal liberty. All the social programs."

"Yes, John. Most of it."

"How? By force?"

"If necessary."

Whyte went on to explain his vision for a new America but Casy did not hear it. He sat in the chair before the fireplace and tuned it all out. Then he went to bed.

Casy did not sleep that night. He felt he had finally come to understand the great, enigmatic idol of his youth, and what he saw appalled and frightened him. Whyte was a simplistic man to whom wealth *was* morality, a man who had elevated capitalism to a religion—a religion in whose defense he would excuse any action, be it killing innocent people in a San Francisco restaurant, destroying his closest friends, or bringing his country to the brink of fascism.

Whyte was a visionary whose vision was so narrow that his mind could not see any evidence that disputed it. He could not see the ugliness and pollution that went with his economic miracle. He could not see that his own financial empire had been founded on the evil of drugs. He could not see that his precious capitalism always evolved in the direction of monopoly—invariably smothering its own principles of freedom and individual initiative—and, above all, he could not see that it always, *always* had to resort to violence and oppression to save itself, as the events of July 4, 1976 so clearly demonstrated.

Casy agonized over this revelation for weeks without knowing what to do about it. Then at 3 A.M.—three days before he was to leave with Whyte on his historic trip to China—it dawned on him what he *must* do. He saw that a great responsibility had been placed on his shoulders and that, for the first time in his life, he could not evade it by telling himself he was an artist. He understood that he was finally going to have to commit a political act. And that act was to see that William Bryan Whyte did not get on that plane to spread his gospel of capitalism to the Mainland of China or to post-Woodstock America.

* * *

It was a bright, wintry morning almost thirty years to the month since Bryan White had left China a penniless refugee. Today he would be returning as a king.

A large crowd came out to see his party off; Whyte and King Lu and John Casy were surrounded by emotional well-wishers. At the forefront of this group were Floyd Harris, David Butler, Warren Stevens and Juan Ortega.

Whyte shook hands with each of them. He paused a moment to give some last-minute instructions to Ortega. He waved to "Terrible" Ding Tze and a party of Greens who had also come down for the occasion.

The pilot signaled them and the three left the crowd. They began walking toward the company jet, Casy leading the way. Several steps out on the runway, Casy suddenly turned around and drew a pistol from his overcoat pocket.

The crowd divided and dived for cover. Greens drew their pistols. King Lu screamed at them to hold their fire.

Whyte stared evenly at Casy. His eyes showed no fear. It was almost as if he had somehow expected this. His mouth seemed almost to form a smile.

"Go ahead, John," he said. "But be sure you're right. Be *positive.*"

Casy's trembling hand aimed the pistol. He saw the calm certainty on Whyte's face. The astonishing, absolute certainty. Then it was all over. He suddenly doubted what he was doing. He suddenly considered that Whyte might be right about everything. What did he, Casy, have to offer that was any better, that hadn't already failed miserably? The gun bounced on the pavement. Whyte stepped closer to him.

"You've won completely now," Casy sobbed.

"No, John. We've won. The Omega Chi."

"There is no Omega Chi. Just you. Everyone else is dead."

Whyte put his arm around the distraught man. "I

want to forget this happened. I want you to put all the past behind you and get on the plane with me."

"I can't be a part of this. I can't live with what you've done."

"None of that matters now. We have a new life and a new world and half of it is yours!"

"I don't want to live in your world. I can't."

"You can. I want you there. I need you there."

"I see their faces at night, Bryan. Alan, Georgie, Mark, all of them."

"I see them, too."

"But they don't haunt you. You don't look at the gray areas in your dream or the human casualties you leave behind."

"I can't look at them. I have to keep focused on the larger picture. Somebody has to, goddammit!"

Casy just stared at Whyte blankly, as the crowd looked on in hushed silence.

"You don't want to believe it," Whyte said, "but you know what I'm doing is right. You know I'm *necessary*. Now get on the fucking plane with me."

"I can't. I can't give you my . . . my approval. That's what you really want from me. That's what you've always wanted. And that's what you can't have."

Whyte could see that it was hopeless. Casy was lost to him forever, just as all the others had been lost to him. He accepted it with an arch of his eyebrow and a slight, stoical nod of acquiescence.

Then he stepped past Casy and walked with King Lu to the waiting plane.

About the Author

WILLIAM ARNOLD lived in Taiwan as a military dependent and graduated from the Taipei American School in 1963. After attending the University of Washington, he worked for the *Seattle Post Intelligencer* as magazine editor, reporter and film critic. His first book, *Shadowland*, was a national best seller. Mr. Arnold lives with his wife and daughter in Washington State, where he is currently at work on a novel set in Asia and Hollywood.

Bestsellers
from
BALLANTINE BOOKS

PAUL THEROUX

"... will successfully startle you ... shock you ... impress you ... but never, never bore you!"*

BESTSELLERS
from
BALLANTINE